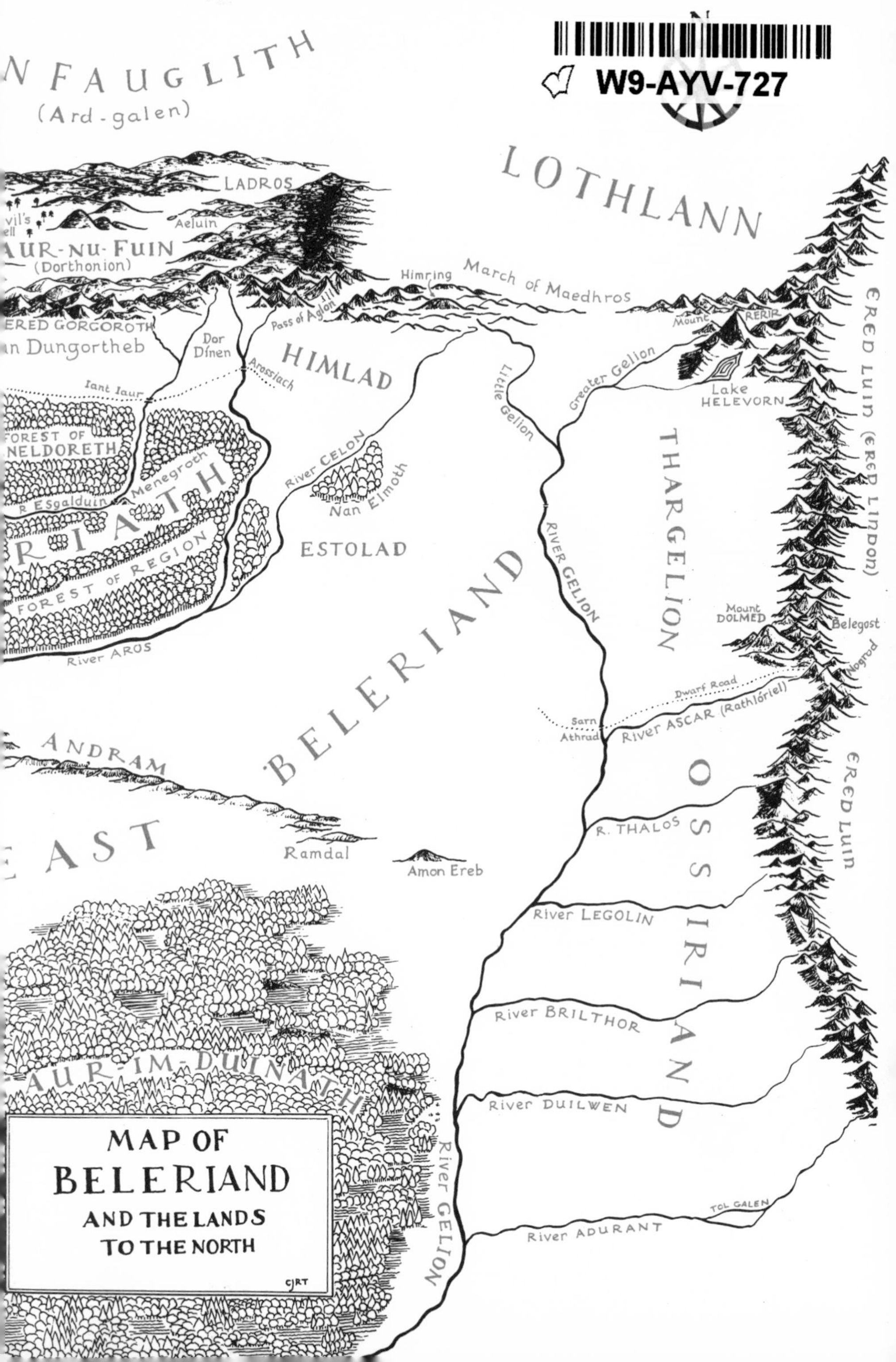

MAP OF BELERIAND AND THE LANDS TO THE NORTH

CJRT

N FAUGLITH
(Ard-galen)
LOTHLANN
LADROS
Aeluin
AUR-NU-FUIN
(Dorthonion)
Himring
March of Maedhros
Pass of Aglon
ERED GORGOROTH
n Dungortheb
Dor Dínen
Arossiach
HIMLAD
Little Gellion
Greater Gellion
Mount RERIR
Lake HELEVORN
Iant Iaur
FOREST OF NELDORETH
Menegroth
R. Esgalduin
FOREST OF REGION
River CELON
Nan Elmoth
ESTOLAD
River AROS
River GELION
THARGELION
ERED LUIN (ERED LINDON)
Mount DOLMED
Belegost
Nogrod
Dwarf Road
Sarn Athrad
River ASCAR (Rathlóriel)
BELERIAND
ANDRAM
EAST
Ramdal
Amon Ereb
OSSIRIAND
ERED LUIN
R. THALOS
River LEGOLIN
River BRILTHOR
River DUILWEN
AUR-IM-DUINATH
River GELION
TOL GALEN
River ADURANT

THE SILMARILLION

BOOKS BY J. R. R. TOLKIEN

The Lord of the Rings
The Fellowship of the Ring
The Two Towers
The Return of the King

The Hobbit

Father Giles of Ham

The Adventures of Tom Bombadil

Smith of Wootton Major

Tree and Leaf

Sir Gawain and the Green Knight,
Pearl *and* Sir Orfeo

The Father Christmas Letters
(edited by Baillie Tolkien)

The Silmarillion
(edited by Christopher Tolkien)

WITH DONALD SWANN

The Road Goes Ever On

J. R. R. TOLKIEN

QUENTA SILMARILLION

(The History of the Silmarils)

together with

AINULINDALË

(The Music of the Ainur)

and

VALAQUENTA

(Account of the Valar)

To which is appended

AKALLABÊTH

(The Downfall of Númenor)

and

OF THE RINGS OF POWER AND THE THIRD AGE

J. R. R. TOLKIEN

The Silmarillion

edited by
CHRISTOPHER TOLKIEN

HOUGHTON MIFFLIN COMPANY BOSTON

Printed in the United States of America

ISBN 0-395-34646-0

FOREWORD

The Silmarillion, now published four years after the death of its author, is an account of the Elder Days, or the First Age of the World. In *The Lord of the Rings* were narrated the great events at the end of the Third Age; but the tales of *The Silmarillion* are legends deriving from a much deeper past, when Morgoth, the first Dark Lord, dwelt in Middle-earth, and the High Elves made war upon him for the recovery of the Silmarils.

Not only, however, does *The Silmarillion* relate the events of a far earlier time than those of *The Lord of the Rings;* it is also, in all the essentials of its conception, far the earlier work. Indeed, although it was not then called *The Silmarillion,* it was already in being half a century ago; and in battered notebooks extending back to 1917 can still be read the earliest versions, often hastily pencilled, of the central stories of the mythology. But it was never published (though some indication of its content could be gleaned from *The Lord of the Rings*), and throughout my father's long life he never abandoned it, nor ceased even in his last years to work on it. In all that time *The Silmarillion,* considered simply as a large narrative structure, underwent relatively little radical change; it became long ago a fixed tradition, and background to later writings. But it was far indeed from being a fixed text, and did not remain unchanged even in certain fundamental ideas concerning the nature of the world it portrays; while the same legends came to be retold in longer and shorter forms, and in different styles. As the years passed the changes and variants, both in detail and in larger perspectives, became so complex, so pervasive, and so many-layered that a final and definitive version seemed unattainable. Moreover the old legends ('old' now not only in their derivation from the remote First Age, but also in terms of my father's life) became the vehicle and depository of his profoundest reflections. In his later writing mythology and poetry sank down behind his theological and philosophical preoccupations: from which arose incompatibilities of tone.

On my father's death it fell to me to try to bring the work into publishable form. It became clear to me that to attempt to present, within the covers of a single book, the diversity of the materials—to show *The Silmarillion* as in truth a continuing and evolving creation extending over more than half a century—would in fact lead only to confusion and the submerging of what is essential. I set myself therefore to work out a single text, selecting and arranging in such a way as seemed to me to produce the most coherent and internally self-consistent narrative. In this work the concluding chapters (from the death of Túrin Turambar) introduced peculiar difficulties, in that they had remained unchanged for many years, and were in some respects in serious disharmony with more developed conceptions in other parts of the book.

A complete consistency (either within the compass of *The Silmarillion* itself or between *The Silmarillion* and other published writings of my father's) is not to be looked for, and could only be achieved, if at all, at heavy and needless cost. Moreover, my father came to conceive *The Silmarillion* as a compilation, a compendious narrative, made long afterwards from sources of great diversity (poems, and annals, and oral tales) that had survived in agelong tradition; and this conception has indeed its parallel in the actual history of the book, for a great deal of earlier prose and poetry does underlie it, and it is to some extent a compendium in fact and not only in theory. To this may be ascribed the varying speed of the narrative and fullness of detail in different parts, the contrast (for example) of the precise recollections of place and motive in the legend of Túrin Turambar beside the high and remote account of the end of the First Age, when Thangorodrim was broken and Morgoth overthrown; and also some differences of tone and portrayal, some obscurities, and, here and there, some lack of cohesion. In the case of the *Valaquenta*, for instance, we have to assume that while it contains much that must go back to the earliest days of the Eldar in Valinor, it was remodelled in later times; and thus explain its continual shifting of tense and viewpoint, so that the divine powers seem now present and active in the world, now remote, a vanished order known only to memory.

The book, though entitled as it must be *The Silmarillion*, contains not only the *Quenta Silmarillion*, or *Silmarillion* proper, but also four other short works. The *Ainulindalë* and *Valaquenta*, which are given at the beginning, are indeed closely associated with *The Silmarillion;* but the *Akallabêth* and *Of the Rings of Power*, which appear at the end, are (it must be emphasised) wholly separate and independent. They are included according to my father's explicit intention; and by their inclusion the entire history is set forth from the Music of the Ainur in which the world began to the passing of the Ringbearers from the Havens of Mithlond at the end of the Third Age.

The number of names that occur in the book is very large, and I have provided a full index; but the number of persons (Elves and Men) who play an important part in the narrative of the First Age is very much smaller, and all of these will be found in the genealogical tables. In addition I have provided a table setting out the rather complex naming of the different Elvish peoples; a note on the pronunciation of Elvish names, and a list of some of the chief elements found in these names; and a map. It may be noted that the great mountain range in the east, Ered Luin or Ered Lindon, the Blue Mountains, appears in the extreme west of the map in *The Lord of the Rings*. In the body of the book there is a smaller map: the intention of this is to make clear at a glance where lay the kingdoms of the Elves after the return of the Noldor to Middle-earth. I have not burdened the book further with any sort of commentary or annotation. There is indeed a wealth of unpublished writing by my father concerning the Three Ages, narrative, linguistic, historical, and philosophical, and I hope that it will prove possible to publish some of this at a later date.

In the difficult and doubtful task of preparing the text of the book I was very greatly assisted by Guy Kay, who worked with me in 1974–1975.

Christopher Tolkien

CONTENTS

AINULINDALË

AINULINDALË

The Music of the Ainur

There was Eru, the One, who in Arda is called Ilúvatar; and he made first the Ainur, the Holy Ones, that were the offspring of his thought, and they were with him before aught else was made. And he spoke to them, propounding to them themes of music; and they sang before him, and he was glad. But for a long while they sang only each alone, or but few together, while the rest hearkened; for each comprehended only that part of the mind of Ilúvatar from which he came, and in the understanding of their brethren they grew but slowly. Yet ever as they listened they came to deeper understanding, and increased in unison and harmony.

And it came to pass that Ilúvatar called together all the Ainur and declared to them a mighty theme, unfolding to them things greater and more wonderful than he had yet revealed; and the glory of its beginning and the splendour of its end amazed the Ainur, so that they bowed before Ilúvatar and were silent.

Then Ilúvatar said to them: 'Of the theme that I have declared to you, I will now that ye make in harmony together a Great Music. And since I have kindled you with the Flame Imperishable, ye shall show forth your powers in adorning this theme, each with his own thoughts and devices, if he will. But I will sit and hearken, and be glad that through you great beauty has been wakened into song.'

Then the voices of the Ainur, like unto harps and lutes, and pipes and trumpets, and viols and organs, and like unto countless choirs singing with words, began to fashion the theme of Ilúvatar to a great music; and a sound arose of endless interchanging melodies woven in harmony that passed beyond hearing into the depths and into the heights, and the places of the dwelling of Ilúvatar were filled to overflowing, and the music and the echo of the music went out into the Void, and it was not void. Never since have the Ainur made any music like to this music, though it has been said that a greater still shall be made before Ilúvatar by the choirs of the Ainur and the Children of Ilúvatar after the end of days. Then the themes of Ilúvatar shall be played aright, and take Being in the moment of their utterance, for all shall then understand fully his intent in their part, and each shall know the comprehension of each, and Ilúvatar shall give to their thoughts the secret fire, being well pleased.

But now Ilúvatar sat and hearkened, and for a great while it seemed good to him, for in the music there were no flaws. But as the theme progressed, it came into the heart of Melkor to interweave matters of his own imagining that were not in accord with the theme of Ilúvatar; for he sought therein to increase the power and glory of the part assigned to himself. To Melkor among the Ainur had been given the greatest gifts of power and knowledge, and he had a share in all the gifts of his brethren. He had gone often alone into the void places seeking the Imperishable Flame; for desire grew hot within him to bring into Being things of his own, and it seemed to him that Ilúvatar took no thought for the Void, and he was impatient of its emptiness. Yet he found not the Fire, for it is with Ilúvatar. But being alone he had begun to conceive thoughts of his own unlike those of his brethren.

Some of these thoughts he now wove into his music, and straightway discord arose about him, and many that sang nigh him grew despondent, and their thought was disturbed and their music faltered; but some began to attune their music to his rather than to the thought which they had at first. Then the discord of Melkor spread ever wider, and the melodies which had been heard before foundered in a sea of turbulent sound. But Ilúvatar sat and hearkened until it seemed that about his throne there was a raging storm, as of dark waters that made war one upon another in an endless wrath that would not be assuaged.

Then Ilúvatar arose, and the Ainur perceived that he smiled; and he lifted up his left hand, and a new theme began amid the storm, like and yet unlike to the former theme, and it gathered power and had new beauty. But the discord of Melkor rose in uproar and contended with it, and again there was a war of sound more violent than before, until many of the Ainur were dismayed and sang no longer, and Melkor had the mastery. Then again Ilúvatar arose, and the Ainur perceived that his countenance was stern; and he lifted up his right hand, and behold! a third theme grew amid the confusion, and it was unlike the others. For it seemed at first soft and sweet, a mere rippling of gentle sounds in delicate melodies; but it could not be quenched, and it took to itself power and profundity. And it seemed at last that there were two musics progressing at one time before the seat of Ilúvatar, and they were utterly at variance. The one was deep and wide and beautiful, but slow and blended with an immeasurable sorrow, from which its beauty chiefly came. The other had now achieved a unity of its own; but it was loud, and vain, and endlessly repeated; and it had little harmony, but rather a clamorous unison as of many trumpets braying upon a few notes. And it essayed to drown the other music by the violence of its voice, but it seemed that its most triumphant notes were taken by the other and woven into its own solemn pattern.

In the midst of this strife, whereat the halls of Ilúvatar shook and a tremor ran out into the silences yet unmoved, Ilúvatar arose a third time, and his face was terrible to behold. Then he raised up both his hands, and in one chord, deeper than the Abyss, higher than the Firmament, piercing as the light of the eye of Ilúvatar, the Music ceased.

Then Ilúvatar spoke, and he said: 'Mighty are the Ainur, and mightiest among them is Melkor; but that he may know, and all the Ainur, that I am Ilúvatar, those things that ye have sung, I will show them forth, that ye may see what ye have done. And thou, Melkor, shalt see that no theme may be played that hath not its uttermost source in me, nor can any alter the music in my despite. For he that attempteth this shall prove but mine instrument in the devising of things more wonderful, which he himself hath not imagined.'

Then the Ainur were afraid, and they did not yet comprehend the words that were said to them; and Melkor was filled with shame, of which came secret anger. But Ilúvatar arose in splendour, and he went forth from the fair regions that he had made for the Ainur; and the Ainur followed him.

But when they were come into the Void, Ilúvatar said to them: 'Behold your Music!' And he showed to them a vision, giving to them sight where before was only hearing; and they saw a new World made visible before them, and it was globed amid the Void, and it was sustained therein, but was not of it. And as they looked and wondered this World began to unfold its history, and it seemed to them that it lived and grew. And when the Ainur had gazed for a while and were silent, Ilúvatar said again: 'Behold your Music! This is your minstrelsy; and each of you shall find contained herein, amid the design that I set before you, all those things which it may seem that he himself devised or added. And thou, Melkor, wilt discover all the secret thoughts of thy mind, and wilt perceive that they are but a part of the whole and tributary to its glory.'

And many other things Ilúvatar spoke to the Ainur at that time, and because of their memory of his words, and the knowledge that each has of the music that he himself made, the Ainur know much of what was, and is, and is to come, and few things are unseen by them. Yet some things there are that they cannot see, neither alone nor taking counsel together; for to none but himself has Ilúvatar revealed all that he has in store, and in every age there come forth things that are new and have no foretelling, for they do not proceed from the past. And so it was that as this vision of the World was played before them, the Ainur saw that it contained things which they had not thought. And they saw with amazement the coming of the Children of Ilúvatar, and the habitation that was prepared for them; and they perceived that they themselves in the labour of their music had been busy with the preparation of this dwelling, and yet knew not that it had any purpose beyond its own beauty. For the Children of Ilúvatar were conceived by him alone; and they came with the third theme, and were not in the theme which Ilúvatar propounded at the beginning, and none of the Ainur had part in their making. Therefore when they beheld them, the more did they love them, being things other than themselves, strange and free, wherein they saw the mind of Ilúvatar reflected anew, and learned yet a little more of his wisdom, which otherwise had been hidden even from the Ainur.

Now the Children of Ilúvatar are Elves and Men, the Firstborn and the Followers. And amid all the splendours of the World, its vast halls and spaces, and its wheeling fires, Ilúvatar chose a place for their habitation in the Deeps of Time and in the midst of the innumerable stars. And this habitation might seem a little thing to those who consider only the majesty of the Ainur, and not their terrible sharpness; as who should take the whole field of Arda for the foundation of a pillar and so raise it until the cone of its summit were more bitter than a needle; or who consider only the immeasurable vastness of the World, which still the Ainur are shaping, and not the minute precision to which they shape all things therein. But when the Ainur had beheld this habitation in a vision and had seen the Children of Ilúvatar arise therein, then many of the most mighty among them bent all their thought and their desire towards that place. And of these Melkor was the chief, even as he was in the beginning the greatest of the Ainur who took part in the Music. And he feigned, even to himself at first, that he desired to go thither and order all things for the good of the Children of Ilúvatar, controlling the turmoils of the heat and the cold that had come to pass through him. But he desired rather to subdue to his will both Elves and Men, envying the gifts with which Ilúvatar promised to endow them; and he wished himself to have subjects and servants, and to be called Lord, and to be a master over other wills.

But the other Ainur looked upon this habitation set within the vast spaces of the World, which the Elves call Arda, the Earth; and their hearts rejoiced in light, and their eyes beholding many colours were filled with gladness; but because of the roaring of the sea they felt a great unquiet. And they observed the winds and the air, and the matters of which Arda was made, of iron and stone and silver and gold and many substances: but of all these water they most greatly praised. And it is said by the Eldar that in water there lives yet the echo of the Music of the Ainur more than in any substance else that is in this Earth; and many of the Children of Ilúvatar hearken still unsated to the voices of the Sea, and yet know not for what they listen.

Now to water had that Ainu whom the Elves call Ulmo turned his thought, and of all most deeply was he instructed by Ilúvatar in music. But of the airs and winds Manwë most had pondered, who is the noblest of the Ainur. Of the fabric of Earth had Aulë thought, to whom Ilúvatar had given skill and knowledge scarce less than to Melkor; but the delight and pride of Aulë is in the deed of making, and in the thing made, and neither in possession nor in his own mastery; wherefore he gives and hoards not, and is free from care, passing ever on to some new work.

And Ilúvatar spoke to Ulmo, and said: 'Seest thou not how here in this little realm in the Deeps of Time Melkor hath made war upon thy province? He hath bethought him of bitter cold immoderate, and yet hath not destroyed the beauty of thy fountains, nor of thy clear pools. Behold the snow, and the cunning work of frost! Melkor hath devised heats and fire without restraint, and hath not dried up thy desire nor utterly quelled the music of the sea. Behold rather the height and glory of the clouds, and the everchanging mists; and listen to the fall of rain upon the Earth! And in these clouds thou art drawn nearer to Manwë, thy friend, whom thou lovest.'

Then Ulmo answered: 'Truly, Water is become now fairer than my heart imagined, neither had my secret thought conceived the snowflake, nor in all my music was contained the falling of the rain. I will seek Manwë, that he and I may make melodies for ever to thy delight!' And Manwë and Ulmo have from the beginning been allied, and in all things have served most faithfully the purpose of Ilúvatar.

But even as Ulmo spoke, and while the Ainur were yet gazing upon this vision, it was taken away and hidden from their sight; and it seemed to them that in that moment they perceived a new thing, Darkness, which they had not known before except in thought. But they had become enamoured of the beauty of the vision and engrossed in the unfolding of the World which came there to being, and their minds were filled with it; for the history was incomplete and the circles of time not full-wrought when the vision was taken away. And some have said that the vision ceased ere the fulfilment of the Dominion of Men and the fading of the Firstborn; wherefore, though the Music is over all, the Valar have not seen as with sight the Later Ages or the ending of the World.

Then there was unrest among the Ainur; but Ilúvatar called to them, and said: 'I know the desire of your minds that what ye have seen should verily be, not only in your thought, but even as ye yourselves are, and yet other. Therefore I say: *Eä!* Let these things Be! And I will send forth into the Void the Flame Imperishable, and it shall be at the heart of the World, and the World shall Be; and those of you that will may go down into it.' And suddenly the Ainur saw afar off a light, as it were a cloud with a living heart of flame; and they knew that this was no vision only, but that Ilúvatar had made a new thing: Eä, the World that Is.

Thus it came to pass that of the Ainur some abode still with Ilúvatar beyond the confines of the World; but others, and among them many of the greatest and most fair, took the leave of Ilúvatar and descended into it. But this condition Ilúvatar made, or it is the necessity of their love, that their power should thenceforward be contained and bounded in the World, to be within it for ever, until it is complete, so that they are its life and it is theirs. And therefore they are named the Valar, the Powers of the World.

But when the Valar entered into Eä they were at first astounded and at a loss, for it was as if naught was yet made which they had seen in vision, and all was but on point to begin and yet unshaped, and it was dark. For the Great Music had been but the growth and flowering of thought in the Timeless Halls, and the Vision only a foreshowing; but now they had entered in at the beginning of Time, and the Valar perceived that the World had been but foreshadowed and foresung, and they must achieve it. So began their great labours in wastes unmeasured and unexplored, and in ages uncounted and forgotten, until in the Deeps of Time and in the midst of the vast halls of Eä there came to be that hour and that place where was made the habitation of the Children of Ilúvatar. And in this work the chief part was taken by Manwë and Aulë and Ulmo; but Melkor too was there from the first, and he meddled in all that was done, turning it if he might to his own desires and purposes; and he kindled great fires. When therefore Earth was yet young and full of flame Melkor coveted it, and he said to the other Valar: 'This shall be my own kingdom; and I name it unto myself!'

But Manwë was the brother of Melkor in the mind of Ilúvatar, and he was the chief instrument of the second theme that Ilúvatar had raised up against the discord of Melkor; and he called unto himself many spirits both greater and less, and they came down into the fields of Arda and aided Manwë, lest Melkor should hinder the fulfilment of their labour for ever, and Earth should wither ere it flowered. And Manwë said unto Melkor: 'This kingdom thou shalt not take for thine own, wrongfully, for many others have laboured here no less than thou.' And there was strife between Melkor and the other Valar; and for that time Melkor withdrew and departed to other regions and did there what he would; but he did not put the desire of the Kingdom of Arda from his heart.

Now the Valar took to themselves shape and hue; and because they were drawn into the World by love of the Children of Ilúvatar, for whom they hoped, they took shape after that manner which they had beheld in the Vision of Ilúvatar, save only in majesty and splendour. Moreover their shape comes of their knowledge of the visible World, rather than of the World itself; and they need it not, save only as we use raiment, and yet we may be naked and suffer no loss of our being. Therefore the Valar may walk, if they will, unclad, and then even the Eldar cannot clearly perceive them, though they be present. But when they desire to clothe themselves the Valar take upon them forms some as of male and some as of female; for that difference of temper they had even from their beginning, and it is but bodied forth in the choice of each, not made by the choice, even as with us male and female may be shown by the raiment but is not made thereby. But the shapes wherein the Great Ones array themselves are not at all times like to the shapes of the kings and queens of the Children of Ilúvatar; for at times they may clothe themselves in their own thought, made visible in forms of majesty and dread.

And the Valar drew unto them many companions, some less, some well nigh as great as themselves, and they laboured together in the ordering of the Earth and the curbing of its tumults. Then Melkor saw what was done, and that the Valar walked on Earth as powers visible, clad in the raiment of the World, and were lovely and glorious to see, and blissful, and that the Earth was becoming as a garden for their delight, for its turmoils were subdued. His envy grew then the greater within him; and he also took visible form, but because of his mood and the malice that burned in him that form was dark and terrible. And he descended upon Arda in power and majesty greater than any other of the Valar, as a mountain that wades in the sea and has its head above the clouds and is clad in ice and crowned with smoke and fire; and the light of the eyes of Melkor was like a flame that withers with heat and pierces with a deadly cold.

Thus began the first battle of the Valar with Melkor for the dominion of Arda; and of those tumults the Elves know but little. For what has here been declared is come from the Valar themselves, with whom the Eldaliё spoke in the land of Valinor, and by whom they were instructed; but little would the Valar ever tell of the wars before the coming of the Elves. Yet it is told among the Eldar that the Valar endeavoured ever, in despite of Melkor, to rule the Earth and to prepare it for the coming of the Firstborn; and they built lands and Melkor destroyed them; valleys they delved and Melkor raised them up; mountains they carved and Melkor threw them down; seas they hollowed and Melkor spilled them; and naught might have peace or come to lasting growth, for as surely as the Valar began a labour so would Melkor undo it or corrupt it. And yet their labour was not all in vain; and though nowhere and in no work was their will and purpose wholly fulfilled, and all things were in hue and shape other than the Valar had at first intended, slowly nonetheless the Earth was fashioned and made firm. And thus was the habitation of the Children of Ilúvatar established at the last in the Deeps of Time and amidst the innumerable stars.

VALAQUENTA

VALAQUENTA

Account of the Valar and Maiar according to the lore of the Eldar

In the beginning Eru, the One, who in the Elvish tongue is named Ilúvatar, made the Ainur of his thought; and they made a great Music before him. In this Music the World was begun; for Ilúvatar made visible the song of the Ainur, and they beheld it as a light in the darkness. And many among them became enamoured of its beauty, and of its history which they saw beginning and unfolding as in a vision. Therefore Ilúvatar gave to their vision Being, and set it amid the Void, and the Secret Fire was sent to burn at the heart of the World; and it was called Eä.

Then those of the Ainur who desired it arose and entered into the World at the beginning of Time; and it was their task to achieve it, and by their labours to fulfil the vision which they had seen. Long they laboured in the regions of Eä, which are vast beyond the thought of Elves and Men, until in the time appointed was made Arda, the Kingdom of Earth. Then they put on the raiment of Earth and descended into it, and dwelt therein.

Of the Valar

The Great among these spirits the Elves name the Valar, the Powers of Arda, and Men have often called them gods. The Lords of the

Valar are seven; and the Valier, the Queens of the Valar, are seven also. These were their names in the Elvish tongue as it was spoken in Valinor, though they have other names in the speech of the Elves in Middle-earth, and their names among Men are manifold. The names of the Lords in due order are: Manwë, Ulmo, Aulë, Oromë, Mandos, Lórien, and Tulkas; and the names of the Queens are: Varda, Yavanna, Nienna, Estë, Vairë, Vána, and Nessa. Melkor is counted no longer among the Valar, and his name is not spoken upon Earth.

Manwë and Melkor were brethren in the thought of Ilúvatar. The mightiest of those Ainur who came into the World was in his beginning Melkor; but Manwë is dearest to Ilúvatar and understands most clearly his purposes. He was appointed to be, in the fullness of time, the first of all Kings: lord of the realm of Arda and ruler of all that dwell therein. In Arda his delight is in the winds and the clouds, and in all the regions of the air, from the heights to the depths, from the utmost borders of the Veil of Arda to the breezes that blow in the grass. Súlimo he is surnamed, Lord of the Breath of Arda. All swift birds, strong of wing, he loves, and they come and go at his bidding.

With Manwë dwells Varda, Lady of the Stars, who knows all the regions of Eä. Too great is her beauty to be declared in the words of Men or of Elves; for the light of Ilúvatar lives still in her face. In light is her power and her joy. Out of the deeps of Eä she came to the aid of Manwë; for Melkor she knew from before the making of the Music and rejected him, and he hated her, and feared her more than all others whom Eru made. Manwë and Varda are seldom parted, and they remain in Valinor. Their halls are above the everlasting snow, upon Oiolossë, the uttermost tower of Taniquetil, tallest of all the mountains upon Earth. When Manwë there ascends his throne and looks forth, if Varda is beside him, he sees further than all other eyes, through mist, and through darkness, and over the leagues of the sea. And if Manwë is with her, Varda hears more clearly than all other ears the sound of voices that cry from east to west, from the hills and the valleys, and from the dark places that Melkor has made upon Earth. Of all the Great Ones who dwell in this world the Elves hold Varda most in reverence and love. Elbereth they name her, and they call upon her name out of the shadows of Middle-earth, and uplift it in song at the rising of the stars.

Ulmo is the Lord of Waters. He is alone. He dwells nowhere long, but moves as he will in all the deep waters about the Earth or under the Earth. He is next in might to Manwë, and before Valinor was made he was closest to him in friendship; but thereafter he went seldom to the councils of the Valar, unless great matters were in debate. For he kept all Arda in thought, and he has no need of any resting-place. Moreover he does not love to walk upon land, and will seldom clothe himself in a body after the manner of his peers. If the Children of Eru beheld him they were filled with a great dread; for the arising of the King of the Sea was terrible, as a mounting wave that strides to the land, with dark helm foam-crested and raiment of mail shimmering from silver down into shadows of green. The trumpets of Manwë are loud, but Ulmo's voice is deep as the deeps of the ocean which he only has seen.

Nonetheless Ulmo loves both Elves and Men, and never abandoned them, not even when they lay under the wrath of the Valar. At times he will come unseen to the shores of Middle-earth, or pass far inland up firths of the sea, and there make music upon his great horns, the Ulumúri, that are wrought of white shell; and those to whom that music comes hear it ever after in their hearts, and longing for the sea never leaves them again. But mostly Ulmo speaks to those who dwell in Middle-earth with voices that are heard only as the music of water. For all seas, lakes, rivers, fountains and springs are in his government; so that the Elves say that the spirit of Ulmo runs in all the veins of the world. Thus news comes to Ulmo, even in the deeps, of all the needs and griefs of Arda, which otherwise would be hidden from Manwë.

Aulë has might little less than Ulmo. His lordship is over all the substances of which Arda is made. In the beginning he wrought much in fellowship with Manwë and Ulmo; and the fashioning of all lands was his labour. He is a smith and a master of all crafts, and he delights in works of skill, however small, as much as in the mighty building of old. His are the gems that lie deep in the Earth and the gold that is fair in the hand, no less than the walls of the mountains and the basins of the sea. The Noldor learned most of him, and he was ever their friend. Melkor was jealous of him, for Aulë was most like himself in thought and in powers; and there was long strife between them, in which Melkor ever marred or undid the works of Aulë, and Aulë grew weary in repairing the tumults and disorders of Melkor. Both, also, desired to make things of their own that should be new and unthought of by others, and delighted in the praise of their skill. But Aulë remained faithful to Eru and submitted all that he did to his will; and he did not envy the works of others, but sought and gave counsel. Whereas Melkor spent his spirit in envy and hate, until at last he could make nothing save in mockery of the thought of others, and all their works he destroyed if he could.

The spouse of Aulë is Yavanna, the Giver of Fruits. She is the lover of all things that grow in the earth, and all their countless forms she holds in her mind, from the trees like towers in forests long ago to the moss upon stones or the small and secret things in the mould. In reverence Yavanna is next to Varda among the Queens of the Valar. In the form of a woman she is tall, and robed in green; but at times she takes other shapes. Some there are who have seen her standing like a tree under heaven, crowned with the Sun; and from all its branches there spilled a golden dew upon the barren earth, and it grew green with corn; but the roots of the tree were in the waters of Ulmo, and the winds of Manwë spoke in its leaves. Kementári, Queen of the Earth, she is surnamed in the Eldarin tongue.

The Fëanturi, masters of spirits, are brethren, and they are called most often Mandos and Lórien. Yet these are rightly the names of the places of their dwelling, and their true names are Námo and Irmo.

Námo the elder dwells in Mandos, which is westward in Valinor. He is the keeper of the Houses of the Dead, and the summoner of the spirits of the slain. He forgets nothing; and he knows all things that shall be, save only those that lie still in the freedom of Ilúvatar. He is the Doomsman of the Valar; but he pronounces his dooms and his judgements only at the bidding of Manwë. Vairë the Weaver is his spouse, who weaves all things that have ever been in Time into her storied webs, and the halls of Mandos that ever widen as the ages pass are clothed with them.

Irmo the younger is the master of visions and dreams. In Lórien are his gardens in the land of the Valar, and they are the fairest of all places in the world, filled with many spirits. Estë the gentle, healer of hurts and of weariness, is his spouse. Grey is her raiment; and rest is her gift. She walks not by day, but sleeps upon an island in the tree-shadowed lake of Lórellin. From the fountains of Irmo and Estë all those who dwell in Valinor draw refreshment; and often the Valar come themselves to Lórien and there find repose and easing of the burden of Arda.

Mightier than Estë is Nienna, sister of the Fëanturi; she dwells alone. She is acquainted with grief, and mourns for every wound that Arda has suffered in the marring of Melkor. So great was her sorrow, as the Music unfolded, that her song turned to lamentation long before its end, and the sound of mourning was woven into the themes of the World before it began. But she does not weep for herself; and those who hearken to her learn pity, and endurance in hope. Her halls are west of West, upon the borders of the world; and she comes seldom to the city of Valimar where all is glad. She goes rather to the halls of Mandos, which are near to her own; and all those who wait in Mandos cry to her, for she brings strength to the spirit and turns sorrow to wisdom. The windows of her house look outward from the walls of the world.

Greatest in strength and deeds of prowess is Tulkas, who is surnamed Astaldo, the Valiant. He came last to Arda, to aid the Valar in the first battles with Melkor. He delights in wrestling and in contests of strength; and he rides no steed, for he can outrun all things that go on feet, and he is tireless. His hair and beard are golden, and his flesh ruddy; his weapons are his hands. He has little heed for either the past or the future, and is of no avail as a counsellor, but is a hardy friend. His spouse is Nessa, the sister of Oromë, and she also is lithe and fleetfooted. Deer she loves, and they follow her train whenever she goes in the wild; but she can outrun them, swift as an arrow with the wind in her hair. In dancing she delights, and she dances in Valimar on lawns of never-fading green.

Oromë is a mighty lord. If he is less strong than Tulkas, he is more dreadful in anger; whereas Tulkas laughs ever, in sport or in war, and even in the face of Melkor he laughed in battles before the Elves were born. Oromë loved the lands of Middle-earth, and he left them unwillingly and came last to Valinor; and often of old he passed back east over the mountains and returned with his host to the hills and the plains. He is a hunter of monsters and fell beasts, and he delights in horses and in hounds; and all trees he loves, for which reason he is called Aldaron, and by the Sindar Tauron, the Lord of Forests. Nahar is the name of his horse, white in the sun, and shining silver at night. The Valaróma is the name of his great horn, the sound of which is like the upgoing of the Sun in scarlet, or the sheer lightning cleaving the clouds. Above all the horns of his host it was heard in the woods that Yavanna brought forth in Valinor; for there Oromë would train his folk and his beasts for the pursuit of the evil creatures of Melkor. The spouse of Oromë is Vána, the Ever-young; she is the younger sister of Yavanna. All flowers spring as she passes and open if she glances upon them; and all birds sing at her coming.

These are the names of the Valar and the Valier, and here is told in brief their likenesses, such as the Eldar beheld them in Aman. But fair and noble as were the forms in which they were manifest to the Children of Ilúvatar, they were but a veil upon their beauty and their power. And if little is here said of all that the Eldar once knew, that is as nothing compared with their true being, which goes back into regions and ages far beyond our thought. Among them Nine were of chief power and reverence; but one is removed from their number, and Eight remain, the Aratar, the High Ones of Arda: Manwë and Varda, Ulmo, Yavanna and Aulë, Mandos, Nienna, and Oromë. Though Manwë is their King and holds their allegiance under Eru, in majesty they are peers, surpassing beyond compare all others, whether of the Valar and the Maiar, or of any other order that Ilúvatar has sent into Eä.

Of the Maiar

With the Valar came other spirits whose being also began before the World, of the same order as the Valar but of less degree. These are the Maiar, the people of the Valar, and their servants and helpers. Their number is not known to the Elves, and few have names in any of the tongues of the Children of Ilúvatar; for though it is otherwise in Aman, in Middle-earth the Maiar have seldom appeared in form visible to Elves and Men.

Chief among the Maiar of Valinor whose names are remembered in the histories of the Elder Days are Ilmarë, the handmaid of Varda, and Eönwë, the banner-bearer and herald of Manwë, whose might in arms is surpassed by none in Arda. But of all the Maiar Ossë and Uinen are best known to the Children of Ilúvatar.

Ossë is a vassal of Ulmo, and he is master of the seas that wash the shores of Middle-earth. He does not go in the deeps, but loves the coasts and the isles, and rejoices in the winds of Manwë; for in storm he delights, and laughs amid the roaring of the waves. His spouse is Uinen, the Lady of the Seas, whose hair lies spread through all waters under sky. All creatures she loves that live in the salt streams, and all weeds that grow there; to her mariners cry, for she can lay calm upon the waves, restraining the wildness of Ossë. The Númenóreans lived long in her protection, and held her in reverence equal to the Valar.

Melkor hated the Sea, for he could not subdue it. It is said that in the making of Arda he endeavoured to draw Ossë to his allegiance, promising to him all the realm and power of Ulmo, if he would serve him. So it was that long ago there arose great tumults in the sea that wrought ruin to the lands. But Uinen, at the prayer of Aulë, restrained Ossë and brought him before Ulmo; and he was pardoned and returned to his allegiance, to which he has remained faithful. For the most part; for the delight in violence has never wholly departed from him, and at times he will rage in his wilfulness without any command from Ulmo his lord. Therefore those who dwell by the sea or go up in ships may love him, but they do not trust him.

Melian was the name of a Maia who served both Vána and Estë; she dwelt long in Lórien, tending the trees that flower in the gardens of Irmo, ere she came to Middle-earth. Nightingales sang about her wherever she went.

Wisest of the Maiar was Olórin. He too dwelt in Lórien, but his ways took him often to the house of Nienna, and of her he learned pity and patience.

Of Melian much is told in the *Quenta Silmarillion*. But of Olórin that tale does not speak; for though he loved the Elves, he walked among them unseen, or in form as one of them, and they did not know whence came the fair visions or the promptings of wisdom that he put into their hearts. In later days he was the friend of all the Children of Ilúvatar, and took pity on their sorrows; and those who listened to him awoke from despair and put away the imaginations of darkness.

Of the Enemies

Last of all is set the name of Melkor, He who arises in Might. But that name he has forfeited; and the Noldor, who among the Elves suffered most from his malice, will not utter it, and they name him Morgoth, the Dark Enemy of the World. Great might was given to him by Ilúvatar, and he was coëval with Manwë. In the powers and knowledge of all the other Valar he had part, but he turned them to evil purposes, and squandered his strength in violence and tyranny. For he coveted Arda and all that was in it, desiring the kingship of Manwë and dominion over the realms of his peers.

From splendour he fell through arrogance to contempt for all things save himself, a spirit wasteful and pitiless. Understanding he turned to subtlety in perverting to his own will all that he would use, until he became a liar without shame. He began with the desire of Light, but when he could not possess it for himself alone, he descended through fire and wrath into a great burning, down into Darkness. And darkness he used most in his evil works upon Arda, and filled it with fear for all living things.

Yet so great was the power of his uprising that in ages forgotten he contended with Manwë and all the Valar, and through long years in Arda held dominion over most of the lands of the Earth. But he was not alone. For of the Maiar many were drawn to his splendour in the days of his greatness, and remained in that allegiance down into his darkness; and others he corrupted afterwards to his service with lies and treacherous gifts. Dreadful among these spirits were the Valaraukar, the scourges of fire that in Middle-earth were called the Balrogs, demons of terror.

Among those of his servants that have names the greatest was that spirit whom the Eldar called Sauron, or Gorthaur the Cruel. In his beginning he was of the Maiar of Aulë, and he remained mighty in the lore of that people. In all the deeds of Melkor the Morgoth upon Arda, in his vast works and in the deceits of his cunning, Sauron had a part, and was only less evil than his master in that for long he served another and not himself. But in after years he rose like a shadow of Morgoth and a ghost of his malice, and walked behind him on the same ruinous path down into the Void.

HERE ENDS THE VALAQUENTA

QUENTA SILMARILLION

The History of the Silmarils

Chapter 1

OF THE BEGINNING OF DAYS

It is told among the wise that the First War began before Arda was full-shaped, and ere yet there was anything that grew or walked upon earth; and for long Melkor had the upper hand. But in the midst of the war a spirit of great strength and hardihood came to the aid of the Valar, hearing in the far heaven that there was battle in the Little Kingdom; and Arda was filled with the sound of his laughter. So came Tulkas the Strong, whose anger passes like a mighty wind, scattering cloud and darkness before it; and Melkor fled before his wrath and his laughter, and forsook Arda, and there was peace for a long age. And Tulkas remained and became one of the Valar of the Kingdom of Arda; but Melkor brooded in the outer darkness, and his hate was given to Tulkas for ever after.

In that time the Valar brought order to the seas and the lands and the mountains, and Yavanna planted at last the seeds that she had long devised. And since, when the fires were subdued or buried beneath the primeval hills, there was need of light, Aulë at the prayer of Yavanna wrought two mighty lamps for the lighting of the Middle-earth which he had built amid the encircling seas. Then Varda filled the lamps and Manwë hallowed them, and the Valar set them upon high pillars, more lofty far than are any mountains of the later days. One lamp they raised near to the north of Middle-earth, and it was named Illuin; and the other was raised in the south, and it was named Ormal; and the light of the Lamps of the Valar flowed out over the Earth, so that all was lit as it were in a changeless day.

Then the seeds that Yavanna had sown began swiftly to sprout and to burgeon, and there arose a multitude of growing things great and small, mosses and grasses and great ferns, and trees whose tops were crowned with cloud as they were living mountains, but whose feet were wrapped in a green twilight. And beasts came forth and dwelt in the grassy plains, or in the rivers and the lakes, or walked in the shadows of the woods. As yet no flower had bloomed nor any bird had sung, for these things waited still their time in the bosom of Yavanna; but wealth there was of her imagining, and nowhere more rich than in the midmost parts of the Earth, where the light of both the Lamps met and blended. And there upon the Isle of Almaren in the Great Lake was the first dwelling of the Valar when all things were young, and new-made green was yet a marvel in the eyes of the makers; and they were long content.

Now it came to pass that while the Valar rested from their labours, and watched the growth and unfolding of the things that they had devised and begun, Manwë ordained a great feast; and the Valar and all their host came at his bidding. But Aulë and Tulkas were weary; for the craft of Aulë and the strength of Tulkas had been at the service of all without ceasing in the days of their labour. And Melkor knew of all that was done, for even then he had secret friends and spies among the Maiar whom he had converted to his cause; and far off in the darkness he was filled with hatred, being jealous of the work of his peers, whom he desired to make subject to himself. Therefore he gathered to himself spirits out of the halls of Eä that he had perverted to his service, and he deemed himself strong. And seeing now his time he drew near again to Arda, and looked down upon it, and the beauty of the Earth in its Spring filled him the more with hate.

Now therefore the Valar were gathered upon Almaren, fearing no evil, and because of the light of Illuin they did not perceive the shadow in the north that was cast from afar by Melkor; for he was grown dark as the Night of the Void. And it is sung that in that feast of the Spring of Arda Tulkas espoused Nessa the sister of Oromë, and she danced before the Valar upon the green grass of Almaren.

Then Tulkas slept, being weary and content, and Melkor deemed that his hour had come. And he passed therefore over the Walls of the Night with his host, and came to Middle-earth far in the north; and the Valar were not aware of him.

Now Melkor began the delving and building of a vast fortress, deep under Earth, beneath dark mountains where the beams of Illuin were cold and dim. That stronghold was named Utumno. And though the

Valar knew naught of it as yet, nonetheless the evil of Melkor and the blight of his hatred flowed out thence, and the Spring of Arda was marred. Green things fell sick and rotted, and rivers were choked with weeds and slime, and fens were made, rank and poisonous, the breeding place of flies; and forests grew dark and perilous, the haunts of fear; and beasts became monsters of horn and ivory and dyed the earth with blood. Then the Valar knew indeed that Melkor was at work again, and they sought for his hiding place. But Melkor, trusting in the strength of Utumno and the might of his servants, came forth suddenly to war, and struck the first blow, ere the Valar were prepared; and he assailed the lights of Illuin and Ormal, and cast down their pillars and broke their lamps. In the overthrow of the mighty pillars lands were broken and seas arose in tumult; and when the lamps were spilled destroying flame was poured out over the Earth. And the shape of Arda and the symmetry of its waters and its lands was marred in that time, so that the first designs of the Valar were never after restored.

In the confusion and the darkness Melkor escaped, though fear fell upon him; for above the roaring of the seas he heard the voice of Manwë as a mighty wind, and the earth trembled beneath the feet of Tulkas. But he came to Utumno ere Tulkas could overtake him; and there he lay hid. And the Valar could not at that time overcome him, for the greater part of their strength was needed to restrain the tumults of the Earth, and to save from ruin all that could be saved of their labour; and afterwards they feared to rend the Earth again, until they knew where the Children of Ilúvatar were dwelling, who were yet to come in a time that was hidden from the Valar.

Thus ended the Spring of Arda. The dwelling of the Valar upon Almaren was utterly destroyed, and they had no abiding place upon the face of the Earth. Therefore they departed from Middle-earth and went to the Land of Aman, the westernmost of all lands upon the borders of the world; for its west shores looked upon the Outer Sea, that is called by the Elves Ekkaia, encircling the Kingdom of Arda. How wide is that sea none know but the Valar; and beyond it are the Walls of the Night. But the east shores of Aman were the uttermost end of Belegaer, the Great Sea of the West; and since Melkor was returned to Middle-earth and they could not yet overcome him, the Valar fortified their dwelling, and upon the shores of the sea they raised the Pelóri, the Mountains of Aman, highest upon Earth. And above all the mountains of the Pelóri was that height upon whose summit Manwë set his throne. Taniquetil the Elves name that holy mountain, and Oiolossë Everlasting Whiteness, and Elerrína Crowned with Stars, and many names beside; but the Sindar spoke of it in their later tongue as Amon Uilos. From their halls upon Taniquetil Manwë and Varda could look out across the Earth even into the furthest East.

Behind the walls of the Pelóri the Valar established their domain in that region which is called Valinor; and there were their houses, their gardens, and their towers. In that guarded land the Valar gathered great store of light and all the fairest things that were saved from the ruin; and many others yet fairer they made anew, and Valinor became more beautiful even than Middle-earth in the Spring of Arda; and it was blessed, for the Deathless dwelt there, and there naught faded nor withered, neither was there any stain upon flower or leaf in that land, nor any corruption or sickness in anything that lived; for the very stones and waters were hallowed.

And when Valinor was full-wrought and the mansions of the Valar were established, in the midst of the plain beyond the mountains they built their city, Valmar of many bells. Before its western gate there was a green mound, Ezellohar, that is named also Corollairë; and Yavanna hallowed it, and she sat there long upon the green grass and sang a song of power, in which was set all her thought of things that grow in the earth. But Nienna thought in silence, and watered the mound with tears. In that time the Valar were gathered together to hear the song of Yavanna, and they sat silent upon their thrones of council in the Máhanaxar, the Ring of Doom near to the golden gates of Valmar; and Yavanna Kementári sang before them and they watched.

And as they watched, upon the mound there came forth two slender shoots; and silence was over all the world in that hour, nor was there any other sound save the chanting of Yavanna. Under her song the saplings grew and became fair and tall, and came to flower; and thus there awoke in the world the Two Trees of Valinor. Of all things which Yavanna made they have most renown, and about their fate all the tales of the Elder Days are woven.

The one had leaves of dark green that beneath were as shining silver, and from each of his countless flowers a dew of silver light was ever falling, and the earth beneath was dappled with the shadows of his fluttering leaves. The other bore leaves of a young green like the new-opened beech; their edges were of glittering gold. Flowers swung upon her branches in clusters of yellow flame, formed each to a glow-ing horn that spilled a golden rain upon the ground; and from the blossom of that tree there came forth warmth and a great light. Telperion the one was called in Valinor, and Silpion, and Ninquelótë, and many other names; but Laurelin the other was, and Malinalda, and Culúrien, and many names in song beside.

In seven hours the glory of each tree waxed to full and waned again to naught; and each awoke once more to life an hour before the other ceased to shine. Thus in Valinor twice every day there came a gentle hour of softer light when both trees were faint and their gold and silver beams were mingled. Telperion was the elder of the trees and came first to full stature and to bloom; and that first hour in which he shone, the white glimmer of a silver dawn, the Valar reckoned not into the tale of hours, but named it the Opening Hour, and counted from it the ages of their reign in Valinor. Therefore at the sixth hour of the First Day, and of all the joyful days thereafter, until the Darkening of Valinor, Telperion ceased his time of flower; and at the twelfth hour Laurelin her blossoming. And each day of the Valar in Aman contained twelve hours, and ended with the second mingling of the lights, in which Laurelin was waning but Telperion was waxing. But the light that was spilled from the trees endured long, ere it was taken up into the airs or sank down into the earth; and the dews of Telperion and the rain that fell from Laurelin Varda hoarded in great vats like shining lakes, that were to all the land of the Valar as wells of water and of light. Thus began the Days of the Bliss of Valinor; and thus began also the Count of Time.

But as the ages drew on to the hour appointed by Ilúvatar for the coming of the Firstborn, Middle-earth lay in a twilight beneath the stars that Varda had wrought in the ages forgotten of her labours in Eä. And in the darkness Melkor dwelt, and still often walked abroad, in many shapes of power and fear, and he wielded cold and fire, from the tops of the mountains to the deep furnaces that are beneath them; and whatsoever was cruel or violent or deadly in those days is laid to his charge.

From the beauty and bliss of Valinor the Valar came seldom over the mountains to Middle-earth, but gave to the land beyond the Pelóri their care and their love. And in the midst of the Blessed Realm were the mansions of Aulë, and there he laboured long. For in the making of all things in that land he had the chief part, and he wrought there many beautiful and shapely works both openly and in secret. Of him comes the lore and knowledge of the Earth and of all things that it contains: whether the lore of those that make not, but seek only for the understanding of what is, or the lore of all craftsmen: the weaver, the shaper of wood, and the worker in metals; and the tiller and husbandman also, though these last and all that deal with things that grow and bear fruit must look also to the spouse of Aulë, Yavanna Kementári. Aulë it is who is named the Friend of the Noldor, for of him they learned much in after days, and they are the most skilled of the Elves; and in their own fashion, according to the gifts which Ilúvatar gave to them, they added much to his teaching, delighting in tongues and in scripts, and in the figures of broidery, of drawing, and of carving. The Noldor also it was who first achieved the making of gems; and the fairest of all gems were the Silmarils, and they are lost.

But Manwë Súlimo, highest and holiest of the Valar, sat upon the borders of Aman, forsaking not in his thought the Outer Lands. For his throne was set in majesty upon the pinnacle of Taniquetil, the highest of the mountains of the world, standing upon the margin of the sea. Spirits in the shape of hawks and eagles flew ever to and from his halls; and their eyes could see to the depths of the seas, and pierce the hidden caverns beneath the world. Thus they brought word to him of well nigh all that passed in Arda; yet some things were hidden even from the eyes of Manwë and the servants of Manwë, for where Melkor sat in his dark thought impenetrable shadows lay.

Manwë has no thought for his own honour, and is not jealous of his power, but rules all to peace. The Vanyar he loved best of all the Elves, and of him they received song and poetry; for poetry is the delight of Manwë, and the song of words is his music. His raiment is blue, and blue is the fire of his eyes, and his sceptre is of sapphire, which the Noldor wrought for him; and he was appointed to be the vicegerent of Ilúvatar, King of the world of Valar and Elves and Men, and the chief defence against the evil of Melkor. With Manwë dwelt Varda the most beautiful, she who in the Sindarin tongue is named Elbereth, Queen of the Valar, maker of the stars; and with them were a great host of spirits in blessedness.

But Ulmo was alone, and he abode not in Valinor, nor ever came thither unless there were need for a great council; he dwelt from the beginning of Arda in the Outer Ocean, and still he dwells there. Thence he governs the flowing of all waters, and the ebbing, the courses of all rivers and the replenishment of springs, the distilling of all dews and rain in every land beneath the sky. In the deep places he gives thought to music great and terrible; and the echo of that music runs through all the veins of the world in sorrow and in joy; for if joyful is the fountain that rises in the sun, its springs are in the wells of sorrow unfathomed at the foundations of the Earth. The Teleri learned much of Ulmo, and for this reason their music has both sadness and enchantment. Salmar came with him to Arda, he who made the horns of Ulmo that none may ever forget who once has heard them; and Ossë and Uinen also, to whom he gave the government of the waves and the movements of the Inner Seas, and many other spirits beside. And thus it was by the power of Ulmo that even under the darkness of Melkor life coursed still through many secret lodes, and the Earth did not die; and to all who were lost in that darkness or wandered far from the light of the Valar the ear of Ulmo was ever open; nor has he ever forsaken Middle-earth, and whatsoever may since have befallen of ruin or of change he has not ceased to take thought for it, and will not until the end of days.

And in that time of dark Yavanna also was unwilling utterly to forsake the Outer Lands; for all things that grow are dear to her, and she mourned for the works that she had begun in Middle-earth but Melkor had marred. Therefore leaving the house of Aulë and the flowering meads of Valinor she would come at times and heal the hurts of Melkor; and returning she would ever urge the Valar to that war with his evil dominion that they must surely wage ere the coming of the Firstborn. And Oromë tamer of beasts would ride too at whiles in the darkness of the unlit forests; as a mighty hunter he came with spear and bow, pursuing to the death the monsters and fell creatures of the kingdom of Melkor, and his white horse Nahar shone like silver in the shadows. Then the sleeping earth trembled at the beat of his golden hooves, and in the twilight of the world Oromë would sound the Valaróma his great horn upon the plains of Arda; whereat the mountains echoed, and the shadows of evil fled away, and Melkor himself quailed in Utumno, foreboding the wrath to come. But even as Oromë passed the servants of Melkor would gather again; and the lands were filled with shadows and deceit.

Now all is said concerning the manner of the Earth and its rulers in the beginning of days, and ere the world became such as the Children of Ilúvatar have known it. For Elves and Men are the Children of Ilúvatar; and since they understood not fully that theme by which the Children entered into the Music, none of the Ainur dared to add anything to their fashion. For which reason the Valar are to these kindreds rather their elders and their chieftains than their masters; and if ever in their dealings with Elves and Men the Ainur have endeavoured to force them when they would not be guided, seldom has this turned to good, howsoever good the intent. The dealings of the Ainur have indeed been mostly with the Elves, for Ilúvatar made them more like in nature to the Ainur, though less in might and stature; whereas to Men he gave strange gifts.

For it is said that after the departure of the Valar there was silence, and for an age Ilúvatar sat alone in thought. Then he spoke and said: 'Behold I love the Earth, which shall be a mansion for the Quendi and the Atani! But the Quendi shall be the fairest of all earthly creatures, and they shall have and shall conceive and bring forth more beauty than all my Children; and they shall have the greater bliss in this world. But to the Atani I will give a new gift.' Therefore he willed that the hearts of Men should seek beyond the world and should find no rest therein; but they should have a virtue to shape their life, amid the powers and chances of the world, beyond the Music of the Ainur, which is as fate to all things else; and of their operation everything should be, in form and deed, completed, and the world fulfilled unto the last and smallest.

But Ilúvatar knew that Men, being set amid the turmoils of the powers of the world, would stray often, and would not use their gifts in harmony; and he said: 'These too in their time shall find that all that they do redounds at the end only to the glory of my work.' Yet the Elves believe that Men are often a grief to Manwë, who knows most of the mind of Ilúvatar; for it seems to the Elves that Men resemble Melkor most of all the Ainur, although he has ever feared and hated them, even those that served him.

It is one with this gift of freedom that the children of Men dwell only a short space in the world alive, and are not bound to it, and depart soon whither the Elves know not. Whereas the Elves remain until the end of days, and their love of the Earth and all the world is more single and more poignant therefore, and as the years lengthen ever more sorrowful. For the Elves die not till the world dies, unless they are slain or waste in grief (and to both these seeming deaths they are subject); neither does age subdue their strength, unless one grow weary of ten thousand centuries; and dying they are gathered to the halls of Mandos in Valinor, whence they may in time return. But the sons of Men die indeed, and leave the world; wherefore they are called the Guests, or the Strangers. Death is their fate, the gift of Ilúvatar, which as Time wears even the Powers shall envy. But Melkor has cast his shadow upon it, and confounded it with darkness, and brought forth evil out of good, and fear out of hope. Yet of old the Valar declared to the Elves in Valinor that Men shall join in the Second Music of the Ainur; whereas Ilúvatar has not revealed what he purposes for the Elves after the World's end, and Melkor has not discovered it.

Chapter 2

OF AULË AND YAVANNA

It is told that in their beginning the Dwarves were made by Aulë in the darkness of Middle-earth; for so greatly did Aulë desire the coming of the Children, to have learners to whom he could teach his lore and his crafts, that he was unwilling to await the fulfilment of the designs of Ilúvatar. And Aulë made the Dwarves even as they still are, because the forms of the Children who were to come were unclear to his mind, and because the power of Melkor was yet over the Earth; and he wished therefore that they should be strong and unyielding. But fearing that the other Valar might blame his work, he wrought in secret: and he made first the Seven Fathers of the Dwarves in a hall under the mountains in Middle-earth.

Now Ilúvatar knew what was done, and in the very hour that Aulë's work was complete, and he was pleased, and began to instruct the Dwarves in the speech that he had devised for them, Ilúvatar spoke to him; and Aulë heard his voice and was silent. And the voice of Ilúvatar said to him: 'Why hast thou done this? Why dost thou attempt a thing which thou knowest is beyond thy power and thy authority? For thou hast from me as a gift thy own being only, and no more; and therefore the creatures of thy hand and mind can live only by that being, moving when thou thinkest to move them, and if thy thought be elsewhere, standing idle. Is that thy desire?'

Then Aulë answered: 'I did not desire such lordship. I desired things other than I am, to love and to teach them, so that they too might perceive the beauty of Eä, which thou hast caused to be. For it seemed to me that there is great room in Arda for many things that might rejoice in it, yet it is for the most part empty still, and dumb. And in my impatience I have fallen into folly. Yet the making of things is in my heart from my own making by thee; and the child of little understanding that makes a play of the deeds of his father may do so without thought of mockery, but because he is the son of his father. But what shall I do now, so that thou be not angry with me for ever? As a child to his father, I offer to thee these things, the work of the hands which thou hast made. Do with them what thou wilt. But should I not rather destroy the work of my presumption?'

Then Aulë took up a great hammer to smite the Dwarves; and he wept. But Ilúvatar had compassion upon Aulë and his desire, because of his humility; and the Dwarves shrank from the hammer and were afraid, and they bowed down their heads and begged for mercy. And the voice of Ilúvatar said to Aulë: 'Thy offer I accepted even as it was made. Dost thou not see that these things have now a life of their own, and speak with their own voices? Else they would not have flinched from thy blow, nor from any command of thy will.' Then Aulë cast down his hammer and was glad, and he gave thanks to Ilúvatar, saying: 'May Eru bless my work and amend it!'

But Ilúvatar spoke again and said: 'Even as I gave being to the thoughts of the Ainur at the beginning of the World, so now I have taken up thy desire and given to it a place therein; but in no other way will I amend thy handiwork, and as thou hast made it, so shall it be. But I will not suffer this: that these should come before the Firstborn of my design, nor that thy impatience should be rewarded. They shall sleep now in the darkness under stone, and shall not come forth until the Firstborn have awakened upon Earth; and until that time thou and they shall wait, though long it seem. But when the time comes I will awaken them, and they shall be to thee as children; and often strife shall arise between thine and mine, the children of my adoption and the children of my choice.'

Then Aulë took the Seven Fathers of the Dwarves, and laid them to rest in far-sundered places; and he returned to Valinor, and waited while the long years lengthened.

Since they were to come in the days of the power of Melkor, Aulë made the Dwarves strong to endure. Therefore they are stone-hard, stubborn, fast in friendship and in enmity, and they suffer toil and hunger and hurt of body more hardily than all other speaking peoples; and they live long, far beyond the span of Men, yet not for ever.

Aforetime it was held among the Elves in Middle-earth that dying the Dwarves returned to the earth and the stone of which they were made; yet that is not their own belief. For they say that Aulë the Maker, whom they call Mahal, cares for them, and gathers them to Mandos in halls set apart; and that he declared to their Fathers of old that Ilúvatar will hallow them and give them a place among the Children in the End. Then their part shall be to serve Aulë and to aid him in the remaking of Arda after the Last Battle. They say also that the Seven Fathers of the Dwarves return to live again in their own kin and to bear once more their ancient names: of whom Durin was the most renowned in after ages, father of that kindred most friendly to the Elves, whose mansions were at Khazad-dûm.

Now when Aulë laboured in the making of the Dwarves he kept this work hidden from the other Valar; but at last he opened his mind to Yavanna and told her of all that had come to pass. Then Yavanna said to him: 'Eru is merciful. Now I see that thy heart rejoiceth, as indeed it may; for thou hast received not only forgiveness but bounty. Yet because thou hiddest this thought from me until its achievement, thy children will have little love for the things of my love. They will love first the things made by their own hands, as doth their father. They will delve in the earth, and the things that grow and live upon the earth they will not heed. Many a tree shall feel the bite of their iron without pity.'

But Aulë answered: 'That shall also be true of the Children of Ilúvatar; for they will eat and they will build. And though the things of thy realm have worth in themselves, and would have worth if no Children were to come, yet Eru will give them dominion, and they shall use all that they find in Arda: though not, by the purpose of Eru, without respect or without gratitude.'

'Not unless Melkor darken their hearts,' said Yavanna. And she was not appeased, but grieved in heart, fearing what might be done upon Middle-earth in days to come. Therefore she went before Manwë, and she did not betray the counsel of Aulë, but she said: 'King of Arda, is it true, as Aulë hath said to me, that the Children when they come shall have dominion over all the things of my labour, to do as they will therewith?'

'It is true,' said Manwë. 'But why dost thou ask, for thou hadst no need of the teaching of Aulë?'

Then Yavanna was silent and looked into her own thought. And she answered: 'Because my heart is anxious, thinking of the days to come.

All my works are dear to me. Is it not enough that Melkor should have marred so many? Shall nothing that I have devised be free from the dominion of others?'

'If thou hadst thy will what wouldst thou reserve?' said Manwë. 'Of all thy realm what dost thou hold dearest?'

'All have their worth,' said Yavanna, 'and each contributes to the worth of the others. But the *kelvar* can flee or defend themselves, whereas the *olvar* that grow cannot. And among these I hold trees dear. Long in the growing, swift shall they be in the felling, and unless they pay toll with fruit upon bough little mourned in their passing. So I see in my thought. Would that the trees might speak on behalf of all things that have roots, and punish those that wrong them!'

'This is a strange thought,' said Manwë.

'Yet it was in the Song,' said Yavanna. 'For while thou wert in the heavens and with Ulmo built the clouds and poured out the rains, I lifted up the branches of great trees to receive them, and some sang to Ilúvatar amid the wind and the rain.'

Then Manwë sat silent, and the thought of Yavanna that she had put into his heart grew and unfolded; and it was beheld by Ilúvatar. Then it seemed to Manwë that the Song rose once more about him, and he heeded now many things therein that though he had heard them he had not heeded before. And at last the Vision was renewed, but it was not now remote, for he was himself within it, and yet he saw that all was upheld by the hand of Ilúvatar; and the hand entered in, and from it came forth many wonders that had until then been hidden from him in the hearts of the Ainur.

Then Manwë awoke, and he went down to Yavanna upon Ezellohar, and he sat beside her beneath the Two Trees. And Manwë said: 'O Kementári, Eru hath spoken, saying: "Do then any of the Valar suppose that I did not hear all the Song, even the least sound of the least voice? Behold! When the Children awake, then the thought of Yavanna will awake also, and it will summon spirits from afar, and they will go among the *kelvar* and the *olvar*, and some will dwell therein, and be held in reverence, and their just anger shall be feared. For a time: while the Firstborn are in their power, and while the Secondborn are young." But dost thou not now remember, Kementári, that thy thought sang not always alone? Did not thy thought and mine meet also, so that we took wing together like great birds that soar above the clouds? That also shall come to be by the heed of Ilúvatar, and before the Children awake there shall go forth with wings like the wind the Eagles of the Lords of the West.'

Then Yavanna was glad, and she stood up, reaching her arms towards the heavens, and she said: 'High shall climb the trees of Kementári, that the Eagles of the King may house therein!'

But Manwë rose also, and it seemed that he stood to such a height that his voice came down to Yavanna as from the paths of the winds. 'Nay,' he said, 'only the trees of Aulë will be tall enough. In the mountains the Eagles shall house, and hear the voices of those who call upon us. But in the forests shall walk the Shepherds of the Trees.'

Then Manwë and Yavanna parted for that time, and Yavanna returned to Aulë; and he was in his smithy, pouring molten metal into a mould. 'Eru is bountiful,' she said. 'Now let thy children beware! For there shall walk a power in the forests whose wrath they will arouse at their peril.'

'Nonetheless they will have need of wood,' said Aulë, and he went on with his smith-work.

Chapter 3

OF THE COMING OF THE ELVES AND THE CAPTIVITY OF MELKOR

Through long ages the Valar dwelt in bliss in the light of the Trees beyond the Mountains of Aman, but all Middle-earth lay in a twilight under the stars. While the Lamps had shone, growth began there which now was checked, because all was again dark. But already the oldest living things had arisen: in the seas the great weeds, and on earth the shadow of great trees; and in the valleys of the night-clad hills there were dark creatures old and strong. To those lands and forests the Valar seldom came, save only Yavanna and Oromë; and Yavanna would walk there in the shadows, grieving because the growth and promise of the Spring of Arda was stayed. And she set a sleep upon many things that had arisen in the Spring, so that they should not age, but should wait for a time of awakening that yet should be.

But in the north Melkor built his strength, and he slept not, but watched, and laboured; and the evil things that he had perverted walked abroad, and the dark and slumbering woods were haunted by monsters and shapes of dread. And in Utumno he gathered his demons about him, those spirits who first adhered to him in the days of his splendour, and became most like him in his corruption: their hearts were of fire, but they were cloaked in darkness, and terror went before them; they had whips of flame. Balrogs they were named in Middle-earth in later days. And in that dark time Melkor bred many other monsters of divers shapes and kinds that long troubled the world; and his realm spread now ever southward over Middle-earth.

And Melkor made also a fortress and armoury not far from the north-western shores of the sea, to resist any assault that might come from Aman. That stronghold was commanded by Sauron, lieutenant of Melkor; and it was named Angband.

It came to pass that the Valar held council, for they became troubled by the tidings that Yavanna and Oromë brought from the Outer Lands; and Yavanna spoke before the Valar, saying: 'Ye mighty of Arda, the Vision of Ilúvatar was brief and soon taken away, so that maybe we cannot guess within a narrow count of days the hour appointed. Yet be sure of this: the hour approaches, and within this age our hope shall be revealed, and the Children shall awake. Shall we then leave the lands of their dwelling desolate and full of evil? Shall they walk in darkness while we have light? Shall they call Melkor lord while Manwë sits upon Taniquetil?'

And Tulkas cried: 'Nay! Let us make war swiftly! Have we not rested from strife overlong, and is not our strength now renewed? Shall one alone contest with us for ever?'

But at the bidding of Manwë Mandos spoke, and he said: 'In this age the Children of Ilúvatar shall come indeed, but they come not yet. Moreover it is doom that the Firstborn shall come in the darkness, and shall look first upon the stars. Great light shall be for their waning. To Varda ever shall they call at need.'

Then Varda went forth from the council, and she looked out from the height of Taniquetil, and beheld the darkness of Middle-earth beneath the innumerable stars, faint and far. Then she began a great labour, greatest of all the works of the Valar since their coming into Arda. She took the silver dews from the vats of Telperion, and therewith she made new stars and brighter against the coming of the Firstborn; wherefore she whose name out of the Deeps of Time and the labours of Eä was Tintallë, the Kindler, was called after by the Elves Elentári, Queen of the Stars. Carnil and Luinil, Nénar and Lumbar, Alcarinquë and Elemmírë she wrought in that time, and many other of the ancient stars she gathered together and set as signs in the heavens of Arda: Wilwarin, Telumendil, Soronúmë, and Anarríma; and Menelmacar with his shining belt, that forebodes the Last Battle that shall be at the end of days. And high in the North as a challenge to Melkor she set the crown of seven mighty stars to swing, Valacirca, the Sickle of the Valar and sign of doom.

It is told that even as Varda ended her labours, and they were long, when first Menelmacar strode up the sky and the blue fire of Helluin flickered in the mists above the borders of the world, in that hour the Children of the Earth awoke, the Firstborn of Ilúvatar. By the starlit mere of Cuiviénen, Water of Awakening, they rose from the sleep of Ilúvatar; and while they dwelt yet silent by Cuiviénen their eyes beheld first of all things the stars of heaven. Therefore they have ever loved the starlight, and have revered Varda Elentári above all the Valar.

In the changes of the world the shapes of lands and of seas have been broken and remade; rivers have not kept their courses, neither have mountains remained steadfast; and to Cuiviénen there is no returning. But it is said among the Elves that it lay far off in the east of Middle-earth, and northward, and it was a bay in the Inland Sea of Helcar; and that sea stood where aforetime the roots of the mountain of Illuin had been before Melkor overthrew it. Many waters flowed down thither from heights in the east, and the first sound that was heard by the Elves was the sound of water flowing, and the sound of water falling over stone.

Long they dwelt in their first home by the water under stars, and they walked the Earth in wonder; and they began to make speech and to give names to all things that they perceived. Themselves they named the Quendi, signifying those that speak with voices; for as yet they had met no other living things that spoke or sang.

And on a time it chanced that Oromë rode eastward in his hunting, and he turned north by the shores of Helcar and passed under the shadows of the Orocarni, the Mountains of the East. Then on a sudden Nahar set up a great neighing, and stood still. And Oromë wondered and sat silent, and it seemed to him that in the quiet of the land under the stars he heard afar off many voices singing.

Thus it was that the Valar found at last, as it were by chance, those whom they had so long awaited. And Oromë looking upon the Elves was filled with wonder, as though they were beings sudden and marvellous and unforeseen; for so it shall ever be with the Valar. From without the World, though all things may be forethought in music or foreshown in vision from afar, to those who enter verily into Eä each in its time shall be met at unawares as something new and unforetold.

In the beginning the Elder Children of Ilúvatar were stronger and greater than they have since become; but not more fair, for though the beauty of the Quendi in the days of their youth was beyond all other beauty that Ilúvatar has caused to be, it has not perished, but lives in the West, and sorrow and wisdom have enriched it. And Oromë loved the Quendi, and named them in their own tongue Eldar, the people of the stars; but that name was after borne only by those who followed him upon the westward road.

Yet many of the Quendi were filled with dread at his coming; and this was the doing of Melkor. For by after-knowledge the wise declare that Melkor, ever watchful, was first aware of the awakening of the Quendi, and sent shadows and evil spirits to spy upon them and waylay them. So it came to pass, some years ere the coming of Oromë, that if any of the Elves strayed far abroad, alone or few together, they would often vanish, and never return; and the Quendi said that the Hunter had caught them, and they were afraid. And indeed the most ancient songs of the Elves, of which echoes are remembered still in the West, tell of the shadow-shapes that walked in the hills above Cuiviénen, or would pass suddenly over the stars; and of the dark Rider upon his wild horse that pursued those that wandered to take them and devour them. Now Melkor greatly hated and feared the riding of Oromë, and either he sent indeed his dark servants as riders, or he set lying whispers abroad, for the purpose that the Quendi should shun Oromë, if ever they should meet.

Thus it was that when Nahar neighed and Oromë indeed came among them, some of the Quendi hid themselves, and some fled and were lost. But those that had courage, and stayed, perceived swiftly that the Great Rider was no shape out of darkness; for the light of Aman was in his face, and all the noblest of the Elves were drawn towards it.

But of those unhappy ones who were ensnared by Melkor little is known of a certainty. For who of the living has descended into the pits of Utumno, or has explored the darkness of the counsels of Melkor? Yet this is held true by the wise of Eressëa, that all those of the Quendi who came into the hands of Melkor, ere Utumno was broken, were put there in prison, and by slow arts of cruelty were corrupted and enslaved; and thus did Melkor breed the hideous race of the Orcs in envy and mockery of the Elves, of whom they were afterwards the bitterest foes. For the Orcs had life and multiplied after the manner of the Children of Ilúvatar; and naught that had life of its own, nor the semblance of life, could ever Melkor make since his rebellion in the Ainulindalë before the Beginning: so say the wise. And deep in their dark hearts the Orcs loathed the Master whom they served in fear, the maker only of their misery. This it may be was the vilest deed of Melkor, and the most hateful to Ilúvatar.

Oromë tarried a while among the Quendi, and then swiftly he rode back over land and sea to Valinor and brought the tidings to Valmar; and he spoke of the shadows that troubled Cuiviénen. Then the Valar rejoiced, and yet they were in doubt amid their joy; and they debated long what counsel it were best to take for the guarding of the Quendi from the shadow of Melkor. But Oromë returned at once to Middle-earth and abode with the Elves.

Manwë sat long in thought upon Taniquetil, and he sought the counsel of Ilúvatar. And coming then down to Valmar he summoned the Valar to the Ring of Doom, and thither came even Ulmo from the Outer Sea.

Then Manwë said to the Valar: 'This is the counsel of Ilúvatar in my heart: that we should take up again the mastery of Arda, at whatsoever cost, and deliver the Quendi from the shadow of Melkor.' Then Tulkas was glad; but Aulë was grieved, foreboding the hurts of the world that must come of that strife. But the Valar made ready and came forth from Aman in strength of war, resolving to assault the fortresses of Melkor and make an end. Never did Melkor forget that this war was made for the sake of the Elves, and that they were the cause of his downfall. Yet they had no part in those deeds, and they know little of the riding of the might of the West against the North in the beginning of their days.

Melkor met the onset of the Valar in the North-west of Middle-earth, and all that region was much broken. But the first victory of the hosts of the West was swift, and the servants of Melkor fled before them to Utumno. Then the Valar passed over Middle-earth, and they set a guard over Cuiviénen; and thereafter the Quendi knew nothing of the great Battle of the Powers, save that the Earth shook and groaned beneath them, and the waters were moved, and in the north there were lights as of mighty fires. Long and grievous was the siege of Utumno, and many battles were fought before its gates of which naught but the rumour is known to the Elves. In that time the shape of Middle-earth was changed, and the Great Sea that sundered it from Aman grew wide and deep; and it broke in upon the coasts and made a deep gulf to the southward. Many lesser bays were made between the Great Gulf and Helcaraxë far in the north, where Middle-earth and Aman came nigh together. Of these the Bay of Balar was the chief; and into it the mighty river Sirion flowed down from the new-raised highlands northwards: Dorthonion, and the mountains about Hithlum. The lands of the far north were all made desolate in those days; for there Utumno was delved exceeding deep, and its pits were filled with fires and with great hosts of the servants of Melkor.

But at the last the gates of Utumno were broken and the halls unroofed, and Melkor took refuge in the uttermost pit. Then Tulkas stood forth as champion of the Valar and wrestled with him, and cast him upon his face; and he was bound with the chain Angainor that Aulë had wrought, and led captive; and the world had peace for a long age.

Nonetheless the Valar did not discover all the mighty vaults and caverns hidden with deceit far under the fortresses of Angband and Utumno. Many evil things still lingered there, and others were dispersed and fled into the dark and roamed in the waste places of the world, awaiting a more evil hour; and Sauron they did not find.

But when the Battle was ended and from the ruin of the North great clouds arose and hid the stars, the Valar drew Melkor back to Valinor, bound hand and foot, and blindfold; and he was brought to the Ring of Doom. There he lay upon his face before the feet of Manwë and sued for pardon; but his prayer was denied, and he was cast into prison in the fastness of Mandos, whence none can escape, neither Vala, nor Elf, nor mortal Man. Vast and strong are those halls, and they were built in the west of the land of Aman. There was Melkor doomed to abide for three ages long, before his cause should be tried anew, or he should plead again for pardon.

Then again the Valar were gathered in council, and they were divided in debate. For some, and of those Ulmo was the chief, held that the Quendi should be left free to walk as they would in Middle-earth, and with their gifts of skill to order all the lands and heal their hurts. But the most part feared for the Quendi in the dangerous world amid the deceits of the starlit dusk; and they were filled moreover with the love of the beauty of the Elves and desired their fellowship. At the last, therefore, the Valar summoned the Quendi to Valinor, there to be gathered at the knees of the Powers in the light of the Trees for ever; and Mandos broke his silence, saying: 'So it is doomed.' From this summons came many woes that afterwards befell.

But the Elves were at first unwilling to hearken to the summons, for they had as yet seen the Valar only in their wrath as they went to war, save Oromë alone; and they were filled with dread. Therefore Oromë was sent again to them, and he chose from among them ambassadors who should go to Valinor and speak for their people; and these were Ingwë, Finwë, and Elwë, who afterwards were kings. And coming they were filled with awe by the glory and majesty of the Valar, and desired greatly the light and splendour of the Trees. Then Oromë brought them back to Cuiviénen, and they spoke before their people, and counselled them to heed the summons of the Valar and remove into the West.

Then befell the first sundering of the Elves. For the kindred of Ingwë, and the most part of the kindreds of Finwë and Elwë, were swayed by the words of their lords, and were willing to depart and follow Oromë; and these were known ever after as the Eldar, by the name that Oromë gave to the Elves in the beginning, in their own tongue. But many refused the summons, preferring the starlight and the wide spaces of Middle-earth to the rumour of the Trees; and these are the Avari, the Unwilling, and they were sundered in that time from the Eldar, and met never again until many ages were past.

The Eldar prepared now a great march from their first homes in the east; and they were arrayed in three hosts. The smallest host and the first to set forth was led by Ingwë, the most high lord of all the Elvish race. He entered into Valinor and sits at the feet of the Powers, and all Elves revere his name; but he came never back, nor looked again upon Middle-earth. The Vanyar were his people; they are the Fair Elves, the beloved of Manwë and Varda, and few among Men have spoken with them.

Next came the Noldor, a name of wisdom, the people of Finwë. They are the Deep Elves, the friends of Aulë; and they are renowned in song, for they fought and laboured long and grievously in the northern lands of old.

The greatest host came last, and they are named the Teleri, for they tarried on the road, and were not wholly of a mind to pass from the dusk to the light of Valinor. In water they had great delight, and those that came at last to the western shores were enamoured of the sea. The Sea-elves therefore they became in the land of Aman, the Falmari, for they made music beside the breaking waves. Two lords they had, for their numbers were great: Elwë Singollo (which signifies Greymantle) and Olwë his brother.

These were the three kindreds of the Eldalië, who passing at length into the uttermost West in the days of the Trees are called the Calaquendi, Elves of the Light. But others of the Eldar there were who set out indeed upon the westward march, but became lost upon the long road, or turned aside, or lingered on the shores of Middle-earth; and these were for the most part of the kindred of the Teleri, as is told hereafter. They dwelt by the sea, or wandered in the woods and mountains of the world, yet their hearts were turned towards the

West. Those Elves the Calaquendi call the Úmanyar, since they came never to the land of Aman and the Blessed Realm; but the Úmanyar and the Avari alike they call the Moriquendi, Elves of the Darkness, for they never beheld the Light that was before the Sun and Moon.

It is told that when the hosts of the Eldaliё departed from Cuiviénen Oromë rode at their head upon Nahar, his white horse shod with gold; and passing northward about the Sea of Helcar they turned towards the west. Before them great clouds hung still black in the North above the ruins of war, and the stars in that region were hidden. Then not a few grew afraid and repented, and turned back, and are forgotten.

Long and slow was the march of the Eldar into the west, for the leagues of Middle-earth were uncounted, and weary and pathless. Nor did the Eldar desire to hasten, for they were filled with wonder at all that they saw, and by many lands and rivers they wished to abide; and though all were yet willing to wander, many feared rather their journey's end than hoped for it. Therefore whenever Oromë departed, having at times other matters to heed, they halted and went forward no more, until he returned to guide them. And it came to pass after many years of journeying in this manner that the Eldar took their course through a forest, and they came to a great river, wider than any they had yet seen; and beyond it were mountains whose sharp horns seemed to pierce the realm of the stars. This river, it is said, was even the river which was after called Anduin the Great, and was ever the frontier of the west-lands of Middle-earth. But the mountains were the Hithaeglir, the Towers of Mist upon the borders of Eriador; yet they were taller and more terrible in those days, and were reared by Melkor to hinder the riding of Oromë. Now the Teleri abode long on the east bank of that river and wished to remain there, but the Vanyar and the Noldor passed over it, and Oromë led them into the passes of the mountains. And when Oromë was gone forward the Teleri looked upon the shadowy heights and were afraid.

Then one arose in the host of Olwë, which was ever the hindmost on the road; Lenwë he was called. He forsook the westward march, and led away a numerous people, southwards down the great river, and they passed out of the knowledge of their kin until long years were past. Those were the Nandor; and they became a people apart, unlike their kin, save that they loved water, and dwelt most beside falls and running streams. Greater knowledge they had of living things, tree and herb, bird and beast, than all other Elves. In after years Denethor, son of Lenwë, turned again west at last, and led a part of that people over the mountains into Beleriand ere the rising of the Moon.

At length the Vanyar and the Noldor came over Ered Luin, the Blue Mountains, between Eriador and the westernmost land of Middle-earth, which the Elves after named Beleriand; and the foremost companies passed over the Vale of Sirion and came down to the shores of the Great Sea between Drengist and the Bay of Balar. But when they beheld it great fear came upon them, and many withdrew into the woods and highlands of Beleriand. Then Oromë departed, and returned to Valinor to seek the counsel of Manwë, and left them.

And the host of the Teleri passed over the Misty Mountains, and crossed the wide lands of Eriador, being urged on by Elwë Singollo, for he was eager to return to Valinor and the Light that he had beheld; and he wished not to be sundered from the Noldor, for he had great friendship with Finwë their lord. Thus after many years the Teleri also came at last over Ered Luin into the eastern regions of Beleriand. There they halted, and dwelt a while beyond the River Gelion.

Chapter 4

OF THINGOL AND MELIAN

Melian was a Maia, of the race of the Valar. She dwelt in the gardens of Lórien, and among all his people there were none more beautiful than Melian, nor more wise, nor more skilled in songs of enchantment. It is told that the Valar would leave their works, and the birds of Valinor their mirth, that the bells of Valmar were silent and the fountains ceased to flow, when at the mingling of the lights Melian sang in Lórien. Nightingales went always with her, and she taught them their song; and she loved the deep shadows of the great trees. She was akin before the World was made to Yavanna herself; and in that time when the Quendi awoke beside the waters of Cuiviénen she departed from Valinor and came to the Hither Lands, and there she filled the silence of Middle-earth before the dawn with her voice and the voices of her birds.

Now when their journey was near its end, as has been told, the people of the Teleri rested long in East Beleriand, beyond the River Gelion; and at that time many of the Noldor still lay to the westward, in those forests that were afterwards named Neldoreth and Region. Elwë, lord of the Teleri, went often through the great woods to seek out Finwë his friend in the dwellings of the Noldor; and it chanced on a time that he came alone to the starlit wood of Nan Elmoth, and there suddenly he heard the song of nightingales. Then an enchantment fell on him, and he stood still; and afar off beyond the voices of the *lómelindi* he heard the voice of Melian, and it filled all his heart with wonder and desire. He forgot then utterly all his people and all the purposes of his mind, and following the birds under the shadow of the trees he passed deep into Nan Elmoth and was lost. But he came at last to a glade open to the stars, and there Melian stood; and out of the darkness he looked at her, and the light of Aman was in her face.

She spoke no word; but being filled with love Elwë came to her and took her hand, and straightway a spell was laid on him, so that they stood thus while long years were measured by the wheeling stars above them; and the trees of Nan Elmoth grew tall and dark before they spoke any word.

Thus Elwë's folk who sought him found him not, and Olwë took the kingship of the Teleri and departed, as is told hereafter. Elwë Singollo came never again across the sea to Valinor so long as he lived, and Melian returned not thither while their realm together lasted; but of her there came among both Elves and Men a strain of the Ainur who were with Ilúvatar before Eä. In after days he became a king renowned, and his people were all the Eldar of Beleriand; the Sindar they were named, the Grey-elves, the Elves of the Twilight, and King Greymantle was he, Elu Thingol in the tongue of that land. And Melian was his Queen, wiser than any child of Middle-earth; and their hidden halls were in Menegroth, the Thousand Caves, in Doriath. Great power Melian lent to Thingol, who was himself great among the Eldar; for he alone of all the Sindar had seen with his own eyes the Trees in the day of their flowering, and king though he was of Úmanyar, he was not accounted among the Moriquendi, but with the Elves of the Light, mighty upon Middle-earth. And of the love of Thingol and Melian there came into the world the fairest of all the Children of Ilúvatar that was or shall ever be.

Chapter 5

OF ELDAMAR AND THE PRINCES OF THE ELDALIË

In time the hosts of the Vanyar and the Noldor came to the last western shores of the Hither Lands. In the north these shores, in the ancient days after the Battle of the Powers, bent ever westward, until in the northernmost parts of Arda only a narrow sea divided Aman, upon which Valinor was built, from the Hither Lands; but this narrow sea was filled with grinding ice, because of the violence of the frosts of Melkor. Therefore Oromë did not lead the hosts of the Eldaliё into the far north, but brought them to the fair lands about the River Sirion, that afterwards were named Beleriand; and from those shores whence first the Eldar looked in fear and wonder on the Sea there stretched an ocean, wide and dark and deep, between them and the Mountains of Aman.

Now Ulmo, by the counsel of the Valar, came to the shores of Middle-earth and spoke with the Eldar who waited there, gazing on the dark waves; and because of his words and the music which he made for them on his horns of shell their fear of the sea was turned rather to desire. Therefore Ulmo uprooted an island which long had stood alone amid the sea, far from either shore, since the tumults of the fall of Illuin; and with the aid of his servants he moved it, as it were a mighty ship, and anchored it in the Bay of Balar, into which Sirion poured his water. Then the Vanyar and the Noldor embarked upon that isle, and were drawn over the sea, and came at last to the long shores beneath the Mountains of Aman; and they entered Valinor and were welcomed to its bliss. But the eastern horn of the island, which was deep-grounded in the shoals off the mouths of Sirion, was broken asunder and remained behind; and that, it is said, was the Isle of Balar, to which afterwards Ossë often came.

But the Teleri remained still in Middle-earth, for they dwelt in East Beleriand far from the sea, and they heard not the summons of Ulmo until too late; and many searched still for Elwë their lord, and without him they were unwilling to depart. But when they learned that Ingwë and Finwë and their peoples were gone, then many of the Teleri pressed on to the shores of Beleriand, and dwelt thereafter near the Mouths of Sirion, in longing for their friends that had departed; and they took Olwë, Elwë's brother, to be their king. Long they remained by the coasts of the western sea, and Ossë and Uinen came to them and befriended them; and Ossë instructed them, sitting upon a rock near to the margin of the land, and of him they learned all manner of sea-lore and sea-music. Thus it came to be that the Teleri, who were from the beginning lovers of water, and the fairest singers of all the Elves, were after enamoured of the seas, and their songs were filled with the sound of waves upon the shore.

When many years had passed, Ulmo hearkened to the prayers of the Noldor and of Finwë their king, who grieved at their long sundering from the Teleri, and besought him to bring them to Aman, if they would come. And most of them proved now willing indeed; but great was the grief of Ossë when Ulmo returned to the coasts of Beleriand, to bear them away to Valinor; for his care was for the seas of Middle-earth and the shores of the Hither Lands, and he was ill-pleased that the voices of the Teleri should be heard no more in his domain. Some he persuaded to remain; and those were the Falathrim, the Elves of the Falas, who in after days had dwellings at the havens of Brithombar and Eglarest, the first mariners in Middle-earth and the first makers of ships. Círdan the Shipwright was their lord.

The kinsfolk and friends of Elwë Singollo also remained in the Hither Lands, seeking him yet, though they would fain have departed to Valinor and the light of the Trees, if Ulmo and Olwë had been willing to tarry longer. But Olwë would be gone; and at last the main host of the Teleri embarked upon the isle, and Ulmo drew them far away. Then the friends of Elwë were left behind; and they called themselves Eglath, the Forsaken People. They dwelt in the woods and hills of Beleriand, rather than by the sea, which filled them with sorrow; but the desire of Aman was ever in their hearts.

But when Elwë awoke from his long trance, he came forth from

Nan Elmoth with Melian, and they dwelt thereafter in the woods in the midst of the land. Greatly though he had desired to see again the light of the Trees, in the face of Melian he beheld the light of Aman as in an unclouded mirror, and in that light he was content. His people gathered about him in joy, and they were amazed; for fair and noble as he had been, now he appeared as it were a lord of the Maiar, his hair as grey silver, tallest of all the Children of Ilúvatar; and a high doom was before him.

Now Ossë followed after the host of Olwë, and when they were come to the Bay of Eldamar (which is Elvenhome) he called to them; and they knew his voice, and begged Ulmo to stay their voyage. And Ulmo granted their request, and at his bidding Ossë made fast the island and rooted it to the foundations of the sea. Ulmo did this the more readily, for he understood the hearts of the Teleri, and in the council of the Valar he had spoken against the summons, thinking that it were better for the Quendi to remain in Middle-earth. The Valar were little pleased to learn what he had done; and Finwë grieved when the Teleri came not, and yet more when he learned that Elwë was forsaken, and knew that he should not see him again, unless it were in the halls of Mandos. But the island was not moved again, and stood there alone in the Bay of Eldamar; and it was called Tol Eressëa, the Lonely Isle. There the Teleri abode as they wished under the stars of heaven, and yet within sight of Aman and the deathless shore; and by that long sojourn apart in the Lonely Isle was caused the sundering of their speech from that of the Vanyar and the Noldor.

To these the Valar had given a land and a dwelling-place. Even among the radiant flowers of the Tree-lit gardens of Valinor they longed still at times to see the stars; and therefore a gap was made in the great walls of the Pelóri, and there in a deep valley that ran down to the sea the Eldar raised a high green hill: Túna it was called. From the west the light of the Trees fell upon it, and its shadow lay ever eastward; and to the east it looked towards the Bay of Elvenhome, and the Lonely Isle, and the Shadowy Seas. Then through the Calacirya, the Pass of Light, the radiance of the Blessed Realm streamed forth, kindling the dark waves to silver and gold, and it touched the Lonely Isle, and its western shore grew green and fair. There bloomed the first flowers that ever were east of the Mountains of Aman.

Upon the crown of Túna the city of the Elves was built, the white walls and terraces of Tirion; and the highest of the towers of that city was the Tower of Ingwë, Mindon Eldaliéva, whose silver lamp shone far out into the mists of the sea. Few are the ships of mortal Men that have seen its slender beam. In Tirion upon Túna the Vanyar and the Noldor dwelt long in fellowship. And since of all things in Valinor they loved most the White Tree, Yavanna made for them a tree like to a lesser image of Telperion, save that it did not give light of its own being; Galathilion it was named in the Sindarin tongue. This tree was planted in the courts beneath the Mindon and there flourished, and its seedlings were many in Eldamar. Of these one was afterwards planted in Tol Eressëa, and it prospered there, and was named Celeborn; thence came in the fullness of time, as is elsewhere told, Nimloth, the White Tree of Númenor.

Manwë and Varda loved most the Vanyar, the Fair Elves; but the Noldor were beloved of Aulë, and he and his people came often among them. Great became their knowledge and their skill; yet even greater was their thirst for more knowledge, and in many things they soon surpassed their teachers. They were changeful in speech, for they had great love of words, and sought ever to find names more fit for all things that they knew or imagined. And it came to pass that the masons of the house of Finwë, quarrying in the hills after stone (for they delighted in the building of high towers), first discovered the earth-gems, and brought them forth in countless myriads; and they devised tools for the cutting and shaping of gems, and carved them in many forms. They hoarded them not, but gave them freely, and by their labour enriched all Valinor.

The Noldor afterwards came back to Middle-earth, and this tale tells mostly of their deeds; therefore the names and kinship of their princes may here be told, in that form which these names later bore in the tongue of the Elves of Beleriand.

Finwë was King of the Noldor. The sons of Finwë were Fëanor, and Fingolfin, and Finarfin; but the mother of Fëanor was Míriel Serindë, whereas the mother of Fingolfin and Finarfin was Indis of the Vanyar.

Fëanor was the mightiest in skill of word and of hand, more learned than his brothers; his spirit burned as a flame. Fingolfin was the strongest, the most steadfast, and the most valiant. Finarfin was the fairest, and the most wise of heart; and afterwards he was a friend of the sons of Olwë, lord of the Teleri, and had to wife Eärwen, the swan-maiden of Alqualondë, Olwë's daughter.

The seven sons of Fëanor were Maedhros the tall; Maglor the mighty singer, whose voice was heard far over land and sea; Celegorm the fair, and Caranthir the dark; Curufin the crafty, who inherited most his father's skill of hand; and the youngest Amrod and Amras, who were twin brothers, alike in mood and face. In later days they were great hunters in the woods of Middle-earth; and a hunter also was Celegorm, who in Valinor was a friend of Oromë, and often followed the Vala's horn.

The sons of Fingolfin were Fingon, who was afterwards King of the Noldor in the north of the world, and Turgon, lord of Gondolin; their sister was Aredhel the White. She was younger in the years of the Eldar than her brothers; and when she was grown to full stature and beauty she was tall and strong, and loved much to ride and hunt in the forests. There she was often in the company of the sons of Fëanor, her kin; but to none was her heart's love given. Ar-Feiniel she was called, the White Lady of the Noldor, for she was pale, though her hair was dark, and she was never arrayed but in silver and white.

The sons of Finarfin were Finrod the faithful (who was afterwards named Felagund, Lord of Caves), Orodreth, Angrod, and Aegnor; these four were as close in friendship with the sons of Fingolfin as though they were all brothers. A sister they had, Galadriel, most beautiful of all the house of Finwë; her hair was lit with gold as though it had caught in a mesh the radiance of Laurelin.

Here must be told how the Teleri came at last to the land of Aman. Through a long age they dwelt in Tol Eressëa; but slowly their hearts were changed, and were drawn towards the light that flowed out over the sea to the Lonely Isle. They were torn between the love of the music of the waves upon their shores, and the desire to see again their kindred and to look upon the splendour of Valinor; but in the end desire of the light was the stronger. Therefore Ulmo, submitting to the will of the Valar, sent to them Ossë, their friend, and he though grieving taught them the craft of ship-building; and when their ships were built he brought them as his parting gift many strong-winged swans. Then the swans drew the white ships of the Teleri over the windless sea; and thus at last and latest they came to Aman and the shores of Eldamar.

There they dwelt, and if they wished they could see the light of the Trees, and could tread the golden streets of Valmar and the crystal stairs of Tirion upon Túna, the green hill; but most of all they sailed in their swift ships on the waters of the Bay of Elvenhome, or walked in the waves upon the shore with their hair gleaming in the light beyond the hill. Many jewels the Noldor gave them, opals and diamonds and pale crystals, which they strewed upon the shores and scattered in the pools; marvellous were the beaches of Elendë in those days. And many pearls they won for themselves from the sea, and their halls were of pearl, and of pearl were the mansions of Olwë at Alqualondë, the Haven of the Swans, lit with many lamps. For that was their city, and the haven of their ships; and those were made in the likeness of swans, with beaks of gold and eyes of gold and jet. The gate of that harbour was an arch of living rock sea-carved; and it lay upon the confines of Eldamar, north of the Calacirya, where the light of the stars was bright and clear.

As the ages passed the Vanyar grew to love the land of the Valar and the full light of the Trees, and they forsook the city of Tirion upon Túna, and dwelt thereafter upon the mountain of Manwë, or about the plains and woods of Valinor, and became sundered from the Noldor. But the memory of Middle-earth under the stars remained in the hearts of the Noldor, and they abode in the Calacirya, and in the hills and valleys within sound of the western sea; and though many of them went often about the land of the Valar, making far journeys in search of the secrets of land and water and all living things, yet the peoples of Túna and Alqualondë drew together in those days. Finwë was king in Tirion and Olwë in Alqualondë; but Ingwë was ever held the High King of all the Elves. He abode thereafter at the feet of Manwë upon Taniquetil.

Fëanor and his sons abode seldom in one place for long, but travelled far and wide upon the confines of Valinor, going even to the borders of the Dark and the cold shores of the Outer Sea, seeking the unknown. Often they were guests in the halls of Aulë; but Celegorm went rather to the house of Oromë, and there he got great knowledge of birds and beasts, and all their tongues he knew. For all living things that are or have been in the Kingdom of Arda, save only the fell and evil creatures of Melkor, lived then in the land of Aman; and there also were many other creatures that have not been seen upon Middle-earth, and perhaps never now shall be, since the fashion of the world was changed.

Chapter 6

OF FËANOR AND THE UNCHAINING OF MELKOR

Now the Three Kindreds of the Eldar were gathered at last in Valinor, and Melkor was chained. This was the Noontide of the Blessed Realm, the fullness of its glory and its bliss, long in tale of years, but in memory too brief. In those days the Eldar became full-grown in stature of body and of mind, and the Noldor advanced ever in skill and knowledge; and the long years were filled with their joyful labours, in which many new things fair and wonderful were devised. Then it was that the Noldor first bethought them of letters, and Rúmil of Tirion was the name of the loremaster who first achieved fitting signs for the recording of speech and song, some for graving upon metal or in stone, others for drawing with brush or with pen.

In that time was born in Eldamar, in the house of the King in Tirion upon the crown of Túna, the eldest of the sons of Finwë, and the most beloved. Curufinwë was his name, but by his mother he was called Fëanor, Spirit of Fire; and thus he is remembered in all the tales of the Noldor.

Míriel was the name of his mother, who was called Serindë, because of her surpassing skill in weaving and needlework; for her hands were more skilled to fineness than any hands even among the Noldor. The love of Finwë and Míriel was great and glad, for it began in the Blessed Realm in the Days of Bliss. But in the bearing of her son Míriel was consumed in spirit and body; and after his birth she yearned for release from the labour of living. And when she had named him, she said to Finwë: 'Never again shall I bear child; for strength that would have nourished the life of many has gone forth into Fëanor.'

Then Finwë was grieved, for the Noldor were in the youth of their days, and he desired to bring forth many children into the bliss of Aman; and he said: 'Surely there is healing in Aman? Here all weariness can find rest.' But when Míriel languished still, Finwë sought the counsel of Manwë, and Manwë delivered her to the care of Irmo in Lórien. At their parting (for a little while as he thought) Finwë was sad, for it seemed an unhappy chance that the mother should depart and miss the beginning at least of the childhood days of her son.

'It is indeed unhappy,' said Míriel, 'and I would weep, if I were not so weary. But hold me blameless in this, and in all that may come after.'

She went then to the gardens of Lórien and lay down to sleep; but though she seemed to sleep, her spirit indeed departed from her body, and passed in silence to the halls of Mandos. The maidens of Estë tended the body of Míriel, and it remained unwithered; but she did not return. Then Finwë lived in sorrow; and he went often to the gardens of Lórien, and sitting beneath the silver willows beside the body of his wife he called her by her names. But it was unavailing; and alone in all the Blessed Realm he was deprived of joy. After a while he went to Lórien no more.

All his love he gave thereafter to his son; and Fëanor grew swiftly, as if a secret fire were kindled within him. He was tall, and fair of face, and masterful, his eyes piercingly bright and his hair raven-dark; in the pursuit of all his purposes eager and steadfast. Few ever changed his courses by counsel, none by force. He became of all the Noldor, then or after, the most subtle in mind and the most skilled in hand. In his youth, bettering the work of Rúmil, he devised those letters which bear his name, and which the Eldar used ever after; and he it was who, first of the Noldor, discovered how gems greater and brighter than those of the Earth might be made with skill. The first gems that Fëanor made were white and colourless, but being set under starlight they would blaze with blue and silver fires brighter than Helluin; and other crystals he made also, wherein things far away could be seen small but clear, as with the eyes of the eagles of Manwë. Seldom were the hands and mind of Fëanor at rest.

While still in his early youth he wedded Nerdanel, the daughter of a great smith named Mahtan, among those of the Noldor most dear to Aulë; and of Mahtan he learned much of the making of things in metal and in stone. Nerdanel also was firm of will, but more patient than Fëanor, desiring to understand minds rather than to master them, and at first she restrained him when the fire of his heart grew too hot; but his later deeds grieved her, and they became estranged. Seven sons she bore to Fëanor; her mood she bequeathed in part to some of them, but not to all.

Now it came to pass that Finwë took as his second wife Indis the Fair. She was a Vanya, close kin of Ingwë the High King, golden-haired and tall, and in all ways unlike Míriel. Finwë loved her greatly, and was glad again. But the shadow of Míriel did not depart from the house of Finwë, nor from his heart; and of all whom he loved Fëanor had ever the chief share of his thought.

The wedding of his father was not pleasing to Fëanor; and he had no great love for Indis, nor for Fingolfin and Finarfin, her sons. He lived apart from them, exploring the land of Aman, or busying himself with the knowledge and the crafts in which he delighted. In those unhappy things which later came to pass, and in which Fëanor was the leader, many saw the effect of this breach within the house of Finwë, judging that if Finwë had endured his loss and been content with the fathering of his mighty son, the courses of Fëanor would have been otherwise, and great evil might have been prevented; for the sorrow and the strife in the house of Finwë is graven in the memory of the Noldorin Elves. But the children of Indis were great and glorious, and their children also; and if they had not lived the history of the Eldar would have been diminished.

Now even while Fëanor and the craftsmen of the Noldor worked with delight, foreseeing no end to their labours, and while the sons of Indis grew to their full stature, the Noontide of Valinor was drawing to its close. For it came to pass that Melkor, as the Valar had decreed, completed the term of his bondage, dwelling for three ages in the duress of Mandos, alone. At length, as Manwë had promised, he was brought again before the thrones of the Valar. Then he looked upon their glory and their bliss, and envy was in his heart; he looked upon the Children of Ilúvatar that sat at the feet of the Mighty, and hatred filled him; he looked upon the wealth of bright gems, and he lusted for them; but he hid his thoughts, and postponed his vengeance.

Before the gates of Valmar Melkor abased himself at the feet of Manwë and sued for pardon, vowing that if he might be made only the least of the free people of Valinor he would aid the Valar in all their works, and most of all in the healing of the many hurts that he had done to the world. And Nienna aided his prayer; but Mandos was silent.

Then Manwë granted him pardon; but the Valar would not yet suffer him to depart beyond their sight and vigilance, and he was constrained to dwell within the gates of Valmar. But fair-seeming were all the words and deeds of Melkor in that time, and both the Valar and the Eldar had profit from his aid and counsel, if they sought it; and therefore in a while he was given leave to go freely about the land, and it seemed to Manwë that the evil of Melkor was cured. For Manwë was free from evil and could not comprehend it, and he knew that in the beginning, in the thought of Ilúvatar, Melkor had been even as he; and he saw not to the depths of Melkor's heart, and did not perceive that all love had departed from him for ever. But Ulmo was not deceived, and Tulkas clenched his hands whenever he saw Melkor his foe go by; for if Tulkas is slow to wrath he is slow also to forget. But they obeyed the judgement of Manwë; for those who will defend authority against rebellion must not themselves rebel.

Now in his heart Melkor most hated the Eldar, both because they were fair and joyful and because in them he saw the reason for the arising of the Valar, and his own downfall. Therefore all the more did he feign love for them and seek their friendship, and he offered them the service of his lore and labour in any great deed that they would do. The Vanyar indeed held him in suspicion, for they dwelt in the light of the Trees and were content; and to the Teleri he gave small heed, thinking them of little worth, tools too weak for his designs. But the Noldor took delight in the hidden knowledge that he could reveal to them; and some hearkened to words that it would have been better for them never to have heard. Melkor indeed declared afterwards that Fëanor had learned much art from him in secret, and had been instructed by him in the greatest of all his works; but he lied in his lust and his envy, for none of the Eldalië ever hated Melkor more than Fëanor son of Finwë, who first named him Morgoth; and snared though he was in the webs of Melkor's malice against the Valar he held no converse with him and took no counsel from him. For Fëanor was driven by the fire of his own heart only, working ever swiftly and alone; and he asked the aid and sought the counsel of none that dwelt in Aman, great or small, save only and for a little while of Nerdanel the wise, his wife.

Chapter 7

OF THE SILMARILS AND THE UNREST OF THE NOLDOR

In that time were made those things that afterwards were most renowned of all the works of the Elves. For Fëanor, being come to his full might, was filled with a new thought, or it may be that some shadow of foreknowledge came to him of the doom that drew near; and he pondered how the light of the Trees, the glory of the Blessed Realm, might be preserved imperishable. Then he began a long and secret labour, and he summoned all his lore, and his power, and his subtle skill; and at the end of all he made the Silmarils.

As three great jewels they were in form. But not until the End, when Fëanor shall return who perished ere the Sun was made, and sits now in the Halls of Awaiting and comes no more among his kin; not until the Sun passes and the Moon falls, shall it be known of what substance they were made. Like the crystal of diamonds it appeared, and yet was more strong than adamant, so that no violence could mar it or break it within the Kingdom of Arda. Yet that crystal was to the Silmarils but as is the body to the Children of Ilúvatar: the house of its inner fire, that is within it and yet in all parts of it, and is its life. And the inner fire of the Silmarils Fëanor made of the blended light of the Trees of Valinor, which lives in them yet, though the Trees have long withered and shine no more. Therefore even in the darkness of the deepest treasury the Silmarils of their own radiance shone like the stars of Varda; and yet, as were they indeed living things, they rejoiced in light and received it and gave it back in hues more marvellous than before.

All who dwelt in Aman were filled with wonder and delight at the work of Fëanor. And Varda hallowed the Silmarils, so that thereafter no mortal flesh, nor hands unclean, nor anything of evil will might touch them, but it was scorched and withered; and Mandos foretold that the fates of Arda, earth, sea, and air, lay locked within them. The heart of Fëanor was fast bound to these things that he himself had made.

Then Melkor lusted for the Silmarils, and the very memory of their radiance was a gnawing fire in his heart. From that time forth, inflamed by this desire, he sought ever more eagerly how he should destroy Fëanor and end the friendship of the Valar and the Elves; but he dissembled his purposes with cunning, and nothing of his malice could yet be seen in the semblance that he wore. Long was he at work, and slow at first and barren was his labour. But he that sows lies in the end shall not lack of a harvest, and soon he may rest from toil indeed while others reap and sow in his stead. Ever Melkor found some ears that would heed him, and some tongues that would enlarge what they had heard; and his lies passed from friend to friend, as secrets of which the knowledge proves the teller wise. Bitterly did the Noldor atone for the folly of their open ears in the days that followed after.

When he saw that many leaned towards him, Melkor would often walk among them, and amid his fair words others were woven, so subtly that many who heard them believed in recollection that they arose from their own thought. Visions he would conjure in their hearts of the mighty realms that they could have ruled at their own will, in power and freedom in the East; and then whispers went abroad that the Valar had brought the Eldar to Aman because of their jealousy, fearing that the beauty of the Quendi and the makers' power that Ilúvatar had bequeathed to them would grow too great for the Valar to govern, as the Elves waxed and spread over the wide lands of the world.

In those days, moreover, though the Valar knew indeed of the coming of Men that were to be, the Elves as yet knew naught of it; for Manwë had not revealed it to them. But Melkor spoke to them in secret of Mortal Men, seeing how the silence of the Valar might be twisted to evil. Little he knew yet concerning Men, for engrossed with his own thought in the Music he had paid small heed to the Third Theme of Ilúvatar; but now the whisper went among the Elves that Manwë held them captive, so that Men might come and supplant

he taught to the husband of Nerdanel all the lore of metalwork that he had learned of Aulë.

Thus with lies and evil whisperings and false counsel Melkor kindled the hearts of the Noldor to strife; and of their quarrels came at length the end of the high days of Valinor and the evening of its ancient glory. For Fëanor now began openly to speak words of rebellion against the Valar, crying aloud that he would depart from Valinor back to the world without, and would deliver the Noldor from thraldom, if they would follow him.

Then there was great unrest in Tirion, and Finwë was troubled; and he summoned all his lords to council. But Fingolfin hastened to his halls and stood before him, saying: 'King and father, wilt thou not restrain the pride of our brother, Curufinwë, who is called the Spirit of Fire, all too truly? By what right does he speak for all our people, as if he were King? Thou it was who long ago spoke before the Quendi, bidding them accept the summons of the Valar to Aman. Thou it was that led the Noldor upon the long road through the perils of Middle-earth to the light of Eldamar. If thou dost not now repent of it, two sons at least thou hast to honour thy words.'

But even as Fingolfin spoke, Fëanor strode into the chamber, and he was fully armed: his high helm upon his head, and at his side a mighty sword. 'So it is, even as I guessed,' he said. 'My half-brother would be before me with my father, in this as in all other matters.' Then turning upon Fingolfin he drew his sword, crying: 'Get thee gone, and take thy due place!'

Fingolfin bowed before Finwë, and without word or glance to Fëanor he went from the chamber. But Fëanor followed him, and at the door of the king's house he stayed him; and the point of his bright sword he set against Fingolfin's breast. 'See, half-brother!' he said. 'This is sharper than thy tongue. Try but once more to usurp my place and the love of my father, and maybe it will rid the Noldor of one who seeks to be the master of thralls.'

These words were heard by many, for the house of Finwë was in the great square beneath the Mindon; but again Fingolfin made no answer, and passing through the throng in silence he went to seek Finarfin his brother.

Now the unrest of the Noldor was not indeed hidden from the Valar, but its seed had been sown in the dark; and therefore, since Fëanor first spoke openly against them, they judged that he was the mover of discontent, being eminent in self-will and arrogance, though all the Noldor had become proud. And Manwë was grieved, but he watched and said no word. The Valar had brought the Eldar to their land freely, to dwell or to depart; and though they might judge departure to be folly, they might not restrain them from it. But now the deeds of Fëanor could not be passed over, and the Valar were angered and dismayed; and he was summoned to appear before them at the gates of Valmar, to answer for all his words and deeds. There also were summoned all others who had any part in this matter, or any knowledge of it; and Fëanor standing before Mandos in the Ring of Doom was commanded to answer all that was asked of him. Then at last the root was laid bare, and the malice of Melkor revealed; and straightway Tulkas left the council to lay hands upon him and bring him again to judgement. But Fëanor was not held guiltless, for he it was that had broken the peace of Valinor and drawn his sword upon his kinsman; and Mandos said to him: 'Thou speakest of thraldom. If thraldom it be, thou canst not escape it; for Manwë is King of Arda, and not of Aman only. And this deed was unlawful, whether in Aman or not in Aman. Therefore this doom is now made: for twelve years thou shalt leave Tirion where this threat was uttered. In that time take counsel with thyself, and remember who and what thou art. But after that time this matter shall be set in peace and held redressed, if others will release thee.'

Then Fingolfin said: 'I will release my brother.' But Fëanor spoke no word in answer, standing silent before the Valar. Then he turned and left the council, and departed from Valmar.

With him into banishment went his seven sons, and northward in Valinor they made a strong place and treasury in the hills; and there at Formenos a multitude of gems were laid in hoard, and weapons also, and the Silmarils were shut in a chamber of iron. Thither also came Finwë the King, because of the love that he bore to Fëanor; and Fingolfin ruled the Noldor in Tirion. Thus the lies of Melkor were made true in seeming, though Fëanor by his own deeds had brought this thing to pass; and the bitterness that Melkor had sown endured, and lived still long afterwards between the sons of Fingolfin and Fëanor.

Now Melkor, knowing that his devices had been revealed, hid himself and passed from place to place as a cloud in the hills; and Tulkas sought for him in vain. Then it seemed to the people of Valinor that the light of the Trees was dimmed, and the shadows of all standing things grew longer and darker in that time.

It is told that for a time Melkor was not seen again in Valinor, nor was any rumour heard of him, until suddenly he came to Formenos, and spoke with Fëanor before his doors. Friendship he feigned with cunning argument, urging him to his former thought of flight from the trammels of the Valar; and he said: 'Behold the truth of all that I have spoken, and how thou art banished unjustly. But if the heart of Fëanor is yet free and bold as were his words in Tirion, then I will aid him, and bring him far from this narrow land. For am I not Vala also? Yea, and more than those who sit in pride in Valimar; and I have ever been a friend to the Noldor, most skilled and most valiant of the people of Arda.'

Now Fëanor's heart was still bitter at his humiliation before Mandos, and he looked at Melkor in silence, pondering if indeed he might yet trust him so far as to aid him in his flight. And Melkor, seeing that Fëanor wavered, and knowing that the Silmarils held his heart in thrall, said at the last: 'Here is a strong place, and well guarded; but think not that the Silmarils will lie safe in any treasury within the realm of the Valar!'

But his cunning overreached his aim; his words touched too deep, and awoke a fire more fierce than he designed; and Fëanor looked upon Melkor with eyes that burned through his fair semblance and pierced the cloaks of his mind, perceiving there his fierce lust for the Silmarils. Then hate overcame Fëanor's fear, and he cursed Melkor and bade him be gone, saying: 'Get thee gone from my gate, thou jail-crow of Mandos!' And he shut the doors of his house in the face of the mightiest of all the dwellers in Eä.

Then Melkor departed in shame, for he was himself in peril, and he saw not his time yet for revenge; but his heart was black with anger. And Finwë was filled with great fear, and in haste he sent messengers to Manwë in Valmar.

Now the Valar were sitting in council before their gates, fearing the lengthening of the shadows, when the messengers came from Formenos. At once Oromë and Tulkas sprang up, but even as they set out in pursuit messengers came from Eldamar, telling that Melkor had fled through the Calacirya, and from the hill of Túna the Elves had seen him pass in wrath as a thundercloud. And they said that thence he had turned northward, for the Teleri in Alqualondë had seen his shadow going by their haven towards Araman.

Thus Melkor departed from Valinor, and for a while the Two Trees shone again unshadowed, and the land was filled with light. But the

Valar sought in vain for tidings of their enemy; and as a cloud far off that looms ever higher, borne upon a slow cold wind, a doubt now marred the joy of all the dwellers in Aman, dreading they knew not what evil that yet might come.

Chapter 8

OF THE DARKENING OF VALINOR

When Manwë heard of the ways that Melkor had taken, it seemed plain to him that he purposed to escape to his old strongholds in the north of Middle-earth; and Oromë and Tulkas went with all speed northward, seeking to overtake him if they might, but they found no trace or rumour of him beyond the shores of the Teleri, in the unpeopled wastes that drew near to the Ice. Thereafter the watch was redoubled along the northern fences of Aman; but to no purpose, for ere ever the pursuit set out Melkor had turned back, and in secrecy passed away far to the south. For he was yet as one of the Valar, and could change his form, or walk unclad, as could his brethren; though that power he was soon to lose for ever.

Thus unseen he came at last to the dark region of Avathar. That narrow land lay south of the Bay of Eldamar, beneath the eastern feet of the Pelóri, and its long and mournful shores stretched away into the south, lightless and unexplored. There, beneath the sheer walls of the mountains and the cold dark sea, the shadows were deepest and thickest in the world; and there in Avathar, secret and unknown, Ungoliant had made her abode. The Eldar knew not whence she came; but some have said that in ages long before she descended from the darkness that lies about Arda, when Melkor first looked down in envy upon the Kingdom of Manwë, and that in the beginning she was one of those that he corrupted to his service. But she had disowned her Master, desiring to be mistress of her own lust, taking all things to herself to feed her emptiness; and she fled to the south, escaping the assaults of the Valar and the hunters of Oromë, for their vigilance had ever been to the north, and the south was long unheeded. Thence she had crept towards the light of the Blessed Realm; for she hungered for light and hated it.

In a ravine she lived, and took shape as a spider of monstrous form, weaving her black webs in a cleft of the mountains. There she sucked up all light that she could find, and spun it forth again in dark nets of strangling gloom, until no light more could come to her abode; and she was famished.

Now Melkor came to Avathar and sought her out; and he put on again the form that he had worn as the tyrant of Utumno: a dark Lord, tall and terrible. In that form he remained ever after. There in the black shadows, beyond the sight even of Manwë in his highest halls, Melkor with Ungoliant plotted his revenge. But when Ungoliant understood the purpose of Melkor, she was torn between lust and great fear; for she was loath to dare the perils of Aman and the power of the dreadful Lords, and she would not stir from her hiding. Therefore Melkor said to her: 'Do as I bid; and if thou hunger still when all is done, then I will give thee whatsoever thy lust may demand. Yea, with both hands.' Lightly he made this vow, as he ever did; and he laughed in his heart. Thus did the great thief set his lure for the lesser.

A cloak of darkness she wove about them when Melkor and Ungoliant set forth: an Unlight, in which things seemed to be no more, and which eyes could not pierce, for it was void. Then slowly she wrought her webs: rope by rope from cleft to cleft, from jutting rock to pinnacle of stone, ever climbing upwards, crawling and clinging, until at last she reached the very summit of Hyarmentir, the highest mountain in that region of the world, far south of great Taniquetil. There the Valar were not vigilant; for west of the Pelóri was an empty land in twilight, and eastward the mountains looked out, save for forgotten Avathar, only upon the dim waters of the pathless sea.

But now upon the mountain-top dark Ungoliant lay; and she made a ladder of woven ropes and cast it down, and Melkor climbed upon it and came to that high place, and stood beside her, looking down upon the Guarded Realm. Below them lay the woods of Oromë, and westward shimmered the fields and pastures of Yavanna, gold beneath the tall wheat of the gods. But Melkor looked north, and saw afar the shining plain, and the silver domes of Valmar gleaming in the mingling of the lights of Telperion and Laurelin. Then Melkor laughed aloud, and leapt swiftly down the long western slopes; and Ungoliant was at his side, and her darkness covered them.

Now it was a time of festival, as Melkor knew well. Though all tides and seasons were at the will of the Valar, and in Valinor there was no winter of death, nonetheless they dwelt then in the Kingdom of Arda, and that was but a small realm in the halls of Eä, whose life is Time, which flows ever from the first note to the last chord of Eru. And even as it was then the delight of the Valar (as is told in the *Ainulindalë*) to clothe themselves as in a vesture in the forms of the Children of Ilúvatar, so also did they eat and drink, and gather the fruits of Yavanna from the Earth, which under Eru they had made.

Therefore Yavanna set times for the flowering and the ripening of all things that grew in Valinor; and at each first gathering of fruits Manwë made a high feast for the praising of Eru, when all the peoples of Valinor poured forth their joy in music and song upon Taniquetil. This now was the hour, and Manwë decreed a feast more glorious than any that had been held since the coming of the Eldar to Aman. For though the escape of Melkor portended toils and sorrows to come, and indeed none could tell what further hurts would be done to Arda ere he could be subdued again, at this time Manwë designed to heal the evil that had arisen among the Noldor; and all were bidden to come to his halls upon Taniquetil, there to put aside the griefs that lay between their princes, and forget utterly the lies of their Enemy.

There came the Vanyar, and there came the Noldor of Tirion, and the Maiar were gathered together, and the Valar were arrayed in their beauty and majesty; and they sang before Manwë and Varda in their lofty halls, or danced upon the green slopes of the Mountain that looked west towards the Trees. In that day the streets of Valmar were empty, and the stairs of Tirion were silent; and all the land lay sleeping in peace. Only the Teleri beyond the mountains still sang upon the shores of the sea; for they recked little of seasons or times, and gave no thought to the cares of the Rulers of Arda, or the shadow that had fallen on Valinor, for it had not touched them, as yet.

One thing only marred the design of Manwë. Fëanor came indeed, for him alone Manwë had commanded to come; but Finwë came not, nor any others of the Noldor of Formenos. For said Finwë: 'While the ban lasts upon Fëanor my son, that he may not go to Tirion, I hold myself unkinged, and I will not meet my people.' And Fëanor came not in raiment of festival, and he wore no ornament, neither silver nor gold nor any gem; and he denied the sight of the Silmarils to the

Valar and the Eldar, and left them locked in Formenos in their chamber of iron. Nevertheless he met Fingolfin before the throne of Manwë, and was reconciled, in word; and Fingolfin set at naught the unsheathing of the sword. For Fingolfin held forth his hand, saying: 'As I promised, I do now. I release thee, and remember no grievance.'

Then Fëanor took his hand in silence; but Fingolfin said: 'Half-brother in blood, full brother in heart will I be. Thou shalt lead and I will follow. May no new grief divide us.'

'I hear thee,' said Fëanor. 'So be it.' But they did not know the meaning that their words would bear.

It is told that even as Fëanor and Fingolfin stood before Manwë there came the mingling of the lights, when both Trees were shining, and the silent city of Valmar was filled with a radiance of silver and gold. And in that very hour Melkor and Ungoliant came hastening over the fields of Valinor, as the shadow of a black cloud upon the wind fleets over the sunlit earth; and they came before the green mound Ezellohar. Then the Unlight of Ungoliant rose up even to the roots of the Trees, and Melkor sprang upon the mound; and with his black spear he smote each Tree to its core, wounded them deep, and their sap poured forth as it were their blood, and was spilled upon the ground. But Ungoliant sucked it up, and going then from Tree to Tree she set her black beak to their wounds, till they were drained; and the poison of Death that was in her went into their tissues and withered them, root, branch, and leaf; and they died. And still she thirsted, and going to the Wells of Varda she drank them dry; but Ungoliant belched forth black vapours as she drank, and swelled to a shape so vast and hideous that Melkor was afraid.

So the great darkness fell upon Valinor. Of the deeds of that day much is told in the *Aldudénië*, that Elemmírë of the Vanyar made and is known to all the Eldar. Yet no song or tale could contain all the grief and terror that then befell. The Light failed; but the Darkness that followed was more than loss of light. In that hour was made a Darkness that seemed not lack but a thing with being of its own: for it was indeed made by malice out of Light, and it had power to pierce the eye, and to enter heart and mind, and strangle the very will.

Varda looked down from Taniquetil, and beheld the Shadow soaring up in sudden towers of gloom; Valmar had foundered in a deep sea of night. Soon the Holy Mountain stood alone, a last island in a world that was drowned. All song ceased. There was silence in Valinor, and no sound could be heard, save only from afar there came on the wind through the pass of the mountains the wailing of the Teleri like the cold cry of gulls. For it blew chill from the East in that hour, and the vast shadows of the sea were rolled against the walls of the shore.

But Manwë from his high seat looked out, and his eyes alone pierced through the night, until they saw a Darkness beyond dark which they could not penetrate, huge but far away, moving now northward with great speed; and he knew that Melkor had come and gone.

Then the pursuit was begun; and the earth shook beneath the horses of the host of Oromë, and the fire that was stricken from the hooves of Nahar was the first light that returned to Valinor. But so soon as any came up with the Cloud of Ungoliant the riders of the Valar were blinded and dismayed, and they were scattered, and went they knew not whither; and the sound of the Valaróma faltered and failed. And Tulkas was as one caught in a black net at night, and he stood powerless and beat the air in vain. But when the Darkness had passed, it was too late: Melkor had gone whither he would, and his vengeance was achieved.

Chapter 9

OF THE FLIGHT OF THE NOLDOR

After a time a great concourse gathered about the Ring of Doom; and the Valar sat in shadow, for it was night. But the stars of Varda now glimmered overhead, and the air was clear; for the winds of Manwë had driven away the vapours of death and rolled back the shadows of the sea. Then Yavanna arose and stood upon Ezellohar, the Green Mound, but it was bare now and black; and she laid her hands upon the Trees, but they were dead and dark, and each branch that she touched broke and fell lifeless at her feet. Then many voices were lifted in lamentation; and it seemed to those that mourned that they had drained to the dregs the cup of woe that Melkor had filled for them. But it was not so.

Yavanna spoke before the Valar, saying: 'The Light of the Trees has passed away, and lives now only in the Silmarils of Fëanor. Foresighted was he! Even for those who are mightiest under Ilúvatar there is some work that they may accomplish once, and once only. The Light of the Trees I brought into being, and within Eä I can do so never again. Yet had I but a little of that light I could recall life to the Trees, ere their roots decay; and then our hurt should be healed, and the malice of Melkor be confounded.'

Then Manwë spoke and said: 'Hearest thou, Fëanor son of Finwë, the words of Yavanna? Wilt thou grant what she would ask?'

There was long silence, but Fëanor answered no word. Then Tulkas cried: 'Speak, O Noldo, yea or nay! But who shall deny Yavanna? And did not the light of the Silmarils come from her work in the beginning?'

But Aulë the Maker said: 'Be not hasty! We ask a greater thing than thou knowest. Let him have peace yet awhile.'

But Fëanor spoke then, and cried bitterly: 'For the less even as for the greater there is some deed that he may accomplish but once only; and in that deed his heart shall rest. It may be that I can unlock my jewels, but never again shall I make their like; and if I must break them, I shall break my heart, and I shall be slain; first of all the Eldar in Aman.'

'Not the first,' said Mandos, but they did not understand his word; and again there was silence, while Fëanor brooded in the dark. It seemed to him that he was beset in a ring of enemies, and the words of Melkor returned to him, saying that the Silmarils were not safe, if the Valar would possess them. 'And is he not Vala as are they,' said his thought, 'and does he not understand their hearts? Yea, a thief shall reveal thieves!' Then he cried aloud: 'This thing I will not do of free will. But if the Valar will constrain me, then shall I know indeed that Melkor is of their kindred.'

Then Mandos said: 'Thou hast spoken.' And Nienna arose and went up onto Ezellohar, and cast back her grey hood, and with her tears washed away the defilements of Ungoliant; and she sang in mourning for the bitterness of the world and the Marring of Arda.

But even as Nienna mourned, there came messengers from Formenos, and they were Noldor and bore new tidings of evil. For they told how a blind Darkness came northward, and in the midst walked some power for which there was no name, and the Darkness issued from it. But Melkor also was there, and he came to the house of Fëanor, and there he slew Finwë King of the Noldor before his doors, and spilled the first blood in the Blessed Realm; for Finwë alone had not fled from the horror of the Dark. And they told that Melkor had broken the stronghold of Formenos, and taken all the jewels of the Noldor that were hoarded in that place; and the Silmarils were gone.

Then Fëanor rose, and lifting up his hand before Manwë he cursed Melkor, naming him *Morgoth*, the Black Foe of the World; and by that name only was he known to the Eldar ever after. And he cursed also the summons of Manwë and the hour in which he came to Taniquetil, thinking in the madness of his rage and grief that had he been at Formenos his strength would have availed more than to be slain also, as Melkor had purposed. Then Fëanor ran from the Ring of Doom, and fled into the night; for his father was dearer to him than the Light of Valinor or the peerless works of his hands; and who among sons, of Elves or of Men, have held their fathers of greater worth?

Many there grieved for the anguish of Fëanor, but his loss was not his alone; and Yavanna wept by the mound, in fear that the Darkness should swallow the last rays of the Light of Valinor for ever. For though the Valar did not yet understand fully what had befallen, they perceived that Melkor had called upon some aid that came from beyond Arda. The Silmarils had passed away, and all one it may seem whether Fëanor had said yea or nay to Yavanna; yet had he said yea at the first, before the tidings came from Formenos, it may be that his after deeds would have been other than they were. But now the doom of the Noldor drew near.

Meanwhile Morgoth escaping from the pursuit of the Valar came to the wastes of Araman. This land lay northward between the Mountains of the Pelóri and the Great Sea, as Avathar lay to the south; but Araman was a wider land, and between the shores and the mountains were barren plains, ever colder as the Ice drew nearer. Through this region Morgoth and Ungoliant passed in haste, and so came through the great mists of Oiomúrë to the Helcaraxë, where the strait between Araman and Middle-earth was filled with grinding ice; and he crossed over, and came back at last to the north of the Outer Lands. Together they went on, for Morgoth could not elude Ungoliant, and her cloud was still about him, and all her eyes were upon him; and they came to those lands that lay north of the Firth of Drengist. Now Morgoth was drawing near to the ruins of Angband, where his great western stronghold had been; and Ungoliant perceived his hope, and knew that here he would seek to escape from her, and she stayed him, demanding that he fulfil his promise.

'Blackheart!' she said. 'I have done thy bidding. But I hunger still.'

'What wouldst thou have more?' said Morgoth. 'Dost thou desire all the world for thy belly? I did not vow to give thee that. I am its Lord.'

'Not so much,' said Ungoliant. 'But thou hast a great treasure from Formenos; I will have all that. Yea, with both hands thou shalt give it.'

Then perforce Morgoth surrendered to her the gems that he bore with him, one by one and grudgingly; and she devoured them, and their beauty perished from the world. Huger and darker yet grew Ungoliant, but her lust was unsated. 'With one hand thou givest,' she said; 'with the left only. Open thy right hand.'

In his right hand Morgoth held close the Silmarils, and though they were locked in a crystal casket, they had begun to burn him, and his hand was clenched in pain; but he would not open it. 'Nay!' he said. 'Thou hast had thy due. For with my power that I put into thee thy work was accomplished. I need thee no more. These things thou shalt not have, nor see. I name them unto myself for ever.'

But Ungoliant had grown great, and he less by the power that had gone out of him; and she rose against him, and her cloud closed about him, and she enmeshed him in a web of clinging thongs to strangle him. Then Morgoth sent forth a terrible cry, that echoed in the mountains. Therefore that region was called Lammoth; for the echoes of his voice dwelt there ever after, so that any who cried aloud in that land awoke them, and all the waste between the hills and the sea was filled with a clamour as of voices in anguish. The cry of Morgoth in that hour was the greatest and most dreadful that was ever heard in the northern world; the mountains shook, and the earth trembled, and rocks were riven asunder. Deep in forgotten places that cry was heard. Far beneath the ruined halls of Angband, in vaults to which the Valar in the haste of their assault had not descended, Balrogs lurked still, awaiting ever the return of their Lord; and now swiftly they arose, and passing over Hithlum they came to Lammoth as a tempest of fire. With their whips of flame they smote asunder the webs of Ungoliant, and she quailed, and turned to flight, belching black vapours to cover her; and fleeing from the north she went down into Beleriand, and dwelt beneath Ered Gorgoroth, in that dark valley that was after called Nan Dungortheb, the Valley of Dreadful Death, because of the horror that she bred there. For other foul creatures of spider form had dwelt there since the days of the delving of Angband, and she mated with them, and devoured them; and even after Ungoliant herself departed, and went whither she would into the forgotten south of the world, her offspring abode there and wove their hideous webs. Of the fate of Ungoliant no tale tells. Yet some have said that she ended long ago, when in her uttermost famine she devoured herself at last.

And thus the fear of Yavanna that the Silmarils would be swallowed up and fall into nothingness did not come to pass; but they remained in the power of Morgoth. And he being freed gathered again all his servants that he could find, and came to the ruins of Angband. There he delved anew his vast vaults and dungeons, and above their gates he reared the threefold peaks of Thangorodrim, and a great reek of dark smoke was ever wreathed about them. There countless became the hosts of his beasts and his demons, and the race of the Orcs, bred long before, grew and multiplied in the bowels of the earth. Dark now fell the shadow on Beleriand, as is told hereafter; but in Angband Morgoth forged for himself a great crown of iron, and he called himself King of the World. In token of this he set the Silmarils in his crown. His hands were burned black by the touch of those hallowed jewels, and black they remained ever after; nor was he ever free from the pain of the burning, and the anger of the pain. That crown he never took from his head, though its weight became a deadly weariness. Never but once only did he depart for a while secretly from his domain in the North; seldom indeed did he leave the deep places of his fortress, but governed his armies from his northern throne. And once only also did he himself wield weapon, while his realm lasted.

For now, more than in the days of Utumno ere his pride was humbled, his hatred devoured him, and in the domination of his servants and the inspiring of them with lust of evil he spent his spirit. Nonetheless his majesty as one of the Valar long remained, though turned to terror, and before his face all save the mightiest sank into a dark pit of fear.

Now when it was known that Morgoth had escaped from Valinor and pursuit was unavailing, the Valar remained long seated in darkness in the Ring of Doom, and the Maiar and the Vanyar stood beside them and wept; but the Noldor for the most part returned to Tirion and mourned for the darkening of their fair city. Through the dim ravine of the Calacirya fogs drifted in from the shadowy seas and mantled its towers, and the lamp of the Mindon burned pale in the gloom.

Then suddenly Fëanor appeared in the city and called on all to come to the high court of the King upon the summit of Túna; but the doom of banishment that had been laid upon him was not yet lifted, and he rebelled against the Valar. A great multitude gathered swiftly, therefore, to hear what he would say; and the hill and all the stairs and streets that climbed upon it were lit with the light of many torches that each one bore in hand. Fëanor was a master of words, and his tongue had great power over hearts when he would use it; and that night he made a speech before the Noldor which they ever remembered. Fierce and fell were his words, and filled with anger and pride; and hearing them the Noldor were stirred to madness. His wrath and his hate were given most to Morgoth, and yet well nigh all that he said came from the very lies of Morgoth himself; but he was distraught with grief for the slaying of his father, and with anguish for the rape of the Silmarils. He claimed now the kingship of all the Noldor, since Finwë was dead, and he scorned the decrees of the Valar.

'Why, O people of the Noldor,' he cried, 'why should we longer serve the jealous Valar, who cannot keep us nor even their own realm secure from their Enemy? And though he be now their foe, are not they and he of one kin? Vengeance calls me hence, but even were it otherwise I would not dwell longer in the same land with the kin of my father's slayer and of the thief of my treasure. Yet I am not the only valiant in this valiant people. And have ye not all lost your King? And what else have ye not lost, cooped here in a narrow land between the mountains and the sea?

'Here once was light, that the Valar begrudged to Middle-earth, but now dark levels all. Shall we mourn here deedless for ever, a shadow-folk, mist-haunting, dropping vain tears in the thankless sea? Or shall we return to our home? In Cuiviénen sweet ran the waters under unclouded stars, and wide lands lay about, where a free people might walk. There they lie still and await us who in our folly forsook them. Come away! Let the cowards keep this city!'

Long he spoke, and ever he urged the Noldor to follow him and by their own prowess to win freedom and great realms in the lands of the East, before it was too late; for he echoed the lies of Melkor, that the Valar had cozened them and would hold them captive so that Men might rule in Middle-earth. Many of the Eldar heard then for the first time of the Aftercomers. 'Fair shall the end be,' he cried, 'though long and hard shall be the road! Say farewell to bondage! But say farewell also to ease! Say farewell to the weak! Say farewell to your treasures! More still shall we make. Journey light: but bring with you your swords! For we will go further than Oromë, endure longer than Tulkas: we will never turn back from pursuit. After Morgoth to the ends of the Earth! War shall he have and hatred undying. But when we have conquered and have regained the Silmarils, then we and we alone shall be lords of the unsullied Light, and masters of the bliss and beauty of Arda. No other race shall oust us!'

Then Fëanor swore a terrible oath. His seven sons leapt straightway to his side and took the selfsame vow together, and red as blood shone their drawn swords in the glare of the torches. They swore an oath which none shall break, and none should take, by the name even of Ilúvatar, calling the Everlasting Dark upon them if they kept it not; and Manwë they named in witness, and Varda, and the hallowed mountain of Taniquetil, vowing to pursue with vengeance and hatred to the ends of the World Vala, Demon, Elf or Man as yet unborn, or any creature, great or small, good or evil, that time should bring forth unto the end of days, whoso should hold or take or keep a Silmaril from their possession.

Thus spoke Maedhros and Maglor and Celegorm, Curufin and Caranthir, Amrod and Amras, princes of the Noldor; and many quailed to hear the dread words. For so sworn, good or evil, an oath may not be broken, and it shall pursue oathkeeper and oathbreaker to the world's end. Fingolfin and Turgon his son therefore spoke against Fëanor, and fierce words awoke, so that once again wrath came near to the edge of swords. But Finarfin spoke softly, as was his wont, and sought to calm the Noldor, persuading them to pause and ponder ere deeds were done that could not be undone; and Orodreth, alone of his sons, spoke in like manner. Finrod was with Turgon, his friend; but Galadriel, the only woman of the Noldor to stand that day tall and valiant among the contending princes, was eager to be gone. No oaths she swore, but the words of Fëanor concerning Middle-earth had kindled in her heart, for she yearned to see the wide unguarded lands and to rule there a realm at her own will. Of like mind with Galadriel was Fingon Fingolfin's son, being moved also by Fëanor's words, though he loved him little; and with Fingon stood as they ever did Angrod and Aegnor, sons of Finarfin. But these held their peace and spoke not against their fathers.

At length after long debate Fëanor prevailed, and the greater part of the Noldor there assembled he set aflame with the desire of new things and strange countries. Therefore when Finarfin spoke yet again for heed and delay, a great shout went up: 'Nay, let us be gone!' And straightway Fëanor and his sons began to prepare for the marching forth.

Little foresight could there be for those who dared to take so dark a road. Yet all was done in over-haste; for Fëanor drove them on, fearing lest in the cooling of their hearts his words should wane and other counsels yet prevail; and for all his proud words he did not forget the power of the Valar. But from Valmar no message came, and Manwë was silent. He would not yet either forbid or hinder Fëanor's purpose; for the Valar were aggrieved that they were charged with evil intent to the Eldar, or that any were held captive by them against their will. Now they watched and waited, for they did not yet believe that Fëanor could hold the host of the Noldor to his will.

And indeed when Fëanor began the marshalling of the Noldor for their setting-out, then at once dissension arose. For though he had brought the assembly in a mind to depart, by no means all were of a mind to take Fëanor as King. Greater love was given to Fingolfin and his sons, and his household and the most part of the dwellers in Tirion refused to renounce him, if he would go with them; and thus at the last as two divided hosts the Noldor set forth upon their bitter road. Fëanor and his following were in the van, but the greater host came behind under Fingolfin; and he marched against his wisdom, because Fingon his son so urged him, and because he would not be sundered from his people that were eager to go, nor leave them to the rash counsels of Fëanor. Nor did he forget his words before the throne of Manwë. With Fingolfin went Finarfin also and for like reasons; but most loath was he to depart. And of all the Noldor in Valinor, who were grown now to a great people, but one tithe refused to take the road: some for the love that they bore to the Valar (and to Aulë not least), some for the love of Tirion and the many things that they had made; none for fear of peril by the way.

But even as the trumpet sang and Fëanor issued from the gates of Tirion a messenger came at last from Manwë, saying: 'Against the folly of Fëanor shall be set my counsel only. Go not forth! For the hour is evil, and your road leads to sorrow that ye do not foresee. No aid will the Valar lend you in this quest; but neither will they hinder you; for this ye shall know: as ye came hither freely, freely shall ye depart. But thou Fëanor Finwë's son, by thine oath art exiled. The lies of Melkor thou shalt unlearn in bitterness. Vala he is, thou saist. Then thou hast sworn in vain, for none of the Valar canst thou overcome now or ever within the halls of Eä, not though Eru whom thou namest had made thee thrice greater than thou art.'

But Fëanor laughed, and spoke not to the herald, but to the Noldor, saying: 'So! Then will this valiant people send forth the heir of their King alone into banishment with his sons only, and return to their bondage? But if any will come with me, I say to them: Is sorrow forboded to you? But in Aman we have seen it. In Aman we have come through bliss to woe. The other now we will try: through sorrow to find joy; or freedom, at the least.'

Then turning to the herald he cried: 'Say this to Manwë Súlimo, High King of Arda: if Fëanor cannot overthrow Morgoth, at least he delays not to assail him, and sits not idle in grief. And it may be that Eru has set in me a fire greater than thou knowest. Such hurt at the least will I do to the Foe of the Valar that even the mighty in the Ring of Doom shall wonder to hear it. Yea, in the end they shall follow me. Farewell!'

In that hour the voice of Fëanor grew so great and so potent that even the herald of the Valar bowed before him as one full-answered, and departed; and the Noldor were over-ruled. Therefore they continued their march; and the House of Fëanor hastened before them along the coasts of Elendë: not once did they turn their eyes back to Tirion on the green hill of Túna. Slower and less eagerly came the host of Fingolfin after them. Of those Fingon was the foremost; but at the rear went Finarfin and Finrod, and many of the noblest and wisest of the Noldor; and often they looked behind them to see their fair city, until the lamp of the Mindon Eldaliéva was lost in the night. More than any others of the Exiles they carried thence memories of the bliss they had forsaken, and some even of the things that they had made there they took with them: a solace and a burden on the road.

Now Fëanor led the Noldor northward, because his first purpose was to follow Morgoth. Moreover Túna beneath Taniquetil was set nigh to the girdle of Arda, and there the Great Sea was immeasurably wide, whereas ever northward the sundering seas grew narrower, as the wasteland of Araman and the coasts of Middle-earth drew together. But as the mind of Fëanor cooled and took counsel he perceived over-late that all these great companies would never overcome the long leagues to the north, nor cross the seas at the last, save with the aid of ships; yet it would need long time and toil to build so great a fleet, even were there any among the Noldor skilled in that craft. He resolved now therefore to persuade the Teleri, ever friends to the Noldor, to join with them; and in his rebellion he thought that thus the bliss of Valinor might be further diminished and his power for war upon Morgoth be increased. He hastened then to Alqualondë, and spoke to the Teleri as he had spoken before in Tirion.

But the Teleri were unmoved by aught that he could say. They were grieved indeed at the going of their kinsfolk and long friends, but would rather dissuade them than aid them; and no ship would they lend, nor help in the building, against the will of the Valar. As for themselves, they desired now no other home but the strands of Eldamar, and no other lord than Olwë, prince of Alqualondë. And he had never lent ear to Morgoth, nor welcomed him to his land, and he trusted still that Ulmo and the other great among the Valar would redress the hurts of Morgoth, and that the night would pass yet to a new dawn.

Then Fëanor grew wrathful, for he still feared delay; and hotly he spoke to Olwë. 'You renounce your friendship, even in the hour of our need,' he said. 'Yet you were glad indeed to receive our aid when you came at last to these shores, fainthearted loiterers, and wellnigh emptyhanded. In huts on the beaches would you be dwelling still, had not the Noldor carved out your haven and toiled upon your walls.'

But Olwë answered: 'We renounce no friendship. But it may be the part of a friend to rebuke a friend's folly. And when the Noldor welcomed us and gave us aid, otherwise then you spoke: in the land of Aman we were to dwell for ever, as brothers whose houses stand side by side. But as for our white ships: those you gave us not. We learned not that craft from the Noldor, but from the Lords of the Sea; and the white timbers we wrought with our own hands, and the white sails were woven by our wives and our daughters. Therefore we will neither give them nor sell them for any league or friendship. For I say to you, Fëanor son of Finwë, these are to us as are the gems of the Noldor: the work of our hearts, whose like we shall not make again.'

Thereupon Fëanor left him, and sat in dark thought beyond the walls of Alqualondë, until his host was assembled. When he judged that his strength was enough, he went to the Haven of the Swans and began to man the ships that were anchored there and to take them away by force. But the Teleri withstood him, and cast many of the Noldor into the sea. Then swords were drawn, and a bitter fight was fought upon the ships, and about the lamplit quays and piers of the Haven, and even upon the great arch of its gate. Thrice the people of Fëanor were driven back, and many were slain upon either side; but the vanguard of the Noldor were succoured by Fingon with the foremost of the host of Fingolfin, who coming up found a battle joined and their own kin falling, and rushed in before they knew rightly the cause of the quarrel; some thought indeed that the Teleri had sought to waylay the march of the Noldor at the bidding of the Valar.

Thus at last the Teleri were overcome, and a great part of their mariners that dwelt in Alqualondë were wickedly slain. For the Noldor were become fierce and desperate, and the Teleri had less strength, and were armed for the most part but with slender bows. Then the Noldor drew away their white ships and manned their oars as best they might, and rowed them north along the coast. And Olwë called upon Ossë, but he came not, for it was not permitted by the Valar that the flight of the Noldor should be hindered by force. But Uinen wept for the mariners of the Teleri; and the sea rose in wrath against the slayers, so that many of the ships were wrecked and those in them drowned. Of the Kinslaying at Alqualondë more is told in that lament which is named *Noldolantë,* the Fall of the Noldor, that Maglor made ere he was lost.

Nonetheless the greater part of the Noldor escaped, and when the storm was past they held on their course, some by ship and some by land; but the way was long and ever more evil as they went forward. After they had marched for a great while in the unmeasured night, they came at length to the northern confines of the Guarded Realm, upon the borders of the empty waste of Araman which were mountainous and cold. There they beheld suddenly a dark figure standing high upon a rock that looked down upon the shore. Some say that it was Mandos himself, and no lesser herald of Manwë. And they heard a loud voice, solemn and terrible, that bade them stand and give ear. Then all halted and stood still, and from end to end of the hosts of the Noldor the voice was heard speaking the curse and prophecy which is called the Prophecy of the North, and the Doom of the Noldor. Much it foretold in dark words, which the Noldor understood not until the woes indeed after befell them; but all heard the curse that was uttered upon those that would not stay nor seek the doom and pardon of the Valar.

'Tears unnumbered ye shall shed; and the Valar will fence Valinor against you, and shut you out, so that not even the echo of your lamentation shall pass over the mountains. On the House of Fëanor the wrath of the Valar lieth from the West unto the uttermost East, and upon all that will follow them it shall be laid also. Their Oath shall drive them, and yet betray them, and ever snatch away the very treasures that they have sworn to pursue. To evil end shall all things turn that they begin well; and by treason of kin unto kin, and the fear of treason, shall this come to pass. The Dispossessed shall they be for ever.

'Ye have spilled the blood of your kindred unrighteously and have stained the land of Aman. For blood ye shall render blood, and beyond Aman ye shall dwell in Death's shadow. For though Eru appointed to you to die not in Eä, and no sickness may assail you, yet slain ye may be, and slain ye shall be: by weapon and by torment and by grief; and your houseless spirits shall come then to Mandos. There long shall ye abide and yearn for your bodies, and find little pity though all whom ye have slain should entreat for you. And those that endure in Middle-earth and come not to Mandos shall grow weary of the world as with a great burden, and shall wane, and become as shadows of regret before the younger race that cometh after. The Valar have spoken.'

Then many quailed; but Fëanor hardened his heart and said: 'We have sworn, and not lightly. This oath we will keep. We are threatened with many evils, and treason not least; but one thing is not said:

that we shall suffer from cowardice, from cravens or the fear of cravens. Therefore I say that we will go on, and this doom I add: the deeds that we shall do shall be the matter of song until the last days of Arda.'

But in that hour Finarfin forsook the march, and turned back, being filled with grief, and with bitterness against the House of Fëanor, because of his kinship with Olwë of Alqualondë; and many of his people went with him, retracing their steps in sorrow, until they beheld once more the far beam of the Mindon upon Túna still shining in the night, and so came at last to Valinor. There they received the pardon of the Valar, and Finarfin was set to rule the remnant of the Noldor in the Blessed Realm. But his sons were not with him, for they would not forsake the sons of Fingolfin; and all Fingolfin's folk went forward still, feeling the constraint of their kinship and the will of Fëanor, and fearing to face the doom of the Valar, since not all of them had been guiltless of the Kinslaying at Alqualondë. Moreover Fingon and Turgon were bold and fiery of heart, and loath to abandon any task to which they had put their hands until the bitter end, if bitter it must be. So the main host held on, and swiftly the evil that was foretold began its work.

The Noldor came at last far into the north of Arda; and they saw the first teeth of the ice that floated in the sea, and knew that they were drawing nigh to the Helcaraxë. For between the land of Aman that in the north curved eastward, and the east-shores of Endor (which is Middle-earth) that bore westward, there was a narrow strait, through which the chill waters of the Encircling Sea and the waves of Belegaer flowed together, and there were vast fogs and mists of deathly cold, and the sea-streams were filled with clashing hills of ice and the grinding of ice deep-sunken. Such was the Helcaraxë, and there none yet had dared to tread save the Valar only and Ungoliant.

Therefore Fëanor halted and the Noldor debated what course they should now take. But they began to suffer anguish from the cold, and the clinging mists through which no gleam of star could pierce; and many repented of the road and began to murmur, especially those that followed Fingolfin, cursing Fëanor, and naming him as the cause of all the woes of the Eldar. But Fëanor, knowing all that was said, took counsel with his sons; and two courses only they saw to escape from Araman and come into Endor: by the straits or by ship. But the Helcaraxë they deemed impassable, whereas the ships were too few. Many had been lost upon their long journey, and there remained now not enough to bear across all the great host together; yet none were willing to abide upon the western coast while others were ferried first: already the fear of treachery was awake among the Noldor. Therefore it came into the hearts of Fëanor and his sons to seize all the ships and depart suddenly; for they had retained the mastery of the fleet since the battle of the Haven, and it was manned only by those who had fought there and were bound to Fëanor. And as though it came at his call, there sprang up a wind from the north-west, and Fëanor slipped away secretly with all whom he deemed true to him, and went aboard, and put out to sea, and left Fingolfin in Araman. And since the sea was there narrow, steering east and somewhat south he passed over without loss, and first of all the Noldor set foot once more upon the shores of Middle-earth; and the landing of Fëanor was at the mouth of the firth which was called Drengist and ran into Dor-lómin.

But when they were landed, Maedhros the eldest of his sons, and on a time the friend of Fingon ere Morgoth's lies came between, spoke to Fëanor, saying: 'Now what ships and rowers will you spare to return, and whom shall they bear hither first? Fingon the valiant?'

Then Fëanor laughed as one fey, and he cried: 'None and none! What I have left behind I count now no loss; needless baggage on the road it has proved. Let those that cursed my name, curse me still, and whine their way back to the cages of the Valar! Let the ships burn!' Then Maedhros alone stood aside, but Fëanor caused fire to be set to the white ships of the Teleri. So in that place which was called Losgar at the outlet of the Firth of Drengist ended the fairest vessels that ever sailed the sea, in a great burning, bright and terrible. And Fingolfin and his people saw the light afar off, red beneath the clouds; and they knew that they were betrayed. This was the firstfruits of the Kinslaying and the Doom of the Noldor.

Then Fingolfin seeing that Fëanor had left him to perish in Araman or return in shame to Valinor was filled with bitterness; but he desired now as never before to come by some way to Middle-earth, and meet Fëanor again. And he and his host wandered long in misery, but their valour and endurance grew with hardship; for they were a mighty people, the elder children undying of Eru Ilúvatar, but new-come from the Blessed Realm, and not yet weary with the weariness of Earth. The fire of their hearts was young, and led by Fingolfin and his sons, and by Finrod and Galadriel, they dared to pass into the bitterest North; and finding no other way they endured at last the terror of the Helcaraxë and the cruel hills of ice. Few of the deeds of the Noldor thereafter surpassed that desperate crossing in hardihood or woe. There Elenwë the wife of Turgon was lost, and many others perished also; and it was with a lessened host that Fingolfin set foot at last upon the Outer Lands. Small love for Fëanor or his sons had those that marched at last behind him, and blew their trumpets in Middle-earth at the first rising of the Moon.

Chapter 10

OF THE SINDAR

Now as has been told the power of Elwë and Melian increased in Middle-earth, and all the Elves of Beleriand, from the mariners of Círdan to the wandering hunters of the Blue Mountains beyond the River Gelion, owned Elwë as their lord; Elu Thingol he was called, King Greymantle, in the tongue of his people. They are called the Sindar, the Grey-elves of starlit Beleriand; and although they were Moriquendi, under the lordship of Thingol and the teaching of Melian they became the fairest and the most wise and skilful of all the Elves of Middle-earth. And at the end of the first age of the Chaining of Melkor, when all the Earth had peace and the glory of Valinor was at its noon, there came into the world Lúthien, the only child of Thingol and Melian. Though Middle-earth lay for the most part in the Sleep of Yavanna, in Beleriand under the power of Melian there was life and joy, and the bright stars shone as silver fires; and there in the forest of Neldoreth Lúthien was born, and the white flowers of *niphredil* came forth to greet her as stars from the earth.

It came to pass during the second age of the captivity of Melkor that Dwarves came over the Blue Mountains of Ered Luin into Beleriand. Themselves they named Khazâd, but the Sindar called them Naugrim, the Stunted People, and Gonnhirrim, Masters of Stone. Far to the east were the most ancient dwellings of the Naugrim, but they had delved for themselves great halls and mansions, after the manner of their kind, in the eastern side of Ered Luin; and those cities were named in their own tongue Gabilgathol and Tumunzahar. To the north of the great height of Mount Dolmed was Gabilgathol, which the Elves interpreted in their tongue Belegost, that is Mickleburg; and southward was delved Tumunzahar, by the Elves named Nogrod, the Hollowbold. Greatest of all the mansions of the Dwarves was Khazad-dûm, the Dwarrowdelf, Hadhodrond in the Elvish tongue, that was afterwards in the days of its darkness called Moria; but it was far off in the Mountains of Mist beyond the wide leagues of Eriador, and to the Eldar came but as a name and a rumour from the words of the Dwarves of the Blue Mountains.

From Nogrod and Belegost the Naugrim came forth into Beleriand; and the Elves were filled with amazement, for they had believed themselves to be the only living things in Middle-earth that spoke with words or wrought with hands, and that all others were but birds and beasts. But they could understand no word of the tongue of the Naugrim, which to their ears was cumbrous and unlovely; and few ever of the Eldar have achieved the mastery of it. But the Dwarves were swift to learn, and indeed were more willing to learn the Elven-tongue than to teach their own to those of alien race. Few of the Eldar went ever to Nogrod and Belegost, save Eöl of Nan Elmoth and Maeglin his son; but the Dwarves trafficked into Beleriand, and they made a great road that passed under the shoulders of Mount Dolmed and followed the course of the River Ascar, crossing Gelion at Sarn Athrad, the Ford of Stones, where battle after befell. Ever cool was the friendship between the Naugrim and the Eldar, though much profit they had one of the other; but at that time those griefs that lay between them had not yet come to pass, and King Thingol welcomed them. But the Naugrim gave their friendship more readily to the Noldor in after days than to any others of Elves and Men, because of their love and reverence for Aulë; and the gems of the Noldor they praised above all other wealth. In the darkness of Arda already the Dwarves wrought great works, for even from the first days of their Fathers they had marvellous skill with metals and with stone; but in that ancient time iron and copper they loved to work, rather than silver or gold.

Now Melian had much foresight, after the manner of the Maiar; and when the second age of the captivity of Melkor had passed, she counselled Thingol that the Peace of Arda would not last for ever. He took thought therefore how he should make for himself a kingly dwelling, and a place that should be strong, if evil were to awake again in Middle-earth; and he sought aid and counsel of the Dwarves of

Belegost. They gave it willingly, for they were unwearied in those days and eager for new works; and though the Dwarves ever demanded a price for all that they did, whether with delight or with toil, at this time they held themselves paid. For Melian taught them much that they were eager to learn, and Thingol rewarded them with many fair pearls. These Círdan gave to him, for they were got in great number in the shallow waters about the Isle of Balar; but the Naugrim had not before seen their like, and they held them dear. One there was as great as a dove's egg, and its sheen was as starlight on the foam of the sea; Nimphelos it was named, and the chieftain of the Dwarves of Belegost prized it above a mountain of wealth.

Therefore the Naugrim laboured long and gladly for Thingol, and devised for him mansions after the fashion of their people, delved deep in the earth. Where the Esgalduin flowed down, and parted Neldoreth from Region, there rose in the midst of the forest a rocky hill, and the river ran at its feet. There they made the gates of the hall of Thingol, and they built a bridge of stone over the river, by which alone the gates could be entered. Beyond the gates wide passages ran down to high halls and chambers far below that were hewn in the living stone, so many and so great that that dwelling was named Menegroth, the Thousand Caves.

But the Elves also had part in that labour, and Elves and Dwarves together, each with their own skill, there wrought out the visions of Melian, images of the wonder and beauty of Valinor beyond the Sea. The pillars of Menegroth were hewn in the likeness of the beeches of Oromë, stock, bough, and leaf, and they were lit with lanterns of gold. The nightingales sang there as in the gardens of Lórien; and there were fountains of silver, and basins of marble, and floors of many-coloured stones. Carven figures of beasts and birds there ran upon the walls, or climbed upon the pillars, or peered among the branches entwined with many flowers. And as the years passed Melian and her maidens filled the halls with woven hangings wherein could be read the deeds of the Valar, and many things that had befallen in Arda since its beginning, and shadows of things that were yet to be. That was the fairest dwelling of any king that has ever been east of the Sea.

And when the building of Menegroth was achieved, and there was peace in the realm of Thingol and Melian, the Naugrim yet came ever and anon over the mountains and went in traffic about the lands; but they went seldom to the Falas, for they hated the sound of the sea and feared to look upon it. To Beleriand there came no other rumour or tidings of the world without.

But as the third age of the captivity of Melkor drew on, the Dwarves became troubled, and they spoke to King Thingol, saying that the Valar had not rooted out utterly the evils of the North, and now the remnant, having long multiplied in the dark, were coming forth once more and roaming far and wide. 'There are fell beasts,' they said, 'in the land east of the mountains, and your ancient kindred that dwell there are flying from the plains to the hills.'

And ere long the evil creatures came even to Beleriand, over passes in the mountains, or up from the south through the dark forests. Wolves there were, or creatures that walked in wolf-shapes, and other fell beings of shadow; and among them were the Orcs, who afterwards wrought ruin in Beleriand: but they were yet few and wary, and did but smell out the ways of the land, awaiting the return of their lord. Whence they came, or what they were, the Elves knew not then, thinking them perhaps to be Avari who had become evil and savage in the wild; in which they guessed all too near, it is said.

Therefore Thingol took thought for arms, which before his people had not needed, and these at first the Naugrim smithied for him; for they were greatly skilled in such work, though none among them surpassed the craftsmen of Nogrod, of whom Telchar the smith was greatest in renown. A warlike race of old were all the Naugrim, and they would fight fiercely against whomsoever aggrieved them: servants of Melkor, or Eldar, or Avari, or wild beasts, or not seldom their own kin, Dwarves of other mansions and lordships. Their smithcraft indeed the Sindar soon learned of them; yet in the tempering of steel alone of all crafts the Dwarves were never outmatched even by the Noldor, and in the making of mail of linked rings, which was first contrived by the smiths of Belegost, their work had no rival.

At this time therefore the Sindar were well-armed, and they drove off all creatures of evil, and had peace again; but Thingol's armouries were stored with axes and with spears and swords, and tall helms, and long coats of bright mail; for the hauberks of the Dwarves were so fashioned that they rusted not but shone ever as if they were new-burnished. And that proved well for Thingol in the time that was to come.

Now as has been told, one Lenwë of the host of Olwë forsook the march of the Eldar at that time when the Teleri were halted by the shores of the Great River upon the borders of the westlands of Middle-earth. Little is known of the wanderings of the Nandor, whom he led away down Anduin: some, it is said, dwelt age-long in the woods of the Vale of the Great River, some came at last to its mouths and there dwelt by the Sea, and yet others passing by Ered Nimrais, the White Mountains, came north again and entered the wilderness of Eriador between Ered Luin and the far Mountains of Mist. Now these were a woodland people and had no weapons of steel, and the coming of the fell beasts of the North filled them with great fear, as the Naugrim declared to King Thingol in Menegroth. Therefore Denethor, the son of Lenwë, hearing rumour of the might of Thingol and his majesty, and of the peace of his realm, gathered such host of his scattered people as he could, and led them over the mountains into Beleriand. There they were welcomed by Thingol, as kin long lost that return, and they dwelt in Ossiriand, the Land of Seven Rivers.

Of the long years of peace that followed after the coming of Denethor there is little tale. In those days, it is said, Daeron the Minstrel, chief loremaster of the kingdom of Thingol, devised his Runes; and the Naugrim that came to Thingol learned them, and were well-pleased with the device, esteeming Daeron's skill higher than did the Sindar, his own people. By the Naugrim the *Cirth* were taken east over the mountains and passed into the knowledge of many peoples; but they were little used by the Sindar for the keeping of records, until the days of the War, and much that was held in memory perished in the ruins of Doriath. But of bliss and glad life there is little to be said, before it ends; as works fair and wonderful, while still they endure for eyes to see, are their own record, and only when they are in peril or broken for ever do they pass into song.

In Beleriand in those days the Elves walked, and the rivers flowed, and the stars shone, and the night-flowers gave forth their scents; and the beauty of Melian was as the noon, and the beauty of Lúthien was as the dawn in spring. In Beleriand King Thingol upon his throne was as the lords of the Maiar, whose power is at rest, whose joy is as an air that they breathe in all their days, whose thought flows in a tide untroubled from the heights to the deeps. In Beleriand still at times rode Oromë the great, passing like a wind over the mountains, and the sound of his horn came down the leagues of the starlight, and the Elves feared him for the splendour of his countenance and the great noise of the onrush of Nahar; but when the Valaróma echoed in the hills, they knew well that all evil things were fled far away.

But it came to pass at last that the end of bliss was at hand, and the noontide of Valinor was drawing to its twilight. For as has been told and as is known to all, being written in lore and sung in many songs,

Melkor slew the Trees of the Valar with the aid of Ungoliant, and escaped, and came back to Middle-earth. Far to the north befell the strife of Morgoth and Ungoliant; but the great cry of Morgoth echoed through Beleriand, and all its people shrank for fear; for though they knew not what it foreboded, they heard then the herald of death. Soon afterwards Ungoliant fled from the north and came into the realm of King Thingol, and a terror of darkness was about her; but by the power of Melian she was stayed, and entered not into Neldoreth, but abode long time under the shadow of the precipices in which Dorthonion fell southward. And they became known as Ered Gorgoroth, the Mountains of Terror, and none dared go thither, or pass nigh them; there life and light were strangled, and there all waters were poisoned. But Morgoth, as has before been told, returned to Angband, and built it anew, and above its doors he reared the reeking towers of Thangorodrim; and the gates of Morgoth were but one hundred and fifty leagues distant from the bridge of Menegroth: far and yet all too near.

Now the Orcs that multiplied in the darkness of the earth grew strong and fell, and their dark lord filled them with a lust of ruin and death; and they issued from Angband's gates under the clouds that Morgoth sent forth, and passed silently into the highlands of the north. Thence on a sudden a great army came into Beleriand and assailed King Thingol. Now in his wide realm many Elves wandered free in the wild, or dwelt at peace in small kindreds far sundered; and only about Menegroth in the midst of the land, and along the Falas in the country of the mariners, were there numerous peoples. But the Orcs came down upon either side of Menegroth, and from camps in the east between Celon and Gelion, and west in the plains between Sirion and Narog, they plundered far and wide; and Thingol was cut off from Círdan at Eglarest. Therefore he called upon Denethor; and the Elves came in force from Region beyond Aros and from Ossiriand, and fought the first battle in the Wars of Beleriand. And the eastern host of the Orcs was taken between the armies of the Eldar, north of the Andram and midway between Aros and Gelion, and there they were utterly defeated, and those that fled north from the great slaughter were waylaid by the axes of the Naugrim that issued from Mount Dolmed: few indeed returned to Angband.

But the victory of the Elves was dear-bought. For those of Ossiriand were light-armed, and no match for the Orcs, who were shod with iron and iron-shielded and bore great spears with broad blades; and Denethor was cut off and surrounded upon the hill of Amon

Ereb. There he fell and all his nearest kin about him, before the host of Thingol could come to his aid. Bitterly though his fall was avenged, when Thingol came upon the rear of the Orcs and slew them in heaps, his people lamented him ever after and took no king again. After the battle some returned to Ossiriand, and their tidings filled the remnant of their people with great fear, so that thereafter they came never forth in open war, but kept themselves by wariness and secrecy; and they were called the Laiquendi, the Green-elves, because of their raiment of the colour of leaves. But many went north and entered the guarded realm of Thingol, and were merged with his people.

And when Thingol came again to Menegroth he learned that the Orc-host in the west was victorious, and had driven Círdan to the rim of the sea. Therefore he withdrew all his people that his summons could reach within the fastness of Neldoreth and Region, and Melian put forth her power and fenced all that dominion round about with an unseen wall of shadow and bewilderment: the Girdle of Melian, that none thereafter could pass against her will or the will of King Thingol, unless one should come with a power greater than that of Melian the Maia. And this inner land, which was long named Eglador, was after called Doriath, the guarded kingdom, Land of the Girdle. Within it there was yet a watchful peace; but without there was peril and great fear, and the servants of Morgoth roamed at will, save in the walled havens of the Falas.

But new tidings were at hand, which none in Middle-earth had foreseen, neither Morgoth in his pits nor Melian in Menegroth; for no news came out of Aman, whether by messenger, or by spirit, or by vision in dream, after the death of the Trees. In this same time Fëanor came over the Sea in the white ships of the Teleri, and landed in the Firth of Drengist, and there burned the ships at Losgar.

Chapter 11

OF THE SUN AND MOON AND THE HIDING OF VALINOR

It is told that after the flight of Melkor the Valar sat long unmoved upon their thrones in the Ring of Doom; but they were not idle, as Fëanor declared in the folly of his heart. For the Valar may work many things with thought rather than with hands, and without voices in silence they may hold council one with another. Thus they held vigil in the night of Valinor, and their thought passed back beyond Eä and forth to the End; yet neither power nor wisdom assuaged their grief, and the knowing of evil in the hour of its being. And they mourned not more for the death of the Trees than for the marring of Fëanor: of the works of Melkor one of the most evil. For Fëanor was made the mightiest in all parts of body and mind, in valour, in endurance, in beauty, in understanding, in skill, in strength and in subtlety alike, of all the Children of Ilúvatar, and a bright flame was in him. The works of wonder for the glory of Arda that he might otherwise have wrought only Manwë might in some measure conceive. And it was told by the Vanyar who held vigil with the Valar that when the messengers declared to Manwë the answers of Fëanor to his heralds, Manwë wept and bowed his head. But at that last word of Fëanor: that at the least the Noldor should do deeds to live in song for ever, he raised his head, as one that hears a voice far off, and he said: 'So shall it be! Dear-bought those songs shall be accounted, and yet shall be well-bought. For the price could be no other. Thus even as Eru spoke to us shall beauty not before conceived be brought into Eä, and evil yet be good to have been.'

But Mandos said: 'And yet remain evil. To me shall Fëanor come soon.'

But when at last the Valar learned that the Noldor had indeed passed out of Aman and were come back into Middle-earth, they arose and began to set forth in deeds those counsels which they had taken in thought for the redress of the evils of Melkor. Then Manwë bade Yavanna and Nienna to put forth all their powers of growth and healing; and they put forth all their powers upon the Trees. But the tears of Nienna availed not to heal their mortal wounds; and for a long while Yavanna sang alone in the shadows. Yet even as hope failed and her song faltered, Telperion bore at last upon a leafless bough one great flower of silver, and Laurelin a single fruit of gold.

These Yavanna took; and then the Trees died, and their lifeless stems stand yet in Valinor, a memorial of vanished joy. But the flower and the fruit Yavanna gave to Aulë, and Manwë hallowed them, and Aulë and his people made vessels to hold them and preserve their radiance: as is said in the *Narsilion*, the Song of the Sun and Moon. These vessels the Valar gave to Varda, that they might become lamps of heaven, outshining the ancient stars, being nearer to Arda; and she gave them power to traverse the lower regions of Ilmen, and set them to voyage upon appointed courses above the girdle of the Earth from the West unto the East and to return.

These things the Valar did, recalling in their twilight the darkness of the lands of Arda; and they resolved now to illumine Middle-earth and with light to hinder the deeds of Melkor. For they remembered the Avari that remained by the waters of their awakening, and they did not utterly forsake the Noldor in exile; and Manwë knew also that the hour of the coming of Men was drawn nigh. And it is said indeed that, even as the Valar made war upon Melkor for the sake of the Quendi, so now for that time they forbore for the sake of the Hildor, the Aftercomers, the younger Children of Ilúvatar. For so grievous had been the hurts of Middle-earth in the war upon Utumno that the Valar feared lest even worse should now befall; whereas the Hildor should be mortal, and weaker than the Quendi to withstand fear and tumult. Moreover it was not revealed to Manwë where the beginning of Men should be, north, south, or east. Therefore the Valar sent forth light, but made strong the land of their dwelling.

Isil the Sheen the Vanyar of old named the Moon, flower of Telperion in Valinor; and Anar the Fire-golden, fruit of Laurelin, they named the Sun. But the Noldor named them also Rána, the Wayward, and Vása, the Heart of Fire, that awakens and consumes; for the Sun was set as a sign for the awakening of Men and the waning of the Elves, but the Moon cherishes their memory.

The maiden whom the Valar chose from among the Maiar to guide the vessel of the Sun was named Arien, and he that steered the island of the Moon was Tilion. In the days of the Trees Arien had tended the golden flowers in the gardens of Vána, and watered them with the bright dews of Laurelin; but Tilion was a hunter of the company of Oromë, and he had a silver bow. He was a lover of silver, and when he would rest he forsook the woods of Oromë, and going into Lórien he lay in dream by the pools of Estë, in Telperion's flickering beams; and he begged to be given the task of tending for ever the last Flower of Silver. Arien the maiden was mightier than he, and she was chosen because she had not feared the heats of Laurelin, and was unhurt by them, being from the beginning a spirit of fire, whom Melkor had not deceived nor drawn to his service. Too bright were the eyes of Arien for even the Eldar to look on, and leaving Valinor she forsook the form and raiment which like the Valar she had worn there, and she was as a naked flame, terrible in the fullness of her splendour.

Isil was first wrought and made ready, and first rose into the realm of the stars, and was the elder of the new lights, as was Telperion of the Trees. Then for a while the world had moonlight, and many things stirred and woke that had waited long in the sleep of Yavanna. The servants of Morgoth were filled with amazement, but the Elves of the Outer Lands looked up in delight; and even as the Moon rose above the darkness in the west, Fingolfin let blow his silver trumpets and began his march into Middle-earth, and the shadows of his host went long and black before them.

Tilion had traversed the heaven seven times, and thus was in the furthest east, when the vessel of Arien was made ready. Then Anar arose in glory, and the first dawn of the Sun was like a great fire upon the towers of the Pelóri: the clouds of Middle-earth were kindled, and there was heard the sound of many waterfalls. Then indeed Morgoth was dismayed, and he descended into the uttermost depths of Angband, and withdrew his servants, sending forth great reek and dark cloud to hide his land from the light of the Daystar.

Now Varda purposed that the two vessels should journey in Ilmen and ever be aloft, but not together; each should pass from Valinor into the east and return, the one issuing from the west as the other turned from the east. Thus the first of the new days were reckoned after the manner of the Trees, from the mingling of the lights when Arien and

Tilion passed in their courses, above the middle of the Earth. But Tilion was wayward and uncertain in speed, and held not to his appointed path; and he sought to come near to Arien, being drawn by her splendour, though the flame of Anar scorched him, and the island of the Moon was darkened.

Because of the waywardness of Tilion, therefore, and yet more because of the prayers of Lórien and Estë, who said that sleep and rest had been banished from the Earth, and the stars were hidden, Varda changed her counsel, and allowed a time wherein the world should still have shadow and half-light. Anar rested therefore a while in Valinor, lying upon the cool bosom of the Outer Sea; and Evening, the time of the descent and resting of the Sun, was the hour of greatest light and joy in Aman. But soon the Sun was drawn down by the servants of Ulmo, and went then in haste under the Earth, and so came unseen to the east and there mounted the heaven again, lest night be over-long and evil walk under the Moon. But by Anar the waters of the Outer Sea were made hot and glowed with coloured fire, and Valinor had light for a while after the passing of Arien. Yet as she journeyed under the Earth and drew towards the east the glow faded and Valinor was dim, and the Valar mourned then most for the death of Laurelin. At dawn the shadows of the Mountains of Defence lay heavy on the Blessed Realm.

Varda commanded the Moon to journey in like manner, and passing under Earth to arise in the east, but only after the Sun had descended from heaven. But Tilion went with uncertain pace, as yet he goes, and was still drawn towards Arien, as he shall ever be; so that often both may be seen above the Earth together, or at times it will chance that he comes so nigh that his shadow cuts off her brightness and there is a darkness amid the day.

Therefore by the coming and going of Anar the Valar reckoned the days thereafter until the Change of the World. For Tilion tarried seldom in Valinor, but more often would pass swiftly over the western land, over Avathar, or Araman, or Valinor, and plunge in the chasm beyond the Outer Sea, pursuing his way alone amid the grots and caverns at the roots of Arda. There he would often wander long, and late would return.

Still therefore, after the Long Night, the light of Valinor was greater and fairer than upon Middle-earth; for the Sun rested there, and the lights of heaven drew nearer to Earth in that region. But neither the Sun nor the Moon can recall the light that was of old, that came from the Trees before they were touched by the poison of Ungoliant. That light lives now in the Silmarils alone.

But Morgoth hated the new lights, and was for a while confounded by this unlooked-for stroke of the Valar. Then he assailed Tilion, sending spirits of shadow against him, and there was strife in Ilmen beneath the paths of the stars; but Tilion was victorious. And Arien Morgoth feared with a great fear, but dared not come nigh her, having indeed no longer the power; for as he grew in malice, and sent forth from himself the evil that he conceived in lies and creatures of wickedness, his might passed into them and was dispersed, and he himself became ever more bound to the earth, unwilling to issue from his dark strongholds. With shadows he hid himself and his servants from Arien, the glance of whose eyes they could not long endure; and the lands near his dwelling were shrouded in fumes and great clouds.

But seeing the assault upon Tilion the Valar were in doubt, fearing what the malice and cunning of Morgoth might yet contrive against them. Being unwilling to make war upon him in Middle-earth, they remembered nonetheless the ruin of Almaren; and they resolved that the like should not befall Valinor. Therefore at that time they fortified their land anew, and they raised up the mountain-walls of the Pelóri to sheer and dreadful heights, east, north, and south. Their outer sides were dark and smooth, without foothold or ledge, and they fell in great precipices with faces hard as glass, and rose up to towers with crowns of white ice. A sleepless watch was set upon them, and no pass led through them, save only at the Calacirya: but that pass the Valar did not close, because of the Eldar that were faithful, and in the city of Tirion upon the green hill Finarfin yet ruled the remnant of the Noldor in the deep cleft of the mountains. For all those of Elven-race, even the Vanyar and Ingwë their lord, must breathe at times the outer air and the wind that comes over the sea from the lands of their birth; and the Valar would not sunder the Teleri wholly from their kin. But in the Calacirya they set strong towers and many sentinels, and at its issue upon the plains of Valmar a host was encamped, so that neither bird nor beast nor elf nor man, nor any creature beside that dwelt in Middle-earth, could pass that leaguer.

And in that time also, which songs call *Nurtalë Valinóreva,* the Hiding of Valinor, the Enchanted Isles were set, and all the seas about them were filled with shadows and bewilderment. And these isles were strung as a net in the Shadowy Seas from the north to the south, before Tol Eressëa, the Lonely Isle, is reached by one sailing west.

Hardly might any vessel pass between them, for in the dangerous sounds the waves sighed for ever upon dark rocks shrouded in mist. And in the twilight a great weariness came upon mariners and a loathing of the sea; but all that ever set foot upon the islands were there entrapped, and slept until the Change of the World. Thus it was that as Mandos foretold to them in Araman the Blessed Realm was shut against the Noldor; and of the many messengers that in after days sailed into the West none came ever to Valinor—save one only: the mightiest mariner of song.

Chapter 12

OF MEN

The Valar sat now behind their mountains at peace; and having given light to Middle-earth they left it for long untended, and the lordship of Morgoth was uncontested save by the valour of the Noldor. Most in mind Ulmo kept the exiles, who gathered news of the Earth through all the waters.

From this time forth were reckoned the Years of the Sun. Swifter and briefer are they than the long Years of the Trees in Valinor. In that time the air of Middle-earth became heavy with the breath of growth and mortality, and the changing and ageing of all things was hastened exceedingly; life teemed upon the soil and in the waters in the Second Spring of Arda, and the Eldar increased, and beneath the new Sun Beleriand grew green and fair.

At the first rising of the Sun the Younger Children of Ilúvatar awoke in the land of Hildórien in the eastward regions of Middle-earth; but the first Sun arose in the West, and the opening eyes of Men were turned towards it, and their feet as they wandered over the Earth for the most part strayed that way. The Atani they were named by the Eldar, the Second People; but they called them also Hildor, the Followers, and many other names: Apanónar, the After-born, Engwar, the Sickly, and Fírimar, the Mortals; and they named them the Usurpers, the Strangers, and the Inscrutable, the Self-cursed, the Heavy-handed, the Night-fearers, the Children of the Sun. Of Men little is told in these tales, which concern the Eldest Days before the waxing of mortals and the waning of the Elves, save of those fathers of men, the Atanatári, who in the first years of the Sun and Moon wandered into the North of the world. To Hildórien there came no Vala to guide Men, or to summon them to dwell in Valinor; and Men have feared the Valar, rather than loved them, and have not understood the purposes of the Powers, being at variance with them, and at strife with the world. Ulmo nonetheless took thought for them, aiding the counsel and will of Manwë; and his messages came often to them by stream and flood. But they have not skill in such matters, and still less had they in those days before they had mingled with the Elves. Therefore they loved the waters, and their hearts were stirred, but they understood not the messages. Yet it is told that ere long they met Dark Elves in many places, and were befriended by them; and Men became the companions and disciples in their childhood of these ancient folk, wanderers of the Elven-race who never set out upon the paths to Valinor, and knew of the Valar only as a rumour and a distant name.

Morgoth had then not long come back into Middle-earth, and his power went not far abroad, and was moreover checked by the sudden coming of great light. There was little peril in the lands and hills; and there new things, devised long ages before in the thought of Yavanna and sown as seed in the dark, came at last to their budding and their bloom. West, North, and South the children of Men spread and wandered, and their joy was the joy of the morning before the dew is dry, when every leaf is green.

But the dawn is brief and the day full often belies its promise; and now the time drew on to the great wars of the powers of the North, when Noldor and Sindar and Men strove against the hosts of Morgoth Bauglir, and went down in ruin. To this end the cunning lies of Morgoth that he sowed of old, and sowed ever anew among his foes, and the curse that came of the slaying at Alqualondë, and the oath of Fëanor, were ever at work. Only a part is here told of the deeds of those days, and most is said of the Noldor, and the Silmarils, and the mortals that became entangled in their fate. In those days Elves and Men were of like stature and strength of body, but the Elves had greater wisdom, and skill, and beauty; and those who had dwelt in Valinor and looked upon the Powers as much surpassed the Dark Elves in these things as they in turn surpassed the people of mortal race. Only in the realm of Doriath, whose queen Melian was of the kindred of Valar, did the Sindar come near to match the Calaquendi of the Blessed Realm.

Immortal were the Elves, and their wisdom waxed from age to age, and no sickness nor pestilence brought death to them. Their bodies indeed were of the stuff of Earth, and could be destroyed; and in those days they were more like to the bodies of Men, since they had not so long been inhabited by the fire of their spirit, which consumes them from within in the courses of time. But Men were more frail, more easily slain by weapon or mischance, and less easily healed; subject to sickness and many ills; and they grew old and died. What may befall their spirits after death the Elves know not. Some say that they too go to the halls of Mandos; but their place of waiting there is not that of the Elves, and Mandos under Ilúvatar alone save Manwë knows whither they go after the time of recollection in those silent halls beside the Outer Sea. None have ever come back from the mansions of the dead, save only Beren son of Barahir, whose hand had touched a Silmaril; but he never spoke afterward to mortal Men. The fate of Men after death, maybe, is not in the hands of the Valar, nor was all foretold in the Music of the Ainur.

In after days, when because of the triumph of Morgoth Elves and Men became estranged, as he most wished, those of the Elven-race that lived still in Middle-earth waned and faded, and Men usurped the sunlight. Then the Quendi wandered in the lonely places of the great lands and the isles, and took to the moonlight and the starlight, and to the woods and caves, becoming as shadows and memories, save those who ever and anon set sail into the West and vanished from Middle-earth. But in the dawn of years Elves and Men were allies and held themselves akin, and there were some among Men that learned the wisdom of the Eldar, and became great and valiant among the captains of the Noldor. And in the glory and beauty of the Elves, and in their fate, full share had the offspring of elf and mortal, Eärendil, and Elwing, and Elrond their child.

Chapter 13

OF THE RETURN OF THE NOLDOR

It has been told that Fëanor and his sons came first of the Exiles to Middle-earth, and landed in the waste of Lammoth, the Great Echo, upon the outer shores of the Firth of Drengist. And even as the Noldor set foot upon the strand their cries were taken up into the hills and multiplied, so that a clamour as of countless mighty voices filled all the coasts of the North; and the noise of the burning of the ships at Losgar went down the winds of the sea as a tumult of great wrath, and far away all who heard that sound were filled with wonder.

Now the flames of that burning were seen not only by Fingolfin, whom Fëanor had deserted in Araman, but also by the Orcs and the watchers of Morgoth. No tale has told what Morgoth thought in his heart at the tidings that Fëanor, his bitterest foe, had brought a host out of the West. It may be that he feared him little, for he had as yet no proof of the swords of the Noldor; and soon it was seen that he purposed to drive them back into the sea.

Under the cold stars before the rising of the Moon the host of Fëanor went up the long Firth of Drengist that pierced the Echoing Hills of Ered Lómin, and passed thus from the shores into the great land of Hithlum; and they came at length to the long lake of Mithrim, and upon its northern shore made their encampment in the region that bore the same name. But the host of Morgoth, aroused by the tumult of Lammoth and the light of the burning at Losgar, came through the passes of Ered Wethrin, the Mountains of Shadow, and assailed

Fëanor on a sudden, before his camp was full-wrought or put in defence; and there on the grey fields of Mithrim was fought the Second Battle in the Wars of Beleriand. Dagor-nuin-Giliath it is named, the Battle-under-Stars, for the Moon had not yet risen; and it is renowned in song. The Noldor, outnumbered and taken at unawares, were yet swiftly victorious; for the light of Aman was not yet dimmed in their eyes, and they were strong and swift, and deadly in anger, and their swords were long and terrible. The Orcs fled before them, and they were driven forth from Mithrim with great slaughter, and hunted over the Mountains of Shadow into the great plain of Ard-galen, that lay northward of Dorthonion. There the armies of Morgoth that had passed south into the Vale of Sirion and beleaguered Círdan in the Havens of the Falas came up to their aid, and were caught in their ruin. For Celegorm, Fëanor's son, having news of them, waylaid them with a part of the Elven-host, and coming down upon them out of the hills near Eithel Sirion drove them into the Fen of Serech. Evil indeed were the tidings that came at last to Angband, and Morgoth was dismayed. Ten days that battle lasted, and from it returned of all the hosts that he had prepared for the conquest of Beleriand no more than a handful of leaves.

Yet cause he had for great joy, though it was hidden from him for a while. For Fëanor, in his wrath against the Enemy, would not halt, but pressed on behind the remnant of the Orcs, thinking so to come at Morgoth himself; and he laughed aloud as he wielded his sword, rejoicing that he had dared the wrath of the Valar and the evils of the road, that he might see the hour of his vengeance. Nothing did he know of Angband or the great strength of defence that Morgoth had so swiftly prepared; but even had he known it would not have deterred him, for he was fey, consumed by the flame of his own wrath. Thus it was that he drew far ahead of the van of his host; and seeing this the servants of Morgoth turned to bay, and there issued from Angband Balrogs to aid them. There upon the confines of Dor Daedeloth, the land of Morgoth, Fëanor was surrounded, with few friends about him. Long he fought on, and undismayed, though he was wrapped in fire and wounded with many wounds; but at the last he was smitten to the ground by Gothmog, Lord of Balrogs, whom Ecthelion after slew in Gondolin. There he would have perished, had not his sons in that moment come up with force to his aid; and the Balrogs left him, and departed to Angband.

Then his sons raised up their father and bore him back towards Mithrim. But as they drew near to Eithel Sirion and were upon the upward path to the pass over the mountains, Fëanor bade them halt; for his wounds were mortal, and he knew that his hour was come. And looking out from the slopes of Ered Wethrin with his last sight he beheld far off the peaks of Thangorodrim, mightiest of the towers of Middle-earth, and knew with the foreknowledge of death that no power of the Noldor would ever overthrow them; but he cursed the name of Morgoth thrice, and laid it upon his sons to hold to their oath, and to avenge their father. Then he died; but he had neither burial nor tomb, for so fiery was his spirit that as it sped his body fell to ash, and was borne away like smoke; and his likeness has never again appeared in Arda, neither has his spirit left the halls of Mandos. Thus ended the mightiest of the Noldor, of whose deeds came both their greatest renown and their most grievous woe.

Now in Mithrim there dwelt Grey-elves, folk of Beleriand that had wandered north over the mountains, and the Noldor met them with gladness, as kinsfolk long sundered; but speech at first was not easy between them, for in their long severance the tongues of the Calaquendi in Valinor and of the Moriquendi in Beleriand had drawn far apart. From the Elves of Mithrim the Noldor learned of the power of Elu Thingol, King in Doriath, and the girdle of enchantment that fenced his realm; and tidings of these great deeds in the north came south to Menegroth, and to the havens of Brithombar and Eglarest. Then all the Elves of Beleriand were filled with wonder and with hope at the coming of their mighty kindred, who thus returned unlooked-for from the West in the very hour of their need, believing indeed at first that they came as emissaries of the Valar to deliver them.

But even in the hour of the death of Fëanor an embassy came to his sons from Morgoth, acknowledging defeat, and offering terms, even to the surrender of a Silmaril. Then Maedhros the tall, the eldest son, persuaded his brothers to feign to treat with Morgoth, and to meet his emissaries at the place appointed; but the Noldor had as little thought of faith as had he. Wherefore each embassy came with greater force than was agreed; but Morgoth sent the more, and there were Balrogs. Maedhros was ambushed, and all his company were slain; but he himself was taken alive by the command of Morgoth, and brought to Angband.

Then the brothers of Maedhros drew back, and fortified a great camp in Hithlum; but Morgoth held Maedhros as hostage, and sent word that he would not release him unless the Noldor would forsake their war, returning into the West, or else departing far from Beleriand into the South of the world. But the sons of Fëanor knew that Morgoth would betray them, and would not release Maedhros, whatsoever they might do; and they were constrained also by their oath, and might not for any cause forsake the war against their Enemy. Therefore Morgoth took Maedhros and hung him from the face of a precipice upon Thangorodrim, and he was caught to the rock by the wrist of his right hand in a band of steel.

Now rumour came to the camp in Hithlum of the march of Fingolfin and those that followed him, who had crossed the Grinding Ice; and all the world lay then in wonder at the coming of the Moon. But as the host of Fingolfin marched into Mithrim the Sun rose flaming in the West; and Fingolfin unfurled his blue and silver banners, and blew his horns, and flowers sprang beneath his marching feet, and the ages of the stars were ended. At the uprising of the great light the servants of Morgoth fled into Angband, and Fingolfin passed unopposed through the fastness of Dor Daedeloth while his foes hid beneath the earth. Then the Elves smote upon the gates of Angband, and the challenge of their trumpets shook the towers of Thangorodrim; and Maedhros heard them amid his torment and cried aloud, but his voice was lost in the echoes of the stone.

But Fingolfin, being of other temper than Fëanor, and wary of the wiles of Morgoth, withdrew from Dor Daedeloth and turned back towards Mithrim, for he had heard tidings that there he should find the sons of Fëanor, and he desired also to have the shield of the Mountains of Shadow while his people rested and grew strong; for he had seen the strength of Angband, and thought not that it would fall to the sound of trumpets only. Therefore coming at length to Hithlum he made his first camp and dwelling by the northern shores of Lake Mithrim. No love was there in the hearts of those that followed Fingolfin for the House of Fëanor, for the agony of those that endured the crossing of the Ice had been great, and Fingolfin held the sons the accomplices of their father. Then there was peril of strife between the hosts; but grievous as were their losses upon the road, the people of Fingolfin and of Finrod son of Finarfin were still more numerous than the followers of Fëanor, and these now withdrew before them, and removed their dwelling to the southern shore; and the lake lay between them. Many of Fëanor's people indeed repented of the burning at Losgar, and were filled with amazement at the valour that had brought the friends whom they had abandoned over the Ice of the North; and they would have welcomed them, but they dared not, for shame.

Thus because of the curse that lay upon them the Noldor achieved nothing, while Morgoth hesitated, and the dread of light was new and strong upon the Orcs. But Morgoth arose from thought, and seeing the division of his foes he laughed. In the pits of Angband he caused vast smokes and vapours to be made, and they came forth from the reeking tops of the Iron Mountains, and afar off they could be seen in Mithrim, staining the bright airs in the first mornings of the world. A wind came out of the east, and bore them over Hithlum, darkening the new Sun; and they fell, and coiled about the fields and hollows, and lay upon the waters of Mithrim, drear and poisonous.

Then Fingon the valiant, son of Fingolfin, resolved to heal the feud that divided the Noldor, before their Enemy should be ready for war; for the earth trembled in the Northlands with the thunder of the forges of Morgoth underground. Long before, in the bliss of Valinor, before Melkor was unchained, or lies came between them, Fingon had been close in friendship with Maedhros; and though he knew not yet that Maedhros had not forgotten him at the burning of the ships, the thought of their ancient friendship stung his heart. Therefore he dared a deed which is justly renowned among the feats of the princes of the Noldor: alone, and without the counsel of any, he set forth in search of Maedhros; and aided by the very darkness that Morgoth had made he came unseen into the fastness of his foes. High upon the shoulders of Thangorodrim he climbed, and looked in despair upon the desolation of the land; but no passage or crevice could he find through which he might come within Morgoth's stronghold. Then in defiance of the Orcs, who cowered still in the dark vaults beneath the earth, he took his harp and sang a song of Valinor that the Noldor made of old, before strife was born among the sons of Finwë; and his voice rang in the mournful hollows that had never heard before aught save cries of fear and woe.

Thus Fingon found what he sought. For suddenly above him far and faint his song was taken up, and a voice answering called to him. Maedhros it was that sang amid his torment. But Fingon climbed to the foot of the precipice where his kinsman hung, and then could go no further; and he wept when he saw the cruel device of Morgoth. Maedhros therefore, being in anguish without hope, begged Fingon to shoot him with his bow; and Fingon strung an arrow, and bent his bow. And seeing no better hope he cried to Manwë, saying: 'O King to whom all birds are dear, speed now this feathered shaft, and recall some pity for the Noldor in their need!'

His prayer was answered swiftly. For Manwë to whom all birds are dear, and to whom they bring news upon Taniquetil from Middle-earth, had sent forth the race of Eagles, commanding them to dwell in the crags of the North, and to keep watch upon Morgoth; for Manwë still had pity for the exiled Elves. And the Eagles brought news of much that passed in those days to the sad ears of Manwë. Now, even as Fingon bent his bow, there flew down from the high airs Thorondor, King of Eagles, mightiest of all birds that have ever been, whose outstretched wings spanned thirty fathoms; and staying Fingon's hand he took him up, and bore him to the face of the rock where Maedhros hung. But Fingon could not release the hell-wrought bond upon his wrist, nor sever it, nor draw it from the stone. Again therefore in his pain Maedhros begged that he would slay him; but Fingon cut off his hand above the wrist, and Thorondor bore them back to Mithrim.

There Maedhros in time was healed; for the fire of life was hot within him, and his strength was of the ancient world, such as those possessed who were nurtured in Valinor. His body recovered from his torment and become hale, but the shadow of his pain was in his heart; and he lived to wield his sword with left hand more deadly than his right had been. By this deed Fingon won great renown, and all the Noldor praised him; and the hatred between the houses of Fingolfin and Fëanor was assuaged. For Maedhros begged forgiveness for the desertion in Araman; and he waived his claim to kingship over all the Noldor, saying to Fingolfin: 'If there lay no grievance between us, lord, still the kingship would rightly come to you, the eldest here of the house of Finwë, and not the least wise.' But to this his brothers did not all in their hearts agree.

Therefore even as Mandos foretold the House of Fëanor were called the Dispossessed, because the overlordship passed from it, the elder, to the House of Fingolfin, both in Elendë and in Beleriand, and because also of the loss of the Silmarils. But the Noldor being again united set a watch upon the borders of Dor Daedeloth, and Angband was beleaguered from west, and south, and east; and they sent forth messengers far and wide to explore the countries of Beleriand, and to treat with the people that dwelt there.

Now King Thingol welcomed not with a full heart the coming of so many princes in might out of the West, eager for new realms; and he would not open his kingdom, nor remove its girdle of enchantment, for wise with the wisdom of Melian he trusted not that the restraint of Morgoth would endure. Alone of the princes of the Noldor those of Finarfin's house were suffered to pass within the confines of Doriath;

for they could claim close kinship with King Thingol himself, since their mother was Eärwen of Alqualondë, Olwë's daughter.

Angrod son of Finarfin was the first of the Exiles to come to Menegroth, as messenger of his brother Finrod, and he spoke long with the King, telling him of the deeds of the Noldor in the north, and of their numbers, and of the ordering of their force; but being true, and wise-hearted, and thinking all griefs now forgiven, he spoke no word concerning the kinslaying, nor of the manner of the exile of the Noldor and the oath of Fëanor. King Thingol hearkened to the words of Angrod; and ere he went he said to him: 'Thus shall you speak for me to those that sent you. In Hithlum the Noldor have leave to dwell, and in the highlands of Dorthonion, and in the lands east of Doriath that are empty and wild; but elsewhere there are many of my people, and I would not have them restrained of their freedom, still less ousted from their homes. Beware therefore how you princes of the West bear yourselves; for I am the Lord of Beleriand, and all who seek to dwell there shall hear my word. Into Doriath none shall come to abide but only such as I call as guests, or who seek me in great need.'

Now the lords of the Noldor held council in Mithrim, and thither came Angrod out of Doriath, bearing the message of King Thingol. Cold seemed its welcome to the Noldor, and the sons of Fëanor were angered at the words; but Maedhros laughed, saying: 'A king is he that can hold his own, or else his title is vain. Thingol does but grant us lands where his power does not run. Indeed Doriath alone would be his realm this day, but for the coming of the Noldor. Therefore in Doriath let him reign, and be glad that he has the sons of Finwë for his neighbours, not the Orcs of Morgoth that we found. Elsewhere it shall go as seems good to us.'

But Caranthir, who loved not the sons of Finarfin, and was the harshest of the brothers and the most quick to anger, cried aloud: 'Yea more! Let not the sons of Finarfin run hither and thither with their tales to this Dark Elf in his caves! Who made them our spokesmen to deal with him? And though they be come indeed to Beleriand, let them not so swiftly forget that their father is a lord of the Noldor, though their mother be of other kin.'

Then Angrod was wrathful and went forth from the council. Maedhros indeed rebuked Caranthir; but the greater part of the Noldor, of both followings, hearing his words were troubled in heart, fearing the fell spirit of the sons of Fëanor that it seemed would ever be like to burst forth in rash word or violence. But Maedhros restrained his brothers, and they departed from the council, and soon afterwards they left Mithrim and went eastward beyond Aros to the wide lands about the Hill of Himring. That region was named thereafter the March of Maedhros; for northwards there was little defence of hill or river against assault from Angband. There Maedhros and his brothers kept watch, gathering all such people as would come to them, and they had few dealings with their kinsfolk westward, save at need. It is said indeed that Maedhros himself devised this plan, to lessen the chances of strife, and because he was very willing that the chief peril of assault should fall upon himself; and he remained for his part in friendship with the houses of Fingolfin and Finarfin, and would come among them at times for common counsel. Yet he also was bound by the oath, though it slept now for a time.

Now the people of Caranthir dwelt furthest east beyond the upper waters of Gelion, about Lake Helevorn under Mount Rerir and to the southward; and they climbed the heights of Ered Luin and looked eastward in wonder, for wild and wide it seemed to them were the lands of Middle-earth. And thus it was that Caranthir's people came upon the Dwarves, who after the onslaught of Morgoth and the coming of the Noldor had ceased their traffic into Beleriand. But though either people loved skill and were eager to learn, no great love was there between them; for the Dwarves were secret and quick to resentment, and Caranthir was haughty and scarce concealed his scorn for the unloveliness of the Naugrim, and his people followed their lord. Nevertheless since both peoples feared and hated Morgoth they made alliance, and had of it great profit; for the Naugrim learned many secrets of craft in those days, so that the smiths and masons of Nogrod and Belegost became renowned among their kin, and when the Dwarves began again to journey into Beleriand all the traffic of the dwarf-mines passed first through the hands of Caranthir, and thus great riches came to him.

When twenty years of the Sun had passed, Fingolfin King of the Noldor made a great feast; and it was held in the spring near to the pools of Ivrin, whence the swift river Narog rose, for there the lands were green and fair at the feet of the Mountains of Shadow that shielded them from the north. The joy of that feast was long remembered in later days of sorrow; and it was called Mereth Aderthad, the Feast of Reuniting. Thither came many of the chieftains and people of Fingolfin and Finrod; and of the sons of Fëanor Maedhros and Maglor, with warriors of the eastern March; and there came also great numbers of the Grey-elves, wanderers of the woods of Beleriand and folk of the Havens, with Círdan their lord. There came even Green-elves from Ossiriand, the Land of Seven Rivers, far off under the walls of the Blue Mountains; but out of Doriath there came but two messengers, Mablung and Daeron, bearing greetings from the King.

At Mereth Aderthad many counsels were taken in good will, and oaths were sworn of league and friendship; and it is told that at this feast the tongue of the Grey-elves was most spoken even by the Noldor, for they learned swiftly the speech of Beleriand, whereas the Sindar were slow to master the tongue of Valinor. The hearts of the Noldor were high and full of hope, and to many among them it seemed that the words of Fëanor had been justified, bidding them seek freedom and fair kingdoms in Middle-earth; and indeed there followed after long years of peace, while their swords fenced Beleriand from the ruin of Morgoth, and his power was shut behind his gates. In those days there was joy beneath the new Sun and Moon, and all the land was glad; but still the Shadow brooded in the north.

And when again thirty years had passed, Turgon son of Fingolfin left Nevrast where he dwelt and sought out Finrod his friend upon the island of Tol Sirion, and they journeyed southward along the river, being weary for a while of the northern mountains; and as they journeyed night came upon them beyond the Meres of Twilight beside the waters of Sirion, and they slept upon his banks beneath the summer stars. But Ulmo coming up the river laid a deep sleep upon them and heavy dreams; and the trouble of the dreams remained after they awoke, but neither said aught to the other, for their memory was not clear, and each believed that Ulmo had sent a message to him alone. But unquiet was upon them ever after, and doubt of what should befall, and they wandered often alone in untrodden lands, seeking far and wide for places of hidden strength; for it seemed to each that he was bidden to prepare for a day of evil, and to establish a retreat, lest Morgoth should burst from Angband and overthrow the armies of the North.

Now on a time Finrod and Galadriel his sister were the guests of Thingol their kinsman in Doriath. Then Finrod was filled with wonder at the strength and majesty of Menegroth, its treasuries and armouries and its many-pillared halls of stone; and it came into his heart that he would build wide halls behind ever-guarded gates in some deep and secret place beneath the hills. Therefore he opened his heart to Thingol, telling him of his dreams; and Thingol spoke to him of the deep gorge of the River Narog, and the caves under the High Faroth in its steep western shore, and when he departed he gave him guides to lead him to that place of which few yet knew. Thus Finrod came to the Caverns of Narog, and began to establish there deep halls and armouries after the fashion of the mansions of Menegroth; and that stronghold was called Nargothrond. In that labour Finrod was aided by the Dwarves of the Blue Mountains; and they were rewarded well, for Finrod had brought more treasures out of Tirion than any other of the princes of the Noldor. And in that time was made for him the Nauglamír, the Necklace of the Dwarves, most renowned of their works in the Elder Days. It was a carcanet of gold, and set therein were gems uncounted from Valinor; but it had a power within it so that it rested lightly on its wearer as a strand of flax, and whatsoever neck it clasped it sat always with grace and loveliness.

There in Nargothrond Finrod made his home with many of his people, and he was named in the tongue of the Dwarves Felagund, Hewer of Caves; and that name he bore thereafter until his end. But Finrod Felagund was not the first to dwell in the caves beside the River Narog.

Galadriel his sister went not with him to Nargothrond, for in Doriath dwelt Celeborn, kinsman of Thingol, and there was great love between them. Therefore she remained in the Hidden Kingdom, and abode with Melian, and of her learned great lore and wisdom concerning Middle-earth.

But Turgon remembered the city set upon a hill, Tirion the fair with its tower and tree, and he found not what he sought, but returned to Nevrast, and sat in peace in Vinyamar by the shores of the sea. And in the next year Ulmo himself appeared to him, and bade him go forth again alone into the Vale of Sirion; and Turgon went forth, and by the guidance of Ulmo he discovered the hidden vale of Tumladen in the Encircling Mountains, in the midst of which there was a hill of stone. Of this he spoke to none as yet, but returned once more to Nevrast, and there began in his secret counsels to devise the plan of a city after the manner of Tirion upon Túna, for which his heart yearned in exile.

Now Morgoth, believing the report of his spies that the lords of the Noldor were wandering abroad with little thought of war, made trial of the strength and watchfulness of his enemies. Once more, with little warning, his might was stirred, and suddenly there were earthquakes in the north, and fire came from fissures in the earth, and the Iron Mountains vomited flame; and Orcs poured forth across the plain of Ard-galen. Thence they thrust down the Pass of Sirion in the west, and in the east they burst through the land of Maglor, in the gap between the hills of Maedhros and the outliers of the Blue Mountains. But Fingolfin and Maedhros were not sleeping, and while others sought out the scattered bands of Orcs that strayed in Beleriand and did great evil they came upon the main host from either side as it was assaulting Dorthonion; and they defeated the servants of Morgoth, and pursuing them across Ard-galen destroyed them utterly, to the least and last, within sight of Angband's gates. That was the third great battle of the Wars of Beleriand, and it was named Dagor Aglareb, the Glorious Battle.

A victory it was, and yet a warning; and the princes took heed of it, and thereafter drew closer their leaguer, and strengthened and ordered their watch, setting the Siege of Angband, which lasted wellnigh four hundred years of the Sun. For a long time after Dagor Aglareb no servant of Morgoth would venture from his gates, for they feared the lords of the Noldor; and Fingolfin boasted that save by treason among themselves Morgoth could never again burst from the leaguer of the Eldar, nor come upon them at unawares. Yet the Noldor could not capture Angband, nor could they regain the Silmarils; and war never wholly ceased in all that time of the Siege, for Morgoth devised new evils, and ever and anon he would make trial of his enemies. Nor could the stronghold of Morgoth be ever wholly encircled; for the Iron Mountains, from whose great curving wall the towers of Thangorodrim were thrust forward, defended it upon either side, and were impassable to the Noldor, because of their snow and ice. Thus in his rear and to the north Morgoth had no foes, and by that way his spies at times went out, and came by devious routes into Beleriand. And desiring above all to sow fear and disunion among the Eldar, he commanded the Orcs to take alive any of them that they could and bring them bound to Angband; and some he so daunted by the terror of his eyes that they needed no chains more, but walked ever in fear of him, doing his will wherever they might be. Thus Morgoth learned much of all that had befallen since the rebellion of Fëanor, and he rejoiced, seeing therein the seed of many dissensions among his foes.

When nearly one hundred years had run since the Dagor Aglareb, Morgoth endeavoured to take Fingolfin at unawares (for he knew of the vigilance of Maedhros); and he sent forth an army into the white north, and they turned west and again south and came down the coasts to the Firth of Drengist, by the route that Fingolfin followed from the Grinding Ice. Thus they would enter into the realm of Hithlum from the west; but they were espied in time, and Fingon fell upon them among the hills at the head of the Firth, and most of the Orcs were driven into the sea. This was not reckoned among the great battles, for the Orcs were not in great number, and only a part of the people of Hithlum fought there. But thereafter there was peace for many years, and no open assault from Angband, for Morgoth perceived now that the Orcs unaided were no match for the Noldor; and he sought in his heart for new counsel.

Again after a hundred years Glaurung, the first of the Urulóki, the fire-drakes of the North, issued from Angband's gates by night. He was yet young and scarce half-grown, for long and slow is the life of the dragons, but the Elves fled before him to Ered Wethrin and Dorthonion in dismay; and he defiled the fields of Ard-galen. Then Fingon prince of Hithlum rode against him with archers on horseback, and hemmed him round with a ring of swift riders; and Glaurung could not endure their darts, being not yet come to his full armoury, and he fled back to Angband, and came not forth again for many years. Fingon won great praise, and the Noldor rejoiced; for few foresaw the full meaning and threat of this new thing. But Morgoth was ill-pleased that Glaurung had disclosed himself oversoon; and after his defeat there was the Long Peace of wellnigh two hundred years. In all that time there were but affrays on the marches, and all Beleriand prospered and grew rich. Behind the guard of their armies in the north the Noldor built their dwellings and their towers, and many fair things they made in those days, and poems and histories and books of lore. In many parts of the land the Noldor and the Sindar became welded into one people, and spoke the same tongue; though this difference remained between them, that the Noldor had the greater power of mind and body, and were the mightier warriors and sages, and they built with stone, and loved the hill-slopes and open lands. But the Sindar had the fairer voices and were more skilled in music, save only Maglor son of Fëanor, and they loved the woods and the riversides; and some of the Grey-elves still wandered far and wide without settled abode, and they sang as they went.

Chapter 14

OF BELERIAND AND ITS REALMS

This is the fashion of the lands into which the Noldor came, in the north of the western regions of Middle-earth, in the ancient days; and here also is told of the manner in which the chieftains of the Eldar held their lands and the leaguer upon Morgoth after the Dagor Aglareb, the third battle in the Wars of Beleriand.

In the north of the world Melkor had in the ages past reared Ered Engrin, the Iron Mountains, as a fence to his citadel of Utumno; and they stood upon the borders of the regions of everlasting cold, in a great curve from east to west. Behind the walls of Ered Engrin in the west, where they bent back northwards, Melkor built another fortress, as a defence against assault that might come from Valinor; and when he came back to Middle-earth, as has been told, he took up his abode in the endless dungeons of Angband, the Hells of Iron, for in the War of the Powers the Valar, in their haste to overthrow him in his great stronghold of Utumno, did not wholly destroy Angband nor search out all its deep places. Beneath Ered Engrin he made a great tunnel, which issued south of the mountains; and there he made a mighty gate. But above this gate, and behind it even to the mountains, he piled the thunderous towers of Thangorodrim, that were made of the ash and slag of his subterranean furnaces, and the vast refuse of his tunnellings. They were black and desolate and exceedingly lofty; and smoke issued from their tops, dark and foul upon the northern sky.

Before the gates of Angband filth and desolation spread southward for many miles over the wide plain of Ard-galen; but after the coming of the Sun rich grass arose there, and while Angband was besieged and its gates shut there were green things even among the pits and broken rocks before the doors of hell.

To the west of Thangorodrim lay Hísilómë, the Land of Mist, for so it was named by the Noldor in their own tongue because of the clouds that Morgoth sent thither during their first encampment; Hithlum it became in the tongue of the Sindar that dwelt in those regions. It was a fair land while the Siege of Angband lasted, although its air was cool and winter there was cold. In the west it was bounded by Ered Lómin, the Echoing Mountains that marched near the sea; and in the east and south by the great curve of Ered Wethrin, the Shadowy Mountains, that looked across Ard-galen and the Vale of Sirion.

Fingolfin and Fingon his son held Hithlum, and the most part of Fingolfin's folk dwelt in Mithrim about the shores of the great lake; to Fingon was assigned Dor-lómin, that lay to the west of the Mountains of Mithrim. But their chief fortress was at Eithel Sirion in the east of Ered Wethrin, whence they kept watch upon Ard-galen; and their cavalry rode upon that plain even to the shadow of Thangorodrim, for from few their horses had increased swiftly, and the grass of Ard-galen was rich and green. Of those horses many of the sires came from Valinor, and they were given to Fingolfin by Maedhros in atonement of his losses, for they had been carried by ship to Losgar.

West of Dor-lómin, beyond the Echoing Mountains, which south of the Firth of Drengist marched inland, lay Nevrast, that signifies the Hither Shore in the Sindarin tongue. That name was given at first to all the coastlands south of the Firth, but afterwards only to the land whose shores lay between Drengist and Mount Taras. There for many years was the realm of Turgon the wise, son of Fingolfin, bounded by the sea, and by Ered Lómin, and by the hills which continued the walls of Ered Wethrin westward, from Ivrin to Mount Taras, which stood upon a promontory. By some Nevrast was held to belong rather to Beleriand than to Hithlum, for it was a milder land, watered by the wet winds from the sea and sheltered from the cold north winds that blew over Hithlum. It was a hollow land, surrounded by mountains and great coast-cliffs higher than the plains behind, and no river flowed thence; and there was a great mere in the midst of Nevrast, with no certain shores, being encircled by wide marshes. Linaewen was the name of that mere, because of the multitude of birds that dwelt there, of such as love tall reeds and shallow pools. At the coming of the Noldor many of the Grey-elves lived in Nevrast near to the coasts, and especially about Mount Taras in the south-west; for to that place Ulmo and Ossë had been wont to come in days of old. All that people took Turgon for their lord, and the mingling of the Noldor and the Sindar came to pass soonest there; and Turgon dwelt long in those halls that he named Vinyamar, under Mount Taras beside the sea.

South of Ard-galen the great highland named Dorthonion stretched for sixty leagues from west to east; great pine forests it bore, especially on its northern and western sides. By gentle slopes from the plain it rose to a bleak and lofty land, where lay many tarns at the feet of bare tors whose heads were higher than the peaks of Ered Wethrin; but southward where it looked towards Doriath it fell suddenly in dreadful precipices. From the northern slopes of Dorthonion Angrod and Aegnor, sons of Finarfin, looked out over the fields of Ard-galen, and were the vassals of their brother Finrod, lord of Nargothrond; their people were few, for the land was barren, and the great highlands behind were deemed to be a bulwark that Morgoth would not lightly seek to cross.

Between Dorthonion and the Shadowy Mountains there was a narrow vale, whose sheer walls were clad with pines; but the vale itself was green, for the River Sirion flowed through it, hastening towards Beleriand. Finrod held the Pass of Sirion, and upon the isle of Tol Sirion in the midst of the river he built a mighty watch-tower, Minas Tirith; but after Nargothrond was made he committed that fortress mostly to the keeping of Orodreth his brother.

Now the great and fair country of Beleriand lay on either side of the mighty River Sirion, renowned in song, which rose at Eithel Sirion and skirted the edge of Ard-galen ere he plunged through the pass, becoming ever fuller with the streams of the mountains. Thence he flowed south for one hundred and thirty leagues, gathering the waters of many tributaries, until with a mighty flood he reached his many mouths and sandy delta in the Bay of Balar. And following Sirion from north to south there lay upon the right hand in West Beleriand the Forest of Brethil between Sirion and Teiglin, and then the realm of Nargothrond, between Teiglin and Narog. And the River Narog rose in the falls of Ivrin in the southern face of Dor-lómin, and flowed some eighty leagues ere he joined Sirion in Nan-tathren, the Land of Willows. South of Nan-tathren was a region of meads filled with many flowers, where few folk dwelt; and beyond lay the marshes and isles

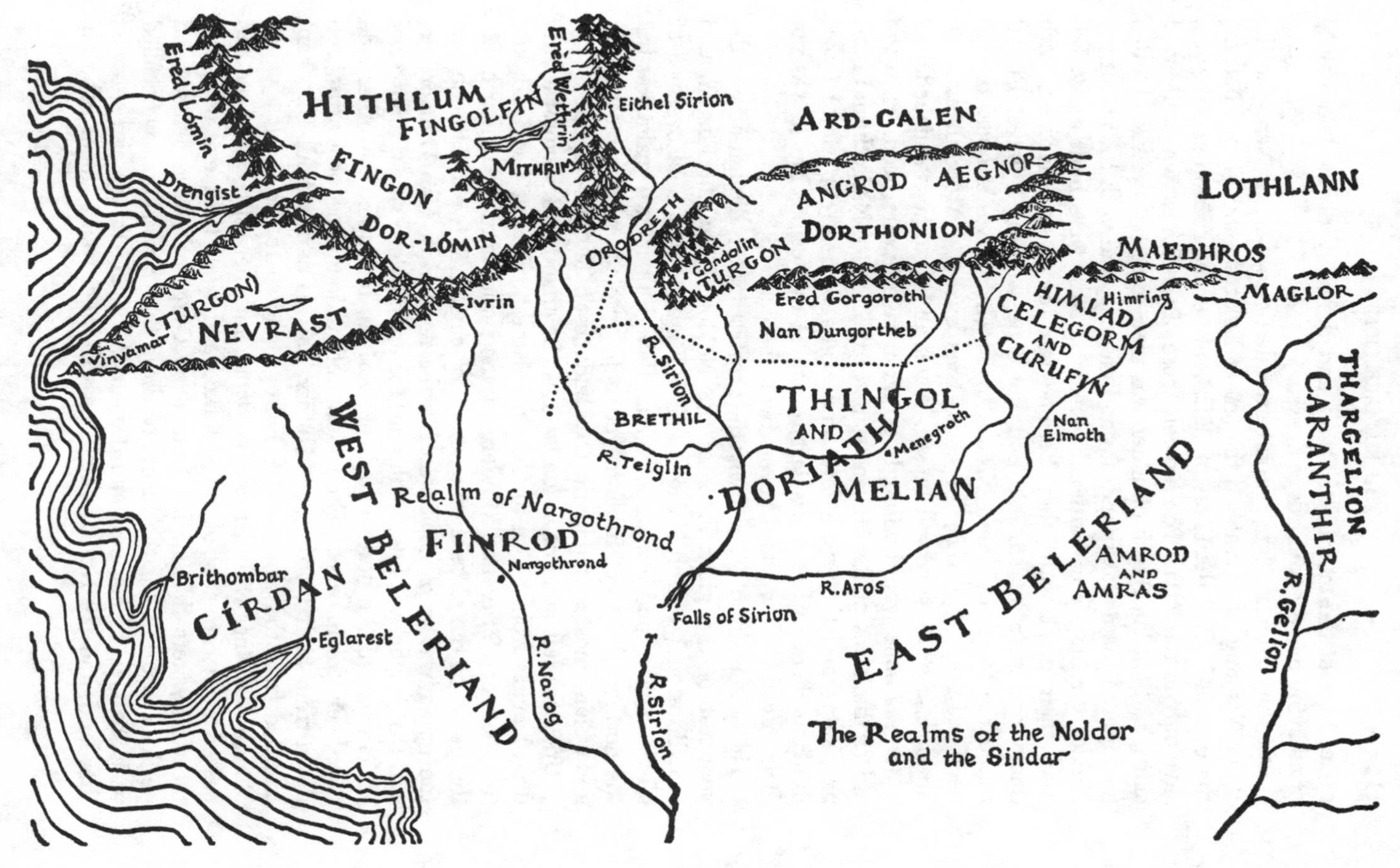

The Realms of the Noldor and the Sindar

of reed about the mouths of Sirion, and the sands of his delta empty of all living things save birds of the sea.

But the realm of Nargothrond extended also west of Narog to the River Nenning, that reached the sea at Eglarest; and Finrod became the overlord of all the Elves of Beleriand between Sirion and the sea, save only in the Falas. There dwelt those of the Sindar who still loved ships, and Círdan the shipbuilder was their lord; but between Círdan and Finrod there was friendship and alliance, and with the aid of the Noldor the havens of Brithombar and Eglarest were built anew. Behind their great walls they became fair towns and harbours with quays and piers of stone. Upon the cape west of Eglarest Finrod raised the tower of Barad Nimras to watch the western sea, though needlessly, as it proved; for at no time ever did Morgoth essay to build ships or to make war by sea. Water all his servants shunned, and to the sea none would willingly go nigh, save in dire need. With the aid of the Elves of the Havens some of the folk of Nargothrond built new ships, and they went forth and explored the great Isle of Balar, thinking there to prepare a last refuge, if evil came; but it was not their fate that they should ever dwell there.

Thus the realm of Finrod was the greatest by far, though he was the youngest of the great lords of the Noldor, Fingolfin, Fingon, and Maedhros, and Finrod Felagund. But Fingolfin was held overlord of all the Noldor, and Fingon after him, though their own realm was but the northern land of Hithlum; yet their people were the most hardy and valiant, most feared by the Orcs and most hated by Morgoth.

Upon the left hand of Sirion lay East Beleriand, at its widest a hundred leagues from Sirion to Gelion and the borders of Ossiriand; and first, between Sirion and Mindeb, lay the empty land of Dimbar under the peaks of the Crissaegrim, abode of eagles. Between Mindeb and the upper waters of Esgalduin lay the no-land of Nan Dungortheb; and that region was filled with fear, for upon its one side the power of Melian fenced the north march of Doriath, but upon the other side the sheer precipices of Ered Gorgoroth, Mountains of Terror, fell down from high Dorthonion. Thither, as was earlier told, Ungoliant had fled from the whips of the Balrogs, and there she dwelt a while, filling the ravines with her deadly gloom, and there still, when she had passed away, her foul offspring lurked and wove their evil nets; and the thin waters that spilled from Ered Gorgoroth were defiled, and perilous to drink, for the hearts of those that tasted them were filled with shadows of madness and despair. All living things else shunned that land, and the Noldor would pass through Nan Dungortheb only at great need, by paths near to the borders of Doriath and furthest from the haunted hills. That way was made long before, in the time ere Morgoth returned to Middle-earth; and if one fared upon it he came eastwards to Esgalduin, where still there stood in the days of the Siege the stone bridge of Iant Iaur. Thence he passed through Dor Dínen, the Silent Land, and crossing the Arossiach (which signifies the Fords of Aros) came to the north marches of Beleriand, where dwelt the sons of Fëanor.

Southward lay the guarded woods of Doriath, abode of Thingol the Hidden King, into whose realm none passed save by his will. Its northern and lesser part, the Forest of Neldoreth, was bounded east and south by the dark river Esgalduin, which bent westward in the midst of the land; and between Aros and Esgalduin lay the denser and greater woods of Region. Upon the southern bank of Esgalduin, where it turned westward towards Sirion, were the Caves of Menegroth; and all Doriath lay east of Sirion save for a narrow region of woodland between the meeting of Teiglin and Sirion and the Meres of Twilight. By the people of Doriath this wood was called Nivrim, the West March; great oak-trees grew there, and it also was encompassed within the Girdle of Melian, that so some portion of Sirion which she loved in reverence of Ulmo should be wholly under the power of Thingol.

In the south-west of Doriath, where Aros flowed into Sirion, lay great pools and marshes on either side of the river, which halted there in his course and strayed in many channels. That region was named Aelin-uial, the Twilight Meres, for they were wrapped in mists, and the enchantment of Doriath lay over them. Now all the northern part of Beleriand sloped southward to this point and then for a while was plain, and the flood of Sirion was stayed. But south of Aelin-uial the land fell suddenly and steeply; and all the lower fields of Sirion were divided from the upper fields by this fall, which to one looking from the south northward appeared as an endless chain of hills running from Eglarest beyond Narog in the west to Amon Ereb in the east, within far sight of Gelion. Narog came through these hills in a deep gorge, and flowed over rapids but had no fall, and on its western bank the land rose into the great wooded highlands of Taur-en-Faroth. On the west side of this gorge, where the short and foaming stream Ringwil tumbled headlong into Narog from the High Faroth, Finrod established Nargothrond. But some twenty-five leagues east of the gorge of Nargothrond Sirion fell from the north in a mighty fall below the Meres, and then he plunged suddenly underground into great tunnels that the weight of his falling waters delved; and he issued again three leagues southward with great noise and smoke through rocky arches at the foot of the hills which were called the Gates of Sirion.

This dividing fall was named Andram, the Long Wall, from Nargothrond to Ramdal, the Wall's End, in East Beleriand. But in the east it became ever less sheer, for the vale of Gelion sloped steadily southward, and Gelion had neither fall nor rapids throughout his course, but was ever swifter than was Sirion. Between Ramdal and Gelion there stood a single hill of great extent and gentle slopes, but seeming mightier than it was, for it stood alone; and that hill was named Amon Ereb. Upon Amon Ereb died Denethor, lord of the Nandor that dwelt in Ossiriand, who marched to the aid of Thingol against Morgoth in those days when the Orcs first came down in force, and broke the starlit peace of Beleriand; and upon that hill Maedhros dwelt after the great defeat. But south of the Andram, between Sirion and Gelion, was a wild land of tangled forest in which no folk went, save here and there a few Dark Elves wandering; Taur-im-Duinath it was named, the Forest between the Rivers.

Gelion was a great river; and he rose in two sources and had at first two branches; Little Gelion that came from the Hill of Himring, and Greater Gelion that came from Mount Rerir. From the meeting of his arms he flowed south for forty leagues before he found his tributaries; and before he found the sea he was twice as long as Sirion, though less wide and full, for more rain fell in Hithlum and Dorthonion, whence Sirion drew his waters, than in the east. From Ered Luin flowed the six tributaries of Gelion: Ascar (that was after named Rathlóriel), Thalos, Legolin, Brilthor, Duilwen, and Adurant, swift and turbulent streams, falling steeply from the mountains; and between Ascar in the north and Adurant in the south, and between Gelion and Ered Luin, lay the far green country of Ossiriand, the Land of Seven Rivers. Now at a point nearly midway in its course the stream of Adurant divided and then joined again; and the island that its waters enclosed was named Tol Galen, the Green Isle. There Beren and Lúthien dwelt after their return.

In Ossiriand dwelt the Green-elves, in the protection of their rivers; for after Sirion Ulmo loved Gelion above all the waters of the western world. The woodcraft of the Elves of Ossiriand was such that a stranger might pass through their land from end to end and see none of them. They were clad in green in spring and summer, and the sound of their singing could be heard even across the waters of

Gelion; wherefore the Noldor named that country Lindon, the land of music, and the mountains beyond they named Ered Lindon, for they first saw them from Ossiriand.

East of Dorthonion the marches of Beleriand were most open to attack, and only hills of no great height guarded the vale of Gelion from the north. In that region, upon the March of Maedhros and in the lands behind, dwelt the sons of Fëanor with many people; and their riders passed often over the vast northern plain, Lothlann the wide and empty, east of Ard-galen, lest Morgoth should attempt any sortie towards East Beleriand. The chief citadel of Maedhros was upon the Hill of Himring, the Ever-cold; and that was wide-shouldered, bare of trees, and flat upon its summit, surrounded by many lesser hills. Between Himring and Dorthonion there was a pass, exceeding steep upon the west, and that was the Pass of Aglon, and was a gate unto Doriath; and a bitter wind blew ever through it from the north. But Celegorm and Curufin fortified Aglon and held it with great strength, and all the land of Himlad southward between the River Aros that rose in Dorthonion and his tributary Celon that came from Himring.

Between the arms of Gelion was the ward of Maglor, and here in one place the hills failed altogether; there it was that the Orcs came into East Beleriand before the Third Battle. Therefore the Noldor held strength of cavalry in the plains at that place; and the people of Caranthir fortified the mountains to the east of Maglor's Gap. There Mount Rerir, and about it many lesser heights, stood out from the main range of Ered Lindon westward; and in the angle between Rerir and Ered Lindon there was a lake, shadowed by mountains on all sides save the south. That was Lake Helevorn, deep and dark, and beside it Caranthir had his abode; but all the great land between Gelion and the mountains, and between Rerir and the River Ascar, was called by the Noldor Thargelion, which signifies the Land beyond Gelion, or Dor Caranthir, the Land of Caranthir; and it was here that the Noldor first met the Dwarves. But Thargelion was before called by the Grey-elves Talath Rhúnen, the East Vale.

Thus the sons of Fëanor under Maedhros were the lords of East Beleriand, but their people were in that time mostly in the north of the land, and southward they rode only to hunt in the greenwoods. But there Amrod and Amras had their abode, and they came seldom northward while the Siege lasted; and there also other of the Elf-lords would ride at times, even from afar, for the land was wild but very fair. Of these Finrod Felagund came most often, for he had great love of wandering, and he came even into Ossiriand, and won the friendship of the Green-elves. But none of the Noldor went ever over Ered Lindon, while their realm lasted; and little news and late came into Beleriand of what passed in the regions of the East.

Chapter 15

OF THE NOLDOR IN BELERIAND

It has been told how by the guidance of Ulmo Turgon of Nevrast discovered the hidden vale of Tumladen; and that (as was after known) lay east of the upper waters of Sirion, in a ring of mountains tall and sheer, and no living thing came there save the eagles of Thorondor. But there was a deep way under the mountains delved in the darkness of the world by waters that flowed out to join the streams of Sirion; and this way Turgon found, and so came to the green plain amid the mountains, and saw the island-hill that stood there of hard smooth stone; for the vale had been a great lake in ancient days. Then Turgon knew that he had found the place of his desire, and he resolved to build there a fair city, a memorial of Tirion upon Túna; but he returned to Nevrast, and remained there in peace, though he pondered ever in his thought how he should accomplish his design.

Now after the Dagor Aglareb the unquiet that Ulmo set in his heart returned to him, and he summoned many of the hardiest and most skilled of his people, and led them secretly to the hidden vale, and there they began the building of the city that Turgon had devised; and they set a watch all about it, that none might come upon their work from without, and the power of Ulmo that ran in Sirion protected them. But Turgon dwelt still for the most part in Nevrast, until it came to pass that at last the city was full-wrought, after two and fifty years of secret toil. It is said that Turgon appointed its name to be Ondolindë in the speech of the Elves of Valinor, the Rock of the

Music of Water, for there were fountains upon the hill; but in the Sindarin tongue the name was changed, and it became Gondolin, the Hidden Rock. Then Turgon prepared to depart from Nevrast and leave his halls in Vinyamar beside the sea; and there Ulmo came to him once again, and spoke with him. And he said: 'Now thou shalt go at last to Gondolin, Turgon; and I will maintain my power in the Vale of Sirion, and in all the waters therein, so that none shall mark thy going, nor shall any find there the hidden entrance against thy will. Longest of all the realms of the Eldalië shall Gondolin stand against Melkor. But love not too well the work of thy hands and the devices of thy heart; and remember that the true hope of the Noldor lieth in the West and cometh from the Sea.'

And Ulmo warned Turgon that he also lay under the Doom of Mandos, which Ulmo had no power to remove. 'Thus it may come to pass,' he said, 'that the curse of the Noldor shall find thee too ere the end, and treason awake within thy walls. Then they shall be in peril of fire. But if this peril draweth nigh indeed, then even from Nevrast one shall come to warn thee, and from him beyond ruin and fire hope shall be born for Elves and Men. Leave therefore in this house arms and a sword, that in years to come he may find them, and thus shalt thou know him, and not be deceived.' And Ulmo declared to Turgon of what kind and stature should be the helm and mail and sword that he left behind.

Then Ulmo returned to the sea, and Turgon sent forth all his people, even to a third part of the Noldor of Fingolfin's following, and a yet greater host of the Sindar; and they passed away, company by company, secretly, under the shadows of Ered Wethrin, and they came unseen to Gondolin, and none knew whither they had gone. And last of all Turgon arose, and went with his household silently through the hills, and passed the gates in the mountains, and they were shut behind him.

Through many long years none passed inward thereafter, save Húrin and Huor only; and the host of Turgon came never forth again until the Year of Lamentation after three hundred and fifty years and more. But behind the circle of the mountains the people of Turgon grew and throve, and they put forth their skill in labour unceasing, so that Gondolin upon Amon Gwareth became fair indeed and fit to compare even with Elven Tirion beyond the sea. High and white were its walls, and smooth its stairs, and tall and strong was the Tower of the King. There shining fountains played, and in the courts of Turgon stood images of the Trees of old, which Turgon himself wrought with elven-craft; and the Tree which he made of gold was named Glingal, and the Tree whose flowers he made of silver was named Belthil. But fairer than all the wonders of Gondolin was Idril, Turgon's daughter, she that was called Celebrindal, the Silver-foot, whose hair was as the gold of Laurelin before the coming of Melkor. Thus Turgon lived long in bliss; but Nevrast was desolate, and remained empty of living folk until the ruin of Beleriand.

Now while the city of Gondolin was building in secret, Finrod Felagund wrought in the deep places of Nargothrond; but Galadriel his sister dwelt, as has been told, in Thingol's realm in Doriath. And at times Melian and Galadriel would speak together of Valinor and the bliss of old; but beyond the dark hour of the death of the Trees Galadriel would not go, but ever fell silent. And on a time Melian said: 'There is some woe that lies upon you and your kin. That I can see in you, but all else is hidden from me; for by no vision or thought can I perceive anything that passed or passes in the West: a shadow lies over all the land of Aman, and reaches far out over the sea. Why will you not tell me more?'

'For that woe is past,' said Galadriel; 'and I would take what joy is here left, untroubled by memory. And maybe there is woe enough yet to come, though still hope may seem bright.'

Then Melian looked in her eyes, and said: 'I believe not that the Noldor came forth as messengers of the Valar, as was said at first: not though they came in the very hour of our need. For they speak never of the Valar, nor have their high lords brought any message to Thingol, whether from Manwë, or Ulmo, or even from Olwë the King's brother, and his own folk that went over the sea. For what cause, Galadriel, were the high people of the Noldor driven forth as exiles from Aman? Or what evil lies on the sons of Fëanor that they are so haughty and so fell? Do I not strike near the truth?'

'Near,' said Galadriel; 'save that we were not driven forth, but came of our own will, and against that of the Valar. And through great peril and in despite of the Valar for this purpose we came: to take vengeance upon Morgoth, and regain what he stole.'

Then Galadriel spoke to Melian of the Silmarils, and of the slaying of King Finwë at Formenos; but still she said no word of the Oath, nor of the Kinslaying, nor of the burning of the ships at Losgar. But Melian said: 'Now much you tell me, and yet more I perceive. A darkness you would cast over the long road from Tirion, but I see evil there, which Thingol should learn for his guidance.'

'Maybe,' said Galadriel; 'but not of me.'

And Melian spoke then no more of these matters with Galadriel; but she told to King Thingol all that she had heard of the Silmarils. 'This is a great matter,' she said, 'greater indeed than the Noldor themselves understand; for the Light of Aman and the fate of Arda lie locked now in these things, the work of Fëanor, who is gone. They shall not be recovered, I foretell, by any power of the Eldar; and the world shall be broken in battles that are to come, ere they are wrested from Morgoth. See now! Fëanor they have slain, and many another, as I guess; but first of all the deaths they have brought and yet shall bring was Finwë your friend. Morgoth slew him, ere he fled from Aman.'

Then Thingol was silent, being filled with grief and foreboding; but at length he said: 'Now at last I understand the coming of the Noldor out of the West, at which I wondered much before. Not to our aid did they come (save by chance); for those that remain in Middle-earth the Valar will leave to their own devices, until the uttermost need. For vengeance and redress of their loss the Noldor came. Yet all the more sure shall they be as allies against Morgoth, with whom it is not now to be thought that they shall ever make treaty.'

But Melian said: 'Truly for these causes they came; but for others also. Beware of the sons of Fëanor! The shadow of the wrath of the Valar lies upon them; and they have done evil, I perceive, both in Aman and to their own kin. A grief but lulled to sleep lies between the princes of the Noldor.'

And Thingol answered: 'What is that to me? Of Fëanor I have heard but report, which makes him great indeed. Of his sons I hear little to my pleasure; yet they are likely to prove the deadliest foes of our foe.'

'Their swords and their counsels shall have two edges,' said Melian; and afterwards they spoke no more of this matter.

It was not long before whispered tales began to pass among the Sindar concerning the deeds of the Noldor ere they came to Beleriand. Certain it is whence they came, and the evil truth was enhanced and poisoned by lies; but the Sindar were yet unwary and trustful of words, and (as may well be thought) Morgoth chose them for this first assault of his malice, for they knew him not. And Círdan, hearing these dark tales, was troubled; for he was wise, and perceived swiftly that true or false they were put about at this time through malice, though the malice he deemed was that of the princes of the Noldor, because of the jealousy of their houses. Therefore he sent messengers to Thingol to tell all that he had heard.

It chanced that at that time the sons of Finarfin were again the guests of Thingol, for they wished to see their sister Galadriel. Then Thingol, being greatly moved, spoke in anger to Finrod, saying: 'Ill have you done to me, kinsman, to conceal so great matters from me. For now I have learned of all the evil deeds of the Noldor.'

But Finrod answered: 'What ill have I done you, lord? Or what evil deed have the Noldor done in all your realm to grieve you? Neither against your kingship nor against any of your people have they thought evil or done evil.'

'I marvel at you, son of Eärwen,' said Thingol, 'that you would come to the board of your kinsman thus red-handed from the slaying of your mother's kin, and yet say naught in defence, nor yet seek any pardon!'

Then Finrod was greatly troubled, but he was silent, for he could not defend himself, save by bringing charges against the other princes of the Noldor; and that he was loath to do before Thingol. But in Angrod's heart the memory of the words of Caranthir welled up again in bitterness, and he cried: 'Lord, I know not what lies you have heard, nor whence; but we came not red-handed. Guiltless we came forth, save maybe of folly, to listen to the words of fell Fëanor, and become as if besotted with wine, and as briefly. No evil did we do on our road, but suffered ourselves great wrong; and forgave it. For this we are named tale-bearers to you and treasonable to the Noldor: untruly as you know, for we have of our loyalty been silent before you, and thus earned your anger. But now these charges are no longer to be borne, and the truth you shall know.'

Then Angrod spoke bitterly against the sons of Fëanor, telling of the blood at Alqualondë, and the Doom of Mandos, and the burning of the ships at Losgar. And he cried: 'Wherefore should we that endured the Grinding Ice bear the name of kinslayers and traitors?'

'Yet the shadow of Mandos lies on you also,' said Melian. But Thingol was long silent ere he spoke. 'Go now!' he said. 'For my heart is hot within me. Later you may return, if you will; for I will not shut my doors for ever against you, my kindred, that were ensnared in an evil that you did not aid. With Fingolfin and his people also I will keep friendship, for they have bitterly atoned for such ill as they did. And in our hatred of the Power that wrought all this woe our griefs shall be lost. But hear my words! Never again in my ears shall be heard the tongue of those who slew my kin in Alqualondë! Nor in all my realm shall it be openly spoken, while my power endures. All the Sindar shall hear my command that they shall neither speak with the tongue of the Noldor nor answer to it. And all such as use it shall be held slayers of kin and betrayers of kin unrepentant.'

Then the sons of Finarfin departed from Menegroth with heavy hearts, perceiving how the words of Mandos would ever be made true, and that none of the Noldor that followed after Fëanor could escape from the shadow that lay upon his house. And it came to pass even as Thingol had spoken; for the Sindar heard his word, and thereafter throughout Beleriand they refused the tongue of the Noldor, and shunned those that spoke it aloud; but the Exiles took the Sindarin tongue in all their daily uses, and the High Speech of the West was spoken only by the lords of the Noldor among themselves. Yet that speech lived ever as a language of lore, wherever any of that people dwelt.

It came to pass that Nargothrond was full-wrought (and yet Turgon still dwelt in the halls of Vinyamar), and the sons of Finarfin were gathered there to a feast; and Galadriel came from Doriath and dwelt a while in Nargothrond. Now King Finrod Felagund had no wife, and Galadriel asked him why this should be; but foresight came upon Felagund as she spoke, and he said: 'An oath I too shall swear, and must be free to fulfil it, and go into darkness. Nor shall anything of my realm endure that a son should inherit.'

But it is said that not until that hour has such cold thoughts ruled him; for indeed she whom he had loved was Amarië of the Vanyar, and she went not with him into exile.

Chapter 16

OF MAEGLIN

Aredhel Ar-Feiniel, the White Lady of the Noldor, daughter of Fingolfin, dwelt in Nevrast with Turgon her brother, and she went with him to the Hidden Kingdom. But she wearied of the guarded city of Gondolin, desiring ever the longer the more to ride again in the wide lands and to walk in the forests, as had been her wont in Valinor; and when two hundred years had passed since Gondolin was full-wrought, she spoke to Turgon and asked leave to depart. Turgon was loath to grant this, and long denied her; but at the last he yielded, saying: 'Go then, if you will, though it is against my wisdom, and I forebode that ill will come of it both to you and to me. But you shall go only to seek Fingon, our brother; and those that I send with you shall return hither to Gondolin as swiftly as they may.'

But Aredhel said: 'I am your sister and not your servant, and beyond your bounds I will go as seems good to me. And if you begrudge me an escort, then I will go alone.'

Then Turgon answered: 'I grudge you nothing that I have. Yet I desire that none shall dwell beyond my walls who know the way hither; and if I trust you, my sister, others I trust less to keep guard on their tongues.'

And Turgon appointed three lords of his household to ride with Aredhel, and he bade them lead her to Fingon in Hithlum, if they might prevail upon her. 'And be wary,' he said; 'for though Morgoth be yet hemmed in the North there are many perils in Middle-earth of which the Lady knows nothing.' Then Aredhel departed from Gondolin, and Turgon's heart was heavy at her going.

But when she came to the Ford of Brithiach in the River Sirion she said to her companions: 'Turn now south and not north, for I will not ride to Hithlum; my heart desires rather to find the sons of Fëanor, my friends of old.' And since she could not be dissuaded they turned south as she commanded, and sought admittance into Doriath. But the march-wardens denied them; for Thingol would suffer none of the Noldor to pass the Girdle, save his kinsfolk of the house of Finarfin, and least of all those that were friends of the sons of Fëanor. Therefore the march-wardens said to Aredhel: 'To the land of Celegorm for which you seek, Lady, you may by no means pass through the realm of King Thingol; you must ride beyond the Girdle of Melian, to the south or to the north. The speediest way is by the paths that lead east from the Brithiach through Dimbar and along the north-march of this kingdom, until you pass the Bridge of Esgalduin and the Fords of Aros, and come to the lands that lie behind the Hill of Himring. There dwell, as we believe, Celegorm and Curufin, and it may be that you will find them; but the road is perilous.'

Then Aredhel turned back and sought the dangerous road between the haunted valleys of Ered Gorgoroth and the north fences of Doriath; and as they drew near to the evil region of Nan Dungortheb the riders became enmeshed in shadows, and Aredhel strayed from her companions and was lost. They sought long for her in vain, fearing that she had been ensnared, or had drunk from the poisoned streams of that land; but the fell creatures of Ungoliant that dwelt in the ravines were aroused and pursued them, and they hardly escaped with their lives. When at last they returned and their tale was told there was great sorrow in Gondolin; and Turgon sat long alone, enduring grief and anger in silence.

But Aredhel, having sought in vain for her companions, rode on, for she was fearless and hardy of heart, as were all the children of Finwë; and she held on her way, and crossing Esgalduin and Aros came to the land of Himlad between Aros and Celon where Celegorm and Curufin dwelt in those days, before the breaking of the Siege of Angband. At that time they were from home, riding with Caranthir east in Thargelion; but the people of Celegorm welcomed her and bade her stay among them with honour until their lord's return. There for a while she was content, and had great joy in wandering free in the woodlands; but as the year lengthened and Celegorm did not return, she became restless again, and took to riding alone ever further abroad, seeking for new paths and untrodden glades. Thus it chanced in the waning of the year that Aredhel came to the south of Himlad, and passed over Celon; and before she was aware she was enmeshed in Nan Elmoth.

In that wood in ages past Melian walked in the twilight of Middle-earth when the trees were young, and enchantment lay upon it still. But now the trees of Nan Elmoth were the tallest and darkest in all Beleriand, and there the sun never came; and there Eöl dwelt, who was named the Dark Elf. Of old he was of the kin of Thingol, but he was restless and ill at ease in Doriath, and when the Girdle of Melian was set about the Forest of Region where he dwelt he fled thence to Nan Elmoth. There he lived in deep shadow, loving the night and the twilight under the stars. He shunned the Noldor, holding them to blame for the return of Morgoth, to trouble the quiet of Beleriand; but for the Dwarves he had more liking than any other of the Elvenfolk of old. From him the Dwarves learned much of what passed in the lands of the Eldar.

Now the traffic of the Dwarves down from the Blue Mountains followed two roads across East Beleriand, and the northern way, going towards the Fords of Aros, passed nigh to Nan Elmoth; and there Eöl would meet the Naugrim and hold converse with them. And as their friendship grew he would at times go and dwell as guest in the deep mansions of Nogrod or Belegost. There he learned much of metal-work, and came to great skill therein; and he devised a metal as hard as the steel of the Dwarves, but so malleable that he could make it thin and supple; and yet it remained resistant to all blades and darts. He named it *galvorn*, for it was black and shining like jet, and he was clad in it whenever he went abroad. But Eöl, though stooped by his smithwork, was no Dwarf, but a tall Elf of a high kin of the Teleri, noble though grim of face; and his eyes could see deep into shadows and dark places. And it came to pass that he saw Aredhel Ar-Feiniel as she strayed among the tall trees near the borders of Nan Elmoth, a gleam of white in the dim land. Very fair she seemed to him, and he desired her; and he set his enchantments about her so that she could not find the ways out, but drew ever nearer to his dwelling in the depths of the wood. There were his smithy, and his dim halls, and such servants as he had, silent and secret as their master. And when Aredhel, weary with wandering, came at last to his doors, he revealed himself; and he welcomed her, and led her into his house. And there she remained; for Eöl took her to wife, and it was long ere any of her kin heard of her again.

It is not said that Aredhel was wholly unwilling, nor that her life in Nan Elmoth was hateful to her for many years. For though at Eöl's command she must shun the sunlight, they wandered far together under the stars or by the light of the sickle moon; or she might fare alone as she would, save that Eöl forbade her to seek the sons of Fëanor, or any others of the Noldor. And Aredhel bore to Eöl a son in the shadows of Nan Elmoth, and in her heart she gave him a name in the forbidden tongue of the Noldor, Lómion, that signifies Child of the Twilight; but his father gave him no name until he was twelve years old. Then he called him Maeglin, which is Sharp Glance, for he perceived that the eyes of his son were more piercing than his own, and his thought could read the secrets of hearts beyond the mist of words.

As Maeglin grew to full stature he resembled in face and form rather his kindred of the Noldor, but in mood and mind he was the son of his father. His words were few save in matters that touched him near, and then his voice had a power to move those that heard him and to overthrow those that withstood him. He was tall and black-haired; his eyes were dark, yet bright and keen as the eyes of the Noldor, and his skin was white. Often he went with Eöl to the cities of the Dwarves in the east of Ered Lindon, and there he learned eagerly what they would teach, and above all the craft of finding the ores of metals in the mountains.

Yet it is said that Maeglin loved his mother better, and if Eöl were abroad he would sit long beside her and listen to all that she could tell him of her kin and their deeds in Eldamar, and of the might and valour of the princes of the House of Fingolfin. All these things he laid to heart, but most of all that which he heard of Turgon, and that he had no heir; for Elenwë his wife perished in the crossing of the Helcaraxë, and his daughter Idril Celebrindal was his only child.

In the telling of these tales there was awakened in Aredhel a desire to see her own kin again, and she marvelled that she had grown weary of the light of Gondolin, and the fountains in the sun, and the green sward of Tumladen under the windy skies of spring; moreover she was often alone in the shadows when both her son and her husband were away. Of these tales also grew the first quarrels of Maeglin and Eöl. For by no means would his mother reveal to Maeglin where Turgon dwelt, nor by what means one might come thither, and he bided his time, trusting yet to wheedle the secret from her, or perhaps to read her unguarded mind; but ere that could be done he desired to look on the Noldor and speak with the sons of Fëanor, his kin, that dwelt not far away. But when he declared his purpose to Eöl, his father was wrathful. 'You are of the house of Eöl, Maeglin, my son,' he said, 'and not of the Golodhrim. All this land is the land of the Teleri, and I will not deal nor have my son deal with the slayers of our kin, the invaders and usurpers of our homes. In this you shall obey me, or I will set you in bonds.' And Maeglin did not answer, but was cold and silent, and went abroad no more with Eöl; and Eöl mistrusted him.

It came to pass that at the midsummer the Dwarves, as was their custom, bade Eöl to a feast in Nogrod; and he rode away. Now Maeglin and his mother were free for a while to go where they wished, and they rode often to the eaves of the wood, seeking the sunlight; and desire grew hot in Maeglin's heart to leave Nan Elmoth for ever. Therefore he said to Aredhel: 'Lady, let us depart while there is time! What hope is there in this wood for you or for me? Here we are held in bondage, and no profit shall I find here; for I have learned all that my father has to teach, or that the Naugrim will reveal to me. Shall we not seek for Gondolin? You shall be my guide, and I will be your guard!'

Then Aredhel was glad, and looked with pride upon her son; and telling the servants of Eöl that they went to seek the sons of Fëanor they departed and rode away to the north eaves of Nan Elmoth. There they crossed the slender stream of Celon into the land of Himlad and rode on to the Fords of Aros, and so westward along the fences of Doriath.

Now Eöl returned out of the east sooner than Maeglin had foreseen, and found his wife and his son but two days gone; and so great was his anger that he followed after them even by the light of day. As he entered the Himlad he mastered his wrath and went warily, remembering his danger, for Celegorm and Curufin were mighty lords who loved Eöl not at all, and Curufin moreover was of perilous mood; but the scouts of Aglon had marked the riding of Maeglin and Aredhel to the Fords of Aros, and Curufin perceiving that strange deeds were afoot came south from the Pass and encamped near the Fords. And before Eöl had ridden far across the Himlad he was waylaid by the riders of Curufin, and taken to their lord.

Then Curufin said to Eöl: 'What errand have you, Dark Elf, in my lands? An urgent matter, perhaps, that keeps one so sun-shy abroad by day.'

And Eöl knowing his peril restrained the bitter words that arose in his mind. 'I have learned, Lord Curufin,' he said, 'that my son and my wife, the White Lady of Gondolin, have ridden to visit you while I was from home; and it seemed to me fitting that I should join them on this errand.'

Then Curufin laughed at Eöl, and he said: 'They might have found their welcome here less warm than they hoped, had you accompanied them; but it is no matter, for that was not their errand. It is not two days since they passed over the Arossiach, and thence rode swiftly westward. It seems that you would deceive me; unless indeed you yourself have been deceived.'

And Eöl answered: 'Then, lord, perhaps you will give me leave to go, and discover the truth of this matter.'

'You have my leave, but not my love,' said Curufin. 'The sooner you depart from my land the better will it please me.'

Then Eöl mounted his horse, saying: 'It is good, Lord Curufin, to find a kinsman thus kindly at need. I will remember it when I return.' Then Curufin looked darkly upon Eöl. 'Do not flaunt the title of your wife before me,' he said. 'For those who steal the daughters of the Noldor and wed them without gift or leave do not gain kinship with their kin. I have given you leave to go. Take it, and be gone. By the laws of the Eldar I may not slay you at this time. And this counsel I add: return now to your dwelling in the darkness of Nan Elmoth; for my heart warns me that if you now pursue those who love you no more, never will you return thither.'

Then Eöl rode off in haste, and he was filled with hatred of all the Noldor; for he perceived now that Maeglin and Aredhel were fleeing to Gondolin. And driven by anger and the shame of his humiliation he crossed the Fords of Aros and rode hard upon the way that they had gone before; but though they knew not that he followed them, and he had the swiftest steed, he came never in sight of them until they reached the Brithiach, and abandoned their horses. Then by ill fate they were betrayed; for the horses neighed loudly, and Eöl's steed heard them, and sped towards them; and Eöl saw from afar the white raiment of Aredhel, and marked which way she went, seeking the secret path into the mountans.

Now Aredhel and Maeglin came to the Outer Gate of Gondolin and the Dark Guard under the mountains; and there she was received with joy, and passing through the Seven Gates she came with Maeglin to Turgon upon Amon Gwareth. Then the King listened with wonder to all that Aredhel had to tell; and he looked with liking upon Maeglin his sister-son, seeing in him one worthy to be accounted among the princes of the Noldor.

'I rejoice indeed that Ar-Feiniel has returned to Gondolin,' he said, 'and now more fair again shall my city seem than in the days when I deemed her lost. And Maeglin shall have the highest honour in my realm.'

Then Maeglin bowed low and took Turgon for lord and king, to do all his will; but thereafter he stood silent and watchful, for the bliss and splendour of Gondolin surpassed all that he had imagined from the tales of his mother, and he was amazed by the strength of the city and the hosts of its people, and the many things strange and beautiful that he beheld. Yet to none were his eyes more often drawn than to Idril the King's daughter, who sat beside him; for she was golden as the Vanyar, her mother's kindred, and she seemed to him as the sun from which all the King's hall drew its light.

But Eöl, following after Aredhel, found the Dry River and the secret path, and so creeping in by stealth he came to the Guard, and was taken and questioned. And when the Guard heard that he claimed Aredhel as wife they were amazed, and sent a swift messenger to the city; and he came to the King's hall.

'Lord,' he cried, 'the Guard have taken captive one that came by stealth to the Dark Gate. Eöl he names himself, and he is a tall Elf, dark and grim, of the kindred of the Sindar; yet he claims the Lady Aredhel as his wife, and demands to be brought before you. His wrath is great and he is hard to restrain; but we have not slain him as your law commands.'

Then Aredhel said: 'Alas! Eöl has followed us, even as I feared. But with great stealth was it done; for we saw and heard no pursuit as we entered upon the Hidden Way.' Then she said to the messenger: 'He speaks but the truth. He is Eöl, and I am his wife, and he is the father of my son. Slay him not, but lead him hither to the King's judgement, if the King so wills.'

And so it was done; and Eöl was brought to Turgon's hall and stood before his high seat, proud and sullen. Though he was amazed no less than his son at all that he saw, his heart was filled the more with anger and with hate of the Noldor. But Turgon treated him with honour, and rose up and would take his hand; and he said: 'Welcome, kinsman, for so I hold you. Here you shall dwell at your pleasure, save only that you must here abide and depart not from my kingdom; for it is my law that none who finds the way hither shall depart.'

But Eöl withdrew his hand. 'I acknowledge not your law,' he said. 'No right have you or any of your kin in this land to seize realms or to set bounds, either here or there. This is the land of the Teleri, to which you bring war and all unquiet, dealing ever proudly and unjustly. I care nothing for your secrets and I came not to spy upon you, but to claim my own: my wife and my son. Yet if in Aredhel your sister you have some claim, then let her remain; let the bird go back to the cage, where soon she will sicken again, as she sickened before. But not so Maeglin. My son you shall not withhold from me. Come, Maeglin son of Eöl! Your father commands you. Leave the house of his enemies and the slayers of his kin, or be accursed!' But Maeglin answered nothing.

Then Turgon sat in his high seat holding his staff of doom, and in a stern voice spoke: 'I will not debate with you, Dark Elf. By the swords of the Noldor alone are your sunless woods defended. Your freedom to wander there wild you owe to my kin; and but for them long since you would have laboured in thraldom in the pits of Angband. And here I am King; and whether you will it or will it not, my doom is law. This choice only is given to you: to abide here, or to die here; and so also for your son.'

Then Eöl looked into the eyes of King Turgon, and he was not daunted, but stood long without word or movement while a still silence fell upon the hall; and Aredhel was afraid, knowing that he was perilous. Suddenly, swift as serpent, he seized a javelin that he held hid beneath his cloak and cast it at Maeglin, crying: 'The second choice I take and for my son also! You shall not hold what is mine!'

But Aredhel sprang before the dart, and it smote her in the shoulder; and Eöl was overborne by many and set in bonds, and led away, while others tended Aredhel. But Maeglin looking upon his father was silent.

It was appointed that Eöl should be brought on the next day to the King's judgement; and Aredhel and Idril moved Turgon to mercy. But in the evening Aredhel sickened, though the wound had seemed little, and she fell into the darkness, and in the night she died; for the point of the javelin was poisoned, though none knew it until too late.

Therefore when Eöl was brought before Turgon he found no mercy; and they led him forth to the Caragdûr, a precipice of black rock upon the north side of the hill of Gondolin, there to cast him down from the sheer walls of the city. And Maeglin stood by and said nothing; but at the last Eöl cried out: 'So you forsake your father and his kin, ill-gotten son! Here shall you fail of all your hopes, and here may you yet die the same death as I.'

Then they cast Eöl over the Caragdûr, and so he ended, and to all in Gondolin it seemed just; but Idril was troubled, and from that day she mistrusted her kinsman. But Maeglin prospered and grew great among the Gondolindrim, praised by all, and high in the favour of Turgon; for if he would learn eagerly and swiftly all that he might, he had much also to teach. And he gathered about him all such as had the most bent to smithcraft and mining; and he sought in the Echoriath (which are the Encircling Mountains), and found rich lodes of ore of divers metals. Most he prized the hard iron of the mine of Anghabar in the north of the Echoriath, and thence he got a wealth of forged metal and of steel, so that the arms of the Gondolindrim were made ever stronger and more keen; and that stood them in good stead in the days to come. Wise in counsel was Maeglin and wary, and yet hardy and valiant at need. And that was seen in after days: for when in the dread year of the Nirnaeth Arnoediad Turgon opened his leaguer and marched forth to the help of Fingon in the north, Maeglin would not remain in Gondolin as regent of the King, but went to the war and fought beside Turgon, and proved fell and fearless in battle.

Thus all seemed well with the fortunes of Maeglin, who had risen to be mighty among the princes of the Noldor, and greatest save one in the most renowned of their realms. Yet he did not reveal his heart; and though not all things went as he would he endured it in silence, hiding his mind so that few could read it, unless it were Idril Celebrindal. For from his first days in Gondolin he had borne a grief, ever worsening, that robbed him of all joy: he loved the beauty of Idril and desired her, without hope. The Eldar wedded not with kin so near, nor ever before had any desired to do so. And however that might be, Idril loved Maeglin not at all; and knowing his thought of her she loved him the less. For it seemed to her a thing strange and crooked in him, as indeed the Eldar ever since have deemed it: an evil fruit of the Kinslaying, whereby the shadow of the curse of Mandos fell upon the last hope of the Noldor. But as the years passed still Maeglin watched Idril, and waited, and his love turned to darkness in his heart. And he sought the more to have his will in other matters, shirking no toil or burden, if he might thereby have power.

Thus it was in Gondolin; and amid all the bliss of that realm, while its glory lasted, a dark seed of evil was sown.

Chapter 17

OF THE COMING OF MEN INTO THE WEST

When three hundred years and more were gone since the Noldor came to Beleriand, in the days of the Long Peace, Finrod Felagund lord of Nargothrond journeyed east of Sirion and went hunting with Maglor and Maedhros, sons of Fëanor. But he wearied of the chase and passed on alone towards the mountains of Ered Lindon that he saw shining afar; and taking the Dwarf-road he crossed Gelion at the ford of Sarn Athrad, and turning south over the upper streams of Ascar, he came into the north of Ossiriand.

In a valley among the foothills of the mountains, below the springs of Thalos, he saw lights in the evening, and far off he heard the sound of song. At this he wondered much, for the Green-elves of that land lit no fires, nor did they sing by night. At first he feared that a raid of Orcs had passed the leaguer of the North, but as he drew near he perceived that it was not so; for the singers used a tongue that he had not heard before, neither that of Dwarves nor of Orcs. Then Felagund, standing silent in the night-shadow of the trees, looked down into the camp, and there he beheld a strange people.

Now these were a part of the kindred and following of Bëor the Old, as he was afterwards called, a chieftain among Men. After many lives of wandering out of the East he had led them at last over the Blue Mountains, the first of the race of Men to enter Beleriand; and they sang because they were glad, and believed that they had escaped from all perils and had come at last to a land without fear.

Long Felagund watched them, and love for them stirred in his heart; but he remained hidden in the trees until they had all fallen asleep. Then he went among the sleeping people, and sat beside their dying fire where none kept watch; and he took up a rude harp which Bëor had laid aside, and he played music upon it such as the ears of Men had not heard; for they had as yet no teachers in the art, save only the Dark Elves in the wild lands.

Now men awoke and listened to Felagund as he harped and sang, and each thought that he was in some fair dream, until he saw that his fellows were awake also beside him; but they did not speak or stir while Felagund still played, because of the beauty of the music and the wonder of the song. Wisdom was in the words of the Elven-king, and the hearts grew wiser that hearkened to him; for the things of which he sang, of the making of Arda, and the bliss of Aman beyond the shadows of the Sea, came as clear visions before their eyes, and his Elvish speech was interpreted in each mind according to its measure.

Thus it was that Men called King Felagund, whom they first met of all the Eldar, Nóm, that is Wisdom, in the language of that people, and after him they named his folk Nómin, the Wise. Indeed they believed at first that Felagund was one of the Valar, of whom they had heard rumour that they dwelt far in the West; and this was (some say) the cause of their journeying. But Felagund dwelt among them and taught them true knowledge, and they loved him, and took him for their lord, and were ever after loyal to the house of Finarfin.

Now the Eldar were beyond all other peoples skilled in tongues; and Felagund discovered also that he could read in the minds of Men such thoughts as they wished to reveal in speech, so that their words were easily interpreted. It is said also that these Men had long had dealings with the Dark Elves east of the mountains, and from them had learned much of their speech; and since all the languages of the Quendi were of one origin, the language of Bëor and his folk resembled the Elven-tongue in many words and devices. It was not long therefore before Felagund could hold converse with Bëor; and while he dwelt with him they spoke much together. But when he questioned him concerning the arising of Men and their journeys, Bëor would say little; and indeed he knew little, for the fathers of his people had told few tales of their past and a silence had fallen upon their memory. 'A darkness lies behind us,' Bëor said; 'and we have turned our backs upon it, and we do not desire to return thither even in thought. Westwards our hearts have been turned, and we believe that there we shall find Light.'

But it was said afterwards among the Eldar that when Men awoke in Hildórien at the rising of the Sun the spies of Morgoth were watchful, and tidings were soon brought to him; and this seemed to him so great a matter that secretly under shadow he himself departed from Angband, and went forth into Middle-earth, leaving to Sauron the command of the War. Of his dealings with Men the Eldar indeed knew nothing, at that time, and learnt but little afterwards; but that a darkness lay upon the hearts of Men (as the shadow of the Kinslaying and the Doom of Mandos lay upon the Noldor) they perceived clearly even in the people of the Elf-friends whom they first knew. To corrupt or destroy whatsoever arose new and fair was ever the chief desire of Morgoth; and doubtless he had this purpose also in his errand: by fear and lies to make Men the foes of the Eldar, and bring them up out of the east against Beleriand. But this design was slow to ripen, and was never wholly achieved; for Men (it is said) were at first very few in number, whereas Morgoth grew afraid of the growing power and union of the Eldar and came back to Angband, leaving behind at that time but few servants, and those of less might and cunning.

Now Felagund learned from Bëor that there were many other Men of like mind who were also journeying westward. 'Others of my own kin have crossed the Mountains,' he said, 'and they are wandering not far away; and the Haladin, a people from whom we are sundered in speech, are still in the valleys on the eastern slopes, awaiting tidings before they venture further. There are yet other Men, whose tongue is more like to ours, with whom we have had dealings at times. They were before us on the westward march, but we passed them; for they are a numerous people, and yet keep together and move slowly, being all ruled by one chieftain whom they call Marach.'

Now the Green-elves of Ossiriand were troubled by the coming of Men, and when they heard that a lord of the Eldar from over the Sea was among them they sent messengers to Felagund. 'Lord,' they said, 'if you have power over these newcomers, bid them return by the ways that they came, or else to go forward. For we desire no strangers in this land to break the peace in which we live. And these folk are hewers of trees and hunters of beasts; therefore we are their unfriends, and if they will not depart we shall afflict them in all ways that we can.'

Then by the advice of Felagund Bëor gathered all the wandering families and kindreds of his people, and they removed over Gelion, and took up their abode in the lands of Amrod and Amras, upon the east banks of the Celon south of Nan Elmoth, near to the borders of Doriath; and the name of that land thereafter was Estolad, the Encampment. But when after a year had passed Felagund wished to return to his own country, Bëor begged leave to come with him; and he remained in the service of the King of Nargothrond while his life lasted. In this way he got his name, Bëor, whereas his name before had been Balan; for Bëor signified 'Vassal' in the tongue of his people. The rule of his folk he committed to Baran his elder son; and he did not return again to Estolad.

Soon after the departure of Felagund the other Men of whom Bëor had spoken came also into Beleriand. First came the Haladin; but meeting the unfriendship of the Green-elves they turned north and dwelt in Thargelion, in the country of Caranthir son of Fëanor; there for a time they had peace, and the people of Caranthir paid little heed to them. In the next year Marach led his people over the mountains; they were a tall and warlike folk, marching in ordered companies, and the Elves of Ossiriand hid themselves and did not waylay them. But Marach, hearing that the people of Bëor were dwelling in a green and fertile land, came down the Dwarf-road, and settled in the country south and east of the dwellings of Baran son of Bëor; and there was great friendship between those peoples.

Felagund himself often returned to visit Men; and many other Elves out of the west-lands, both Noldor and Sindar, journeyed to Estolad, being eager to see the Edain, whose coming had long been foretold. Now Atani, the Second People, was the name given to Men in Valinor in the lore that told of their coming; but in the speech of Beleriand that name became Edain, and it was there used only of the three kindreds of the Elf-friends.

Fingolfin, as King of all the Noldor, sent messengers of welcome to them; and then many young and eager men of the Edain went away and took service with the kings and lords of the Eldar. Among them was Malach son of Marach, and he dwelt in Hithlum for fourteen years; and he learned the Elven-tongue and was given the name of Aradan.

The Edain did not long dwell content in Estolad, for many still desired to go westward; but they did not know the way. Before them lay the fences of Doriath, and southward lay Sirion and its impassable fens. Therefore the kings of the three houses of the Noldor, seeing hope of strength in the sons of Men, sent word that any of the Edain that wished might remove and come to dwell among their people. In this way the migration of the Edain began: at first little by little, but later in families and kindreds, they arose and left Estolad, until after some fifty years many thousands had entered the lands of the Kings. Most of these took the long road northwards, until the ways became well known to them. The people of Bëor came to Dorthonion and dwelt in lands ruled by the house of Finarfin. The people of Aradan (for Marach his father remained in Estolad until his death) for the most part went on westward; and some came to Hithlum, but Magor son of Aradan and many of the people passed down Sirion into Beleriand and dwelt a while in the vales of the southern slopes of Ered Wethrin.

It is said that in all these matters none save Finrod Felagund took counsel with King Thingol, and he was ill pleased, both for that reason, and because he was troubled by dreams concerning the coming of Men, ere ever the first tidings of them were heard. Therefore he commanded that Men should take no lands to dewll in save in the north, and that the princes whom they served should be answerable for all that they did; and he said: 'Into Doriath shall no Man come while my realm lasts, not even those of the house of Bëor who serve Finrod the beloved.' Melian said nothing to him at that time, but afterwards she said to Galadriel: 'Now the world runs on swiftly to great tidings. And one of Men, even of Bëor's house, shall indeed come, and the Girdle of Melian shall not restrain him, for doom greater than my power shall send him; and the songs that shall spring from that coming shall endure when all Middle-earth is changed.'

But many Men remained in Estolad, and there was still a mingled people living there long years after, until in the ruin of Beleriand they were overwhelmed or fled back into the East. For beside the old who deemed that their wandering days were over there were not a few who desired to go their own ways, and they feared the Eldar and the light of their eyes; and then dissensions awoke among the Edain, in which the shadow of Morgoth may be discerned, for certain it is that he knew of the coming of Men into Beleriand and of their growing friendship with the Elves.

The leaders of discontent were Bereg of the house of Bëor, and Amlach, one of the grandsons of Marach; and they said openly: 'We took long roads, desiring to escape the perils of Middle-earth and the dark things that dwell there; for we heard that there was Light in the West. But now we learn that the Light is beyond the Sea. Thither we cannot come where the Gods dwell in bliss. Save one; for the Lord of the Dark is here before us, and the Eldar, wise but fell, who make endless war upon him. In the North he dwells, they say; and there is the pain and death from which we fled. We will not go that way.'

Then a council and assembly of Men was called, and great numbers came together. And the Elf-friends answered Bereg, saying: 'Truly from the Dark King come all the evils from which we fled; but he seeks dominion over all Middle-earth, and whither now shall we turn and he will not pursue us? Unless he be vanquished here, or at least held in leaguer. Only by the valour of the Eldar is he restrained, and maybe it was for this purpose, to aid them at need, that we were brought into this land.'

To this Bereg answered: 'Let the Eldar look to it! Our lives are short enough.' But there arose one who seemed to all to be Amlach son of Imlach, speaking fell words that shook the hearts of all who heard him: 'All this is but Elvish lore, tales to beguile newcomers that are unwary. The Sea has no shore. There is no Light in the West. You have followed a fool-fire of the Elves to the end of the world! Which of you has seen the least of the Gods? Who has beheld the Dark King in the North? Those who seek the dominion of Middle-earth are the Eldar. Greedy for wealth they have delved in the earth for its secrets and have stirred to wrath the things that dwell beneath it, as they have ever done and ever shall. Let the Orcs have the realm that is theirs, and we will have ours. There is room in the world, if the Eldar will let us be!'

Then those that listened sat for a while astounded, and a shadow of fear fell on their hearts; and they resolved to depart far from the lands of the Eldar. But afterwards Amlach returned among them, and denied that he had been present at their debate or had spoken such words as they reported; and there was doubt and bewilderment among Men. Then the Elf-friends said: 'You will now believe this at least: there is indeed a Dark Lord, and his spies and emissaries are among us; for he fears us, and the strength that we may give to his foes.'

But some still answered: 'He hates us, rather, and ever the more the longer we dwell here, meddling in his quarrel with the Kings of the Eldar, to no gain of ours.' Many therefore of those that yet remained in Estolad made ready to depart; and Bereg led a thousand of the people of Bëor away southwards, and they passed out of the songs of those days. But Amlach repented, saying: 'I have now a quarrel of my own with this Master of Lies, which will last to my life's end'; and he went away north and entered the service of Maedhros. But those of his people who were of like mind with Bereg chose a new leader, and they went back over the mountains into Eriador, and are forgotten.

During this time the Haladin remained in Thargelion and were content. But Morgoth, seeing that by lies and deceits he could not yet wholly estrange Elves and Men, was filled with wrath, and endeavoured to do Men what hurt he could. Therefore he sent out an Orc-raid, and passing east it escaped the leaguer, and came in stealth back over Ered Lindon by the passes of the Dwarf-road, and fell upon the Haladin in the southern woods of the land of Caranthir.

Now the Haladin did not live under the rule of lords or many together, but each homestead was set apart and governed its own affairs, and they were slow to unite. But there was among them a man named Haldad, who was masterful and fearless; and he gathered all the brave men that he could find, and retreated to the angle of land between Ascar and Gelion, and in the utmost corner he built a stockade across from water to water; and behind it they led all the women and children that they could save. There they were besieged, until their food was gone.

Haldad had twin children: Haleth his daughter, and Haldar his son; and both were valiant in the defence, for Haleth was a woman of great heart and strength. But at last Haldad was slain in a sortie against the Orcs; and Haldar, who rushed out to save his father's body from their butchery, was hewn down beside him. Then Haleth held the people together, though they were without hope; and some cast themselves in the rivers and were drowned. But seven days later, as the Orcs made their last assault and had already broken through the stockade, there came suddenly a music of trumpets, and Caranthir with his host came down from the north and drove the Orcs into the rivers.

Then Caranthir looked kindly upon Men and did Haleth great honour; and he offered her recompense for her father and brother. And seeing, over late, what valour there was in the Edain, he said to her: 'If you will remove and dwell further north, there you shall have the friendship and protection of the Eldar, and free lands of your own.'

But Haleth was proud, and unwilling to be guided or ruled, and most of the Haladin were of like mood. Therefore she thanked Caranthir, but answered: 'My mind is now set, lord, to leave the shadow of the mountains, and go west, whither others of our kin have gone.' When therefore the Haladin had gathered all whom they could find alive of their folk who had fled wild into the woods before the

Orcs, and had gleaned what remained of their goods in their burned homesteads, they took Haleth for their chief; and she led them at last to Estolad, and there dwelt for a time.

But they remained a people apart, and were ever after known to Elves and Men as the People of Haleth. Haleth remained their chief while her days lasted, but she did not wed, and the headship afterwards passed to Haldan son of Haldar her brother. Soon however Haleth desired to move westward again; and though most of her people were against this counsel, she led them forth once more; and they went without help or guidance of the Eldar, and passing over Celon and Aros they journeyed in the perilous land between the Mountains of Terror and the Girdle of Melian. That land was even then not yet so evil as it after became, but it was no road for mortal Men to take without aid, and Haleth only brought her people through it with hardship and loss, constraining them to go forward by the strength of her will. At last they crossed over the Brithiach, and many bitterly repented of their journey; but there was now no returning. Therefore in new lands they went back to their old life as best they could; and they dwelt in free homesteads in the woods of Talath Dirnen beyond Teiglin, and some wandered far into the realm of Nargothrond. But there were many who loved the Lady Haleth and wished to go whither she would, and dwell under her rule; and these she led into the Forest of Brethil, between Teiglin and Sirion. Thither in the evil days that followed many of her scattered folk returned.

Now Brethil was claimed as part of his realm by King Thingol, though it was not within the Girdle of Melian, and he would have denied it to Haleth; but Felagund, who had the friendship of Thingol, hearing of all that had befallen the People of Haleth, obtained this grace for her: that she should dwell free in Brethil, upon the condition only that her people should guard the Crossings of Teiglin against all enemies of the Eldar, and allow no Orcs to enter their woods. To this Haleth answered: 'Where are Haldad my father, and Haldar my brother? If the King of Doriath fears a friendship between Haleth and those who have devoured her kin, then the thoughts of the Eldar are strange to Men.' And Haleth dwelt in Brethil until she died; and her people raised a green mound over her in the heights of the forest, Tûr Haretha, the Ladybarrow, Haudh-en-Arwen in the Sindarin tongue.

In this way it came to pass that the Edain dwelt in the lands of the Eldar, some here, some there, some wandering, some settled in kindreds or small peoples; and the most part of them soon learned the Grey-elven tongue, both as a common speech among themselves and because many were eager to learn the lore of the Elves. But after a time the Elf-kings, seeing that it was not good for Elves and Men to dwell mingled together without order, and that Men needed lords of their own kind, set regions apart where Men could live their own lives, and appointed chieftains to hold these lands freely. They were the allies of the Eldar in war, but marched under their own leaders. Yet many of the Edain had delight in the friendship of the Elves, and dwelt among them for so long as they had leave; and the young men often took service for a time in the hosts of the kings.

Now Hador Lórindol, son of Hathol, son of Magor, son of Malach Aradan, entered the household of Fingolfin in his youth, and was loved by the King. Fingolfin therefore gave to him the lordship of Dor-lómin, and into that land he gathered most of the people of his kin, and became the mightiest of the chieftains of the Edain. In his house only the Elven-tongue was spoken; but their own speech was not forgotten, and from it came the common tongue of Númenor. But in Dorthonion the lordship of the people of Bëor and the country of Ladros was given to Boromir, son of Boron, who was the grandson of Bëor the Old.

The sons of Hador were Galdor and Gundor; and the sons of Galdor were Húrin and Huor; and the son of Húrin was Túrin the Bane of Glaurung; and the son of Huor was Tuor, father of Eärendil the Blessed. The son of Boromir was Bregor, whose sons were Bregolas and Barahir; and the sons of Bregolas were Baragund and Belegund. The daughter of Baragund was Morwen, the mother of Túrin, and the daughter of Belegund was Rían, the mother of Tuor. But the son of Barahir was Beren One-hand, who won the love of Lúthien Thingol's daughter, and returned from the Dead; from them came Elwing the wife of Eärendil, and all the Kings of Númenor after.

All these were caught in the net of the Doom of the Noldor; and they did great deeds which the Eldar remember still among the histories of the Kings of old. And in those days the strength of Men was added to the power of the Noldor, and their hope was high; and Morgoth was straitly enclosed, for the people of Hador, being hardy to endure cold and long wandering, feared not at times to go far into the north and there keep watch upon the movements of the Enemy. The Men of the Three Houses throve and multiplied, but greatest among them was the house of Hador Goldenhead, peer of Elven-lords. His people were of great strength and stature, ready in mind, bold and steadfast, quick to anger and to laughter, mighty among the Children of Ilúvatar in the youth of Mankind. Yellow-haired they were for the most part, and blue-eyed; but not so was Túrin, whose mother was Morwen of the house of Bëor. The Men of that house were dark or brown of hair, with grey eyes; and of all Men they were most like to the Noldor and most loved by them; for they were eager of mind, cunning-handed, swift in understanding, long in memory, and they were moved sooner to pity than to laughter. Like to them were the woodland folk of Haleth, but they were of lesser stature, and less eager for lore. They used few words, and did not love great concourse of Men; and many among them delighted in solitude, wandering free in the greenwoods while the wonder of the lands of the Eldar was new upon them. But in the realms of the West their time was brief and their days unhappy.

The years of the Edain were lengthened, according to the reckoning of Men, after their coming to Beleriand; but at last Bëor the Old died when he had lived three and ninety years, for four and forty of which he had served King Felagund. And when he lay dead, of no wound or grief, but stricken by age, the Eldar saw for the first time the swift waning of the life of Men, and the death of weariness which they knew not in themselves; and they grieved greatly for the loss of their friends. But Bëor at the last had relinquished his life willingly and passed in peace; and the Eldar wondered much at the strange fate of Men, for in all their lore there was no account of it, and its end was hidden from them.

Nonetheless the Edain of old learned swiftly of the Eldar all such art and knowledge as they could receive, and their sons increased in wisdom and skill, until they far surpassed all others of Mankind, who dwelt still east of the mountains and had not seen the Eldar, nor looked upon the faces that had beheld the Light of Valinor.

Chapter 18

OF THE RUIN OF BELERIAND AND THE FALL OF FINGOLFIN

Now Fingolfin, King of the North, and High King of the Noldor, seeing that his people were become numerous and strong, and that the Men allied to them were many and valiant, pondered once more an assault upon Angband; for he knew that they lived in danger while the circle of the siege was incomplete, and Morgoth was free to labour in his deep mines, devising what evils none could foretell ere he should reveal them. This counsel was wise according to the measure of his knowledge; for the Noldor did not yet comprehend the fullness of the power of Morgoth, nor understand that their unaided war upon him was without final hope, whether they hasted or delayed. But because the land was fair and their kingdoms wide, most of the Noldor were content with things as they were, trusting them to last, and slow to begin an assault in which many must surely perish were it in victory or in defeat. Therefore they were little disposed to hearken to Fingolfin, and the sons of Fëanor at that time least of all. Among the chieftains of the Noldor Angrod and Aegnor alone were of like mind with the King; for they dwelt in regions whence Thangorodrim could be descried, and the threat of Morgoth was present to their thought. Thus the designs of Fingolfin came to naught, and the land had peace yet for a while.

But when the sixth generation of Men after Bëor and Marach were not yet come to full manhood, it being then four hundred years and five and fifty since the coming of Fingolfin, the evil befell that he had long dreaded, and yet more dire and sudden than his darkest fear. For Morgoth had long prepared his force in secret, while ever the malice of his heart grew greater, and his hatred of the Noldor more bitter; and he desired not only to end his foes but to destroy also and defile the lands that they had taken and made fair. And it is said that his hate overcame his counsel, so that if he had but endured to wait longer, until his designs were full, then the Noldor would have perished utterly. But on his part he esteemed too lightly the valour of the Elves, and of Men he took yet no account.

There came a time of winter, when night was dark and without moon; and the wide plain of Ard-galen stretched dim beneath the cold stars, from the hill-forts of the Noldor to the feet of Thangorodrim. The watchfires burned low, and the guards were few; on the plain few were waking in the camps of the horsemen of Hithlum. Then suddenly Morgoth sent forth great rivers of flame that ran down swifter than Balrogs from Thangorodrim, and poured over all the plain; and the Mountains of Iron belched forth fires of many poisonous hues, and the fume of them stank upon the air, and was deadly. Thus Ard-galen perished, and fire devoured its grasses; and it became a burned and desolate waste, full of a choking dust, barren and lifeless. Thereafter its name was changed, and it was called Anfauglith, the Gasping Dust. Many charred bones had there their roofless grave; for many of the Noldor perished in that burning, who were caught by the running flame and could not fly to the hills. The heights of Dorthonion and Ered Wethrin held back the fiery torrents, but their woods upon the slopes that looked towards Angband were all kindled, and the smoke wrought confusion among the defenders. Thus began the fourth of the great battles, Dagor Bragollach, the Battle of Sudden Flame.

In the front of that fire came Glaurung the golden, father of dragons, in his full might; and in his train were Balrogs, and behind them came the black armies of the Orcs in multitudes such as the Noldor had never before seen or imagined. And they assaulted the fortresses of the Noldor, and broke the leaguer about Angband, and slew wherever they found them the Noldor and their allies, Grey-elves and Men. Many of the stoutest of the foes of Morgoth were destroyed in the first days of that war, bewildered and dispersed and unable to muster their strength. War ceased not wholly ever again in Beleriand; but the Battle of Sudden Flame is held to have ended with the coming of spring, when the onslaught of Morgoth grew less.

Thus ended the Siege of Angband; and the foes of Morgoth were scattered and sundered one from another. The most part of the Grey-elves fled south and forsook the northern war; many were received into Doriath, and the kingdom and strength of Thingol grew greater in that time, for the power of Melian the queen was woven about his borders and evil could not yet enter that hidden realm. Others took refuge in the fortresses by the sea, and in Nargothrond; and some fled the land and hid themselves in Ossiriand, or passing the mountains wandered homeless in the wild. And rumour of the war and the breaking of the siege reached the ears of Men in the east of Middle-earth.

The sons of Finarfin bore most heavily the brunt of the assault, and Angrod and Aegnor were slain; beside them fell Bregolas lord of the house of Bëor, and a great part of the warriors of that people. But Barahir the brother of Bregolas was in the fighting further westward, near to the Pass of Sirion. There King Finrod Felagund, hastening from the south, was cut off from his people and surrounded with small company in the Fen of Serech; and he would have been slain or taken, but Barahir came up with the bravest of his men and rescued him, and made a wall of spears about him; and they cut their way out of the battle with great loss. Thus Felagund escaped, and returned to his deep fortress of Nargothrond; but he swore an oath of abiding friendship and aid in every need to Barahir and all his kin, and in token of his vow he gave to Barahir his ring. Barahir was now by right lord of the house of Bëor, and he returned to Dorthonion; but most of his people fled from their homes and took refuge in the fastness of Hithlum.

So great was the onslaught of Morgoth that Fingolfin and Fingon could not come to the aid of the sons of Finarfin; and the hosts of Hithlum were driven back with great loss to the fortresses of Ered Wethrin, and these they hardly defended against the Orcs. Before the walls of Eithel Sirion fell Hador the Golden-haired, defending the rearguard of his lord Fingolfin, being then sixty and six years of age, and with him fell Gundor his younger son, pierced with many arrows; and they were mourned by the Elves. Then Galdor the Tall took the lordship of his father. And because of the strength and height of the Shadowy Mountains, which withstood the torrent of fire, and by the valour of the Elves and the Men of the North, which neither Orc nor Balrog could yet overcome, Hithlum remained unconquered, a threat upon the flank of Morgoth's attack; but Fingolfin was sundered from his kinsmen by a sea of foes.

For the war had gone ill with the sons of Fëanor, and well nigh all the east marches were taken by assault. The Pass of Aglon was forced, though with great cost to the hosts of Morgoth; and Celegorm and Curufin being defeated fled south and west by the marches of Doriath, and coming at last to Nargothrond sought harbour with Finrod Felagund. Thus it came to pass that their people swelled the strength of Nargothrond; but it would have been better, as was after seen, if they had remained in the east among their own kin. Maedhros did deeds of surpassing valour, and the Orcs fled before his face; for since his torment upon Thangorodrim his spirit burned like a white fire within, and he was as one that returns from the dead. Thus the great fortress upon the Hill of Himring could not be taken, and many of the most valiant that remained, both of the people of Dorthonion and of the east marches, rallied there to Maedhros; and for a while he closed once more the Pass of Aglon, so that the Orcs could not enter Beleriand by that road. But they overwhelmed the riders of the people of Fëanor upon Lothlann, for Glaurung came thither, and passed through Maglor's Gap, and destroyed all the land between the arms of Gelion. And the Orcs took the fortress upon the west slopes of Mount Rerir, and ravaged all Thargelion, the land of Caranthir; and they defiled Lake Helevorn. Thence they passed over Gelion with fire and terror and came far into East Beleriand. Maglor joined Maedhros upon Himring; but Caranthir fled and joined the remnant of his people to the scattered folk of the hunters, Amrod and Amras, and they retreated and passed Ramdal in the south. Upon Amon Ereb they maintained a watch and some strength of war, and they had aid of the Green-elves; and the Orcs came not into Ossiriand, nor to Taur-im-Duinath and the wilds of the south.

Now news came to Hithlum that Dorthonion was lost and the sons of Finarfin overthrown, and that the sons of Fëanor were driven from their lands. Then Fingolfin beheld (as it seemed to him) the utter ruin of the Noldor, and the defeat beyond redress of all their houses; and filled with wrath and despair he mounted upon Rochallor his great horse and rode forth alone, and none might restrain him. He passed over Dor-nu-Fauglith like a wind amid the dust, and all that beheld his onset fled in amaze, thinking that Oromë himself was come: for a great madness of rage was upon him, so that his eyes shone like the eyes of the Valar. Thus he came alone to Angband's gates, and he sounded his horn, and smote once more upon the brazen doors, and challenged Morgoth to come forth to single combat. And Morgoth came.

That was the last time in those wars that he passed the doors of his stronghold, and it is said that he took not the challenge willingly; for though his might was greatest of all things in this world, alone of the Valar he knew fear. But he could not now deny the challenge before the face of his captains; for the rocks rang with the shrill music of Fingolfin's horn, and his voice came keen and clear down into the depths of Angband; and Fingolfin named Morgoth craven, and lord of slaves. Therefore Morgoth came, climbing slowly from his subterranean throne, and the rumour of his feet was like thunder underground. And he issued forth clad in black armour; and he stood before the King like a tower, iron-crowned, and his vast shield, sable unblazoned, cast a shadow over him like a stormcloud. But Fingolfin gleamed beneath it as a star; for his mail was overlaid with silver, and his blue shield was set with crystals; and he drew his sword Ringil, that glittered like ice.

Then Morgoth hurled aloft Grond, the Hammer of the Underworld, and swung it down like a bolt of thunder. But Fingolfin sprang aside, and Grond rent a mighty pit in the earth, whence smoke and fire darted. Many times Morgoth essayed to smite him, and each time Fingolfin leaped away, as a lightning shoots from under a dark cloud; and he wounded Morgoth with seven wounds, and seven times Morgoth gave a cry of anguish, whereat the hosts of Angband fell upon their faces in dismay, and the cries echoed in the Northlands.

But at the last the King grew weary, and Morgoth bore down his shield upon him. Thrice he was crushed to his knees, and thrice arose again and bore up his broken shield and stricken helm. But the earth was all rent and pitted about him, and he stumbled and fell backward before the feet of Morgoth; and Morgoth set his left foot upon his neck, and the weight of it was like a fallen hill. Yet with his last and desperate stroke Fingolfin hewed the foot with Ringil, and the blood gushed forth black and smoking and filled the pits of Grond.

Thus died Fingolfin, High King of the Noldor, most proud and valiant of the Elven-kings of old. The Orcs made no boast of that duel at the gate; neither do the Elves sing of it, for their sorrow is too deep. Yet the tale of it is remembered still, for Thorondor King of Eagles brought the tidings to Gondolin, and to Hithlum afar off. And Morgoth took the body of the Elven-king and broke it, and would cast it to his wolves; but Thorondor came hasting from his eyrie among the peaks of the Crissaegrim, and he stooped upon Morgoth and marred his face. The rushing of the wings of Thorondor was like the noise of the winds of Manwë, and he seized the body in his mighty talons, and soaring suddenly above the darts of the Orcs he bore the King away. And he laid him upon a mountain-top that looked from the north upon the hidden valley of Gondolin; and Turgon coming built a high cairn over his father. No Orc dared ever after to pass over the mount of Fingolfin or draw nigh his tomb, until the doom of Gondolin was come and treachery was born among his kin. Morgoth went ever halt of one foot after that day, and the pain of his wounds could not be healed; and in his face was the scar that Thorondor made.

Great was the lamentation in Hithlum when the fall of Fingolfin became known, and Fingon in sorrow took the lordship of the house of Fingolfin and the kingdom of the Noldor; but his young son Ereinion (who was after named Gil-galad) he sent to the Havens.

Now Morgoth's power overshadowed the Northlands; but Barahir would not flee from Dorthonion, and remained contesting the land foot by foot with his enemies. Then Morgoth pursued his people to the death, until few remained; and all the forest of the northward slopes of that land was turned little by little into a region of such dread and dark enchantment that even the Orcs would not enter it unless need drove them, and it was called Deldúwath, and Taur-nu-Fuin, The Forest under Nightshade. The trees that grew there after the burning were black and grim, and their roots were tangled, groping in the dark like claws; and those who strayed among them became lost and blind, and were strangled or pursued to madness by phantoms of terror. At last so desperate was the case of Barahir that Emeldir the Manhearted his wife (whose mind was rather to fight beside her son and her husband than to flee) gathered together all the women and children that were left, and gave arms to those that would bear them; and she led them into the mountains that lay behind, and so by perilous paths, until they came at last with loss and misery to Brethil. Some were there received among the Haladin, but some passed on over the mountains to Dor-lómin and the people of Galdor, Hador's son; and among those were Rían, daughter of Belegund, and Morwen, who was named Eledhwen, that is Elfsheen, daughter of Baragund. But none ever saw again the men that they had left. For these were slain one by one, until at last only twelve men remained to Barahir: Beren his son, and Baragund and Belegund his nephews, the sons of Bregolas, and nine faithful servants of his house whose names were long remembered in the songs of the Noldor: Radhruin and Dairuin they were, Dagnir and Ragnor, Gildor and Gorlim the unhappy, Arthad and Urthel, and Hathaldir the young. Outlaws without hope they became, a desperate band that could not escape and would not yield, for their dwellings were destroyed, and their wives and children captured, slain, or fled. From Hithlum there came neither news nor help, and Barahir and his men were hunted like wild beasts; and they retreated to the barren highland above the forest, and wandered among the tarns and rocky moors of that region, furthest from the spies and spells of Morgoth. Their bed was the heather and their roof the cloudy sky.

For nigh on two years after the Dagor Bragollach the Noldor still defended the western pass about the sources of Sirion, for the power of Ulmo was in that water, and Minas Tirith withstood the Orcs. But at length, after the fall of Fingolfin, Sauron, greatest and most terrible of the servants of Morgoth, who in the Sindarin tongue was named Gorthaur, came against Orodreth, the warden of the tower upon Tol Sirion. Sauron was become now a sorcerer of dreadful power, master of shadows and of phantoms, foul in wisdom, cruel in strength, misshaping what he touched, twisting what he ruled, lord of werewolves; his dominion was torment. He took Minas Tirith by assault, for a dark cloud of fear fell upon those that defended it; and Orodreth was driven out, and fled to Nargothrond. Then Sauron made it into a watchtower for Morgoth, a stronghold of evil, and a menace; and the fair isle of Tol Sirion became accursed, and it was called Tol-in-Gaurhoth, the Isle of Werewolves. No living creature could pass through that vale that Sauron did not espy from the tower where he sat. And Morgoth held now the western pass, and his terror filled the fields and woods of Beleriand. Beyond Hithlum he pursued his foes relentlessly, and he searched out their hiding-places and took their strongholds one by one. The Orcs growing ever bolder wandered at will far and wide, coming down Sirion in the west and Celon in the east, and they encompassed Doriath; and they harried the lands so that beast and bird fled before them, and silence and desolation spread steadily from the North. Many of the Noldor and the Sindar they took captive and led to Angband, and made them thralls, forcing them to use their skill and their knowledge in the service of Morgoth. And Morgoth sent out his spies, and they were clad in false forms and deceit was in their speech; they made lying promises of reward, and with cunning words sought to arouse fear and jealousy among the peoples, accusing their kings and chieftains of greed, and of treachery one to another. And because of the curse of the Kinslaying at Alqualondë these lies were often believed; and indeed as the time darkened they had a measure of truth, for the hearts and minds of the Elves of Beleriand became clouded with despair and fear. But ever the Noldor feared most the treachery of those of their own kin, who had been thralls in Angband; for Morgoth used some of these for his evil purposes, and feigning to give them liberty sent them abroad, but their wills were chained to his, and they strayed only to come back to him again. Therefore if any of his captives escaped in truth, and returned to their own people, they had little welcome, and wandered alone outlawed and desperate.

To Men Morgoth feigned pity, if any would hearken to his messages, saying that their woes came only of their servitude to the rebel Noldor, but at the hands of the rightful Lord of Middle-earth they would get honour and a just reward of valour, if they would leave rebellion. But few men of the Three Houses of the Edain would give ear to him, not even were they brought to the torment of Angband. Therefore Morgoth pursued them with hatred; and he sent his messengers over the mountains.

It is told that at this time the Swarthy Men came first into Beleriand. Some were already secretly under the dominion of Morgoth, and came at his call; but not all, for the rumour of Beleriand, of its lands and waters, of its wars and riches, went now far and wide, and the wandering feet of Men were ever set westward in those days. These Men were short and broad, long and strong in the arm; their skins were swart or sallow, and their hair was dark as were their eyes. Their houses were many, and some had greater liking for the Dwarves of the mountains than for the Elves. But Maedhros, knowing the weakness of the Noldor and the Edain, whereas the pits of Angband seemed to hold store inexhaustible and ever-renewed, made alliance with these new-come Men, and gave his friendship to the greatest of their chieftains, Bór and Ulfang. And Morgoth was well content; for this was as he had designed. The sons of Bór were Borlad, Borlach, and Borthand; and they followed Maedhros and Maglor, and cheated the hope of Morgoth, and were faithful. The sons of Ulfang the Black were Ulfast, and Ulwarth, and Uldor the accursed; and they followed Caranthir and swore allegiance to him, and proved faithless.

There was small love between the Edain and the Easterlings, and they met seldom; for the newcomers abode long in East Beleriand, but Hador's folk were shut in Hithlum, and Bëor's house was well-nigh destroyed. The People of Haleth were at first untouched by the northern war, for they dwelt to the southward in the Forest of Brethil; but now there was battle between them and the invading Orcs, for they were stout-hearted men and would not lightly forsake the woods that they loved. And amid the tale of defeats of that time the deeds of the

Haladin are remembered with honour: for after the taking of Minas Tirith the Orcs came through the western pass, and maybe would have ravaged even to the mouths of Sirion; but Halmir lord of the Haladin sent swift word to Thingol, for he had friendship with the Elves that guarded the borders of Doriath. Then Beleg Strongbow, chief of the marchwardens of Thingol, brought great strength of the Sindar armed with axes into Brethil; and issuing from the deeps of the forest Halmir and Beleg took an Orc-legion at unawares and destroyed it. Thereafter the black tide out of the North was stemmed in that region, and the Orcs dared not cross the Teiglin for many years after. The People of Haleth dwelt yet in watchful peace in the Forest of Brethil, and behind their guard the Kingdom of Nargothrond had respite, and mustered its strength.

At this time Húrin and Huor, the sons of Galdor of Dor-lómin, were dwelling with the Haladin, for they were akin. In the days before the Dagor Bragollach those two houses of the Edain were joined at a great feast, when Galdor and Glóredhel the children of Hador Goldenhead were wedded to Hareth and Haldir the children of Halmir lord of the Haladin. Thus it was that the sons of Galdor were fostered in Brethil by Haldir their uncle, according to the custom of Men in that time; and they went both to that battle with the Orcs, even Huor, for he would not be restrained, though he was but thirteen years old. But being with a company that was cut off from the rest they were pursued to the Ford of Brithiach, and there they would have been taken or slain but for the power of Ulmo, that was still strong in Sirion. A mist arose from the river and hid them from their enemies, and they escaped over the Brithiach into Dimbar, and wandered among the hills beneath the sheer walls of the Crissaegrim, until they were bewildered in the deceits of that land and knew not the way to go on or to return. There Thorondor espied them, and he sent two of his eagles to their aid; and the eagles bore them up and brought them beyond the Encircling Mountains to the secret vale of Tumladen and the hidden city of Gondolin, which no Man yet had seen.

There Turgon the King received them well, when he learned of their kin; for messages and dreams had come to him up Sirion from the sea, from Ulmo, Lord of Waters, warning him of woe to come and counselling him to deal kindly with the sons of the house of Hador, from whom help should come to him at need. Húrin and Huor dwelt as guests in the King's house for well nigh a year; and it is said that in this time Húrin learned much lore of the Elves, and understood also something of the counsels and purposes of the King. For Turgon took great liking for the sons of Galdor, and spoke much with them; and he wished indeed to keep them in Gondolin out of love, and not only for his law that no stranger, be he Elf or Man, who found the way to the secret kingdom and looked upon the city should ever depart again, until the King should open the leaguer, and the hidden people should come forth.

But Húrin and Huor desired to return to their own people and share in the wars and griefs that now beset them. And Húrin said to Turgon: 'Lord, we are but mortal Men, and unlike the Eldar. They may endure for long years awaiting battle with their enemies in some far distant day; but for us the time is short, and our hope and strength soon wither. Moreover we did not find the road to Gondolin, and indeed we do not know surely where this city stands; for we were brought in fear and wonder by the high ways of the air, and in mercy our eyes were veiled.' Then Turgon granted his prayer, and he said: 'By the way that you came you have leave to depart, if Thorondor is willing. I grieve at this parting; yet in a little while, as the Eldar account it, we may meet again.'

But Maeglin, the King's sister-son, who was mighty in Gondolin, grieved not at all at their going, though he begrudged them the favour of the King, for he had no love for any of the kindred of Men; and he said to Húrin: 'The King's grace is greater than you know, and the law is become less stern than aforetime; or else no choice would be given you but to abide here to your life's end.'

Then Húrin answered him: 'The King's grace is great indeed; but if our word is not enough, then we will swear oaths to you.' And the brothers swore never to reveal the counsels of Turgon, and to keep secret all that they had seen in his realm. Then they took their leave, and the eagles coming bore them away by night, and set them down in Dor-lómin before the dawn. Their kinsfolk rejoiced to see them, for messengers from Brethil had reported that they were lost; but they would not declare even to their father where they had been, save that they were rescued in the wilderness by the eagles that brought them home. But Galdor said: 'Did you then dwell a year in the wild? Or did the eagles house you in their eyries? But you found food and fine raiment, and return as young princes, not as waifs of the wood.' And Húrin answered: 'Be content that we have returned; for only under an oath of silence was this permitted.' Then Galdor questioned them no more, but he and many others guessed at the truth; and in time the strange fortune of Húrin and Huor reached the ears of the servants of Morgoth.

Now when Turgon learned of the breaking of the leaguer of Angband he would not suffer any of his own people to issue forth to war; for he deemed that Gondolin was strong, and the time not yet ripe for its revealing. But he believed also that the ending of the Siege was the beginning of the downfall of the Noldor, unless aid should come; and he sent companies of the Gondolindrim in secret to the mouths of Sirion and the Isle of Balar. There they built ships, and set sail into the uttermost West upon Turgon's errand, seeking for Valinor, to ask for pardon and aid of the Valar; and they besought the birds of the sea to guide them. But the seas were wild and wide, and shadow and enchantment lay upon them; and Valinor was hidden. Therefore none of the messengers of Turgon came into the West, and many were lost and few returned; but the doom of Gondolin drew nearer.

Rumour came to Morgoth of these things, and he was unquiet amid his victories; and he desired greatly to learn tidings of Felagund and Turgon. For they had vanished out of knowledge, and yet were not dead; and he feared what they might yet accomplish against him. Of Nargothrond he knew indeed the name, but neither its place nor its strength; and of Gondolin he knew nothing, and the thought of Turgon troubled him the more. Therefore he sent forth ever more spies into Beleriand; but he recalled the main hosts of the Orcs to Angband, for he perceived that he could not yet make a final and victorious battle until he had gathered new strength, and that he had not measured rightly the valour of the Noldor nor the might in arms of the Men that fought beside them. Great though his victory had been in the Bragollach and in the years after, and grievous the harm that he had done to his enemies, his own loss had been no less; and though he held Dorthonion and the Pass of Sirion, the Eldar recovering from their first dismay began now to regain what they had lost. Thus Beleriand in the south had a semblance of peace again for a few brief years; but the forges of Angband were full of labour.

When seven years had passed since the Fourth Battle, Morgoth renewed his assault, and he sent a great force against Hithlum. The attack on the passes of the Shadowy Mountains was bitter, and in the siege of Eithel Sirion Galdor the tall, Lord of Dor-lómin, was slain by an arrow. That fortress he held on behalf of Fingon the High King; and in that same place his father Hador Lórindol died but a little time before. Húrin his son was then newly come to manhood, but he was great in strength both of mind and body; and he drove the Orcs with heavy slaughter from Ered Wethrin, and pursued them far across the sands of Anfauglith.

But King Fingon was hard put to it to hold back the army of Angband that came down from the north; and battle was joined upon the very plains of Hithlum. There Fingon was outnumbered; but the ships of Círdan sailed in great strength up the Firth of Drengist, and in the hour of need the Elves of the Falas came upon the host of Morgoth from the west. Then the Orcs broke and fled, and the Eldar had the victory, and their horsed archers pursued them even into the Iron Mountains.

Thereafter Húrin son of Galdor ruled the house of Hador in Dor-lómin, and served Fingon. Húrin was of less stature than his fathers, or his son after him; but he was tireless and enduring in body, lithe and swift after the manner of his mother's kin, Hareth of the Haladin. His wife was Morwen Eledhwen, daughter of Baragund of the house of Bëor, she who fled from Dorthonion with Rían daughter of Belegund and Emeldir the mother of Beren.

In that time also the outlaws of Dorthonion were destroyed, as is told hereafter; and Beren son of Barahir alone escaping came hardly into Doriath.

Chapter 19

OF BEREN AND LÚTHIEN

Among the tales of sorrow and of ruin that come down to us from the darkness of those days there are yet some in which amid weeping there is joy and under the shadow of death light that endures. And of these histories most fair still in the ears of the Elves is the tale of Beren and Lúthien. Of their lives was made the Lay of Leithian, Release from Bondage, which is the longest save one of the songs concerning the world of old; but here the tale is told in fewer words and without song.

It has been told that Barahir would not forsake Dorthonion, and there Morgoth pursued him to the death, until at last there remained to him only twelve companions. Now the forest of Dorthonion rose southward into mountainous moors; and in the east of those highlands there lay a lake, Tarn Aeluin, with wild heaths about it, and all that land was pathless and untamed, for even in the days of the Long Peace none had dwelt there. But the waters of Tarn Aeluin were held in reverence, for they were clear and blue by day and by night were a mirror for the stars; and it was said that Melian herself had hallowed that water in days of old. Thither Barahir and his outlaws withdrew, and there made their lair, and Morgoth could not discover it. But the rumour of the deeds of Barahir and his companions went far and wide; and Morgoth commanded Sauron to find them and destroy them.

Now among the companions of Barahir was Gorlim son of Angrim.

His wife was named Eilinel, and their love was great, ere evil befell. But Gorlim returning from the war upon the marches found his house plundered and forsaken, and his wife gone; whether slain or taken he knew not. Then he fled to Barahir, and of his companions he was the most fierce and desperate; but doubt gnawed his heart, thinking that perhaps Eilinel was not dead. At times he would depart alone and secretly, and visit his house that still stood amid the fields and woods he had once possessed; and this became known to the servants of Morgoth.

On a time of autumn he came in the dusk of evening, and drawing near he saw as he thought a light at the window; and coming warily he looked within. There he saw Eilinel, and her face was worn with grief and hunger, and it seemed to him that he heard her voice lamenting that he had forsaken her. But even as he cried aloud the light was blown out in the wind; wolves howled, and on his shoulders he felt suddenly the heavy hands of Sauron's hunters. Thus Gorlim was ensnared; and taking him to their camp they tormented him, seeking to learn the hidings of Barahir and all his ways. But nothing would Gorlim tell. Then they promised him that he should be released and restored to Eilinel, if he would yield; and being at last worn with pain, and yearning for his wife, he faltered. Then straightway they brought him into the dreadful presence of Sauron; and Sauron said: 'I hear now that thou wouldst barter with me. What is thy price?'

And Gorlim answered that he should find Eilinel again, and with her be set free; for he thought that Eilinel also had been made captive.

Then Sauron smiled, saying: 'That is a small price for so great a treachery. So shall it surely be. Say on!'

Now Gorlim would have drawn back, but daunted by the eyes of Sauron he told at last all that he would know. Then Sauron laughed; and he mocked Gorlim, and revealed to him that he had seen only a phantom devised by wizardry to entrap him; for Eilinel was dead. 'Nonetheless I will grant thy prayer,' said Sauron; 'and thou shalt go to Eilinel, and be set free of my service.' Then he put him cruelly to death.

In this way the hiding of Barahir was revealed, and Morgoth drew his net about it; and the Orcs coming in the still hours before dawn surprised the Men of Dorthonion and slew them all, save one. For Beren son of Barahir had been sent by his father on a perilous errand to spy upon the ways of the Enemy, and he was far afield when the lair was taken. But as he slept benighted in the forest he dreamed that carrion-birds sat thick as leaves upon bare trees beside a mere, and blood dripped from their beaks. Then Beren was aware in his dream of a form that came to him across the water, and it was a wraith of Gorlim; and it spoke to him declaring his treachery and death, and bade him make haste to warn his father.

Then Beren awoke, and sped through the night, and came back to the lair of the outlaws on the second morning. But as he drew near the carrion-birds rose from the ground and sat in the alder-trees beside Tarn Aeluin, and croaked in mockery.

There Beren buried his father's bones, and raised a cairn of boulders above him, and swore upon it an oath of vengeance. First therefore he pursued the Orcs that had slain his father and his kinsmen, and he found their camp by night at Rivil's Well above the Fen of Serech, and because of his woodcraft he came near to their fire unseen. There their captain made boast of his deeds, and he held up the hand of Barahir that he had cut off as a token for Sauron that their mission was fulfilled; and the ring of Felagund was on that hand. Then Beren sprang from behind a rock, and slew the captain, and taking the hand and the ring he escaped, being defended by fate; for the Orcs were dismayed, and their arrows wild.

Thereafter for four years more Beren wandered still upon Dorthonion, a solitary outlaw; but he became the friend of birds and beasts, and they aided him, and did not betray him, and from that time forth he ate no flesh nor slew any living thing that was not in the service of Morgoth. He did not fear death, but only captivity, and being bold and desperate he escaped both death and bonds; and the deeds of lonely daring that he achieved were noised abroad throughout Beleriand, and the tale of them came even into Doriath. At length Morgoth set a price upon his head no less than the price upon the head of Fingon, High King of the Noldor; but the Orcs fled rather at the rumour of his approach than sought him out. Therefore an army was sent against him under the command of Sauron; and Sauron brought werewolves, fell beasts inhabited by dreadful spirits that he had imprisoned in their bodies.

All that land was now become filled with evil, and all clean things were departing from it; and Beren was pressed so hard that at last he was forced to flee from Dorthonion. In time of winter and snow he forsook the land and grave of his father, and climbing into the high regions of Gorgoroth, the Mountains of Terror, he descried afar the land of Doriath. There it was put into his heart that he would go down into the Hidden Kingdom, where no mortal foot had yet trodden.

Terrible was his southward journey. Sheer were the precipices of Ered Gorgoroth, and beneath their feet were shadows that were laid before the rising of the Moon. Beyond lay the wilderness of Dungortheb, where the sorcery of Sauron and the power of Melian came together, and horror and madness walked. There spiders of the fell race of Ungoliant abode, spinning their unseen webs in which all living things were snared; and monsters wandered there that were born in the long dark before the Sun, hunting silently with many eyes. No food for Elves or Men was there in that haunted land, but death only. That journey is not accounted least among the great deeds of Beren, but he spoke of it to no one after, lest the horror return into his mind; and none know how he found a way, and so came by paths that no Man nor Elf else ever dared to tread to the borders of Doriath. And he passed through the mazes that Melian wove about the kingdom of Thingol, even as she had foretold; for a great doom lay upon him.

It is told in the Lay of Leithian that Beren came stumbling into Doriath grey and bowed as with many years of woe, so great had been the torment of the road. But wandering in the summer in the woods of Neldoreth he came upon Lúthien, daughter of Thingol and Melian, at a time of evening under moonrise, as she danced upon the unfading grass in the glades beside Esgalduin. Then all memory of his pain departed from him, and he fell into an enchantment; for Lúthien was the most beautiful of all the Children of Ilúvatar. Blue was her raiment as the unclouded heaven, but her eyes were grey as the starlit evening; her mantle was sewn with golden flowers, but her hair was dark as the shadows of twilight. As the light upon the leaves of trees, as the voice of clear waters, as the stars above the mists of the world, such was her glory and her loveliness; and in her face was a shining light.

But she vanished from his sight; and he became dumb, as one that is bound under a spell, and he strayed long in the woods, wild and wary as a beast, seeking for her. In his heart he called her Tinúviel, that signifies Nightingale, daughter of twilight, in the Grey-elven tongue, for he knew no other name for her. And he saw her afar as leaves in the winds of autumn, and in winter as a star upon a hill, but a chain was upon his limbs.

There came a time near dawn on the eve of spring, and Lúthien danced upon a green hill; and suddenly she began to sing. Keen, heart-piercing was her song as the song of the lark that rises from the gates of night and pours its voice among the dying stars, seeing the sun behind the walls of the world; and the song of Lúthien released the bonds of winter, and the frozen waters spoke, and flowers sprang from the cold earth where her feet had passed.

Then the spell of silence fell from Beren, and he called to her, crying Tinúviel; and the woods echoed the name. Then she halted in wonder, and fled no more, and Beren came to her. But as she looked on him, doom fell upon her, and she loved him; yet she slipped from his arms and vanished from his sight even as the day was breaking. Then Beren lay upon the ground in a swoon, as one slain at once by bliss and grief; and he fell into a sleep as it were into an abyss of shadow, and waking he was cold as stone, and his heart barren and forsaken. And wandering in mind he groped as one that is stricken with sudden blindness, and seeks with hands to grasp the vanished light. Thus he began the payment of anguish for the fate that was laid on him; and in his fate Lúthien was caught, and being immortal she shared in his mortality, and being free received his chain; and her anguish was greater than any other of the Eldalië has known.

Beyond his hope she returned to him where he sat in darkness, and long ago in the Hidden Kingdom she laid her hand in his. Thereafter often she came to him, and they went in secret through the woods together from spring to summer; and no others of the Children of Ilúvatar have had joy so great, though the time was brief.

But Daeron the minstrel also loved Lúthien, and he espied her meetings with Beren, and betrayed them to Thingol. Then the King was filled with anger, for Lúthien he loved above all things, setting her above all the princes of the Elves; whereas mortal Men he did not even take into his service. Therefore he spoke in grief and amazement to Lúthien; but she would reveal nothing, until he swore an oath to her that he would neither slay Beren nor imprison him. But he sent his servants to lay hands on him and lead him to Menegroth as a malefactor; and Lúthien forestalling them led Beren herself before the throne of Thingol, as if he were an honoured guest.

Then Thingol looked upon Beren in scorn and anger; but Melian was silent. 'Who are you,' said the King, 'that come hither as a thief, and unbidden dare to approach my throne?'

But Beren being filled with dread, for the splendour of Menegroth and the majesty of Thingol were very great, answered nothing. Therefore Lúthien spoke, and said: 'He is Beren son of Barahir, lord of Men, mighty foe of Morgoth, the tale of whose deeds is become a song even among the Elves.'

'Let Beren speak!' said Thingol. 'What would you here, unhappy mortal, and for what cause have you left your own land to enter this, which is forbidden to such as you? Can you show reason why my power should not be laid on you in heavy punishment for your insolence and folly?'

Then Beren looking up beheld the eyes of Lúthien, and his glance went also to the face of Melian; and it seemed to him that words were put into his mouth. Fear left him, and the pride of the eldest house of Men returned to him; and he said: 'My fate, O King, led me hither, through perils such as few even of the Elves would dare. And here I have found what I sought not indeed, but finding I would possess for ever. For it is above all gold and silver, and beyond all jewels. Neither rock, nor steel, nor the fires of Morgoth, nor all the powers of the Elf-kingdoms, shall keep from me the treasure that I desire. For Lúthien your daughter is the fairest of all the Children of the World.'

Then silence fell upon the hall, for those that stood there were astounded and afraid, and they thought that Beren would be slain. But Thingol spoke slowly, saying: 'Death you have earned with these words; and death you should find suddenly, had I not sworn an oath in haste; of which I repent, baseborn mortal, who in the realm of Morgoth has learnt to creep in secret as his spies and thralls.'

Then Beren answered: 'Death you can give me earned or unearned; but the names I will not take from you of baseborn, nor spy, nor thrall. By the ring of Felagund, that he gave to Barahir my father on the battlefield of the North, my house has not earned such names from any Elf, be he king or no.'

His words were proud, and all eyes looked upon the ring; for he held it now aloft, and the green jewels gleamed there that the Noldor had devised in Valinor. For this ring was like to twin serpents, whose eyes were emeralds, and their heads met beneath a crown of golden flowers, that the one upheld and the other devoured; that was the badge of Finarfin and his house. Then Melian leaned to Thingol's side, and in whispered counsel bade him forgo his wrath. 'For not by you,' she said, 'shall Beren be slain; and far and free does his fate lead him in the end, yet it is wound with yours. Take heed!'

But Thingol looked in silence upon Lúthien; and he thought in his heart: 'Unhappy Men, children of little lords and brief kings, shall such as these lay hands on you, and yet live?' Then breaking the silence he said: 'I see the ring, son of Barahir, and I perceive that you are proud, and deem yourself mighty. But a father's deeds, even had his service been rendered to me, avail not to win the daughter of

Thingol and Melian. See now! I too desire a treasure that is withheld. For rock and steel and the fires of Morgoth keep the jewel that I would possess against all the powers of the Elf-kingdoms. Yet I hear you say that bonds such as these do not daunt you. Go your way therefore! Bring to me in your hand a Silmaril from Morgoth's crown; and then, if she will, Lúthien may set her hand in yours. Then you shall have my jewel; and though the fate of Arda lie within the Silmarils, yet you shall hold me generous.'

Thus he wrought the doom of Doriath, and was ensnared within the curse of Mandos. And those that heard these words perceived that Thingol would save his oath, and yet send Beren to his death; for they knew that not all the power of the Noldor, before the Siege was broken, had availed even to see from afar the shining Silmarils of Fëanor. For they were set in the Iron Crown, and treasured in Angband above all wealth; and Balrogs were about them, and countless swords, and strong bars, and unassailable walls, and the dark majesty of Morgoth.

But Beren laughed. 'For little price,' he said, 'do Elven-kings sell their daughters: for gems, and things made by craft. But if this be your will, Thingol, I will perform it. And when we meet again my hand shall hold a Silmaril from the Iron Crown; for you have not looked the last upon Beren son of Barahir.'

Then he looked in the eyes of Melian, who spoke not; and he bade farewell to Lúthien Tinúviel, and bowing before Thingol and Melian he put aside the guards about him, and departed from Menegroth alone.

Then at last Melian spoke, and she said to Thingol: 'O King, you have devised cunning counsel. But if my eyes have not lost their sight, it is ill for you, whether Beren fail in his errand, or achieve it. For you have doomed either your daughter, or yourself. And now is Doriath drawn within the fate of a mightier realm.'

But Thingol answered: 'I sell not to Elves or Men those whom I love and cherish above all treasure. And if there were hope or fear that Beren should come ever back alive to Menegroth, he should not have looked again upon the light of heaven, though I had sworn it.'

But Lúthien was silent, and from that hour she sang not again in Doriath. A brooding silence fell upon the woods, and the shadows lengthened in the kingdom of Thingol.

It is told in the Lay of Leithian that Beren passed through Doriath unhindered, and came at length to the region of the Twilight Meres, and the Fens of Sirion; and leaving Thingol's land he climbed the hills above the Falls of Sirion, where the river plunged underground with great noise. Thence he looked westward, and through the mist and rains that lay upon those hills he saw Talath Dirnen, the Guarded Plain, stretching between Sirion and Narog; and beyond he descried afar the highlands of Taur-en-Faroth that rose above Nargothrond. And being destitute, without hope or counsel, he turned his feet thither.

Upon all that plain the Elves of Nargothrond kept unceasing watch; and every hill upon its borders was crowned with hidden towers, and through all its woods and fields archers ranged secretly and with great craft. Their arrows were sure and deadly, and nothing crept there against their will. Therefore, ere Beren had come far upon his road, they were aware of him, and his death was nigh. But knowing his danger he held ever aloft the ring of Felagund; and though he saw no living thing, because of the stealth of the hunters, he felt that he was watched, and cried often aloud: 'I am Beren son of Barahir, friend of Felagund. Take me to the King!'

Therefore the hunters slew him not, but assembling they waylaid him, and commanded him to halt. But seeing the ring they bowed before him, though he was in evil plight, wild and wayworn; and they led him northward and westward, going by night lest their paths should be revealed. For at that time there was no ford or bridge over the torrent of Narog before the gates of Nargothrond; but further to the north, where Ginglith joined Narog, the flood was less, and crossing there and turning again southward the Elves led Beren under the light of the moon to the dark gates of their hidden halls.

Thus Beren came before King Finrod Felagund; and Felagund knew him, needing no ring to remind him of the kin of Bëor and of Barahir. Behind closed doors they sat, and Beren told of the death of Barahir, and of all that had befallen him in Doriath; and he wept, recalling Lúthien and their joy together. But Felagund heard his tale in wonder and disquiet; and he knew that the oath he had sworn was come upon him for his death, as long before he had foretold to Galadriel. He spoke then to Beren in heaviness of heart. 'It is plain that Thingol desires your death; but it seems that this doom goes beyond his purpose, and that the Oath of Fëanor is again at work. For the Silmarils are cursed with an oath of hatred, and he that even names them in desire moves a great power from slumber; and the sons of Fëanor would lay all the Elf-kingdoms in ruin rather than suffer any other than themselves to win or possess a Silmaril, for the Oath drives them. And now Celegorm and Curufin are dwelling in my halls; and though I, Finarfin's son, am King, they have won a strong power in the realm, and lead many of their own people. They have shown friendship to me in every need, but I fear that they will show neither love nor mercy to you, if your quest be told. Yet my own oath holds; and thus we are all ensnared.'

Then King Felagund spoke before his people, recalling the deeds of Barahir, and his vow; and he declared that it was laid upon him to aid the son of Barahir in his need, and he sought the help of his chieftains. Then Celegorm arose amid the throng, and drawing his sword he cried: 'Be he friend or foe, whether demon of Morgoth, or Elf, or child of Men, or any other living thing in Arda, neither law, nor love, nor league of hell, nor might of the Valar, nor any power of wizardry, shall defend him from the pursuing hate of Fëanor's sons, if he take or find a Silmaril and keep it. For the Silmarils we alone claim, until the world ends.'

Many other words he spoke, as potent as were long before in Tirion the words of his father that first inflamed the Noldor to rebellion. And after Celegorm Curufin spoke, more softly but with no less power, conjuring in the minds of the Elves a vision of war and the ruin of Nargothrond. So great a fear did he set in their hearts that never after until the time of Túrin would any Elf of that realm go into open battle; but with stealth and ambush, with wizardry and venomed dart, they pursued all strangers, forgetting the bonds of kinship. Thus they fell from the valour and freedom of the Elves of old, and their land was darkened.

And now they murmured that Finarfin's son was not as a Vala to command them, and they turned their faces from him. But the curse of Mandos came upon the brothers, and dark thoughts arose in their hearts, thinking to send forth Felagund alone to his death, and to usurp, it might be, the throne of Nargothrond; for they were of the eldest line of the princes of the Noldor.

And Felagund seeing that he was forsaken took from his head the silver crown of Nargothrond and cast it at his feet, saying: 'Your oaths of faith to me you may break, but I must hold my bond. Yet if there be any on whom the shadow of our curse has not yet fallen, I should find at least a few to follow me, and should not go hence as a beggar that is thrust from the gates.' There were ten that stood by him; and the chief of them, who was named Edrahil, stooping lifted the crown and asked that it be given to a steward until Felagund's return. 'For you remain my king, and theirs,' he said, 'whatever betide.'

Then Felagund gave the crown of Nargothrond to Orodreth his

brother to govern in his stead; and Celegorm and Curufin said nothing, but they smiled and went from the halls.

On an evening of autumn Felagund and Beren set out from Nargothrond with their ten companions; and they journeyed beside Narog to his source in the Falls of Ivrin. Beneath the Shadowy Mountains they came upon a company of Orcs, and slew them all in their camp by night; and they took their gear and their weapons. By the arts of Felagund their own forms and faces were changed into the likeness of Orcs; and thus disguised they came far upon their northward road, and ventured into the western pass, between Ered Wethrin and the highlands of Taur-nu-Fuin. But Sauron in his tower was ware of them, and doubt took him; for they went in haste, and stayed not to report their deeds, as was commanded to all the servants of Morgoth that passed that way. Therefore he sent to waylay them, and bring them before him.

Thus befell the contest of Sauron and Felagund which is renowned. For Felagund strove with Sauron in songs of power, and the power of the King was very great; but Sauron had the mastery, as is told in the Lay of Leithian:

He chanted a song of wizardry,
Of piercing, opening, of treachery,
Revealing, uncovering, betraying.
Then sudden Felagund there swaying
Sang in answer a song of staying,
Resisting, battling against power,
Of secrets kept, strength like a tower,
And trust unbroken, freedom, escape;
Of changing and of shifting shape,
Of snares eluded, broken traps,
The prison opening, the chain that snaps.
Backwards and forwards swayed their song.
Reeling and foundering, as ever more strong
The chanting swelled, Felagund fought,
And all the magic and might he brought
Of Elvenesse into his words.
Softly in the gloom they heard the birds
Singing afar in Nargothrond,
The sighing of the Sea beyond,
Beyond the western world, on sand,

On sand of pearls in Elvenland.
Then the gloom gathered; darkness growing
In Valinor, the red blood flowing
Beside the Sea, where the Noldor slew
The Foamriders, and stealing drew
Their white ships with their white sails
From lamplit havens. The wind wails,
The wolf howls. The ravens flee.
The ice mutters in the mouths of the Sea.
The captives sad in Angband mourn.
Thunder rumbles, the fires burn—
And Finrod fell before the throne.

Then Sauron stripped from them their disguise, and they stood before him naked and afraid. But though their kinds were revealed, Sauron could not discover their names or their purposes.

He cast them therefore into a deep pit, dark and silent, and threatened to slay them cruelly, unless one would betray the truth to him. From time to time they saw two eyes kindled in the dark, and a werewolf devoured one of the companions; but none betrayed their lord.

In the time when Sauron cast Beren into the pit a weight of horror came upon Lúthien's heart; and going to Melian for counsel she learned that Beren lay in the dungeons of Tol-in-Gaurhoth without hope of rescue. Then Lúthien, perceiving that no help would come from any other on earth, resolved to fly from Doriath and come herself to him; but she sought the aid of Daeron, and he betrayed her purpose to the King. Then Thingol was filled with fear and wonder; and because he would not deprive Lúthien of the lights of heaven, lest she fail and fade, and yet would restrain her, he caused a house to be built from which she should not escape. Not far from the gates of Menegroth stood the greatest of all the trees in the Forest of Neldoreth; and that was a beech-forest and the northern half of the kingdom. This mighty beech was named Hírilorn, and it had three trunks, equal in girth, smooth in rind, and exceeding tall; no branches grew from them for a great height above the ground. Far aloft between the shafts of Hírilorn a wooden house was built, and there Lúthien was made to dwell; and the ladders were taken away and guarded, save only when the servants of Thingol brought her such things as she needed.

It is told in the Lay of Leithian how she escaped from the house in

Hírilorn; for she put forth her arts of enchantment, and caused her hair to grow to great length, and of it she wove a dark robe that wrapped her beauty like a shadow, and it was laden with a spell of sleep. Of the strands that remained she twined a rope, and she let it down from her window; and as the end swayed above the guards that sat beneath the tree they fell into a deep slumber. Then Lúthien climbed from her prison, and shrouded in her shadowy cloak she escaped from all eyes, and vanished out of Doriath.

It chanced that Celegorm and Curufin went on a hunt through the Guarded Plain; and this they did because Sauron, being filled with suspicion, sent forth many wolves into the Elf-lands. Therefore they took their hounds and rode forth; and they thought that ere they returned they might also hear tidings concerning King Felagund. Now the chief of the wolfhounds that followed Celegorm was named Huan. He was not born in Middle-earth, but came from the Blessed Realm; for Oromë had given him to Celegorm long ago in Valinor, and there he had followed the horn of his master, before evil came. Huan followed Celegorm into exile, and was faithful; and thus he too came under the doom of woe set upon the Noldor, and it was decreed that he should meet death, but not until he encountered the mightiest wolf that would ever walk the world.

Huan it was that found Lúthien flying like a shadow surprised by the daylight under the trees, when Celegorm and Curufin rested a while near to the western eaves of Doriath; for nothing could escape the sight and scent of Huan, not could any enchantment stay him, and he slept not, neither by night nor day. He brought her to Celegorm, and Lúthien, learning that he was a prince of the Noldor and a foe of Morgoth, was glad; and she declared herself, casting aside her cloak. So great was her sudden beauty revealed beneath the sun that Celegorm became enamoured of her; but he spoke her fair, and promised that she would find help in her need, if she returned with him now to Nargothrond. By no sign did he reveal that he knew already of Beren and the quest, of which she told, nor that it was a matter which touched him near.

Thus they broke off the hunt and returned to Nargothrond, and Lúthien was betrayed; for they held her fast, and took away her cloak, and she was not permitted to pass the gates or to speak with any save the brothers, Celegorm and Curufin. For now, believing that Beren and Felagund were prisoners beyond hope of aid, they purposed to let the King perish, and to keep Lúthien, and force Thingol to give her hand to Celegorm. Thus they would advance their power, and become the mightiest of the princes of the Noldor. And they did not purpose to seek the Silmarils by craft or war, or to suffer any others to do so, until they had all the might of the Elf-kingdoms under their hands. Orodreth had no power to withstand them, for they swayed the hearts of the people of Nargothrond; and Celegorm sent messengers to Thingol urging his suit.

But Huan the hound was true of heart, and the love of Lúthien had fallen upon him in the first hour of their meeting; and he grieved at her captivity. Therefore he came often to her chamber; and at night he lay before her door, for he felt that evil had come to Nargothrond. Lúthien spoke often to Huan in her loneliness, telling of Beren, who was the friend of all birds and beasts that did not serve Morgoth; and Huan understood all that was said. For he comprehended the speech of all things with voice; but it was permitted to him thrice only ere his death to speak with words.

Now Huan devised a plan for the aid of Lúthien; and coming at a time of night he brought her cloak, and for the first time he spoke, giving her counsel. Then he led her by secret ways out of Nargothrond, and they fled north together; and he humbled his pride and suffered her to ride upon him in the fashion of a steed, even as the Orcs did at times upon great wolves. Thus they made great speed, for Huan was swift and tireless.

In the pits of Sauron Beren and Felagund lay, and all their companions were now dead; but Sauron purposed to keep Felagund to the last, for he perceived that he was a Noldo of great might and wisdom, and he deemed that in him lay the secret of their errand. But when the wolf came for Beren, Felagund put forth all his power, and burst his bonds; and he wrestled with the werewolf, and slew it with his hands and teeth; yet he himself was wounded to the death. Then he spoke to Beren, saying: 'I go now to my long rest in the timeless halls beyond the seas and the Mountains of Aman. It will be long ere I am seen among the Noldor again; and it may be that we shall not meet a second time in death or life, for the fates of our kindreds are apart. Farewell!' He died then in the dark, in Tol-in-Gaurhoth, whose great tower he himself had built. Thus King Finrod Felagund, fairest and most beloved of the house of Finwë, redeemed his oath; but Beren mourned beside him in despair.

In that hour Lúthien came, and standing upon the bridge that led to Sauron's isle she sang a song that no walls of stone could hinder. Beren heard, and he thought that he dreamed; for the stars shone above him, and in the trees nightingales were singing. And in answer he sang a song of challenge that he had made in praise of the Seven Stars, the Sickle of the Valar that Varda hung above the North as a sign for the fall of Morgoth. Then all strength left him and he fell down into darkness.

But Lúthien heard his answering voice, and she sang then a song of greater power. The wolves howled, and the isle trembled. Sauron stood in the high tower, wrapped in his black thought; but he smiled hearing her voice, for he knew that it was the daughter of Melian. The fame of the beauty of Lúthien and the wonder of her song had long gone forth from Doriath; and he thought to make her captive and hand her over to the power of Morgoth, for his reward would be great.

Therefore he sent a wolf to the bridge. But Huan slew it silently. Still Sauron sent others one by one; and one by one Huan took them by the throat and slew them. Then Sauron sent Draugluin, a dread beast, old in evil, lord and sire of the werewolves of Angband. His might was great; and the battle of Huan and Draugluin was long and fierce. Yet at length Draugluin escaped, and fleeing back into the tower he died before Sauron's feet; and as he died he told his master: 'Huan is there!' Now Sauron knew well, as did all in that land, the fate that was decreed for the hound of Valinor, and it came into his thought that he himself would accomplish it. Therefore he took upon himself the form of a werewolf, and made himself the mightiest that had yet walked the world; and he came forth to win the passage of the bridge.

So great was the horror of his approach that Huan leaped aside. Then Sauron sprang upon Lúthien; and she swooned before the menace of the fell spirit in his eyes and the foul vapour of his breath. But even as he came, falling she cast a fold of her dark cloak before his eyes; and he stumbled, for a fleeting drowsiness came upon him. Then Huan sprang. There befell the battle of Huan and Wolf-Sauron, and the howls and baying echoed in the hills, and the watchers on the walls of Ered Wethrin across the valley heard it afar and were dismayed.

But no wizardry nor spell, neither fang nor venom, nor devil's art nor beast-strength, could overthrow Huan of Valinor; and he took his foe by the throat and pinned him down. Then Sauron shifted shape, from wolf to serpent, and from monster to his own accustomed form; but he could not elude the grip of Huan without forsaking his body utterly. Ere his foul spirit left its dark house, Lúthien came to him, and said that he should be stripped of his raiment of flesh, and his ghost be sent quaking back to Morgoth; and she said: 'There everlastingly thy naked self shall endure the torment of his scorn, pierced by his eyes, unless thou yield to me the mastery of thy tower.'

Then Sauron yielded himself, and Lúthien took the mastery of the isle and all that was there; and Huan released him. And immediately he took the form of a vampire, great as a dark cloud across the moon, and he fled, dripping blood from his throat upon the trees, and came to Taur-nu-Fuin, and dwelt there, filling it with horror.

Then Lúthien stood upon the bridge, and declared her power: and the spell was loosed that bound stone to stone, and the gates were thrown down, and the walls opened, and the pits laid bare; and many thralls and captives came forth in wonder and dismay, shielding their eyes against the pale moonlight, for they had lain long in the darkness of Sauron. But Beren came not. Therefore Huan and Lúthien sought him in the isle; and Lúthien found him mourning by Felagund. So deep was his anguish that he lay still, and did not hear her feet. Then thinking him already dead she put her arms about him and fell into a dark forgetfulness. But Beren coming back to the light out of the pits of despair lifted her up, and they looked again upon one another; and the day rising over the dark hills shone upon them.

They buried the body of Felagund upon the hill-top of his own isle, and it was clean again; and the green grave of Finrod Finarfin's son, fairest of all the princes of the Elves, remained inviolate, until the land was changed and broken, and foundered under destroying seas. But Finrod walks with Finarfin his father beneath the trees in Eldamar.

Now Beren and Lúthien Tinúviel went free again and together walked through the woods renewing for a time their joy; and though winter came it hurt them not, for flowers lingered where Lúthien went, and the birds sang beneath the snowclad hills. But Huan being faithful went back to Celegorm his master; yet their love was less than before.

There was tumult in Nargothrond. For thither now returned many Elves that had been prisoners in the isle of Sauron; and a clamour arose that no words of Celegorm could still. They lamented bitterly the fall of Felagund their king, saying that a maiden had dared that which the sons of Fëanor had not dared to do; but many perceived that it was treachery rather than fear that had guided Celegorm and Curufin. Therefore the hearts of the people of Nargothrond were released from their dominion, and turned again to the house of Finarfin; and they obeyed Orodreth. But he would not suffer them to slay the brothers, as some desired, for the spilling of kindred blood by kin would bind the curse of Mandos more closely upon them all. Yet neither bread nor rest would he grant to Celegorm and Curufin within his realm, and he swore that there should be little love between Nargothrond and the sons of Fëanor thereafter.

'Let it be so!' said Celegorm, and there was a light of menace in his eyes; but Curufin smiled. Then they took horse and rode away like fire, to find if they might their kindred in the east. But none would go with them, not even those that were of their own people; for all perceived that the curse lay heavily upon the brothers, and that evil followed them. In that time Celebrimbor the son of Curufin repudiated the deeds of his father, and remained in Nargothrond; yet Huan followed still the horse of Celegorm his master.

Northward they rode, for they intended in their haste to pass through Dimbar, and along the north marches of Doriath, seeking the swiftest road to Himring, where Maedhros their brother dwelt; and still they might hope with speed to traverse it, since it lay close to Doriath's borders, shunning Nan Dungortheb and the distant menace of the Mountains of Terror.

Now it is told that Beren and Lúthien came in their wandering into the Forest of Brethil, and drew near at last to the borders of Doriath. Then Beren took thought of his vow; and against his heart he resolved, when Lúthien was come again within the safety of her own land, to set forth once more. But she was not willing to be parted from him again, saying: 'You must choose, Beren, between these two: to relinquish the quest and your oath and seek a life of wandering upon the face of the earth; or to hold to your word and challenge the power of darkness upon its throne. But on either road I shall go with you, and our doom shall be alike.'

Even as they spoke together of these things, walking without heed of aught else, Celegorm and Curufin rode up, hastening through the forest; and the brothers espied them and knew them from afar. Then Celegorm turned his horse, and spurred it upon Beren, purposing to ride him down; but Curufin swerving stooped and lifted Lúthien to his saddle, for he was a strong and cunning horseman. Then Beren sprang from before Celegorm full upon the speeding horse of Curufin that had passed him; and the Leap of Beren is renowned among Men and Elves. He took Curufin by the throat from behind, and hurled him backward, and they fell to the ground together. The horse reared and fell, but Lúthien was flung aside, and lay upon the grass.

Then Beren throttled Curufin; but death was near him, for Celegorm rode upon him with a spear. In that hour Huan forsook the service of Celegorm, and sprang upon him, so that his horse swerved aside, and would not approach Beren because of the terror of the great hound. Celegorm cursed both hound and horse, but Huan was unmoved. Then Lúthien rising forbade the slaying of Curufin; but Beren despoiled him of his gear and weapons, and took his knife, Angrist. That knife was made by Telchar of Nogrod, and hung sheathless by his side; iron it would cleave as if it were green wood. Then Beren lifting Curufin flung him from him, and bade him walk now back to his noble kinsfolk, who might teach him to turn his valour to worthier use. 'Your horse,' he said, 'I keep for the service of Lúthien, and it may be accounted happy to be free of such a master.'

Then Curufin cursed Beren under cloud and sky. 'Go hence,' he said, 'unto a swift and bitter death.' Celegorm took him beside him on his horse, and the brothers made then as if to ride away; and Beren turned away and took no heed of their words. But Curufin, being filled with shame and malice, took the bow of Celegorm and shot back as they went; and the arrow was aimed at Lúthien. Huan leaping caught it in his mouth; but Curufin shot again, and Beren sprang before Lúthien, and the dart smote him in the breast.

It is told that Huan pursued the sons of Fëanor, and they fled in fear; and returning he brought to Lúthien an herb out of the forest. With that leaf she staunched Beren's wound, and by her arts and by her love she healed him; and thus at last they returned to Doriath. There Beren, being torn between his oath and his love, and knowing Lúthien to be now safe, arose one morning before the sun, and committed her to the care of Huan; then in great anguish he departed while she yet slept upon the grass.

He rode northward again with all speed to the Pass of Sirion, and coming to the skirts of Taur-nu-Fuin he looked out across the waste of Anfauglith and saw afar the peaks of Thangorodrim. There he dismissed the horse of Curufin, and bade it leave now dread and servitude and run free upon the green grass in the lands of Sirion. Then being now alone and upon the threshold of the final peril he made the Song of Parting, in praise of Lúthien and the lights of heaven; for he believed that he must now say farewell to both love and light. Of that song these words were part:

Farewell sweet earth and northern sky,
for ever blest, since here did lie
and here with lissom limbs did run
beneath the Moon, beneath the Sun,
Lúthien Tinúviel
more fair than mortal tongue can tell.
Though all to ruin fell the world
and were dissolved and backward hurled
unmade into the old abyss,
yet were its making good, for this—
the dusk, the dawn, the earth, the sea—
that Lúthien for a time should be.

And he sang aloud, caring not what ear should overhear him, for he was desperate and looked for no escape.

But Lúthien heard his song, and she sang in answer, as she came through the woods unlooked for. For Huan, consenting once more to be her steed, had borne her swiftly hard upon Beren's trail. Long he had pondered in his heart what counsel he could devise for the lightening of the peril of these two whom he loved. He turned aside therefore at Sauron's isle, as they ran northward again, and he took thence the ghastly wolf-hame of Draugluin, and the bat-fell of Thuringwethil. She was the messenger of Sauron, and was wont to fly in vampire's form to Angband; and her great fingered wings were barbed at each joint's end with an iron claw. Clad in these dreadful garments Huan and Lúthien ran through Taur-nu-Fuin, and all things fled before them.

Beren seeing their approach was dismayed; and he wondered, for he had heard the voice of Tinúviel, and he thought it now a phantom for his ensnaring. But they halted and cast aside their disguise, and Lúthien ran towards him. Thus Beren and Lúthien met again between the desert and the wood. For a while he was silent, and was glad; but after a space he strove once more to dissuade Lúthien from her journey.

'Thrice now I curse my oath to Thingol,' he said, 'and I would that he had slain me in Menegroth, rather than I should bring you under the shadow of Morgoth.'

Then for the second time Huan spoke with words; and he counselled Beren, saying: 'From the shadow of death you can no longer save Lúthien, for by her love she is now subject to it. You can turn from your fate and lead her into exile, seeking peace in vain while your life lasts. But if you will not deny your doom, then either Lúthien, being forsaken, must assuredly die alone, or she must with you challenge the fate that lies before you—hopeless, yet not certain. Further counsel I cannot give, nor may I go further on your road. But my heart forebodes that what you find at the Gate I shall myself see. All else is dark to me; yet it may be that our three paths lead back to Doriath, and we may meet before the end.'

Then Beren perceived that Lúthien could not be divided from the doom that lay upon them both, and he sought no longer to dissuade her. By the counsel of Huan and the arts of Lúthien he was arrayed now in the hame of Draugluin, and she in the winged fell of Thuringwethil. Beren became in all things like a werewolf to look upon, save that in his eyes there shone a spirit grim indeed but clean; and horror was in his glance as he saw upon his flank a bat-like creature clinging with creased wings. Then howling under the moon he leaped down the hill, and the bat wheeled and flittered above him.

They passed through all perils, until they came with the dust of their long and weary road upon them to the drear dale that lay before the Gate of Angband. Black chasms opened beside the road, whence forms as of writhing serpents issued. On either hand the cliffs stood as embattled walls, and upon them sat carrion fowl crying with fell voices. Before them was the impregnable Gate, an arch wide and dark at the foot of the mountain; above it reared a thousand feet of precipice.

There dismay took them, for at the gate was a guard of whom no tidings had yet gone forth. Rumour of he knew not what designs abroad among the princes of the Elves had come to Morgoth, and ever down the aisles of the forest was heard the baying of Huan, the great hound of war, whom long ago the Valar unleashed. Then Morgoth recalled the doom of Huan, and he chose one from among the whelps of the race of Draugluin; and he fed him with his own hand upon living flesh, and put his power upon him. Swiftly the wolf grew, until he could creep into no den, but lay huge and hungry before the feet of Morgoth. There the fire and anguish of hell entered into him, and he became filled with a devouring spirit, tormented, terrible, and strong. Carcharoth, the Red Maw, he is named in the tales of those days, and Anfauglir, the Jaws of Thirst. And Morgoth set him to lie unsleeping before the doors of Angband, lest Huan come.

Now Carcharoth espied them from afar, and he was filled with doubt; for news had long been brought to Angband that Draugluin was dead. Therefore when they approached he denied them entry, and bade them stand; and he drew near with menace, scenting something strange in the air about them. But suddenly some power, descended from of old from divine race, possessed Lúthien, and casting back her foul raiment she stood forth, small before the might of Carcharoth, but radiant and terrible. Lifting up her hand she commanded him to sleep, saying: 'O woe-begotten spirit, fall now into dark oblivion, and forget for a while the dreadful doom of life.' And Carcharoth was felled, as though lightning had smitten him.

Then Beren and Lúthien went through the Gate, and down the labyrinthine stairs; and together wrought the greatest deed that has been dared by Elves or Men. For they came to the seat of Morgoth in his nethermost hall, that was upheld by horror, lit by fire, and filled with weapons of death and torment. There Beren slunk in wolf's form beneath his throne; but Lúthien was stripped of her disguise by the will of Morgoth, and he bent his gaze upon her. She was not daunted by his eyes; and she named her own name, and offered her service to sing before him, after the manner of a minstrel. Then Morgoth looking upon her beauty conceived in his thought an evil lust, and a design more dark than any that had yet come into his heart since he fled from Valinor. Thus he was beguiled by his own malice, for he watched her, leaving her free for a while, and taking secret pleasure in his thought. Then suddenly she eluded his sight, and out of the shadows began a song of such surpassing loveliness, and of such blinding power, that he listened perforce; and a blindness came upon him, as his eyes roamed to and fro, seeking her.

All his court were cast down in slumber, and all the fires faded and were quenched; but the Silmarils in the crown on Morgoth's head blazed forth suddenly with a radiance of white flame; and the burden of that crown and of the jewels bowed down his head, as though the world were set upon it, laden with a weight of care, of fear, and of desire, that even the will of Morgoth could not support. Then Lúthien catching up her winged robe sprang into the air, and her voice came dropping down like rain into pools, profound and dark. She cast her cloak before his eyes, and set upon him a dream, dark as the Outer Void where once he walked alone. Suddenly he fell, as a hill sliding in avalanche, and hurled like thunder from his throne lay prone upon the floors of hell. The iron crown rolled echoing from his head. All things were still.

As a dead beast Beren lay upon the ground; but Lúthien touching him with her hand aroused him, and he cast aside the wolf-hame.

Then he drew forth the knife Angrist; and from the iron claws that held it he cut a Silmaril.

As he closed it in his hand, the radiance welled through his living flesh, and his hand became as a shining lamp; but the jewel suffered his touch and hurt him not. It came then into Beren's mind that he would go beyond his vow, and bear out of Angband all three of the Jewels of Fëanor; but such was not the doom of the Silmarils. The knife Angrist snapped, and a shard of the blade flying smote the cheek of Morgoth. He groaned and stirred, and all the host of Angband moved in sleep.

Then terror fell upon Beren and Lúthien, and they fled, heedless and without disguise, desiring only to see the light once more. They were neither hindered nor pursued, but the Gate was held against their going out; for Carcharoth had arisen from sleep, and stood now in wrath upon the threshold of Angband. Before they were aware of him, he saw them, and sprang upon them as they ran.

Lúthien was spent, and she had not time nor strength to quell the wolf. But Beren strode forth before her, and in his right hand he held aloft the Silmaril. Carcharoth halted, and for a moment was afraid. 'Get you gone, and fly!' cried Beren; 'for here is a fire that shall consume you, and all evil things.' And he thrust the Silmaril before the eyes of the wolf.

But Carcharoth looked upon that holy jewel and was not daunted, and the devouring spirit within him awoke to sudden fire; and gaping he took suddenly the hand within his jaws, and he bit it off at the wrist. Then swiftly all his inwards were filled with a flame of anguish, and the Silmaril seared his accursed flesh. Howling he fled before them, and the walls of the valley of the Gate echoed with the clamour of his torment. So terrible did he become in his madness that all the creatures of Morgoth that abode in that valley, or were upon any of the roads that led thither, fled far away; for he slew all living things that stood in his path, and burst from the North with ruin upon the world. Of all the terrors that came ever into Beleriand ere Angband's fall the madness of Carcharoth was the most dreadful; for the power of the Silmaril was hidden within him.

Now Beren lay in a swoon within the perilous Gate, and death drew nigh him, for there was venom on the fangs of the wolf. Lúthien with her lips drew out the venom, and she put forth her failing power to staunch the hideous wound. But behind her in the depths of Angband the rumour grew of great wrath aroused. The hosts of Morgoth were awakened.

Thus the quest of the Silmaril was like to have ended in ruin and despair; but in that hour above the wall of the valley three mighty birds appeared, flying northward with wings swifter than the wind. Among all birds and beasts the wandering and need of Beren had been noised, and Huan himself had bidden all things watch, that they might bring him aid. High above the realm of Morgoth Thorondor and his vassals soared, and seeing now the madness of the Wolf and Beren's fall they came swiftly down, even as the powers of Angband were released from the toils of sleep.

Then they lifted up Lúthien and Beren from the earth, and bore them aloft into the clouds. Below them suddenly thunder rolled, lightnings leaped upward, and the mountains quaked. Fire and smoke belched forth from Thangorodrim, and flaming bolts were hurled far abroad, falling ruinous upon the lands; and the Noldor in Hithlum trembled. But Thorondor took his way far above the earth, seeking the high roads of heaven, where the sun daylong shines unveiled and the moon walks amid the cloudless stars. Thus they passed swiftly over Dor-nu-Fauglith, and over Taur-nu-Fuin, and came above the hidden valley of Tumladen. No cloud nor mist lay there, and looking down Lúthien saw far below, as a white light starting from a green jewel, the radiance of Gondolin the fair where Turgon dwelt. But she wept, for she thought that Beren would surely die; he spoke no word, nor opened his eyes, and knew thereafter nothing of his flight. And at the last the eagles set them down upon the borders of Doriath; and they were come to that same dell whence Beren had stolen in despair and left Lúthien asleep.

There the eagles laid her at Beren's side and returned to the peaks of Crissaegrim and their high eyries; but Huan came to her, and together they tended Beren, even as before when she healed him of the wound that Curufin gave to him. But this wound was fell and poisonous. Long Beren lay, and his spirit wandered upon the dark borders of death, knowing ever an anguish that pursued him from dream to dream. Then suddenly, when her hope was almost spent, he woke again, and looked up, seeing leaves against the sky; and he heard beneath the leaves singing soft and slow beside him Lúthien Tinúviel. And it was spring again.

Thereafter Beren was named Erchamion, which is the One-handed; and suffering was graven in his face. But at last he was drawn back to life by the love of Lúthien, and he arose, and together they walked in the woods once more. And they did not hasten from that place, for it seemed fair to them. Lúthien indeed was willing to wander in the wild without returning, forgetting house and people and all the glory of the Elf-kingdoms, and for a time Beren was content; but he could not for long forget his oath to return to Menegroth, nor would he withhold Lúthien from Thingol for ever. For he held by the law of Men, deeming it perilous to set at naught the will of the father, save at the last need; and it seemed also to him unfit that one so royal and fair as Lúthien should live always in the woods, as the rude hunters among Men, without home or honour or the fair things which are the delight of the queens of the Eldalië. Therefore after a while he persuaded her, and their footsteps forsook the houseless lands; and he passed into Doriath, leading Lúthien home. So their doom willed it.

Upon Doriath evil days had fallen. Grief and silence had come upon all its people when Lúthien was lost. Long they had sought for her in vain. And it is told that in that time Daeron the minstrel of Thingol strayed from the land, and was seen no more. He it was that made music for the dance and song of Lúthien, before Beren came to Doriath; and he had loved her, and set all his thought of her in his music. He became the greatest of all the minstrels of the Elves east of the Sea, named even before Maglor son of Fëanor. But seeking for Lúthien in despair he wandered upon strange paths, and passing over the mountains he came into the East of Middle-earth, where for many ages he made lament beside dark waters for Lúthien, daughter of Thingol, most beautiful of all living things.

In that time Thingol turned to Melian; but now she withheld her counsel from him, saying that the doom that he had devised must work to its appointed end, and that he must wait now upon time. But Thingol learned that Lúthien had journeyed far from Doriath, for messages came secretly from Celegorm, as has been told, saying that Felagund was dead, and Beren was dead, but Lúthien was in Nargothrond, and that Celegorm would wed her. Then Thingol was wrathful, and he sent forth spies, thinking to make war upon Nargothrond; and thus he learned that Lúthien was again fled, and that Celegorm and Curufin were driven from Nargothrond. Then his counsel was in doubt, for he had not the strength to assail the seven sons of Fëanor; but he sent messengers to Himring to summon their aid in seeking for Lúthien, since Celegorm had not sent her to the house of her father, nor had he kept her safely.

But in the north of his realm his messengers met with a peril sudden and unlooked for: the onslaught of Carcharoth, the Wolf of Angband. In his madness he had run ravening from the north, and passing at length over Taur-nu-Fuin upon its eastern side he came down from the sources of Esgalduin like a destroying fire. Nothing hindered him, and the might of Melian upon the borders of the land stayed him not; for fate drove him, and the power of the Silmaril that he bore to his torment. Thus he burst into the inviolate woods of Doriath, and all fled away in fear. Alone of the messengers Mablung, chief captain of the King, escaped, and he brought the dread tidings to Thingol.

Even in that dark hour Beren and Lúthien returned, hastening from the west, and the news of their coming went before them like a sound of music borne by the wind into dark houses where men sit sorrowful. They came at last to the gates of Menegroth, and a great host followed them. Then Beren led Lúthien before the throne of Thingol her father; and he looked in wonder upon Beren, whom he had thought dead; but he loved him not, because of the woes that he had brought upon Doriath. But Beren knelt before him, and said: 'I return according to my word. I am come now to claim my own.'

And Thingol answered: 'What of your quest, and of your vow?'

But Beren said: 'It is fulfilled. Even now a Silmaril is in my hand.'

Then Thingol said: 'Show it to me!'

And Beren put forth his left hand, slowly opening its fingers; but it was empty. Then he held up his right arm; and from that hour he named himself Camlost, the Empty-handed.

Then Thingol's mood was softened; and Beren sat before his throne upon the left, and Lúthien upon the right, and they told all the tale of the Quest, while all there listened and were filled with amazement. And it seemed to Thingol that this Man was unlike all other mortal Men, and among the great in Arda, and the love of Lúthien a thing new and strange; and he perceived that their doom might not be withstood by any power of the world. Therefore at the last he yielded his will, and Beren took the hand of Lúthien before the throne of her father.

But now a shadow fell upon the joy of Doriath at the return of Lúthien the fair; for learning of the cause of the madness of Carcharoth the people grew the more afraid, perceiving that his danger was fraught with dreadful power because of the holy jewel, and hardly might be overthrown. And Beren, hearing of the onslaught of the Wolf, understood that the Quest was not yet fulfilled.

Therefore, since daily Carcharoth drew nearer to Menegroth, they prepared the Hunting of the Wolf; of all pursuits of beasts whereof tales tell the most perilous. To that chase went Huan the Hound of Valinor, and Mablung of the Heavy Hand, and Beleg Strongbow, and Beren Erchamion, and Thingol King of Doriath. They rode forth in the morning and passed over the River Esgalduin; but Lúthien remained behind at the gates of Menegroth. A dark shadow fell upon her and it seemed to her that the sun had sickened and turned black.

The hunters turned east and north, and following the course of the river they came at last upon Carcharoth the Wolf in a dark valley, down the northern side whereof Esgalduin fell in a torrent over steep falls. At the foot of the falls Carcharoth drank to ease his consuming thirst, and he howled, and thus they were aware of him. But he, espying their approach, rushed not suddenly to attack them. It may be that the devil's cunning of his heart awoke, being for a moment eased of his pain by the sweet waters of Esgalduin; and even as they rode towards him he slunk aside into a deep brake, and there lay hid. But they set a guard about all that place, and waited, and the shadows grew long in the forest.

Beren stood beside Thingol, and suddenly they were aware that Huan had left their side. Then a great baying awoke in the thicket; for Huan becoming impatient and desiring to look upon this wolf had gone in alone to dislodge him. But Carcharoth avoided him, and bursting from the thorns leaped suddenly upon Thingol. Swiftly Beren strode before him with a spear, but Carcharoth swept it aside and felled him, biting at his breast. In that moment Huan leaped from the thicket upon the back of the Wolf, and they fell together fighting bitterly; and no battle of wolf and hound has been like to it, for in the baying of Huan was heard the voice of the horns of Oromë and the wrath of the Valar, but in the howls of Carcharoth was the hate of Morgoth and malice crueller than teeth of steel; and the rocks were rent by their clamour and fell from on high and choked the falls of Esgalduin. There they fought to the death; but Thingol gave no heed, for he knelt by Beren, seeing that he was sorely hurt.

Huan in that hour slew Carcharoth; but there in the woven woods of Doriath his own doom long spoken was fulfilled, and he was wounded mortally, and the venom of Morgoth entered into him. Then he came, and falling beside Beren spoke for the third time with words; and he bade Beren farewell before he died. Beren spoke not, but laid his hand upon the head of the hound, and so they parted.

Mablung and Beleg came hastening to the King's aid, but when they looked upon what was done they cast aside their spears and wept. Then Mablung took a knife and ripped up the belly of the Wolf; and within he was wellnigh all consumed as with a fire, but the hand of Beren that held the jewel was yet incorrupt. But when Mablung reached forth to touch it, the hand was no more, and the Silmaril lay there unveiled, and the light of it filled the shadows of the forest all about them. Then quickly and in fear Mablung took it and set it in Beren's living hand; and Beren was aroused by the touch of the Silmaril, and held it aloft, and bade Thingol receive it. 'Now is the Quest achieved,' he said, 'and my doom full-wrought'; and he spoke no more.

They bore back Beren Camlost son of Barahir upon a bier of branches with Huan the wolfhound at his side; and night fell ere they returned to Menegroth. At the feet of Hírilorn the great beech Lúthien met them walking slow, and some bore torches beside the bier. There she set her arms about Beren, and kissed him, bidding him await her beyond the Western Sea; and he looked upon her eyes ere the spirit left him. But the starlight was quenched and darkness had fallen even upon Lúthien Tinúviel. Thus ended the Quest of the Silmaril; but the Lay of Leithian, Release from Bondage, does not end.

For the spirit of Beren at her bidding tarried in the halls of Mandos, unwilling to leave the world, until Lúthien came to say her last farewell upon the dim shores of the Outer Sea, whence Men that die set out never to return. But the spirit of Lúthien fell down into darkness, and at the last it fled, and her body lay like a flower that is suddenly cut off and lies for a while unwithered on the grass.

Then a winter, as it were the hoar age of mortal Men, fell upon Thingol. But Lúthien came to the halls of Mandos, where are the appointed places of the Eldalië, beyond the mansions of the West upon the confines of the world. There those that wait sit in the shadow of their thought. But her beauty was more than their beauty, and her sorrow deeper than their sorrows; and she knelt before Mandos and sang to him.

The song of Lúthien before Mandos was the song most fair that ever in words was woven, and the song most sorrowful that ever the world shall hear. Unchanged, imperishable, it is sung still in Valinor beyond the hearing of the world, and listening the Valar are grieved. For Lúthien wove two themes of words, of the sorrow of the Eldar and the grief of Men, of the Two Kindreds that were made by Ilúvatar to dwell in Arda, the Kingdom of Earth amid the innumerable stars. And as she knelt before him her tears fell upon his feet like rain upon the stones; and Mandos was moved to pity, who never before was so moved, nor has been since.

Therefore he summoned Beren, and even as Lúthien had spoken in the hour of his death they met again beyond the Western Sea. But

Mandos had no power to withhold the spirits of Men that were dead within the confines of the world, after their time of waiting; nor could he change the fates of the Children of Ilúvatar. He went therefore to Manwë, Lord of the Valar, who governed the world under the hand of Ilúvatar; and Manwë sought counsel in his inmost thought, where the will of Ilúvatar was revealed.

These were the choices that he gave to Lúthien. Because of her labours and her sorrow, she should be released from Mandos, and go to Valimar, there to dwell until the world's end among the Valar, forgetting all griefs that her life had known. Thither Beren could not come. For it was not permitted to the Valar to withhold Death from him, which is the gift of Ilúvatar to Men. But the other choice was this: that she might return to Middle-earth, and take with her Beren, there to dwell again, but without certitude of life or joy. Then she would become mortal, and subject to a second death, even as he; and ere long she would leave the world for ever, and her beauty become only a memory in song.

This doom she chose, forsaking the Blessed Realm, and putting aside all claim to kinship with those that dwell there; that thus whatever grief might lie in wait, the fates of Beren and Lúthien might be joined, and their paths lead together beyond the confines of the world. So it was that alone of the Eldalië she has died indeed, and left the world long ago. Yet in her choice the Two Kindreds have been joined; and she is the forerunner of many in whom the Eldar see yet, though all the world is changed, the likeness of Lúthien the beloved, whom they have lost.

Chapter 20

OF THE FIFTH BATTLE: NIRNAETH ARNOEDIAD

It is said that Beren and Lúthien returned to the northern lands of Middle-earth, and dwelt together for a time as living man and woman; and they took up again their mortal form in Doriath. Those that saw them were both glad and fearful; and Lúthien went to Menegroth and healed the winter of Thingol with the touch of her hand. But Melian looked in her eyes and read the doom that was written there, and turned away; for she knew that a parting beyond the end of the world had come between them, and no grief of loss has been heavier than the grief of Melian the Maia in that hour. Then Beren and Lúthien went forth alone, fearing neither thirst nor hunger; and they passed beyond the River Gelion into Ossiriand, and dwelt there in Tol Galen the green isle, in the midst of Adurant, until all tidings of them ceased. The Eldar afterwards called that country Dor Firn-i-Guinar, the Land of the Dead that Live; and there was born Dior Aranel the beautiful, who was after known as Dior Eluchíl, which is Thingol's Heir. No mortal man spoke ever again with Beren son of Barahir; and none saw Beren or Lúthien leave the world, or marked where at last their bodies lay.

In those days Maedhros son of Fëanor lifted up his heart, perceiving that Morgoth was not unassailable; for the deeds of Beren and Lúthien were sung in many songs throughout Beleriand. Yet Morgoth would destroy them all, one by one, if they could not again unite, and make new league and common council; and he began those counsels for the raising of the fortunes of the Eldar that are called the Union of Maedhros.

Yet the oath of Fëanor and the evil deeds that it had wrought did injury to the design of Maedhros, and he had less aid than should have been. Orodreth would not march forth at the word of any son of Fëanor, because of the deeds of Celegorm and Curufin; and the Elves of Nargothrond trusted still to defend their hidden stronghold by secrecy and stealth. Thence came only a small company, following Gwindor son of Guilin, a very valiant prince; and against the will of Orodreth he went to the northern war, because he grieved for the loss of Gelmir his brother in the Dagor Bragollach. They took the badge of the house of Fingolfin, and marched beneath the banners of Fingon; and they came never back, save one.

From Doriath came little help. For Maedhros and his brothers, being constrained by their oath, had before sent to Thingol and reminded him with haughty words of their claim, summoning him to yield the Silmaril, or become their enemy. Melian counselled him to surrender it; but the words of the sons of Fëanor were proud and threatening, and Thingol was filled with anger, thinking of the anguish of Lúthien and the blood of Beren whereby the jewel had been won, despite the malice of Celegorm and Curufin. And every day that he looked upon the Silmaril the more he desired to keep it for ever; for such was its power. Therefore he sent back the messengers with scornful words. Maedhros made no answer, for he had now begun to devise the league and union of the Elves; but Celegorm and Curufin vowed openly to slay Thingol and destroy his people, if they came victorious from war, and the jewel were not surrendered of free will. Then Thingol fortified the marches of his realm, and went not to war, nor any out of Doriath save Mablung and Beleg, who were unwilling to have no part in these great deeds. To them Thingol gave leave to go, so long as they served not the sons of Fëanor; and they joined themselves to the host of Fingon.

But Maedhros had the help of the Naugrim, both in armed force and in great store of weapons; and the smithies of Nogrod and Belegost were busy in those days. And he gathered together again all his brothers and all the people who would follow them; and the Men of Bór and Ulfang were marshalled and trained for war, and they summoned yet more of their kinsfolk out of the East. Moreover in the west Fingon, ever the friend of Maedhros, took counsel with Himring, and in Hithlum the Noldor and the Men of the house of Hador prepared for war. In the forest of Brethil Halmir, lord of the People of Haleth, gathered his men, and they whetted their axes; but Halmir died ere the war came, and Haldir his son ruled that people. And to Gondolin also the tidings came, to Turgon, the hidden king.

But Maedhros made trial of his strength too soon, ere his plans were full-wrought; and though the Orcs were driven out of all the northward regions of Beleriand, and even Dorthonion was freed for a while, Morgoth was warned of the uprising of the Eldar and the Elf-friends, and took counsel against them. Many spies and workers of treason he sent forth among them, as he was the better able now to do, for the faithless Men of his secret allegiance were yet deep in the secrets of the sons of Fëanor.

At length Maedhros, having gathered all the strength that he could of Elves and Men and Dwarves, resolved to assault Angband from east and west; and he purposed to march with banners displayed in open force over Anfauglith. But when he had drawn forth, as he hoped, the armies of Morgoth in answer, then Fingon should issue forth from the passes of Hithlum; and thus they thought to take the might of Morgoth as between anvil and hammer, and break it to pieces. And the signal for this was to be the firing of a great beacon in Dorthonion.

On the appointed day, on the morning of Midsummer, the trumpets of the Eldar greeted the rising of the sun; and in the east was raised the standard of the sons of Fëanor, and in the west the standard of Fingon, High King of the Noldor. Then Fingon looked out from the walls of Eithel Sirion, and his host was arrayed in the valleys and the woods upon the east of Ered Wethrin, well hid from the eyes of the Enemy; but he knew that it was very great. For there all the Noldor of Hithlum were assembled, together with Elves of the Falas and Gwindor's company from Nargothrond, and he had great strength of Men: upon the right were the host of Dor-lómin and all the valour of Húrin and Huor his brother, and to them had come Haldir of Brethil with many men of the woods.

Then Fingon looked towards Thangorodrim, and there was a dark cloud about it, and a black smoke went up; and he knew that the wrath of Morgoth was aroused, and that their challenge was accepted. A shadow of doubt fell upon Fingon's heart; and he looked eastwards, seeking if he might see with elven-sight the dust of Anfauglith rising beneath the hosts of Maedhros. He knew not that Maedhros was hindered in his setting-forth by the guile of Uldor the accursed, who deceived him with false warnings of assault from Angband.

But now a cry went up, passing up the wind from the south from vale to vale, and Elves and Men lifted their voices in wonder and joy. For unsummoned and unlooked for Turgon had opened the leaguer of Gondolin, and was come with an army ten thousand strong, with bright mail and long swords and spears like a forest. Then when Fingon heard afar the great trumpet of Turgon his brother, the shadow passed and his heart was uplifted, and he shouted aloud: *'Utúlie'n aurë! Aiya Eldalië ar Atanatári, utúlie'n aurë!* The day has come! Behold, people of the Eldar and Fathers of Men, the day has come!' And all those who heard his great voice echo in the hills answered crying: '*Auta i lómë!* The night is passing!'

Now Morgoth, who knew much of what was done and designed by his enemies, chose his hour, and trusting in his treacherous servants to hold back Maedhros and prevent the union of his foes he sent a force seeming great (and yet but part of all that he had made ready) towards Hithlum; and they were clad all in dun raiment and showed no naked steel, and thus were already far over the sands of Anfauglith before their approach was seen.

Then the hearts of the Noldor grew hot, and their captains wished to assail their foes upon the plain; but Húrin spoke against it, and bade them beware of the guile of Morgoth, whose strength was always greater than it seemed, and his purpose other than he revealed. And though the signal of the approach of Maedhros came not, and the host grew impatient, Húrin urged them still to await it, and to let the Orcs break themselves in assault upon the hills.

But the Captain of Morgoth in the west had been commanded to draw out Fingon swiftly from his hills by whatever means he could. He marched on therefore until the front of his battle was drawn up before the stream of Sirion, from the walls of the fortress of Eithel Sirion to the inflowing of Rivil at the Fen of Serech; and the outposts of Fingon could see the eyes of their enemies. But there was no answer to his challenge, and the taunts of the Orcs faltered as they looked upon the silent walls and the hidden threat of the hills. Then the Captain of Morgoth sent out riders with tokens of parley, and they rode up before the outworks of the Barad Eithel. With them they brought Gelmir son of Guilin, that lord of Nargothrond whom they had captured in the Bragollach; and they had blinded him. Then the heralds of Angband showed him forth, crying: 'We have many more such at home, but you must make haste if you would find them; for we shall deal with them all when we return even so.' And they hewed off Gelmir's hands and feet, and his head last, within sight of the Elves, and left him.

By ill chance, at that place in the outworks stood Gwindor of Nargothrond, the brother of Gelmir. Now his wrath was kindled to madness, and he leapt forth on horseback, and many riders with him; and they pursued the heralds and slew them, and drove on deep into the main host. And seeing this all the host of the Noldor was set on fire, and Fingon put on his white helm and sounded his trumpets, and all the host of Hithlum leapt forth from the hills in sudden onslaught. The light of the drawing of the swords of the Noldor was like a fire in a field of reeds; and so fell and swift was their onset that almost the designs of Morgoth went astray. Before the army that he sent westward could be strengthened it was swept away, and the banners of Fingon passed over Anfauglith and were raised before the walls of Angband. Ever in the forefront of that battle went Gwindor and the Elves of Nargothrond, and even now they could not be restrained; and they burst through the Gate and slew the guards upon the very stairs of Angband, and Morgoth trembled upon his deep throne, hearing them beat upon his doors. But they were trapped there, and all were slain save Gwindor only, whom they took alive; for Fingon could not come to their aid. By many secret doors in Thangorodrim Morgoth had let issue forth his main host that he held in waiting, and Fingon was beaten back with great loss from the walls.

Then in the plain of Anfauglith, on the fourth day of the war, there began Nirnaeth Arnoediad, Unnumbered Tears, for no song or tale can contain all its grief. The host of Fingon retreated over the sands, and Haldir lord of the Haladin was slain in the rearguard; with him fell most of the Men of Brethil, and came never back to their woods. But on the fifth day as night fell, and they were still far from Ered Wethrin, the Orcs surrounded the host of Hithlum, and they fought until day, pressed ever closer. In the morning came hope, when the horns of Turgon were heard as he marched up with the main host of Gondolin; for they had been stationed southward guarding the Pass of Sirion, and Turgon restrained most of his people from the rash onslaught. Now he hastened to the aid of his brother; and the Gondolindrim were strong and clad in mail, and their ranks shone like a river of steel in the sun.

Now the phalanx of the guard of the King broke through the ranks of the Orcs, and Turgon hewed his way to the side of his brother; and it is told that the meeting of Turgon with Húrin, who stood beside Fingon, was glad in the midst of battle. Then hope was renewed in the hearts of the Elves; and in that very time, at the third hour of morning, the trumpets of Maedhros were heard at last coming up from the east, and the banners of the sons of Fëanor assailed the enemy in the rear. Some have said that even then the Eldar might have won the day, had all their hosts proved faithful; for the Orcs wavered, and their onslaught was stayed, and already some were turning to flight. But even as the vanguard of Maedhros came upon the Orcs, Morgoth loosed his last strength, and Angband was emptied. There came wolves, and wolfriders, and there came Balrogs, and dragons, and Glaurung father of dragons. The strength and terror of the Great Worm were now great indeed, and Elves and Men withered before him; and he came between the hosts of Maedhros and Fingon and swept them apart.

Yet neither by wolf, nor by Balrog, nor by Dragon, would Morgoth have achieved his end, but for the treachery of Men. In this hour the plots of Ulfang were revealed. Many of the Easterlings turned and fled, their hearts being filled with lies and fear; but the sons of Ulfang went over suddenly to Morgoth and drove in upon the rear of the sons of Fëanor, and in the confusion that they wrought they came near to the standard of Maedhros. They reaped not the reward that Morgoth promised them, for Maglor slew Uldor the accursed, the leader in treason, and the sons of Bór slew Ulfast and Ulwarth ere they themselves were slain. But new strength of evil Men came up that Uldor had summoned and kept hidden in the eastern hills, and the host of Maedhros was assailed now on three sides, and it broke, and was scattered, and fled this way and that. Yet fate saved the sons of Fëanor, and though all were wounded none were slain, for they drew together, and gathering a remnant of the Noldor and the Naugrim about them they hewed a way out of the battle and escaped far away towards Mount Dolmed in the east.

Last of all the eastern force to stand firm were the Dwarves of Belegost, and thus they won renown. For the Naugrim withstood fire more hardily than either Elves or Men, and it was their custom moreover to wear great masks in battle hideous to look upon; and those stood them in good stead against the dragons. And but for them Glaurung and his brood would have withered all that was left of the Noldor. But the Naugrim made a circle about him when he assailed them, and even his mighty armour was not full proof against the blows of their great axes; and when in his rage Glaurung turned and struck down Azaghâl, Lord of Belegost, and crawled over him, with his last stroke Azaghâl drove a knife into his belly, and so wounded him that he fled the field, and the beasts of Angband in dismay followed after him. Then the Dwarves raised up the body of Azaghâl and bore it away; and with slow steps they walked behind singing a dirge in deep voices, as it were a funeral pomp in their country, and gave no heed more to their foes; and none dared to stay them.

But now in the western battle Fingon and Turgon were assailed by a tide of foes thrice greater than all the force that was left to them. Gothmog, Lord of Balrogs, high-captain of Angband, was come; and he drove a dark wedge between the Elvenhosts, surrounding King Fingon, and thrusting Turgon and Húrin aside towards the Fen of Serech. Then he turned upon Fingon. That was a grim meeting. At last Fingon stood alone with his guard dead about him; and he fought with Gothmog, until another Balrog came behind and cast a thong of fire about him. Then Gothmog hewed him with his black axe, and a white flame sprang up from the helm of Fingon as it was cloven. Thus fell the High King of the Noldor; and they beat him into the dust with their maces, and his banner, blue and silver, they trod into the mire of his blood.

The field was lost; but still Húrin and Huor and the remnant of the house of Hador stood firm with Turgon of Gondolin, and the hosts of Morgoth could not yet win the Pass of Sirion. Then Húrin spoke to Turgon, saying: 'Go now, lord, while time is! For in you lives the last hope of the Eldar, and while Gondolin stands Morgoth shall still know fear in his heart.'

But Turgon answered: 'Not long now can Gondolin be hidden; and being discovered it must fall.'

Then Huor spoke and said: 'Yet if it stands but a little while, then out of your house shall come the hope of Elves and Men. This I say to you, lord, with the eyes of death: though we part here for ever, and I shall not look on your white walls again, from you and from me a new star shall arise. Farewell!'

And Maeglin, Turgon's sister-son, who stood by, heard these words, and did not forget them; but he said nothing.

Then Turgon took the counsel of Húrin and Huor, and summoning all that remained of the host of Gondolin and such of Fingon's people as could be gathered he retreated towards the Pass of Sirion; and his captains Ecthelion and Glorfindel guarded the flanks to right and left, so that none of the enemy should pass them by. But the Men of Dor-lómin held the rearguard, as Húrin and Huor desired; for they did not wish in their hearts to leave the Northlands, and if they could not win back to their homes, there they would stand to the end. Thus was the treachery of Uldor redressed; and of all the deeds of war that the fathers of Men wrought in behalf of the Eldar, the last stand of the Men of Dor-lómin is most renowned.

So it was that Turgon fought his way southward, until coming behind the guard of Húrin and Huor he passed down Sirion and escaped; and he vanished into the mountains and was hidden from the eyes of Morgoth. But the brothers drew the remnant of the Men of the house of Hador about them, and foot by foot they withdrew, until they came behind the Fen of Serech, and had the stream of Rivil before them. There they stood and gave way no more.

Then all the hosts of Angband swarmed against them, and they bridged the stream with their dead, and encircled the remnant of Hithlum as a gathering tide about a rock. There as the sun westered on the sixth day, and the shadow of Ered Wethrin grew dark, Huor fell pierced with a venomed arrow in his eye, and all the valiant Men of Hador were slain about him in a heap; and the Orcs hewed their heads and piled them as a mound of gold in the sunset.

Last of all Húrin stood alone. Then he cast aside his shield, and wielded an axe two-handed; and it is sung that the axe smoked in the black blood of the troll-guard of Gothmog until it withered, and each time that he slew Húrin cried: '*Aurë entuluva!* Day shall come again!' Seventy times he uttered that cry; but they took him at last alive, by the command of Morgoth, for the Orcs grappled him with their hands, which clung to him still though he hewed off their arms; and ever their numbers were renewed, until at last he fell buried beneath them. Then Gothmog bound him and dragged him to Angband with mockery.

Thus ended Nirnaeth Arnoediad, as the sun went down beyond the sea. Night fell in Hithlum, and there came a great storm of wind out of the West.

Great was the triumph of Morgoth, and his design was accomplished in a manner after his own heart; for Men took the lives of Men, and betrayed the Eldar, and fear and hatred were aroused among those that should have been united against him. From that day the hearts of the Elves were estranged from Men, save only those of the Three Houses of the Edain.

The realm of Fingon was no more; and the sons of Fëanor wandered as leaves before the wind. Their arms were scattered, and their league broken; and they took to a wild and woodland life beneath the feet of Ered Lindon, mingling with the Green-elves of Ossiriand, bereft of their power and glory of old. In Brethil some few of the Haladin yet dwelt in the protection of their woods, and Handir son of Haldir was their lord; but to Hithlum came back never one of Fingon's host, nor any of the Men of Hador's house, nor any tidings of the battle and the fate of their lords. But Morgoth sent thither the Easterlings that had served him, denying them the rich lands of Beleriand which they coveted; and he shut them in Hithlum and forbade them to leave it. Such was the reward he gave them for their treachery to Maedhros: to plunder and harass the old and the women and the children of Hador's people. The remnant of the Eldar of Hithlum were taken to the mines of the north and laboured there as thralls, save some that eluded him and escaped into the wilds and the mountains.

The Orcs and the wolves went freely through all the North, and came ever further southward into Beleriand, even as far as Nan-tathren, the Land of Willows, and the borders of Ossiriand, and none were safe in field or wild. Doriath indeed remained, and the halls of Nargothrond were hidden; but Morgoth gave small heed to them, either because he knew little of them, or because their hour was not yet come in the deep purposes of his malice. Many now fled to the Havens and took refuge behind Círdan's walls, and the mariners passed up and down the coast and harried the enemy with swift landings. But in the next year, ere the winter was come, Morgoth sent great strength over Hithlum and Nevrast, and they came down the rivers Brithon and Nenning and ravaged all the Falas, and besieged the walls of Brithombar and Eglarest. Smiths and miners and makers of fire they brought with them, and they set up great engines; and valiantly though they were resisted they broke the walls at last. Then the Havens were laid in ruin, and the tower of Barad Nimras cast down; and the most part of Círdan's people were slain or enslaved. But some went aboard ship and escaped by sea; and among them was Ereinion Gil-galad, the son of Fingon, whom his father had sent to the Havens after the Dagor Bragollach. This remnant sailed with Círdan south to the Isle of Balar, and they made a refuge for all that could come thither; for they kept a foothold also at the Mouths of Sirion, and there many light and swift ships lay hid in the creeks and waters where the reeds were dense as a forest.

And when Turgon heard of this he sent again his messengers to Sirion's mouths, and besought the aid of Círdan the Shipwright. At the bidding of Turgon Círdan built seven swift ships, and they sailed out into the West; but no tidings of them came ever back to Balar, save of one, and the last. The mariners of that ship toiled long in the sea, and returning at last in despair they foundered in a great storm within sight of the coasts of Middle-earth; but one of them was saved by Ulmo from the wrath of Ossë, and the waves bore him up, and cast him ashore in Nevrast. His name was Voronwë; and he was one of those that Turgon sent forth as messengers from Gondolin.

Now the thought of Morgoth dwelt ever upon Turgon; for Turgon had escaped him, of all his foes that one whom he most desired to take or to destroy. And that thought troubled him, and marred his victory, for Turgon of the mighty house of Fingolfin was now by right King of all the Noldor; and Morgoth feared and hated the house of Fingolfin, because they had the friendship of Ulmo his foe, and because of the wounds that Fingolfin gave him with his sword. And most of all his kin Morgoth feared Turgon; for of old in Valinor his eye had lighted upon him, and whenever he drew near a shadow had fallen on his spirit, foreboding that in some time that yet lay hidden, from Turgon ruin should come to him.

Therefore Húrin was brought before Morgoth, for Morgoth knew that he had the friendship of the King of Gondolin; but Húrin defied him, and mocked him. Then Morgoth cursed Húrin and Morwen and their offspring, and set a doom upon them of darkness and sorrow; and taking Húrin from prison he set him in a chair of stone upon a high place of Thangorodrim. There he was bound by the power of Morgoth, and Morgoth standing beside him cursed him again; and he said: 'Sit now there; and look out upon the lands where evil and despair shall come upon those whom thou lovest. Thou hast dared to mock me, and to question the power of Melkor, Master of the fates of Arda. Therefore with my eyes thou shalt see, and with my ears thou shalt hear; and never shalt thou move from this place until all is fulfilled unto its bitter end.'

And even so it came to pass; but it is not said that Húrin asked ever of Morgoth either mercy or death, for himself or for any of his kin.

By the command of Morgoth the Orcs with great labour gathered all the bodies of those who had fallen in the great battle, and all their harness and weapons, and piled them in a great mound in the midst of Anfauglith; and it was like a hill that could be seen from afar. Haudh-en-Ndengin the Elves named it, the Hill of Slain, and Haudh-en-Nirnaeth, the Hill of Tears. But grass came there and grew again long and green upon that hill, alone in all the desert that Morgoth made; and no creature of Morgoth trod thereafter upon the earth beneath which the swords of the Eldar and the Edain crumbled into rust.

Chapter 21

OF TÚRIN TURAMBAR

Rían, daughter of Belegund, was the wife of Huor, son of Galdor; and she was wedded to him two months before he went with Húrin his brother to the Nirnaeth Arnoediad. When no tidings came of her lord she fled into the wild; but she was aided by the Grey-elves of Mithrim, and when her son Tuor was born they fostered him. Then Rían departed from Hithlum, and going to the Haudh-en-Ndengin she laid herself down upon it and died.

Morwen, daughter of Baragund, was the wife of Húrin, Lord of Dor-lómin; and their son was Túrin, who was born in the year that Beren Erchamion came upon Lúthien in the Forest of Neldoreth. A daughter they had also who was called Lalaith, which is Laughter, and she was beloved by Túrin her brother; but when she was three years old there came a pestilence to Hithlum, borne on an evil wind out of Angband, and she died.

Now after the Nirnaeth Arnoediad Morwen abode still in Dor-lómin, for Túrin was but eight years old, and she was again with child. Those days were evil; for the Easterlings that came into Hithlum despised the remnant of the people of Hador, and they oppressed them, and took their lands and their goods, and enslaved their children. But so great was the beauty and majesty of the Lady of Dor-lómin that the Easterlings were afraid, and dared not to lay hands upon her or her household; and they whispered among themselves, saying that she was perilous, and a witch skilled in magic and in league with the Elves. Yet she was now poor and without aid, save that she was succoured secretly by a kinswoman of Húrin named Aerin, whom Brodda, an Easterling, had taken as his wife; and Morwen feared greatly that Túrin would be taken from her and enslaved. Therefore it came into her heart to send him away in secret, and to beg King Thingol to harbour him, for Beren son of Barahir was her father's kinsman, and he had been moreover a friend of Húrin, ere evil befell. Therefore in the autumn of the Year of Lamentation Morwen sent Túrin forth over the mountains with two aged servants, bidding them find entry, if they could, into the kingdom of Doriath. Thus was the fate of Túrin woven, which is fulltold in that lay that is called *Narn i Hîn Húrin,* the Tale of the Children of Húrin, and is the longest of all the lays that speak of those days. Here that tale is told in brief, for it is woven with the fate of the Silmarils and of the Elves; and it is called the Tale of Grief, for it is sorrowful, and in it are revealed most evil works of Morgoth Bauglir.

In the first beginning of the year Morwen gave birth to her child, the daughter of Húrin; and she named her Nienor, which is Mourning. But Túrin and his companions passing through great perils came at last to the borders of Doriath; and there they were found by Beleg Strongbow, chief of the marchwardens of King Thingol, who led them to Menegroth. Then Thingol received Túrin, and took him even to his own fostering, in honour of Húrin the Steadfast; for Thingol's mood was changed towards the houses of the Elf-friends. Thereafter messengers went north to Hithlum, bidding Morwen leave Dor-lómin and return with them to Doriath; but still she would not leave the house in which she had dwelt with Húrin. And when the Elves departed she sent with them the Dragon-helm of Dor-lómin, greatest of the heirlooms of the house of Hador.

Túrin grew fair and strong in Doriath, but he was marked with sorrow. For nine years he dwelt in Thingol's halls, and during that time his grief grew less; for messengers went at times to Hithlum, and returning they brought better tidings of Morwen and Nienor. But there came a day when the messengers did not return out of the north, and Thingol would send no more. Then Túrin was filled with fear for his mother and his sister, and in grimness of heart he went before the King and asked for mail and sword; and he put on the Dragon-helm of Dor-lómin and went out to battle on the marches of Doriath, and became the companion in arms of Beleg Cúthalion.

And when three years had passed, Túrin returned again to Menegroth; but he came from the wild, and was unkempt, and his gear and garments were wayworn. Now one there was in Doriath, of the people of the Nandor, high in the counsels of the King; Saeros was his name. He had long begrudged to Túrin the honour he received as Thingol's fosterson; and seated opposite to him at the board he taunted him, saying: 'If the Men of Hithlum are so wild and fell, of what sort are the women of that land? Do they run like deer clad only in their hair?' Then Túrin in great anger took up a drinking-vessel, and cast it at Saeros; and he was grievously hurt.

On the next day Saeros waylaid Túrin as he set out from Menegroth to return to the marches; but Túrin overcame him, and set him to run naked as a hunted beast through the woods. Then Saeros fleeing in terror before him fell into the chasm of a stream, and his body was broken on a great rock in the water. But others coming saw what was done, and Mablung was among them; and he bade Túrin return with him to Menegroth and abide the judgement of the King, seeking his pardon. But Túrin, deeming himself now an outlaw and fearing to be held captive, refused Mablung's bidding, and turned swiftly away; and passing through the Girdle of Melian he came into the woods west of Sirion. There he joined himself to a band of such houseless and desperate men as could be found in those evil days lurking in the wild; and their hands were turned against all who came in their path, Elves and Men and Orcs.

But when all that had befallen was told and searched out before Thingol, the King pardoned Túrin, holding him wronged. In that time Beleg Strongbow returned from the north marches and came to Menegroth, seeking him; and Thingol spoke to Beleg, saying: 'I grieve, Cúthalion; for I took Húrin's son as my son, and so he shall remain, unless Húrin himself should return out of the shadows to claim his own. I would not have any say that Túrin was driven forth unjustly into the wild, and gladly would I welcome him back; for I loved him well.'

And Beleg answered: 'I will seek Túrin until I find him, and I will bring him back to Menegroth, if I can; for I love him also.'

Then Beleg departed from Menegroth, and far across Beleriand he sought in vain for tidings of Túrin through many perils.

But Túrin abode long among the outlaws, and became their captain; and he named himself Neithan, the Wronged. Very warily they dwelt in the wooded lands south of Teiglin; but when a year had passed since Túrin fled from Doriath, Beleg came upon their lair by night. It chanced that at that time Túrin was gone from the camp; and the outlaws seized Beleg and bound him, and treated him cruelly, for they feared him as a spy of the King of Doriath. But Túrin returning and seeing what was done, was stricken with remorse for all their evil and lawless deeds; and he released Beleg, and they renewed their friendship, and Túrin foreswore thenceforward war or plunder against all save the servants of Angband.

Then Beleg told Túrin of King Thingol's pardon; and he sought to persuade him by all means that he might to return with him to Doriath, saying that there was great need of his strength and valour on the north marches of the realm. 'Of late the Orcs have found a way down out of Taur-nu-Fuin,' he said; 'they have made a road through the Pass of Anach.'

'I do not remember it,' said Túrin.

'Never did we go so far from the borders,' said Beleg. 'But you have seen the peaks of the Crissaegrim far off, and to the east the dark walls of the Gorgoroth. Anach lies between, above the high springs of Mindeb, a hard and dangerous road; yet many come by it now, and Dimbar which used to be in peace is falling under the Black Hand, and the Men of Brethil are troubled. We are needed there.'

But in the pride of his heart Túrin refused the pardon of the King, and the words of Beleg were of no avail to change his mood. And he for his part urged Beleg to remain with him in the lands west of Sirion; but that Beleg would not do, and he said: 'Hard you are, Túrin, and stubborn. Now the turn is mine. If you wish indeed to have the Strongbow beside you, look for me in Dimbar; for thither I shall return.'

On the next day Beleg set out, and Túrin went with him a bowshot from the camp; but he said nothing. 'Is it farewell, then, son of Húrin?' said Beleg. Then Túrin looked out westward, and he saw far off the great height of Amon Rûdh; and unwitting of what lay before him he answered: 'You have said, seek me in Dimbar. But I say, seek for me on Amon Rûdh! Else, this is our last farewell.' Then they parted, in friendship, yet in sadness.

Now Beleg returned to the Thousand Caves, and coming before Thingol and Melian he told them of all that had befallen, save only of his evil handling by Túrin's companions. Then Thingol sighed, and he said: 'What more would Túrin have me do?'

'Give me leave, lord,' said Beleg, 'and I will guard him and guide him as I may; then no man shall say that elven-words are lightly spoken. Nor would I wish to see so great a good run to nothing in the wild.'

Then Thingol gave Beleg leave to do as he would; and he said: 'Beleg Cúthalion! For many deeds you have earned my thanks; but not the least is the finding of my fosterson. At this parting ask for any gift, and I will not deny it to you.'

'I ask then for a sword of worth,' said Beleg; 'for the Orcs come now too thick and close for a bow only, and such blade as I have is no match for their armour.'

'Choose from all that I have,' said Thingol, 'save only Aranrúth, my own.'

Then Beleg chose Anglachel; and that was a sword of great worth, and it was so named because it was made of iron that fell from heaven as a blazing star; it would cleave all earth-delved iron. One other sword only in Middle-earth was like to it. That sword does not enter into this tale, though it was made of the same ore by the same smith; and that smith was Eöl the Dark Elf, who took Aredhel Turgon's sister to wife. He gave Anglachel to Thingol as fee, which he begrudged, for leave to dwell in Nan Elmoth; but its mate Anguirel he kept, until it was stolen from him by Maeglin, his son.

But as Thingol turned the hilt of Anglachel towards Beleg, Melian looked at the blade; and she said: 'There is malice in this sword. The dark heart of the smith still dwells in it. It will not love the hand it serves; neither will it abide with you long.'

'Nonetheless I will wield it while I may,' said Beleg.

'Another gift I will give to you, Cúthalion,' said Melian, 'that shall be your help in the wild, and the help also of those whom you choose.' And she gave him store of *lembas,* the waybread of the Elves, wrapped in leaves of silver, and the threads that bound it were sealed at the knots with the seal of the Queen, a wafer of white wax shaped as a single flower of Telperion; for according to the customs of the Eldalië the keeping and giving of *lembas* belonged to the Queen alone. In nothing did Melian show greater favour to Túrin than in this gift; for the Eldar had never before allowed Men to use this waybread, and seldom did so again.

Then Beleg departed with these gifts from Menegroth and went back to the north marches, where he had his lodges, and many friends. Then in Dimbar the Orcs were driven back, and Anglachel rejoiced to be unsheathed; but when the winter came, and war was stilled, suddenly his companions missed Beleg, and he returned to them no more.

Now when Beleg parted from the outlaws and returned into Doriath, Túrin led them away westward out of Sirion's vale; for they grew weary of their life without rest, ever watchful and in fear of pursuit, and they sought for a safer lair. And it chanced at a time of evening that they came upon three Dwarves, who fled before them; but one that lagged behind was seized and thrown down, and a man of the company took his bow and let fly an arrow at the others as they vanished in the dusk. Now the dwarf that they had taken was named Mîm; and he pleaded for his life before Túrin, and offered as ransom to lead them to his hidden halls which none might find without his aid. Then Túrin pitied Mîm, and spared him; and he said: 'Where is your house?'

Then Mîm answered: 'High above the lands lies the house of Mîm, upon the great hill; Amon Rûdh is that hill called now, since the Elves changed all the names.'

Then Túrin was silent, and he looked long upon the dwarf; and at last he said: 'You shall bring us to that place.'

On the next day they set out thither, following Mîm to Amon Rûdh. Now that hill stood upon the edge of the moorlands that rose between the vales of Sirion and Narog, and high above the stony heath it reared its crown; but its steep grey head was bare, save for the red *seregon* that mantled the stone. And as the men of Túrin's band drew near, the sun westering broke through the clouds, and fell upon the crown; and the *seregon* was all in flower. Then one among them said: 'There is blood on the hill-top.'

But Mîm led them by secret paths up the steep slopes of Amon Rûdh; and at the mouth of his cave he bowed to Túrin, saying: 'Enter into Bar-en-Danwedh, the House of Ransom; for so it shall be called.'

And now there came another dwarf bearing light to greet him, and they spoke together, and passed swiftly down into the darkness of the cave; but Túrin followed after, and came at length to a chamber far within, lit by dim lamps hanging upon chains. There he found Mîm kneeling at a stone couch beside the wall, and he tore his beard, and wailed, crying one name unceasingly; and on the couch there lay a third. But Túrin entering stood beside Mîm, and offered him aid. Then Mîm looked up at him, and said: 'You can give no aid. For this is Khîm, my son; and he is dead, pierced by an arrow. He died at sunset. Ibun my son has told me.'

Then pity rose in Túrin's heart, and he said to Mîm: 'Alas! I would recall that shaft, if I could. Now Bar-en-Danwedh this house shall be called in truth; and if ever I come to any wealth, I will pay you a ransom of gold for your son, in token of sorrow, though it gladden your heart no more.'

Then Mîm rose, and looked long at Túrin. 'I hear you,' he said. 'You speak like a dwarf-lord of old; and at that I marvel. Now my heart is cooled, though it is not glad; and in this house you may dwell, if you will; for I will pay my ransom.'

So began the abiding of Túrin in the hidden house of Mîm upon Amon Rûdh; and he walked on the greensward before the mouth of the cave, and looked out east, and west, and north. Northward he looked, and descried the Forest of Brethil climbing green about Amon Obel in its midst, and thither his eyes were drawn ever and again, he knew not why; for his heart was set rather to the north-west, where league upon league away on the skirts of the sky it seemed to him that he could glimpse the Mountains of Shadow, the walls of his home. But at evening Túrin looked west into the sunset, as the sun rode down red into the hazes above the distant coasts, and the Vale of Narog lay deep in the shadows between.

In the time that followed Túrin spoke much with Mîm, and sitting with him alone he listened to his lore and the tale of his life. For Mîm came of Dwarves that were banished in ancient days from the great Dwarf-cities of the east, and long before the return of Morgoth they wandered westward into Beleriand; but they became diminished in stature and in smith-craft, and they took to lives of stealth, walking with bowed shoulders and furtive steps. Before the Dwarves of Nogrod and Belegost came west over the mountains the Elves of Beleriand knew not what these others were, and they hunted them, and slew them; but afterwards they let them alone, and they were called Noegyth Nibin, the Petty-Dwarves, in the Sindarin tongue. They loved none but themselves, and if they feared and hated the Orcs, they hated the Eldar no less, and the Exiles most of all; for the Noldor, they said, had stolen their lands and their homes. Long ere King Finrod Felagund came over the Sea, the caves of Nargothrond were discovered by them, and by them its delving was begun; and beneath the crown of Amon Rûdh, the Bald Hill, the slow hands of the Petty-Dwarves had bored and deepened the caves through the long years that they dwelt there, untroubled by the Grey-elves of the woods. But now at last they had dwindled and died out of Middle-earth, all save Mîm and his two sons; and Mîm was old even in the reckoning of Dwarves, old and forgotten. And in his halls the smithies were idle, and the axes rusted, and their name was remembered only in ancient tales of Doriath and Nargothrond.

But when the year drew on to midwinter, snow came down from the north heavier than they had known it in the river-vales, and Amon Rûdh was covered deep; and they said that the winters worsened in Beleriand as the power of Angband grew. Then only the hardiest dared stir abroad; and some fell sick, and all were pinched with hunger. But in the dim dusk of a winter's day there appeared suddenly among them a man, as it seemed, of great bulk and girth, cloaked and hooded in white; and he walked up to the fire without a word. And when men sprang up in fear, he laughed, and threw back his hood, and beneath his wide cloak he bore a great pack; and in the light of the fire Túrin looked again on the face of Beleg Cúthalion.

Thus Beleg returned once more to Túrin, and their meeting was glad; and with him he brought out of Dimbar the Dragon-helm of Dor-lómin, thinking that it might lift Túrin's thought again above his life in the wilderness as the leader of a petty company. But still Túrin would not return to Doriath; and Beleg yielding to his love against his wisdom remained with him, and did not depart, and in that time he laboured much for the good of Túrin's company. Those that were hurt or sick he tended, and gave to them the *lembas* of Melian; and they were quickly healed, for though the Grey-elves were less in skill and knowledge than the Exiles from Valinor, in the ways of the life of Middle-earth they had a wisdom beyond the reach of Men. And because Beleg was strong and enduring, farsighted in mind as in eye, he came to be held in honour among the outlaws; but the hatred of Mîm for the Elf that had come into Bar-en-Danwedh grew ever greater, and he sat with Ibun his son in the deepest shadows of his house, speaking to none. But Túrin paid now little heed to the Dwarf; and when winter passed, and spring came, they had sterner work to do.

Who knows now the counsels of Morgoth? Who can measure the reach of his thought, who had been Melkor, mighty among the Ainur of the Great Song, and sat now, a dark lord upon a dark throne in the North, weighing in his malice all the tidings that came to him, and perceiving more of the deeds and purposes of his enemies than even the wisest of them feared, save only Melian the Queen? To her often the thought of Morgoth reached out, and there was foiled.

And now again the might of Angband was moved; and as the long fingers of a groping hand the forerunners of his armies probed the ways into Beleriand. Through Anach they came, and Dimbar was taken, and all the north marches of Doriath. Down the ancient road they came that led through the long defile of Sirion, past the isle where Minas Tirith of Finrod had stood, and so through the land between Malduin and Sirion, and on through the eaves of Brethil to the Crossings of Teiglin. Thence the road went on into the Guarded Plain; but the Orcs did not go far upon it, as yet, for there dwelt now in the wild a terror that was hidden, and upon the red hill were watchful eyes of which they had not been warned. For Túrin put on again the Helm of Hador; and far and wide in Beleriand the whisper went, under wood and over stream and through the passes of the hills, saying that the Helm and Bow that had fallen in Dimbar had arisen again beyond hope. Then many who went leaderless, dispossessed but undaunted, took heart again, and came to seek the Two Captains. Dor-Cúarthol, the Land of Bow and Helm, was in that time named all the region between Teiglin and the west march of Doriath; and Túrin named himself anew, Gorthol, the Dread Helm, and his heart was high again. In Menegroth, and in the deep halls of Nargothrond, and even in the hidden realm of Gondolin, the fame of the deeds of the Two Captains was heard; and in Angband also they were known. Then Morgoth laughed, for now by the Dragon-helm was Húrin's son revealed to him again; and ere long Amon Rûdh was ringed with spies.

In the waning of the year Mîm the Dwarf and Ibun his son went out from Bar-en-Danwedh to gather roots in the wild for their winter store; and they were taken captive by Orcs. Then for a second time Mîm promised to guide his enemies by the secret paths to his home on Amon Rûdh; but yet he sought to delay the fulfilment of his promise, and demanded that Gorthol should not be slain. Then the Orc-captain laughed, and he said to Mîm: 'Assuredly Túrin son of Húrin shall not be slain.'

Thus was Bar-en-Danwedh betrayed, for the Orcs came upon it by night at unawares, guided by Mîm. There many of Túrin's company were slain as they slept; but some fleeing by an inner stair came out upon the hill-top, and there they fought until they fell, and their blood flowed out upon the *seregon* that mantled the stone. But a net was cast over Túrin as he fought, and he was enmeshed in it, and overcome, and led away.

And at length when all was silent again Mîm crept out of the shadows of his house; and as the sun rose over the mists of Sirion he stood beside the dead men on the hill-top. But he perceived that not all those that lay there were dead; for by one his gaze was returned, and he looked in the eyes of Beleg the Elf. Then with hatred long-stored Mîm stepped up to Beleg, and drew forth the sword Anglachel that lay beneath the body of one that had fallen beside him; but Beleg stumbling up seized back the sword and thrust it at the Dwarf, and Mîm in terror fled wailing from the hill-top. And Beleg cried after him: 'The vengeance of the house of Hador will find you yet!'

Now Beleg was sorely wounded, but he was mighty among the Elves of Middle-earth, and he was moreover a master of healing.

Therefore he did not die, and slowly his strength returned; and he sought in vain among the dead for Túrin, to bury him. But he found him not; and then he knew that Húrin's son was yet alive, and taken to Angband.

With little hope Beleg departed from Amon Rûdh and set out northward, towards the Crossings of Teiglin, following in the track of the Orcs; and he crossed over the Brithiach and journeyed through Dimbar towards the Pass of Anach. And now he was not far behind them, for he went without sleeping, whereas they had tarried on their road, hunting in the lands and fearing no pursuit as they came northward; and not even in the dreadful woods of Taur-nu-Fuin did he swerve from the trail, for the skill of Beleg was greater than any that have been in Middle-earth. But as he passed by night through that evil land he came upon one lying asleep at the foot of a great dead tree; and Beleg staying his steps beside the sleeper saw that it was an Elf. Then he spoke to him, and gave him *lembas,* and asked him what fate had brought him to that terrible place; and he named himself Gwindor, son of Guilin.

Grieving Beleg looked upon him; for Gwindor was now but a bent and fearful shadow of his former shape and mood, when in the Nirnaeth Arnoediad that lord of Nargothrond rode with rash courage to the very doors of Angband, and there was taken. For few of the Noldor whom Morgoth captured were put to death, because of their skill in forging and in mining for metals and gems; and Gwindor was not slain, but put to labour in the mines of the North. By secret tunnels known only to themselves the mining Elves might sometimes escape; and thus it came to pass that Beleg found him, spent and bewildered in the mazes of Taur-nu-Fuin.

And Gwindor told him that as he lay and lurked among the trees he saw a great company of Orcs passing northwards, and wolves went with them; and among them was a Man, whose hands were chained, and they drove him onward with whips. 'Very tall he was,' said Gwindor, 'as tall as are the Men from the misty hills of Hithlum.' Then Beleg told him of his own errand in Taur-nu-Fuin; and Gwindor sought to dissuade him from his quest, saying that he would but join Túrin in the anguish that awaited him. But Beleg would not abandon Túrin, and despairing himself he aroused hope again in Gwindor's heart; and together they went on, following the Orcs until they came out of the forest on the high slopes that ran down to the barren dunes of Anfauglith. There within sight of the peaks of Thangorodrim the Orcs made their encampment in a bare dell as the light of day was failing, and setting wolf-sentinels all about they fell to carousing. A great storm rode up out of the west, and lightning glittered on the Shadowy Mountains far away, as Beleg and Gwindor crept towards the dell.

When all in the camp were sleeping Beleg took his bow, and in the darkness shot the wolf-sentinels, one by one and silently. Then in great peril they entered in, and they found Túrin fettered hand and foot and tied to a withered tree; and all about him knives that had been cast at him were embedded in the trunk, and he was senseless in a sleep of great weariness. But Beleg and Gwindor cut the bonds that held him, and lifting him they carried him out of the dell; yet they could bear him no further than to a thicket of thorn-trees a little way above. There they laid him down; and now the storm drew very near. Beleg drew his sword Anglachel, and with it he cut the fetters that bound Túrin; but fate was that day more strong, for the blade slipped as he cut the shackles, and Túrin's foot was pricked. Then he was aroused into a sudden wakefulness of rage and fear, and seeing one bending over him with naked blade he leapt up with a great cry, believing that Orcs were come again to torment him; and grappling with him in the darkness he seized Anglachel, and slew Beleg Cúthalion thinking him a foe.

But as he stood, finding himself free, and ready to sell his life dearly against imagined foes, there came a great flash of lightning above them; and in its light he looked down on Beleg's face. Then Túrin stood stonestill and silent, staring on that dreadful death, knowing what he had done; and so terrible was his face, lit by the lightning that flickered all about them, that Gwindor cowered down upon the ground and dared not raise his eyes.

But now in the dell beneath the Orcs were aroused, and all the camp was in a tumult; for they feared the thunder that came out of the west, believing that it was sent against them by the great Enemies beyond the Sea. Then a wind arose, and great rains fell, and torrents swept down from the heights of Taur-nu-Fuin; and though Gwindor cried out to Túrin, warning him of their utmost peril, he made no answer, but sat unmoving and unweeping in the tempest beside the body of Beleg Cúthalion.

When morning came the storm was passed away eastward over Lothlann, and the sun of autumn rose hot and bright; but believing that Túrin would have fled far away from that place and all trace of his flight be washed away, the Orcs departed in haste without longer search, and far off Gwindor saw them marching away over the steaming sands of Anfauglith. Thus it came to pass that they returned to Morgoth emptyhanded, and left behind them the son of Húrin, who sat crazed and unwitting on the slopes of Taur-nu-Fuin, bearing a burden heavier than their bonds.

Then Gwindor roused Túrin to aid him in the burial of Beleg, and he rose as one that walked in sleep; and together they laid Beleg in a shallow grave, and placed beside him Belthronding his great bow, that was made of black yew-wood. But the dread sword Anglachel Gwindor took, saying that it were better that it should take vengeance on the servants of Morgoth than lie useless in the earth; and he took also the *lembas* of Melian to strengthen them in the wild.

Thus ended Beleg Strongbow, truest of friends, greatest in skill of all that harboured in the woods of Beleriand in the Elder Days, at the hand of him whom he most loved; and that grief was graven on the face of Túrin and never faded. But courage and strength were renewed in the Elf of Nargothrond, and departing from Taur-nu-Fuin he led Túrin far away. Never once as they wandered together on long and grievous paths did Túrin speak, and he walked as one without wish or purpose, while the year waned and winter drew on over the northern lands. But Gwindor was ever beside him to guard him and guide him; and thus they passed westward over Sirion and came at length to Eithel Ivrin, the springs whence Narog rose beneath the Mountains of Shadow. There Gwindor spoke to Túrin, saying: 'Awake, Túrin son of Húrin Thalion! On Ivrin's lake is endless laughter. She is fed from crystal fountains unfailing, and guarded from defilement by Ulmo, Lord of Waters, who wrought her beauty in ancient days.' Then Túrin knelt and drank from that water; and suddenly he cast himself down, and his tears were unloosed at last, and he was healed of his madness.

There he made a song for Beleg, and he named it *Laer Cú Beleg*, the Song of the Great Bow, singing it aloud heedless of peril. And Gwindor gave the sword Anglachel into his hands, and Túrin knew that it was heavy and strong and had great power; but its blade was black and dull and its edges blunt. Then Gwindor said: 'This is a strange blade, and unlike any that I have seen in Middle-earth. It mourns for Beleg even as you do. But be comforted; for I return to Nargothrond of the house of Finarfin, and you shall come with me, and be healed and renewed.'

'Who are you?' said Túrin.

'A wandering Elf, a thrall escaped, whom Beleg met and comforted,' said Gwindor. 'Yet once I was Gwindor son of Guilin, a lord of

Nargothrond, until I went to the Nirnaeth Arnoediad, and was enslaved in Angband.'

'Then have you seen Húrin son of Galdor, the warrior of Dor-lómin?' said Túrin.

'I have not seen him,' said Gwindor. 'But rumour of him runs through Angband that he still defies Morgoth; and Morgoth has laid a curse upon him and all his kin.'

'That I do believe,' said Túrin.

And now they arose, and departing from Eithel Ivrin they journeyed southward along the banks of Narog, until they were taken by scouts of the Elves and brought as prisoners to the hidden stronghold. Thus did Túrin come to Nargothrond.

At first his own people did not know Gwindor, who went out young and strong, and returned now seeming as one of the aged among mortal Men, because of his torments and his labours; but Finduilas daughter of Orodreth the King knew him and welcomed him, for she had loved him before the Nirnaeth, and so greatly did Gwindor love her beauty that he named her Faelivrin, which is the gleam of the sun on the pools of Ivrin. For Gwindor's sake Túrin was admitted with him into Nargothrond, and he dwelt there in honour. But when Gwindor would tell his name, Túrin checked him, saying: 'I am Agarwaen the son of Úmarth (which is the Bloodstained, son of Ill-fate), a hunter in the woods'; and the Elves of Nargothrond questioned him no more.

In the time that followed Túrin grew high in favour with Orodreth, and well-nigh all hearts were turned to him in Nargothrond. For he was young, and only now reached his full manhood; and he was in truth the son of Morwen Eledhwen to look upon: dark-haired and pale-skinned, with grey eyes, and his face more beautiful than any other among mortal Men, in the Elder Days. His speech and bearing were that of the ancient kingdom of Doriath, and even among the Elves he might be taken for one from the great houses of the Noldor; therefore many called him Adanedhel, the Elf-Man. The sword Anglachel was forged anew for him by cunning smiths of Nargothrond, and though ever black its edges shone with pale fire; and he named it Gurthang, Iron of Death. So great was his prowess and skill in warfare on the confines of the Guarded Plain that he himself became known as Mormegil, the Black Sword; and the Elves said: 'The Mormegil cannot be slain, save by mischance, or an evil arrow from afar.' Therefore they gave him dwarf-mail, to guard him; and in a grim mood he found also in the armouries a dwarf-mask all gilded, and he put it on before battle, and his enemies fled before his face.

Then the heart of Finduilas was turned from Gwindor and against her will her love was given to Túrin; but Túrin did not perceive what had befallen. And being torn in heart Finduilas became sorrowful; and she grew wan and silent. But Gwindor sat in dark thought; and on a time he spoke to Finduilas, saying: 'Daughter of the house of Finarfin, let no grief lie between us; for though Morgoth has laid my life in ruin, you still I love. Go whither love leads you; yet beware! It is not fitting that the Elder Children of Ilúvatar should wed with the Younger; nor is it wise, for they are brief, and soon pass, to leave us in widowhood while the world lasts. Neither will fate suffer it, unless it be once or twice only, for some high cause of doom that we do not perceive. But this Man is not Beren. A doom indeed lies on him, as seeing eyes may well read in him, but a dark doom. Enter not into it! And if you will, your love shall betray you to bitterness and death. For hearken to me! Though he be indeed *agarwaen* son of *úmarth*, his right name is Túrin son of Húrin, whom Morgoth holds in Angband, and whose kin he has cursed. Doubt not the power of Morgoth Bauglir! Is it not written in me?'

Then Finduilas sat long in thought; but at the last she said only: 'Túrin son of Húrin loves me not; nor will.'

Now when Túrin learnt from Finduilas of what had passed, he was wrathful, and he said to Gwindor: 'In love I hold you for rescue and safe-keeping. But now you have done ill to me, friend, to betray my right name, and call my doom upon me, from which I would lie hid.'

But Gwindor answered: 'The doom lies in yourself, not in your name.'

When it became known to Orodreth that the Mormegil was in truth the son of Húrin Thalion he gave him great honour, and Túrin became mighty among the people of Nargothrond. But he had no liking for their manner of warfare, of ambush and stealth and secret arrow, and he yearned for brave strokes and battle in the open; and his counsels weighed with the King ever the longer the more. In those days the Elves of Nargothrond forsook their secrecy and went openly to battle, and great store of weapons were made; and by the counsel of Túrin the Noldor built a mighty bridge over the Narog from the Doors of Felagund, for the swifter passage of their arms. Then the servants of Angband were driven out of all the land between Narog and Sirion eastward, and westward to the Nenning and the desolate Falas; and though Gwindor spoke ever against Túrin in the council of the King, holding it an ill policy, he fell into dishonour and none heeded him, for his strength was small and he was no longer forward in arms. Thus Nargothrond was revealed to the wrath and hatred of Morgoth; but still at Túrin's prayer his true name was not spoken, and though the fame of his deeds came into Doriath and to the ears of Thingol, rumour spoke only of the Black Sword of Nargothrond.

In that time of respite and hope, when because of the deeds of the Mormegil the power of Morgoth was stemmed west of Sirion, Morwen fled at last from Dor-lómin with Nienor her daughter, and adventured the long journey to Thingol's halls. There new grief awaited her, for she found Túrin gone, and to Doriath there had come no tidings since the Dragon-helm had vanished from the lands west of Sirion; but Morwen remained in Doriath with Nienor as guests of Thingol and Melian, and were treated with honour.

Now it came to pass, when four hundred and ninety-five years had passed since the rising of the Moon, in the spring of the year, there came to Nargothrond two Elves, named Gelmir and Arminas; they were of Angrod's people, but since the Dagor Bragollach they dwelt in the south with Círdan the Shipwright. From their far journeys they brought tidings of a great mustering of Orcs and evil creatures under the eaves of Ered Wethrin and in the Pass of Sirion; and they told also that Ulmo had come to Círdan, giving warning that great peril drew nigh to Nargothrond.

'Hear the words of the Lord of Waters!' said they to the King. 'Thus he spoke to Círdan the Shipwright: "The Evil of the North has defiled the springs of Sirion, and my power withdraws from the fingers of the flowing waters. But a worse thing is yet to come forth. Say therefore to the Lord of Nargothrond: Shut the doors of the fortress and go not abroad. Cast the stones of your pride into the loud river, that the creeping evil may not find the gate."'

Orodreth was troubled by the dark words of the messengers, but Túrin would by no means hearken to these counsels, and least of all would he suffer the great bridge to be cast down; for he was become proud and stern, and would order all things as he wished.

Soon afterwards Handir Lord of Brethil was slain, for the Orcs invaded his land, and Handir gave them battle; but the Men of Brethil were worsted, and driven back into their woods. And in the autumn of the year, biding his hour, Morgoth loosed upon the people of Narog the great host that he had long prepared; and Glaurung the Urulóki passed over Anfauglith, and came thence into the north vales of Sirion and there did great evil. Under the shadows of Ered Wethrin he defiled the Eithel Ivrin, and thence he passed into the realm of Nargothrond, and burned the Talath Dirnen, the Guarded Plain, between Narog and Teiglin.

Then the warriors of Nargothrond went forth, and tall and terrible on that day looked Túrin, and the heart of the host was upheld, as he rode on the right hand of Orodreth. But greater far was the host of Morgoth than any scouts had told, and none but Túrin defended by his dwarf-mask could withstand the approach of Glaurung; and the Elves were driven back and pressed by the Orcs into the field of Tumhalad, between Ginglith and Narog, and there they were penned. On that day all the pride and host of Nargothrond withered away; and Orodreth was slain in the forefront of the battle, and Gwindor son of Guilin was wounded to the death. But Túrin came to his aid, and all fled before him; and he bore Gwindor out of the rout, and escaping into a wood there laid him on the grass.

Then Gwindor said to Túrin: 'Let bearing pay for bearing! But ill-fated was mine, and vain is thine; for my body is marred beyond healing, and I must leave Middle-earth. And though I love thee, son of Húrin, yet I rue the day that I took thee from the Orcs. But for thy prowess and thy pride, still I should have love and life, and Nargothrond should yet stand a while. Now if thou love me, leave me! Haste thee to Nargothrond, and save Finduilas. And this last I say to thee: she alone stands between thee and thy doom. If thou fail her, it shall not fail to find thee. Farewell!'

Then Túrin sped back to Nargothrond, mustering such of the rout as he met with on the way; and the leaves fell from the trees in a great wind as they went, for the autumn was passing to a dire winter. But the host of the Orcs and Glaurung the Dragon were there before him, and they came suddenly, ere those that were left on guard were aware of what had befallen on the field of Tumhalad. In that day the bridge over Narog proved an evil; for it was great and mightily made and could not swiftly be destroyed, and the enemy came readily over the deep river, and Glaurung came in full fire against the Doors of Felagund, and overthrew them, and passed within.

And even as Túrin came up the dreadful sack of Nargothrond was well nigh achieved. The Orcs had slain or driven off all that remained in arms, and were even then ransacking the great halls and chambers, plundering and destroying; but those of the women and maidens that were not burned or slain they had herded on the terraces before the doors, as slaves to be taken into Morgoth's thraldom. Upon this ruin and woe Túrin came, and none could withstand him; or would not, though he struck down all before him, and passed over the bridge, and hewed his way towards the captives.

And now he stood alone, for the few that followed him had fled. But in that moment Glaurung issued from the gaping doors, and lay behind, between Túrin and the bridge. Then suddenly he spoke, by the evil spirit that was in him, saying: 'Hail, son of Húrin. Well met!'

Then Túrin sprang about, and strode against him, and the edges of Gurthang shone as with flame; but Glaurung withheld his blast, and opened wide his serpent-eyes and gazed upon Túrin. Without fear Túrin looked into them as he raised up the sword; and straightway he fell under the binding spell of the lidless eyes of the dragon, and was halted moveless. Then for a long time he stood as one graven of stone; and they two were alone, silent before the doors of Nargothrond. But Glaurung spoke again, taunting Túrin, and he said: 'Evil have been all thy ways, son of Húrin. Thankless fosterling, outlaw, slayer of thy friend, thief of love, usurper of Nargothrond, captain foolhardy, and deserter of thy kin. As thralls thy mother and thy sister live in Dor-lómin, in misery and want. Thou art arrayed as a prince, but they go in rags; and for thee they yearn, but thou carest not for that. Glad may thy father be to learn that he hath such a son; as learn he shall.' And Túrin being under the spell of Glaurung hearkened to his words, and he saw himself as in a mirror misshapen by malice, and loathed that which he saw.

And while he was yet held by the eyes of the dragon in torment of mind, and could not stir, the Orcs drove away the herded captives, and they passed nigh to Túrin and crossed over the bridge. Among them was Finduilas, and she cried out to Túrin as she went; but not until her cries and the wailing of the captives was lost upon the northward road did Glaurung release Túrin, and he might not stop his ears against that voice that haunted him after.

Then suddenly Glaurung withdrew his glance, and waited; and Túrin stirred slowly, as one waking from a hideous dream. Then coming to himself he sprang upon the dragon with a cry. But Glaurung laughed, saying: 'If thou wilt be slain, I will slay thee gladly. But small help will that be to Morwen and Nienor. No heed didst thou give to the cries of the Elf-woman. Wilt thou deny also the bond of thy blood?'

But Túrin drawing back his sword stabbed at the dragon's eyes; and Glaurung coiling back swiftly towered above him, and said: 'Nay! At least thou art valiant; beyond all whom I have met. And they lie who say that we of our part do not honour the valour of foes. See now! I offer thee freedom. Go to thy kin, if thou canst. Get thee gone! And if Elf or Man be left to make tale of these days, then surely in scorn they will name thee, if thou spurnest this gift.'

Then Túrin, being yet bemused by the eyes of the dragon, as were he treating with a foe that could know pity, believed the words of Glaurung; and turning away he sped over the bridge. But as he went Glaurung spoke behind him, saying in a fell voice: 'Haste thee now, son of Húrin, to Dor-lómin! Or perhaps the Orcs shall come before thee, once again. And if thou tarry for Finduilas, then never shalt thou see Morwen again, and never at all shalt thou see Nienor thy sister; and they will curse thee.'

But Túrin passed away on the northward road, and Glaurung laughed once more, for he had accomplished the errand of his Master. Then he turned to his own pleasure, and sent forth his blast, and burned all about him. But all the Orcs that were busy in the sack he routed forth, and drove them away, and denied them their plunder even to the last thing of worth. The bridge then he broke down and cast into the foam of Narog; and being thus secure he gathered all the hoard and riches of Felagund and heaped them, and lay upon them in the innermost hall, and rested a while.

And Túrin hastened along the ways to the north, through the lands now desolate between Narog and Teiglin, and the Fell Winter came down to meet him; for in that year snow fell ere autumn was passed, and spring came late and cold. Ever it seemed to him as he went that he heard the cries of Finduilas, calling his name by wood and hill, and great was his anguish; but his heart being hot with the lies of Glaurung, and seeing ever in his mind the Orcs burning the house of Húrin or putting Morwen and Nienor to torment, he held on his way, and turned never aside.

At last worn by haste and the long road (for forty leagues and more had he journeyed without rest) he came with the first ice of winter to the pools of Ivrin, where before he had been healed. But they were now but a frozen mire, and he could drink there no more.

Thus he came hardly by the passes of Dor-lómin, through bitter snows from the north, and found again the land of his childhood. Bare and bleak it was; and Morwen was gone. Her house stood empty, broken and cold; and no living thing dwelt nigh. Therefore Túrin departed, and came to the house of Brodda the Easterling, he that had to wife Aerin, Húrin's kinswoman; and there he learned of an old servant that Morwen was long gone, for she had fled with Nienor out of Dor-lómin, none but Aerin knew where.

Then Túrin strode to Brodda's table, and seizing him he drew his sword, and demanded that he be told whither Morwen had gone; and Aerin declared to him that she went to Doriath to seek her son. 'For the lands were freed then from evil,' she said, 'by the Black Sword of the south, who now has fallen, they say.' Then Túrin's eyes were opened, and the last threads of Glaurung's spell were loosed; and for anguish, and wrath at the lies that had deluded him, and hatred of the oppressors of Morwen, a black rage seized him, and he slew Brodda in his hall, and other Easterlings that were his guests. Thereafter he fled out into the winter, a hunted man; but he was aided by some that remained of Hador's people and knew the ways of the wild, and with them he escaped through the falling snow and came to an outlaws' refuge in the southern mountains of Dor-lómin. Thence Túrin passed again from the land of his childhood, and returned to Sirion's vale. His heart was bitter, for to Dor-lómin he had brought only greater woe upon the remnant of his people, and they were glad of his going; and this comfort alone he had: that by the prowess of the Black Sword the ways to Doriath had been laid open to Morwen. And he said in his thought: 'Then those deeds wrought not evil to all. And where else might I have better bestowed my kin, even had I come sooner? For if the Girdle of Melian be broken, then last hope is ended. Nay, it is better indeed as things be; for a shadow I cast wheresoever I come. Let Melian keep them! And I will leave them in peace unshadowed for a while.'

Now Túrin coming down from Ered Wethrin sought for Finduilas in vain, roaming the woods beneath the mountains, wild and wary as a beast; and he waylaid all the roads that went north to the Pass of Sirion. But he was too late; for all the trails had grown old, or were washed away by the winter. Yet thus it was that passing southwards down Teiglin Túrin came upon some of the Men of Brethil that were surrounded by Orcs; and he delivered them, for the Orcs fled from Gurthang. He named himself Wildman of the Woods, and they besought him to come and dwell with them; but he said that he had an errand yet unachieved, to seek Finduilas, Orodreth's daughter of Nargothrond. Then Dorlas, the leader of those woodmen, told the grievous tidings of her death. For the Men of Brethil had waylaid at the Crossings of Teiglin the Orc-host that led the captives of Nargothrond, hoping to rescue them; but the Orcs had at once cruelly slain their prisoners, and Finduilas they pinned to a tree with a spear. So she died, saying at the last: 'Tell the Mormegil that Finduilas is here.' Therefore they had laid her in a mound near that place, and named it Haudh-en-Elleth, the Mound of the Elf-maid.

Túrin bade them lead him thither, and there he fell down into a darkness of grief that was near death. Then Dorlas by his black sword, the fame whereof had come even into the deeps of Brethil, and by his quest of the King's daughter, knew that this Wildman was indeed the Mormegil of Nargothrond, whom rumour said was the son of Húrin of Dor-lómin. Therefore the woodmen lifted him up, and bore him away to their homes. Now those were set in a stockade upon a high place in the forest, Ephel Brandir upon Amon Obel; for the People of Haleth were now dwindled by war, and Brandir son of Handir who ruled them was a man of gentle mood, and lame also from childhood, and he trusted rather in secrecy than in deeds of war to save them from the power of the North. Therefore he feared the tidings that Dorlas brought, and when he beheld the face of Túrin as he lay on the bier a cloud of foreboding lay on his heart. Nonetheless being moved by his woe he took him into his own house and tended him, for he had skill in healing. And with the beginning of spring Túrin cast off his darkness, and grew hale again; and he arose, and he thought that he would remain in Brethil hidden, and put his shadow behind him, forsaking the past. He took therefore a new name, Turambar, which in the High-elven speech signified Master of Doom; and he besought the woodmen to forget that he was a stranger among them or ever bore any other name. Nonetheless he would not wholly leave deeds of war; for he could not endure that the Orcs should come to the Crossings of Teiglin or draw nigh to Haudh-en-Elleth, and he made that a place of dread for them, so that they shunned it. But he laid his black sword by, and wielded rather the bow and the spear.

Now new tidings came to Doriath concerning Nargothrond, for some that had escaped from the defeat and the sack, and had survived the Fell Winter in the wild, came at last to Thingol seeking refuge; and the march-wardens brought them to the King. And some said that all the enemy had withdrawn northwards, and others that Glaurung abode still in the halls of Felagund; and some said that the Mormegil was slain, and others that he was cast under a spell by the dragon and dwelt there yet, as one changed to stone. But all declared that it was known to many in Nargothrond ere the end that the Mormegil was none other than Túrin son of Húrin of Dor-lómin.

Then Morwen was distraught, and refusing the counsel of Melian she rode forth alone into the wild to seek her son, or some true tidings of him. Thingol therefore sent Mablung after her, with many hardy march-wards, to find her and guard her, and to learn what news they might; but Nienor was bidden to remain behind. Yet the fearlessness of her house was hers; and in an evil hour, in hope that Morwen would return when she saw that her daughter would go with her into peril, Nienor disguised herself as one of Thingol's people, and went with that ill-fated riding.

They came upon Morwen by the banks of Sirion, and Mablung besought her to return to Menegroth; but she was fey, and would not be persuaded. Then also the coming of Nienor was revealed, and despite Morwen's command she would not go back; and Mablung perforce brought them to the hidden ferries at the Meres of Twilight, and they passed over Sirion. And after three days' journeying they came to Amon Ethir, the Hill of Spies, that long ago Felagund had caused to be raised with great labour, a league before the doors of Nargothrond. There Mablung set a guard of riders about Morwen and her daughter, and forbade them to go further. But he, seeing from the hill no sign of any enemy, went down with his scouts to the Narog, as stealthily as they could go.

But Glaurung was aware of all that they did, and he came forth in heat of wrath, and lay into the river; and a vast vapour and foul reek went up, in which Mablung and his company were blinded and lost. Then Glaurung passed east over Narog.

Seeing the onset of the dragon the guards upon Amon Ethir sought to lead Morwen and Nienor away, and fly with them with all speed back eastwards; but the wind bore the blank mists upon them, and their horses were maddened by the dragon-stench, and were ungovernable, and ran this way and that, so that some were dashed against trees and were slain, and others were borne far away. Thus the ladies were lost, and of Morwen indeed no sure tidings came ever to Doriath after. But Nienor, being thrown by her steed, yet unhurt, made her way back to Amon Ethir, there to await Mablung, and came thus above the reek into the sunlight; and looking westward she stared straight into the eyes of Glaurung, whose head lay upon the hill-top.

Her will strove with him for a while, but he put forth his power, and having learned who she was he constrained her to gaze into his eyes, and he laid a spell of utter darkness and forgetfulness upon her, so that she could remember nothing that had ever befallen her, nor her own name, nor the name of any other thing; and for many days she could neither hear, nor see, nor stir by her own will. Then Glaurung left her standing alone upon Amon Ethir, and went back to Nargothrond.

Now Mablung, who greatly daring had explored the halls of Felagund when Glaurung left them, fled from them at the approach of the dragon, and returned to Amon Ethir. The sun sank and night fell as he climbed the hill, and he found none there save Nienor, standing alone under the stars as an image of stone. No word she spoke or heard, but would follow, if he took up her hand. Therefore in great grief he led her away, though it seemed to him vain; for they were both like to perish, succourless in the wild.

But they were found by three of Mablung's companions, and slowly they journeyed northward and eastward towards the fences of the land of Doriath beyond Sirion, and the guarded bridge nigh to the inflowing of Esgalduin. Slowly the strength of Nienor returned as they drew nearer to Doriath; but still she could not speak or hear, and walked blindly as she was led. But even as they drew near the fences at last she closed her staring eyes, and would sleep; and they laid her down, and rested also, unheedfully, for they were utterly outworn. There they were assailed by an Orc-band, such as now roamed often as nigh the fences of Doriath as they dared. But Nienor in that hour recovered hearing and sight, and being awakened by the cries of the Orcs she sprang up in terror, and fled ere they could come to her.

Then the Orcs gave chase, and the Elves after; and they overtook the Orcs and slew them ere they could harm her, but Nienor escaped them. For she fled as in a madness of fear, swifter than a deer, and tore off all her clothing as she ran, until she was naked; and she passed out of their sight, running northward, and though they sought her long they found her not, nor any trace of her. And at last Mablung in despair returned to Menegroth and told the tidings. Then Thingol and Melian were filled with grief; but Mablung went forth, and sought long in vain for tidings of Morwen and Nienor.

But Nienor ran on into the woods until she was spent, and then fell, and slept, and awoke; and it was a sunlit morning, and she rejoiced in light as it were a new thing, and all things else that she saw seemed new and strange, for she had no names for them. Nothing did she remember save a darkness that lay behind her, and a shadow of fear; therefore she went warily as a hunted beast, and became famished, for she had no food and knew not how to seek it. But coming at last to the Crossings of Teiglin she passed over, seeking the shelter of the great trees of Brethil, for she was afraid, and it seemed to her that the darkness was overtaking her again from which she had fled.

But it was a great storm of thunder that came up from the south, and in terror she cast herself down upon the mound of Haudh-en-Elleth, stopping her ears from the thunder; but the rain smote her and drenched her, and she lay like a wild beast that is dying. There Turambar found her, as he came to the Crossings of Teiglin, having heard rumour of Orcs that roamed near; and seeing in a flare of lightning the body as it seemed of a slain maiden lying upon the mound of Finduilas he was stricken to the heart. But the woodmen lifted her up, and Turambar cast his cloak about her, and they took her to a lodge nearby, and warmed her, and gave her food. And as soon as she looked upon Turambar she was comforted, for it seemed to her that she had found at last something that she had sought in her darkness; and she would not be parted from him. But when he asked her concerning her name and her kin and her misadventure, then she became troubled as a child that perceives that something is demanded but cannot understand what it may be; and she wept. Therefore Turambar said: 'Do not be troubled. The tale shall wait. But I will give you a name, and I will call you Níniel, Tear-maiden.' And at that name she shook her head, but said: Níniel. That was the first word she spoke after her darkness, and it remained her name among the woodmen ever after.

On the next day they bore her towards Ephel Brandir; but when they came to Dimrost, the Rainy Stair, where the tumbling stream of Celebros fell towards Teiglin, a great shuddering came upon her, wherefore afterwards that place was called Nen Girith, the Shuddering Water. Ere she came to the home of the woodmen upon Amon Obel she was sick of a fever; and long she lay thus, tended by the women of Brethil, and they taught her language as to an infant. But ere the autumn came by the skill of Brandir she was healed of her sickness, and she could speak; but nothing did she remember of the time before she was found by Turambar on the mound of Haudh-en-Elleth. And Brandir loved her; but all her heart was given to Turambar.

In that time the woodmen were not troubled by the Orcs, and Turambar went not to war, and there was peace in Brethil. His heart turned to Níniel, and he asked her in marriage; but for that time she delayed in spite of her love. For Brandir foreboded he knew not what, and sought to restrain her, rather for her sake than his own or rivalry with Turambar; and he revealed to her that Turambar was Túrin son of Húrin, and though she knew not the name a shadow fell upon her mind.

But when three years were passed since the sack of Nargothrond Turambar asked Níniel again, and vowed that now he would wed her, or else go back to war in the wild. And Níniel took him with joy, and they were wedded at the midsummer, and the woodmen of Brethil made a great feast. But ere the end of the year Glaurung sent Orcs of his dominion against Brethil; and Turambar sat at home deedless, for he had promised to Níniel that he would go to battle only if their homes were assailed. But the woodmen were worsted, and Dorlas upbraided him that he would not aid the people that he had taken for his own. Then Turambar arose and brought forth again his black sword, and he gathered a great company of the Men of Brethil, and they defeated the Orcs utterly. But Glaurung heard tidings that the Black Sword was in Brethil, and he pondered what he heard, devising new evil.

In the spring of the year after Níniel conceived, and she became wan and sad; and at the same time there came to Ephel Brandir the first rumours that Glaurung had issued from Nargothrond. Then Turambar sent out scouts far afield, for now he ordered things as he would, and few gave heed to Brandir. As it drew near to summer Glaurung came to the borders of Brethil, and lay near the west shores of Teiglin; and then there was great fear among the woodfolk, for it was now plain that the Great Worm would assail them and ravage their land, and not pass by, returning to Angband, as they had hoped. They sought therefore the counsel of Turambar; and he counselled them that it was vain to go against Glaurung with all their force, for only by cunning and good fortune could they defeat him. He offered therefore himself to seek the dragon on the borders of the land, and bade the rest of the people to remain at Ephel Brandir, but to prepare for flight. For if Glaurung had the victory, he would come first to the woodmen's homes to destroy them, and they could not hope to withstand him; but if they then scattered far and wide, then many might escape, for Glaurung would not take up his dwelling in Brethil, and would return soon to Nargothrond.

Then Turambar asked for companions willing to aid him in his peril; and Dorlas stood forth, but no others. Therefore Dorlas upbraided the people, and spoke scorn of Brandir, who could not play the part of the heir of the house of Haleth; and Brandir was shamed before his people, and was bitter at heart. But Hunthor, kinsman of

Brandir, asked his leave to go in his stead. Then Turambar said farewell to Níniel, and she was filled with fear and foreboding, and their parting was sorrowful; but Turambar set out with his two companions and went to Nen Girith.

Then Níniel being unable to endure her fear, and unwilling to wait in the Ephel tidings of Turambar's fortune, set forth after him, and a great company went with her. At this Brandir was filled all the more with dread, and he sought to dissuade her and the people that would go with her from this rashness, but they heeded him not. Therefore he renounced his lordship, and all love for the people that had scorned him, and having naught left but his love for Níniel he girt himself with a sword and went after her; but being lame he fell far behind.

Now Turambar came to Nen Girith at sundown, and there he learned that Glaurung lay on the brink of the high shores of Teiglin, and was like to move when night fell. Then he called those tidings good; for the dragon lay at Cabed-en-Aras, where the river ran in a deep and narrow gorge that a hunted deer might overleap, and Turambar thought that he would seek no further, but would attempt to pass over the gorge. Therefore he purposed to creep down at dusk, and descend into the ravine under night, and cross over the wild water; and then to climb up the further cliff, and so come to the dragon beneath his guard.

This counsel he took, but the heart of Dorlas failed when they came to the races of Teiglin in the dark, and he dared not attempt the perilous crossing, but drew back and lurked in the woods, burdened with shame. Turambar and Hunthor, nonetheless, crossed over in safety, for the loud roaring of the water drowned all other sounds, and Glaurung slept. But ere the middle-night the dragon roused, and with a great noise and blast cast his forward part across the chasm, and began to draw his bulk after. Turambar and Hunthor were well-nigh overcome by the heat and the stench, as they sought in haste for a way up to come at Glaurung; and Hunthor was slain by a great stone that was dislodged from on high by the passage of the dragon, and smote him on the head and cast him into the river. So he ended, of the house of Haleth not the least valiant.

Then Turambar summoned all his will and courage and climbed the cliff alone, and came beneath the dragon. Then he drew Gurthang, and with all the might of his arm, and of his hate, he thrust it into the soft belly of the Worm, even up to the hilts. But when Glaurung felt his death-pang, he screamed, and in his dreadful throe he heaved up his bulk and hurled himself across the chasm, and there lay lashing and coiling in his agony. And he set all in a blaze about him, and beat all to ruin, until at last his fires died, and he lay still.

Now Gurthang had been wrested from Turambar's hand in the throe of Glaurung, and it clave to the belly of the dragon. Turambar therefore crossed the water once more, desiring to recover his sword and to look upon his foe; and he found him stretched at his length, and rolled upon one side, and the hilts of Gurthang stood in his belly. Then Turambar seized the hilts and set his foot upon the belly, and cried in mockery of the dragon and his words at Nargothrond: 'Hail, Worm of Morgoth! Well met again! Die now and the darkness have thee! Thus is Túrin son of Húrin avenged.'

Then he wrenched out the sword, but a spout of black blood followed it, and fell on his hand, and the venom burned it. And thereupon Glaurung opened his eyes and looked upon Turambar with such malice that it smote him as a blow; and by that stroke and the anguish of the venom he fell into a dark swoon, and lay as one dead, and his sword was beneath him.

The screams of Glaurung rang in the woods, and came to the people that waited at Nen Girith; and when those that looked forth heard them, and saw afar the ruin and burning that the dragon made, they deemed that he had triumphed and was destroying those that assailed him. And Níniel sat and shuddered beside the falling water, and at the voice of Glaurung her darkness crept upon her again, so that she could not stir from that place of her own will.

Even so Brandir found her, for he came to Nen Girith at last, limping wearily; and when he heard that the dragon had crossed the river and had beaten down his foes, his heart yearned towards Níniel in pity. Yet he thought also: 'Turambar is dead, but Níniel lives. Now it may be that she will come with me, and I will lead her away, and so we shall escape from the dragon together.' After a while therefore he stood by Níniel, and he said: 'Come! It is time to go. If you will, I will lead you.' And he took her hand, and she arose silently, and followed him; and in the darkness none saw them go.

But as they went down the path to the Crossings the moon rose, and cast a grey light on the land, and Níniel said: 'Is this the way?' And Brandir answered that he knew no way, save to flee as they might from Glaurung, and escape into the wild. But Níniel said: 'The Black Sword was my beloved and my husband. To seek him only do I go. What else could you think?' And she sped on before him. Thus she came towards the Crossings of Teiglin and beheld Haudh-en-Elleth in the white moonlight, and great dread came on her. Then with a cry she turned away, casting off her cloak, and fled southward along the river, and her white raiment shone in the moon.

Thus Brandir saw her from the hill-side, and turned to cross her path, but he was still behind her when she came to the ruin of Glaurung nigh the brink of Cabed-en-Aras. There she saw the dragon lying, but she heeded him not, for a man lay beside him; and she ran to Turambar, and called his name in vain. Then finding that his hand was burned she washed it with tears and bound it about with a strip of her raiment, and she kissed him and cried on him again to awake. Thereat Glaurung stirred for the last time ere he died, and he spoke with his last breath, saying: 'Hail, Nienor, daughter of Húrin. We meet again ere the end. I give thee joy that thou hast found thy brother at last. And now thou shalt know him: a stabber in the dark, treacherous to foes, faithless to friends, and a curse unto his kin, Túrin son of Húrin! But the worst of all his deeds thou shalt feel in thyself.'

Then Glaurung died, and the veil of his malice was taken from her, and she remembered all the days of her life. Looking down upon Túrin she cried: 'Farewell, O twice beloved! *A Túrin Turambar turun ambartanen:* master of doom by doom mastered! O happy to be dead!' Then Brandir who had heard all, standing stricken upon the edge of ruin, hastened towards her; but she ran from him distraught with horror and anguish, and coming to the brink of Cabed-en-Aras she cast herself over, and was lost in the wild water.

Then Brandir came and looked down, and turned away in horror; and though he no longer desired life, he could not seek death in that roaring water. And thereafter no man looked again upon Cabed-en-Aras, nor would any beast or bird come there, nor any tree grow; and it was named Cabed Naeramarth, the Leap of Dreadful Doom.

But Brandir made his way back to Nen Girith, to bring tidings to the people; and he met Dorlas in the woods, and slew him: the first blood that ever he had spilled, and the last. And he came to Nen Girith, and men cried to him: 'Have you seen her? For Níniel is gone.'

And he answered: 'Níniel is gone for ever. The Dragon is dead, and Turambar is dead; and those tidings are good.' The people murmured at these words, saying that he was crazed; but Brandir said: 'Hear me to the end! Níniel the beloved is also dead. She cast herself into Teiglin, desiring life no more; for she learned that she was none other than Nienor daughter of Húrin of Dor-lómin, ere her forgetfulness came upon her, and that Turambar was her brother, Túrin son of Húrin.'

But even as he ceased, and the people wept, Túrin himself came before them. For when the dragon died, his swoon left him, and he fell into a deep sleep of weariness. But the cold of the night troubled him, and the hilts of Gurthang drove into his side, and he awoke. Then he saw that one had tended his hand, and he wondered much that he was left nonetheless to lie upon the cold ground; and he called, and hearing no answer he went in search of aid, for he was weary and sick.

But when the people saw him they drew back in fear, thinking that it was his unquiet spirit; and he said: 'Nay, be glad; for the Dragon is dead, and I live. But wherefore have you scorned my counsel, and come into peril? And where is Níniel? For her I would see. And surely you did not bring her from her home?'

Then Brandir told him that it was so, and Níniel was dead. But the wife of Dorlas cried out: 'Nay, lord, he is crazed. For he came here saying that you were dead, and he called it good tidings. But you live.'

Then Turambar was wrathful, and believed that all Brandir said or did was done in malice towards himself and Níniel, begrudging their love; and he spoke evilly to Brandir, calling him Club-foot. Then Brandir reported all that he had heard, and named Níniel Nienor daughter of Húrin, and he cried out upon Turambar with the last words of Glaurung, that he was a curse unto his kin and to all that harboured him.

Then Turambar fell into a fury, for in those words he heard the feet of his doom overtaking him; and he charged Brandir with leading Níniel to her death, and publishing with delight the lies of Glaurung, if indeed he devised them not himself. Then he cursed Brandir, and slew him; and he fled from the people into the woods. But after a while his madness left him, and he came to Haudh-en-Elleth, and there sat, and pondered all his deeds. And he cried upon Finduilas to bring him counsel; for he knew not whether he would do now more ill to go to Doriath to seek his kin, or to forsake them for ever and seek death in battle.

And even as he sat there Mablung with a company of Grey-elves came over the Crossings of Teiglin, and he knew Túrin, and hailed him, and was glad indeed to find him yet living; for he had learned of the coming forth of Glaurung and that his path led to Brethil, and also he had heard report that the Black Sword of Nargothrond now dwelt there. Therefore he came to give warning to Túrin, and help if need be; but Túrin said: 'You come too late. The Dragon is dead.'

Then they marvelled, and gave him great praise; but he cared nothing for it, and said: 'This only I ask: give me news of my kin, for in Dor-lómin I learned that they had gone to the Hidden Kingdom.'

Then Mablung was dismayed, but needs must tell to Túrin how Morwen was lost, and Nienor cast into a spell of dumb forgetfulness, and how she escaped them upon the borders of Doriath and fled northwards. Then at last Túrin knew that doom had overtaken him, and that he had slain Brandir unjustly; so that the words of Glaurung were fulfilled in him. And he laughed as one fey, crying: 'This is a bitter jest indeed!' But he bade Mablung go, and return to Doriath, with curses upon it. 'And a curse too upon your errand!' he cried. 'This only was wanting. Now comes the night.'

Then he fled from them like the wind, and they were amazed, wondering what madness had seized him; and they followed after him. But Túrin far out-ran them; and he came to Cabed-en-Aras, and heard the roaring of the water, and saw that all the leaves fell sere from the trees, as though winter had come. There he drew forth his sword, that now alone remained to him of all his possessions, and he said: 'Hail Gurthang! No lord or loyalty dost thou know, save the hand that wieldeth thee. From no blood wilt thou shrink. Wilt thou therefore take Túrin Turambar, wilt thou slay me swiftly?'

And from the blade rang a cold voice in answer: 'Yea, I will drink thy blood gladly, that so I may forget the blood of Beleg my master, and the blood of Brandir slain unjustly. I will slay thee swiftly.'

Then Túrin set the hilts upon the ground, and cast himself upon the point of Gurthang, and the black blade took his life. But Mablung and the Elves came and looked on the shape of Glaurung lying dead, and upon the body of Túrin, and they grieved; and when Men of Brethil came thither, and they learned the reasons of Túrin's madness and death, they were aghast; and Mablung said bitterly: 'I also have been meshed in the doom of the Children of Húrin, and thus with my tidings have slain one that I loved.'

Then they lifted up Túrin, and found that Gurthang had broken asunder. But Elves and Men gathered there great store of wood, and they made a mighty burning, and the Dragon was consumed to ashes. Túrin they laid in a high mound where he had fallen, and the shards of Gurthang were laid beside him. And when all was done, the Elves sang a lament for the Children of Húrin, and a great grey stone was set upon the mound, and thereon was carven in runes of Doriath:

TÚRIN TURAMBAR DAGNIR GLAURUNGA

and beneath they wrote also:

NIENOR NÍNIEL

But she was not there, nor was it ever known whither the cold waters of Teiglin had taken her.

Chapter 22

OF THE RUIN OF DORIATH

So ended the tale of Túrin Turambar; but Morgoth did not sleep nor rest from evil, and his dealings with the house of Hador were not yet ended. Against them his malice was unsated, though Húrin was under his eye, and Morwen wandered distraught in the wild.

Unhappy was the lot of Húrin; for all that Morgoth knew of the working of his malice Húrin knew also, but lies were mingled with the truth, and aught that was good was hidden or distorted. In all ways Morgoth sought most to cast an evil light on those things that Thingol and Melian had done, for he hated them, and feared them. When therefore he judged the time to be ripe, he released Húrin from his bondage, bidding him go whither he would; and he feigned that in this he was moved by pity as for an enemy utterly defeated. But he lied, for his purpose was that Húrin should still further his hatred for Elves and Men, ere he died.

Then little though he trusted the words of Morgoth, knowing indeed that he was without pity, Húrin took his freedom, and went forth in grief, embittered by the words of the Dark Lord; and a year was now gone since the death of Túrin his son. For twenty-eight years he had been captive in Angband, and he was grown grim to look upon. His hair and beard were white and long, but he walked unbowed, bearing a great black staff; and he was girt with a sword. Thus he passed into Hithlum, and tidings came to the chieftains of the Easterlings that there was a great riding of captains and black soldiers of

Angband over the sands of Anfauglith, and with them came an old man, as one that was held in high honour. Therefore they did not lay hands on Húrin, but let him walk at will in those lands; in which they were wise, for the remnant of his own people shunned him, because of his coming from Angband as one in league and honour with Morgoth.

Thus his freedom did but increase the bitterness of Húrin's heart; and he departed from the land of Hithlum and went up into the mountains. Thence he descried far off amid the clouds the peaks of the Crissaegrim, and he remembered Turgon; and he desired to come again to the hidden realm of Gondolin. He went down therefore from Ered Wethrin, and he knew not that the creatures of Morgoth watched all his steps; and crossing over the Brithiach he passed into Dimbar, and came to the dark feet of the Echoriath. All the land was cold and desolate, and he looked about him with little hope, standing at the foot of a great fall of stones beneath a sheer rock-wall; and he knew not that this was all that was now left to see of the old Way of Escape: the Dry River was blocked, and the arched gate was buried. Then Húrin looked up to the grey sky, thinking that he might once more descry the eagles, as he had done long ago in his youth; but he saw only the shadows blown from the east, and clouds swirling about the inaccessible peaks, and he heard only the wind hissing over the stones.

But the watch of the great eagles was now redoubled, and they marked Húrin well, far below, forlorn in the fading light; and straightway Thorondor himself, since the tidings seemed great, brought word to Turgon. But Turgon said: 'Does Morgoth sleep? You were mistaken.'

'Not so,' said Thorondor. 'If the Eagles of Manwë were wont to err thus, then long ago, lord, your hiding would have been in vain.'

'Then your words bode ill,' said Turgon; 'for they can bear but one meaning. Even Húrin Thalion has surrendered to the will of Morgoth. My heart is shut.'

But when Thorondor was gone, Turgon sat long in thought, and he was troubled, remembering the deeds of Húrin of Dor-lómin; and he opened his heart, and sent to the eagles to seek for Húrin, and to bring him if they might to Gondolin. But it was too late, and they never saw him again in light or in shadow.

For Húrin stood in despair before the silent cliffs of the Echoriath, and the westering sun, piercing the clouds, stained his white hair with red. Then he cried aloud in the wilderness, heedless of any ears, and he cursed the pitiless land; and standing at last upon a high rock he looked towards Gondolin and called in a great voice: 'Turgon, Turgon, remember the Fen of Serech! O Turgon, will you not hear in your hidden halls?' But there was no sound save the wind in the dry grasses. 'Even so they hissed in Serech at the sunset,' he said; and as he spoke the sun went behind the Mountains of Shadow, and a darkness fell about him, and the wind ceased, and there was silence in the waste.

Yet there were ears that heard the words that Húrin spoke, and report of all came soon to the Dark Throne in the north; and Morgoth smiled, for he knew now clearly in what region Turgon dwelt, though because of the eagles no spy of his could yet come within sight of the land behind the Encircling Mountains. This was the first evil that the freedom of Húrin achieved.

As darkness fell Húrin stumbled from the rock, and fell into a heavy sleep of grief. But in his sleep he heard the voice of Morwen lamenting, and often she spoke his name; and it seemed to him that her voice came out of Brethil. Therefore when he awoke with the coming of day he arose, and went back to the Brithiach; and passing along the eaves of Brethil he came at a time of night to the Crossings of Teiglin. The night-sentinels saw him, but they were filled with dread, for they thought that they saw a ghost out of some ancient battle-mound that walked with darkness about it; and therefore Húrin was not stayed, and he came at last to the place of the burning of Glaurung, and saw the tall stone standing near the brink of Cabed Naeramarth.

But Húrin did not look at the stone, for he knew what was written there; and his eyes had seen that he was not alone. Sitting in the shadow of the stone there was a woman, bent over her knees; and as Húrin stood there silent she cast back her tattered hood and lifted her face. Grey she was and old, but suddenly her eyes looked into his, and he knew her; for though they were wild and full of fear, that light still gleamed in them that long ago had earned for her the name Eledhwen, proudest and most beautiful of mortal women in the days of old.

'You come at last,' she said. 'I have waited too long.'

'It was a dark road. I have come as I could,' he answered.

'But you are too late,' said Morwen. 'They are lost.'

'I know it,' he said. 'But you are not.'

But Morwen said: 'Almost. I am spent. I shall go with the sun. Now little time is left: if you know, tell me! How did she find him?'

But Húrin did not answer, and they sat beside the stone, and did not speak again; and when the sun went down Morwen sighed and clasped his hand, and was still; and Húrin knew that she had died. He looked down at her in the twilight and it seemed to him that the lines of grief and cruel hardship were smoothed away. 'She was not conquered,' he said; and he closed her eyes, and sat unmoving beside her as the night drew down. The waters of Cabed Naeramarth roared on, but he heard no sound, and he saw nothing, and felt nothing, for his heart was stone within him. But there came a chill wind that drove sharp rain into his face; and he was roused, and anger rose in him like smoke, mastering reason, so that all his desire was to seek vengeance for his wrongs and for the wrongs of his kin, accusing in his anguish all those who ever had dealings with them. Then he rose up, and he made a grave for Morwen above Cabed Naeramarth on the west side of the stone; and upon it he cut these words: *Here lies also Morwen Eledhwen.*

It is told that a seer and harp-player of Brethil named Glirhuin made a song, saying that the Stone of the Hapless should not be defiled by Morgoth nor ever thrown down, not though the sea should drown all the land; as after indeed befell, and still Tol Morwen stands alone in the water beyond the new coasts that were made in the days of the wrath of the Valar. But Húrin does not lie there, for his doom drove him on, and the Shadow still followed him.

Now Húrin crossed over Teiglin and passed southwards down the ancient road that led to Nargothrond; and he saw far off to the eastward the lonely height of Amon Rûdh, and knew what had befallen there. At length he came to the banks of Narog, and ventured the passage of the wild river upon the fallen stones of the bridge, as Mablung of Doriath had ventured it before him; and he stood before the broken Doors of Felagund, leaning upon his staff.

Here it must be told that after the departure of Glaurung Mîm the Petty-Dwarf had found his way to Nargothrond, and crept within the ruined halls; and he took possession of them, and sat there fingering the gold and the gems, letting them run ever through his hands, for none came nigh to despoil him, from dread of the spirit of Glaurung and his very memory. But now one had come, and stood upon the threshold; and Mîm came forth, and demanded to know his purpose. But Húrin said: 'Who are you, that would hinder me from entering the house of Finrod Felagund?'

Then the Dwarf answered: 'I am Mîm; and before the proud ones came from over the Sea, Dwarves delved the halls of Nulukkizdîn. I have but returned to take what is mine; for I am the last of my people.'

'Then you shall enjoy your inheritance no longer,' said Húrin; 'for I am Húrin son of Galdor, returned out of Angband, and my son was Túrin Turambar, whom you have not forgotten; and he it was that slew Glaurung the Dragon, who wasted these halls where now you sit; and not unknown is it to me by whom the Dragon-helm of Dor-lómin was betrayed.'

Then Mîm in great fear besought Húrin to take what he would, but to spare his life; but Húrin gave no heed to his prayer, and slew him there before the doors of Nargothrond. Then he entered in, and stayed a while in that dreadful place, where the treasures of Valinor lay strewn upon the floors in darkness and decay; but it is told that when Húrin came forth from the wreck of Nargothrond and stood again beneath the sky he bore with him out of all that great hoard but one thing only.

Now Húrin journeyed eastward, and he came to the Meres of Twilight above the Falls of Sirion; and there he was taken by the Elves that guarded the western marches of Doriath, and brought before King Thingol in the Thousand Caves. Then Thingol was filled with wonder and grief when he looked on him, and knew that grim and aged man for Húrin Thalion, the captive of Morgoth; but he greeted him fairly and showed him honour. Húrin made no answer to the King, but drew forth from beneath his cloak that one thing which he had taken with him out of Nargothrond; and that was no lesser treasure than the Nauglamír, the Necklace of the Dwarves, that was made for Finrod Felagund long years before by the craftsmen of Nogrod and Belegost, most famed of all their works in the Elder Days, and prized by Finrod while he lived above all the treasures of Nargothrond. And Húrin cast it at the feet of Thingol with wild and bitter words.

'Receive thou thy fee,' he cried, 'for thy fair keeping of my children and my wife! For this is the Nauglamír, whose name is known to many among Elves and Men; and I bring it to thee out of the darkness of Nargothrond, where Finrod thy kinsman left it behind him when he set forth with Beren son of Barahir to fulfil the errand of Thingol of Doriath!'

Then Thingol looked upon the great treasure, and knew it for the Nauglamír, and well did he understand Húrin's intent; but being filled with pity he restrained his wrath, and endured Húrin's scorn. And at the last Melian spoke, and said: 'Húrin Thalion, Morgoth hath bewitched thee; for he that seeth through Morgoth's eyes, willing or unwilling, seeth all things crooked. Long was Túrin thy son fostered in the halls of Menegroth, and shown love and honour as the son of the

King; and it was not by the King's will nor by mine that he came never back to Doriath. And afterwards thy wife and thy daughter were harboured here with honour and goodwill; and we sought by all means that we might to dissuade Morwen from the road to Nargothrond. With the voice of Morgoth thou dost now upbraid thy friends.'

And hearing the words of Melian Húrin stood moveless, and he gazed long into the eyes of the Queen; and there in Menegroth, defended still by the Girdle of Melian from the darkness of the Enemy, he read the truth of all that was done, and tasted at last the fullness of woe that was measured for him by Morgoth Bauglir. And he spoke no more of what was past, but stooping lifted up the Nauglamír from where it lay before Thingol's chair, and he gave it to him, saying: 'Receive now, lord, the Necklace of the Dwarves, as a gift from one who has nothing, and as a memorial of Húrin of Dor-lómin. For now my fate is fulfilled, and the purpose of Morgoth achieved; but I am his thrall no longer.'

Then he turned away, and passed out from the Thousand Caves, and all that saw him fell back before his face; and none sought to withstand his going, nor did any know whither he went. But it is said that Húrin would not live thereafter, being bereft of all purpose and desire, and cast himself at last into the western sea; and so ended the mightiest of the warriors of mortal Men.

But when Húrin was gone from Menegroth, Thingol sat long in silence, gazing upon the great treasure that lay upon his knees; and it came into his mind that it should be remade, and in it should be set the Silmaril. For as the years passed Thingol's thought turned unceasingly to the jewel of Fëanor, and became bound to it, and he liked not to let it rest even behind the doors of his inmost treasury; and he was minded now to bear it with him always, waking and sleeping.

In those days the Dwarves still came on their journeys into Beleriand from their mansions in Ered Lindon, and passing over Gelion at Sarn Athrad, the Ford of Stones, they travelled the ancient road to Doriath; for their skill in the working of metal and stone was very great, and there was much need of their craft in the halls of Menegroth. But they came now no longer in small parties as aforetime, but in great companies well armed for their protection in the perilous lands between Aros and Gelion; and they dwelt in Menegroth at such times in chambers and smithies set apart for them. At that very time great craftsmen of Nogrod were lately come into Doriath; and the King therefore summoning them declared his desire, that if their skill were great enough they should remake the Nauglamír, and in it set the Silmaril. Then the Dwarves looked upon the work of their fathers, and they beheld with wonder the shining jewel of Fëanor; and they were filled with a great lust to possess them, and carry them off to their far homes in the mountains. But they dissembled their mind, and consented to the task.

Long was their labour; and Thingol went down alone to their deep smithies, and sat ever among them as they worked. In time his desire was achieved, and the greatest of the works of Elves and Dwarves were brought together and made one; and its beauty was very great, for now the countless jewels of the Nauglamír did reflect and cast abroad in marvellous hues the light of the Silmaril amidmost. Then Thingol, being alone among them, made to take it up and clasp it about his neck; but the Dwarves in that moment withheld it from him, and demanded that he yield it up to them, saying: 'By what right does the Elvenking lay claim to the Nauglamír, that was made by our fathers for Finrod Felagund who is dead? It has come to him but by the hand of Húrin the Man of Dor-lómin, who took it as a thief out of the darkness of Nargothrond.' But Thingol perceived their hearts, and saw well that desiring the Silmaril they sought but a pretext and fair cloak for their true intent; and in his wrath and pride he gave no heed to his peril, but spoke to them in scorn, saying: 'How do ye of uncouth race dare to demand aught of me, Elu Thingol, Lord of Beleriand, whose life began by the waters of Cuiviénen years uncounted ere the fathers of the stunted people awoke?' And standing tall and proud among them he bade them with shameful words be gone unrequited out of Doriath.

Then the lust of the Dwarves was kindled to rage by the words of the King; and they rose up about him, and laid hands on him, and slew him as he stood. So died in the deep places of Menegroth Elwë Singollo, King of Doriath, who alone of all the Children of Ilúvatar was joined with one of the Ainur; and he who, alone of the Forsaken Elves, had seen the light of the Trees of Valinor, with his last sight gazed upon the Silmaril.

Then the Dwarves taking the Nauglamír passed out of Menegroth and fled eastwards through Region. But tidings went swiftly through the forest, and few of that company came over Aros, for they were pursued to the death as they sought the eastward road; and the Nauglamír was retaken, and brought back in bitter grief to Melian the Queen. Yet two there were of the slayers of Thingol who escaped from the pursuit on the eastern marches, and returned at last to their city far off in the Blue Mountains; and there in Nogrod they told somewhat of all that had befallen, saying that the Dwarves were slain in Doriath by command of the Elvenking, who thus would cheat them of their reward.

Then great was the wrath and lamentation of the Dwarves of Nogrod for the death of their kin and their great craftsmen, and they tore their beards, and wailed; and long they sat taking thought for vengeance. It is told that they asked aid from Belegost, but it was denied them, and the Dwarves of Belegost sought to dissuade them from their purpose; but their counsel was unavailing, and ere long a great host came forth from Nogrod, and crossing over Gelion marched westward through Beleriand.

Upon Doriath a heavy change had fallen. Melian sat long in silence beside Thingol the King, and her thought passed back into the starlit years and to their first meeting among the nightingales of Nan Elmoth in ages past; and she knew that her parting from Thingol was the forerunner of a greater parting, and that the doom of Doriath was drawing nigh. For Melian was of the divine race of the Valar, and she was a Maia of great power and wisdom; but for love of Elwë Singollo she took upon herself the form of the Elder Children of Ilúvatar, and in that union she became bound by the chain and trammels of the flesh of Arda. In that form she bore to him Lúthien Tinúviel; and in that form she gained a power over the substance of Arda, and by the Girdle of Melian was Doriath defended through long ages from the evils without. But now Thingol lay dead, and his spirit had passed to the halls of Mandos; and with his death a change came also upon Melian. Thus it came to pass that her power was withdrawn in that time from the forests of Neldoreth and Region, and Esgalduin the enchanted river spoke with a different voice, and Doriath lay open to its enemies.

Thereafter Melian spoke to none save to Mablung only, bidding him take heed to the Silmaril, and to send word speedily to Beren and Lúthien in Ossiriand; and she vanished out of Middle-earth, and passed to the land of the Valar beyond the western sea, to muse upon her sorrows in the gardens of Lórien, whence she came, and this tale speaks of her no more.

Thus it was that the host of the Naugrim crossing over Aros passed unhindered into the woods of Doriath; and none withstood them, for they were many and fierce, and the captains of the Grey-elves were cast into doubt and despair, and went hither and thither purposeless. But the Dwarves held on their way, and passed over the great bridge, and entered into Menegroth; and there befell a thing most grievous among the sorrowful deeds of the Elder Days. For there was battle in the Thousand Caves, and many Elves and Dwarves were slain; and it has not been forgotten. But the Dwarves were victorious, and the halls of Thingol were ransacked and plundered. There fell Mablung of the Heavy Hand before the doors of the treasury wherein lay the Nauglamír; and the Silmaril was taken.

At that time Beren and Lúthien yet dwelt in Tol Galen, the Green Isle, in the River Adurant, southernmost of the streams that falling from Ered Lindon flowed down to join with Gelion; and their son Dior Eluchíl had to wife Nimloth, kinswoman of Celeborn, prince of Doriath, who was wedded to the Lady Galadriel. The sons of Dior and Nimloth were Eluréd and Elurín; and a daughter also was born to them, and she was named Elwing, which is Star-spray, for she was born on a night of stars, whose light glittered in the spray of the waterfall of Lanthir Lamath beside her father's house.

Now word went swiftly among the Elves of Ossiriand that a great host of Dwarves bearing gear of war had come down out of the mountains and passed over Gelion at the Ford of Stones. These tidings came soon to Beren and Lúthien; and in that time also a messenger came to them out of Doriath telling of what had befallen there. Then Beren arose and left Tol Galen, and summoning to him Dior his son they went north to the River Ascar; and with them went many of the Green-elves of Ossiriand.

Thus it came to pass that when the Dwarves of Nogrod, returning from Menegroth with diminished host, came again to Sarn Athrad, they were assailed by unseen enemies; for as they climbed up Gelion's banks burdened with the spoils of Doriath, suddenly all the woods were filled with the sound of elven-horns, and shafts sped upon them from every side. There very many of the Dwarves were slain in the first onset; but some escaping from the ambush held together, and fled eastwards towards the mountains. And as they climbed the long slopes beneath Mount Dolmed there came forth the Shepherds of the Trees, and they drove the Dwarves into the shadowy woods of Ered Lindon: whence, it is said, came never one to climb the high passes that led to their homes.

In that battle by Sarn Athrad Beren fought his last fight, and himself slew the Lord of Nogrod, and wrested from him the Necklace of the Dwarves; but he dying laid his curse upon all the treasure. Then Beren gazed in wonder on the selfsame jewel of Fëanor that he had cut from Morgoth's iron crown, now shining set amid gold and gems by the cunning of the Dwarves; and he washed it clean of blood in the waters of the river. And when all was finished the treasure of Doriath was drowned in the River Ascar, and from that time the river was named anew, Rathlóriel, the Goldenbed; but Beren took the Nauglamír and returned to Tol Galen. Little did it ease the grief of Lúthien to learn that the Lord of Nogrod was slain and many Dwarves beside; but it is said and sung that Lúthien wearing that necklace and that immortal jewel was the vision of greatest beauty and glory that has ever been outside the realm of Valinor; and for a little while the Land of the Dead that Live became like a vision of the land of the Valar, and no place has been since so fair, so fruitful, or so filled with light.

Now Dior Thingol's heir bade farewell to Beren and Lúthien, and departing from Lanthir Lamath with Nimloth his wife he came to Menegroth, and abode there; and with them went their young sons Eluréd and Elurín, and Elwing their daughter. Then the Sindar received them with joy, and they arose from the darkness of their grief for fallen kin and King and for the departure of Melian; and Dior Eluchíl set himself to raise anew the glory of the kingdom of Doriath.

There came a night of autumn, and when it grew late, one came and smote upon the doors of Menegroth, demanding admittance to the King. He was a lord of the Green-elves hastening from Ossiriand, and the door-wards brought him to where Dior sat alone in his chamber; and there in silence he gave to the King a coffer, and took his leave. But in that coffer lay the Necklace of the Dwarves, wherein was set the Silmaril; and Dior looking upon it knew it for a sign that Beren Erchamion and Lúthien Tinúviel had died indeed, and gone where go the race of Men to a fate beyond the world.

Long did Dior gaze upon the Silmaril, which his father and mother had brought beyond hope out of the terror of Morgoth; and his grief was great that death had come upon them so soon. But the wise have said that the Silmaril hastened their end; for the flame of the beauty of Lúthien as she wore it was too bright for mortal lands.

Then Dior arose, and about his neck he clasped the Nauglamír; and now he appeared as the fairest of all the children of the world, of threefold race: of the Edain, and of the Eldar, and of the Maiar of the Blessed Realm.

But now the rumour ran among the scattered Elves of Beleriand that Dior Thingol's heir wore the Nauglamír, and they said: 'A Silmaril of Fëanor burns again in the woods of Doriath'; and the oath of the sons of Fëanor was waked again from sleep. For while Lúthien wore the Necklace of the Dwarves no Elf would dare to assail her; but now hearing of the renewal of Doriath and of Dior's pride the seven gathered again from wandering, and they sent to him to claim their own.

But Dior returned no answer to the sons of Fëanor; and Celegorm stirred up his brothers to prepare an assault upon Doriath. They came at unawares in the middle of winter, and fought with Dior in the Thousand Caves; and so befell the second slaying of Elf by Elf. There fell Celegorm by Dior's hand, and there fell Curufin, and dark Caranthir; but Dior was slain also, and Nimloth his wife, and the cruel servants of Celegorm seized his young sons and left them to starve in the forest. Of this Maedhros indeed repented, and sought for them long in the woods of Doriath; but his search was unavailing, and of the fate of Eluréd and Elurín no tale tells.

Thus Doriath was destroyed, and never rose again. But the sons of Fëanor gained not what they sought; for a remnant of the people fled before them, and with them was Elwing Dior's daughter, and they escaped, and bearing with them the Silmaril they came in time to the mouths of the River Sirion by the sea.

Chapter 23

OF TUOR AND THE FALL OF GONDOLIN

It has been told that Huor the brother of Húrin was slain in the Battle of Unnumbered Tears; and in the winter of that year Rían his wife bore a child in the wilds of Mithrim, and he was named Tuor, and was taken to foster by Annael of the Grey-elves, who yet lived in those hills. Now when Tuor was sixteen years old the Elves were minded to leave the caves of Androth where they dwelt, and to make their way secretly to the Havens of Sirion in the distant south; but they were assailed by Orcs and Easterlings before they made good their escape, and Tuor was taken captive and enslaved by Lorgan, chief of the Easterlings of Hithlum. For three years he endured that thraldom, but at the end of that time he escaped; and returning to the caves of Androth he dwelt there alone, and did such great hurt to the Easterlings that Lorgan set a price upon his head.

But when Tuor had lived thus in solitude as an outlaw for four years, Ulmo set it in his heart to depart from the land of his fathers, for he had chosen Tuor as the instrument of his designs; and leaving once more the caves of Androth he went westwards across Dor-lómin, and found Annon-in-Gelydh, the Gate of the Noldor, which the people of Turgon built when they dwelt in Nevrast long years before. Thence a dark tunnel led beneath the mountains, and issued into Cirith Ninniach, the Rainbow Cleft, through which a turbulent water ran towards the western sea. Thus it was that Tuor's flight from Hithlum was marked by neither Man nor Orc, and no knowledge of it came to the ears of Morgoth.

And Tuor came into Nevrast, and looking upon Belegaer the Great Sea he was enamoured of it, and the sound of it and the longing for it were ever in his heart and ear, and an unquiet was on him that took him at last into the depths of the realms of Ulmo. Then he dwelt in Nevrast alone, and the summer of that year passed, and the doom of Nargothrond drew near; but when the autumn came he saw seven great swans flying south, and he knew them for a sign that he had tarried overlong, and he followed their flight along the shores of the sea. Thus he came at length to the deserted halls of Vinyamar beneath Mount Taras, and he entered in, and found there the shield and hauberk, and the sword and helm, that Turgon had left there by the command of Ulmo long before; and he arrayed himself in those arms, and went down to the shore. But there came a great storm out of the west, and out of that storm Ulmo the Lord of Waters arose in majesty and spoke to Tuor as he stood beside the sea. And Ulmo bade him depart from that place and seek out the hidden kingdom of Gondolin; and he gave Tuor a great cloak, to mantle him in shadow from the eyes of his enemies.

But in the morning when the storm was passed, Tuor came upon an Elf standing beside the walls of Vinyamar; and he was Voronwë, son of Aranwë, of Gondolin, who sailed in the last ship that Turgon sent into the West. But when that ship returning at last out of the deep ocean foundered in the great storm within sight of the coasts of Middle-earth, Ulmo took him up, alone of all its mariners, and cast him onto the land near Vinyamar; and learning of the command laid upon Tuor by the Lord of Waters Voronwë was filled with wonder, and did not refuse him his guidance to the hidden door of Gondolin. Therefore they set out together from that place, and as the Fell Winter of that year came down upon them out of the north they went warily eastward under the eaves of the Mountains of Shadow.

At length they came in their journeying to the Pools of Ivrin, and looked with grief on the defilement wrought there by the passage of Glaurung the Dragon; but even as they gazed upon it they saw one going northward in haste, and he was a tall Man, clad in black, and bearing a black sword. But they knew not who he was, nor anything of what had befallen in the south; and he passed them by, and they said no word.

And at the last by the power that Ulmo set upon them they came to the hidden door of Gondolin, and passing down the tunnel they reached the inner gate, and were taken by the guard as prisoners. Then they were led up the mighty ravine of Orfalch Echor, barred by seven gates, and brought before Ecthelion of the Fountain, the warden of the great gate at the end of the climbing road; and there Tuor cast aside his cloak, and from the arms that he bore from Vinyamar it was seen that he was in truth one sent by Ulmo. Then Tuor looked down upon the fair vale of Tumladen, set as a green jewel amid the encircling hills; and he saw far off upon the rocky height of Amon Gwareth Gondolin the great, city of seven names, whose fame and glory is mightiest in song of all dwellings of the Elves in the Hither Lands. At the bidding of Ecthelion trumpets were blown on the towers of the great gate, and they echoed in the hills; and far off but clear there came a sound of answering trumpets blown upon the white walls of the city, flushed with the rose of dawn upon the plain.

Thus it was that the son of Huor rode across Tumladen, and came to the gate of Gondolin; and passing up the wide stairways of the city he was brought at last to the Tower of the King, and looked upon the images of the Trees of Valinor. Then Tuor stood before Turgon son of Fingolfin, High King of the Noldor, and upon the King's right hand there stood Maeglin his sister-son, but upon his left hand sat Idril Celebrindal his daughter; and all that heard the voice of Tuor marvelled, doubting that this were in truth a Man of mortal race, for his words were the words of the Lord of Waters that came to him in that hour. And he gave warning to Turgon that the Curse of Mandos now hastened to its fulfilment, when all the works of the Noldor should perish; and he bade him depart, and abandon the fair and mighty city that he had built, and go down Sirion to the sea.

Then Turgon pondered long the counsel of Ulmo, and there came into his mind the words that were spoken to him in Vinyamar: 'Love not too well the work of thy hands and the devices of thy heart; and remember that the true hope of the Noldor lieth in the West, and cometh from the Sea.' But Turgon was become proud, and Gondolin as beautiful as a memory of Elven Tirion, and he trusted still in its secret and impregnable strength, though even a Vala should gainsay it; and after the Nirnaeth Arnoediad the people of that city desired never again to mingle in the woes of Elves and Men without, nor to return through dread and danger into the West. Shut behind their pathless and enchanted hills they suffered none to enter, though he fled from Morgoth hate-pursued; and tidings of the lands beyond came to them faint and far, and they heeded them little. The spies of Angband sought for them in vain; and their dwelling was as a rumour, and a secret that none could find. Maeglin spoke ever against Tuor in the councils of the King, and his words seemed the more weighty in that they went with Turgon's heart; and at the last he rejected the bidding of Ulmo and refused his counsel. But in the warning of the Vala he heard again the words that were spoken before the departing Noldor on the coast of Araman long ago; and the fear of treason was wakened in Turgon's heart. Therefore in that time the very entrance to the hidden door in the Encircling Mountains was caused to be blocked up; and thereafter none went ever forth from Gondolin on any errand of peace or war, while that city stood. Tidings were brought by Thorondor Lord of Eagles of the fall of Nargothrond, and after of the slaying of Thingol and of Dior his heir, and of the ruin of Doriath; but Turgon shut his ear to word of the woes without, and vowed to march never at the side of any son of Fëanor; and his people he forbade ever to pass the leaguer of the hills.

And Tuor remained in Gondolin, for its bliss and its beauty and the wisdom of its people held him enthralled; and he became mighty in stature and in mind, and learned deeply of the lore of the exiled Elves. Then the heart of Idril was turned to him, and his to her; and Maeglin's secret hatred grew ever greater, for he desired above all things to possess her, the only heir of the King of Gondolin. But so high did Tuor stand in the favour of the King that when he had dwelt there for seven years Turgon did not refuse him even the hand of his daughter; for though he would not heed the bidding of Ulmo, he perceived that the fate of the Noldor was wound with the one whom Ulmo had sent; and he did not forget the words that Huor spoke to him before the host of Gondolin departed from the Battle of Unnumbered Tears.

Then there was made a great and joyful feast, for Tuor had won the hearts of all that people, save only of Maeglin and his secret following; and thus there came to pass the second union of Elves and Men.

In the spring of the year after was born in Gondolin Eärendil Half-elven, the son of Tuor and Idril Celebrindal; and that was five hundred years and three since the coming of the Noldor to Middle-earth. Of surpassing beauty was Eärendil, for a light was in his face as the light of heaven, and he had the beauty and the wisdom of the Eldar and the strength and hardihood of the Men of old; and the Sea spoke ever in his ear and heart, even as with Tuor his father.

Then the days of Gondolin were yet full of joy and peace; and none knew that the region wherein the Hidden Kingdom lay had been at last revealed to Morgoth by the cries of Húrin, when standing in the wilderness beyond the Encircling Mountains and finding no entrance he called on Turgon in despair. Thereafter the thought of Morgoth was bent unceasing on the mountainous land between Anach and the upper waters of Sirion, whither his servants had never passed; yet still no spy or creature out of Angband could come there because of the vigilance of the eagles, and Morgoth was thwarted in the fulfilment of his designs. But Idril Celebrindal was wise and far-seeing, and her heart misgave her, and foreboding crept upon her spirit as a cloud. Therefore in that time she let prepare a secret way, that should lead down from the city and passing out beneath the surface of the plain issue far beyond the walls, northward of Amon Gwareth; and she contrived it that the work was known but to few, and no whisper of it came to Maeglin's ears.

Now on a time, when Eärendil was yet young, Maeglin was lost. For he, as has been told, loved mining and quarrying after metals above all other craft; and he was master and leader of the Elves who worked in the mountains distant from the city, seeking after metals for their smithying of things both of peace and war. But often Maeglin went with few of his folk beyond the leaguer of the hills, and the King knew not that his bidding was defied; and thus it came to pass, as fate willed, that Maeglin was taken prisoner by Orcs, and brought to Angband. Maeglin was no weakling or craven, but the torment wherewith he was threatened cowed his spirit, and he purchased his life and freedom by revealing to Morgoth the very place of Gondolin and the ways whereby it might be found and assailed. Great indeed was the joy of Morgoth, and to Maeglin he promised the lordship of Gondolin as his vassal, and the possession of Idril Celebrindal, when the city should be taken; and indeed desire for Idril and hatred for Tuor led Maeglin the easier to his treachery, most infamous in all the histories of the Elder Days. But Morgoth sent him back to Gondolin, lest any should suspect the betrayal, and so that Maeglin should aid the assault from within, when the hour came; and he abode in the halls of the King with smiling face and evil in his heart, while the darkness gathered ever deeper upon Idril.

At last, in the year when Eärendil was seven years old, Morgoth was ready, and he loosed upon Gondolin his Balrogs, and his Orcs, and his wolves; and with them came dragons of the brood of Glaurung, and they were become now many and terrible. The host of Morgoth came over the northern hills where the height was greatest and the watch least vigilant, and it came at night upon a time of festival, when all the people of Gondolin were upon the walls to await the rising sun, and sing their songs at its uplifting; for the morrow was the great feast that they named the Gates of Summer. But the red light mounted the hills in the north and not in the east; and there was no stay in the advance of the foe until they were beneath the very walls of Gondolin, and the city was beleaguered without hope. Of the deeds of desperate valour there done, by the chieftains of the noble houses and their warriors, and not least by Tuor, much is told in *The Fall of Gondolin:* of the battle of Ecthelion of the Fountain with Gothmog Lord of Balrogs in the very square of the King, where each slew the other, and of the defence of the tower of Turgon by the people of his household, until the tower was overthrown; and mighty was its fall and the fall of Turgon in its ruin.

Tuor sought to rescue Idril from the sack of the city, but Maeglin had laid hands on her, and on Eärendil; and Tuor fought with Maeglin on the walls, and cast him far out, and his body as it fell smote the rocky slopes of Amon Gwareth thrice ere it pitched into the flames below. Then Tuor and Idril led such remnants of the people of Gondolin as they could gather in the confusion of the burning down the secret way which Idril had prepared; and of that passage the captains of Angband knew nothing, and thought not that any fugitives would take a path towards the north and the highest parts of the mountains and the nighest to Angband. The fume of the burning, and the steam of the fair fountains of Gondolin withering in the flame of the dragons of the north, fell upon the vale of Tumladen in mournful mists; and thus was the escape of Tuor and his company aided, for there was still a long and open road to follow from the tunnel's mouth to the foothills of the mountains. Nonetheless they came thither, and beyond hope they climbed, in woe and misery, for the high places were cold and terrible, and they had among them many that were wounded, and women and children.

There was a dreadful pass, Cirith Thoronath it was named, the Eagles' Cleft, where beneath the shadow of the highest peaks a narrow path wound its way; on the right hand it was walled by a precipice, and on the left a dreadful fall leapt into emptiness. Along that narrow way their march was strung, when they were ambushed by Orcs, for Morgoth had set watchers all about the encircling hills; and a Balrog was with them. Then dreadful was their plight, and hardly would they have been saved by the valour of yellow-haired Glorfindel, chief of the House of the Golden Flower of Gondolin, had not Thorondor come timely to their aid.

Many are the songs that have been sung of the duel of Glorfindel with the Balrog upon a pinnacle of rock in that high place; and both fell to ruin in the abyss. But the eagles coming stooped upon the Orcs, and drove them shrieking back; and all were slain or cast into the deeps, so that rumour of the escape from Gondolin came not until long after to Morgoth's ears. Then Thorondor bore up Glorfindel's body out of the abyss, and they buried him in a mound of stones beside the pass; and a green turf came there, and yellow flowers bloomed upon it amid the barrenness of stone, until the world was changed.

Thus led by Tuor son of Huor the remnant of Gondolin passed over the mountains, and came down into the Vale of Sirion; and fleeing southward by weary and dangerous marches they came at length to Nan-tathren, the Land of Willows, for the power of Ulmo yet ran in the great river, and it was about them. There they rested a while, and were healed of their hurts and weariness; but their sorrow could not be healed. And they made a feast in memory of Gondolin and of the Elves that had perished there, the maidens, and the wives, and the warriors of the King; and for Glorfindel the beloved many were the songs they sang, under the willows of Nan-tathren in the waning of the year. There Tuor made a song for Eärendil his son, concerning the coming of Ulmo the Lord of Waters to the shores of Nevrast aforetime; and the sea-longing woke in his heart, and in his son's also. Therefore Idril and Tuor departed from Nan-tathren, and went southwards down the river to the sea; and they dwelt there by the mouths of Sirion, and joined their people to the company of Elwing Dior's daughter, that had fled thither but a little while before. And when the tidings came to Balar of the fall of Gondolin and the death of Turgon, Ereinion Gil-galad son of Fingon was named High King of the Noldor in Middle-earth.

But Morgoth thought that his triumph was fulfilled, recking little of the sons of Fëanor, and of their oath, which had harmed him never and turned always to his mightiest aid; and in his black thought he laughed, regretting not the one Silmaril that he had lost, for by it as he deemed the last shred of the people of the Eldar should vanish from Middle-earth and trouble it no more. If he knew of the dwelling by the waters of Sirion, he gave no sign, biding his time, and waiting upon the working of oath and lie. Yet by Sirion and the sea there grew up an Elven-folk, the gleanings of Doriath and Gondolin; and from Balar the mariners of Círdan came among them, and they took to the waves and the building of ships, dwelling ever nigh to the coasts of Arvernien, under the shadow of Ulmo's hand.

And it is said that in that time Ulmo came to Valinor out of the deep waters, and spoke there to the Valar of the need of the Elves; and he called on them to forgive them, and rescue them from the overmastering might of Morgoth, and win back the Simarils, wherein alone now bloomed the light of the Days of Bliss when the Two Trees still shone in Valinor. But Manwë moved not; and of the counsels of his heart what tale shall tell? The wise have said that the hour was not yet come, and that only one speaking in person for the cause of both Elves and Men, pleading for pardon on their misdeeds and pity on their woes, might move the counsels of the Powers; and the oath of Fëanor perhaps even Manwë could not loose, until it found its end, and the sons of Fëanor relinquished the Silmarils, upon which they had laid their ruthless claim. For the light which lit the Silmarils the Valar themselves had made.

In those days Tuor felt old age creep upon him, and ever a longing for the deeps of the Sea grew stronger in his heart. Therefore he built a great ship, and he named it Eärrámë, which is Sea-Wing; and with Idril Celebrindal he set sail into the sunset and the West, and came no more into any tale or song. But in after days it was sung that Tuor alone of mortal Men was numbered among the elder race, and was joined with the Noldor, whom he loved; and his fate is sundered from the fate of Men.

Chapter 24

OF THE VOYAGE OF EÄRENDIL AND THE WAR OF WRATH

Bright Eärendil was then lord of the people that dwelt nigh to Sirion's mouths; and he took to wife Elwing the fair, and she bore to him Elrond and Elros, who are called the Half-elven. Yet Eärendil could not rest, and his voyages about the shores of the Hither Lands eased not his unquiet. Two purposes grew in his heart, blended as one in longing for the wide Sea: he sought to sail thereon, seeking after Tuor and Idril who returned not; and he thought to find perhaps the last shore, and bring ere he died the message of Elves and Men to the Valar in the West, that should move their hearts to pity for the sorrows of Middle-earth.

Now Eärendil became fast in friendship with Círdan the Shipwright, who dwelt on the Isle of Balar with those of his people who escaped from the sack of the Havens of Brithombar and Eglarest. With the aid of Círdan Eärendil built Vingilot, the Foam-flower, fairest of the ships of song; golden were its oars and white its timbers, hewn in the birchwoods of Nimbrethil, and its sails were as the argent moon. In the *Lay of Eärendil* is many a thing sung of his adventures in the deep and in lands untrodden, and in many seas and in many isles; but Elwing was not with him, and she sat in sorrow by the mouths of Sirion.

Eärendil found not Tuor nor Idril, nor came he ever on that journey to the shores of Valinor, defeated by shadows and enchantment, driven by repelling winds, until in longing for Elwing he turned homeward towards the coast of Beleriand. And his heart bade him haste, for a sudden fear had fallen on him out of dreams; and the winds that before he had striven with might not now bear him back as swift as his desire.

Now when first the tidings came to Maedhros that Elwing yet lived, and dwelt in possession of the Silmaril by the mouths of Sirion, he repenting of the deeds in Doriath withheld his hand. But in time the knowledge of their oath unfulfilled returned to torment him and his brothers, and gathering from their wandering hunting-paths they sent messages to the Havens of friendship and yet of stern demand. Then Elwing and the people of Sirion would not yield the jewel which Beren had won and Lúthien had worn, and for which Dior the fair was slain; and least of all while Eärendil their lord was on the sea, for it seemed to them that in the Silmaril lay the healing and the blessing that had come upon their houses and their ships. And so there came to pass the last and cruellest of the slayings of Elf by Elf; and that was the third of the great wrongs achieved by the accursed oath.

For the sons of Fëanor that yet lived came down suddenly upon the exiles of Gondolin and the remnant of Doriath, and destroyed them. In that battle some of their people stood aside, and some few rebelled and were slain upon the other part aiding Elwing against their own lords (for such was the sorrow and confusion in the hearts of the Eldar in those days); but Maedhros and Maglor won the day, though they alone remained thereafter of the sons of Fëanor, for both Amrod and Amras were slain. Too late the ships of Círdan and Gil-galad the High King came hasting to the aid of the Elves of Sirion; and Elwing was gone, and her sons. Then such few of that people as did not perish in the assault joined themselves to Gil-galad, and went with him to Balar; and they told that Elros and Elrond were taken captive, but Elwing with the Silmaril upon her breast had cast herself into the sea.

Thus Maedhros and Maglor gained not the jewel; but it was not lost. For Ulmo bore up Elwing out of the waves, and he gave her the likeness of a great white bird, and upon her breast there shone as a star the Silmaril, as she flew over the water to seek Eärendil her beloved. On a time of night Eärendil at the helm of his ship saw her come towards him, as a white cloud exceeding swift beneath the moon, as a star over the sea moving in strange course, a pale flame on wings of storm. And it is sung that she fell from the air upon the timbers of Vingilot, in a swoon, nigh unto death for the urgency of her speed, and Eärendil took her to his bosom; but in the morning with marvelling eyes he beheld his wife in her own form beside him with her hair upon his face, and she slept.

Great was the sorrow of Eärendil and Elwing for the ruin of the havens of Sirion, and the captivity of their sons, and they feared that they would be slain; but it was not so. For Maglor took pity upon Elros and Elrond, and he cherished them, and love grew after between them, as little might be thought; but Maglor's heart was sick and weary with the burden of the dreadful oath.

Yet Eärendil saw now no hope left in the lands of Middle-earth, and he turned again in despair and came not home, but sought back once more to Valinor with Elwing at his side. He stood now most often at the prow of Vingilot, and the Silmaril was bound upon his brow; and ever its light grew greater as they drew into the West. And the wise have said that it was by reason of the power of that holy jewel that they came in time to waters that no vessels save those of the Teleri had known; and they came to the Enchanted Isles and escaped their enchantment; and they came into the Shadowy Seas and passed their shadows, and they looked upon Tol Eressëa the Lonely Isle, but tarried not; and at the last they cast anchor in the Bay of Eldamar, and the Teleri saw the coming of that ship out of the East and they were amazed, gazing from afar upon the light of the Silmaril, and it was very great. Then Eärendil, first of living Men, landed on the immortal shores; and he spoke there to Elwing and to those that were with him, and they were three mariners who had sailed all the seas besides him: Falathar, Erellont, and Aerandir were their names. And Eärendil said to them: 'Here none but myself shall set foot, lest you fall under the wrath of the Valar. But that peril I will take on myself alone, for the sake of the Two Kindreds.'

But Elwing answered: 'Then would our paths be sundered for ever; but all thy perils I will take on myself also.' And she leaped into the white foam and ran towards him; but Eärendil was sorrowful, for he feared the anger of the Lords of the West upon any of Middle-earth that should dare to pass the leaguer of Aman. And there they bade farewell to the companions of their voyage, and were taken from them for ever.

Then Eärendil said to Elwing: 'Await me here; for one only may bring the message that it is my fate to bear.' And he went up alone into the land, and came into the Calacirya, and it seemed to him empty and silent; for even as Morgoth and Ungoliant came in ages past, so now Eärendil had come at a time of festival, and wellnigh all the Elvenfolk were gone to Valimar, or were gathered in the halls of

Manwë upon Taniquetil, and few were left to keep watch upon the walls of Tirion.

But some there were who saw him from afar, and the great light that he bore; and they went in haste to Valimar. But Eärendil climbed the green hill of Túna and found it bare; and he entered into the streets of Tirion, and they were empty; and his heart was heavy, for he feared that some evil had come even to the Blessed Realm. He walked in the deserted ways of Tirion, and the dust upon his raiment and his shoes was a dust of diamonds, and he shone and glistened as he climbed the long white stairs. And he called aloud in many tongues, both of Elves and Men, but there were none to answer him. Therefore he turned back at last towards the sea; but even as he took the shoreward road one stood upon the hill and called to him in a great voice, crying:

'Hail Eärendil, of mariners most renowned, the looked for that cometh at unawares, the longed for that cometh beyond hope! Hail Eärendil, bearer of light before the Sun and Moon! Splendour of the Children of Earth, star in the darkness, jewel in the sunset, radiant in the morning!'

That voice was the voice of Eönwë, herald of Manwë, and he came from Valimar, and summoned Eärendil to come before the Powers of Arda. And Eärendil went into Valinor and to the halls of Valimar, and never again set foot upon the lands of Men. Then the Valar took counsel together, and they summoned Ulmo from the deeps of the sea; and Eärendil stood before their faces, and delivered the errand of the Two Kindreds. Pardon he asked for the Noldor and pity for their great sorrows, and mercy upon Men and Elves and succour in their need. And his prayer was granted.

It is told among the Elves that after Eärendil had departed, seeking Elwing his wife, Mandos spoke concerning his fate; and he said: 'Shall mortal Man step living upon the undying lands, and yet live?' But Ulmo said: 'For this he was born into the world. And say unto me: whether is he Eärendil Tuor's son of the line of Hador, or the son of Idril, Turgon's daughter, of the Elven-house of Finwë?' And Mandos answered: 'Equally the Noldor, who went wilfully into exile, may not return hither.'

But when all was spoken, Manwë gave judgement, and he said: 'In this matter the power of doom is given to me. The peril that he ventured for love of the Two Kindreds shall not fall upon Eärendil, nor shall it fall upon Elwing his wife, who entered into peril for love of him; but they shall not walk again ever among Elves or Men in the

Outer Lands. And this is my decree concerning them: to Eärendil and to Elwing, and to their sons, shall be given leave each to choose freely to which kindred their fates shall be joined, and under which kindred they shall be judged.'

Now when Eärendil was long time gone Elwing became lonely and afraid; and wandering by the margin of the sea she came near to Alqualondë, where lay the Telerin fleets. There the Teleri befriended her, and they listened to her tales of Doriath and Gondolin and the griefs of Beleriand, and they were filled with pity and wonder; and there Eärendil returning found her, at the Haven of the Swans. But ere long they were summoned to Valimar; and there the decree of the Elder King was declared to them.

Then Eärendil said to Elwing: 'Choose thou, for now I am weary of the world.' And Elwing chose to be judged among the Firstborn Children of Ilúvatar, because of Lúthien; and for her sake Eärendil chose alike, though his heart was rather with the kindred of Men and the people of his father. Then at the bidding of the Valar Eönwë went to the shore of Aman, where the companions of Eärendil still remained, awaiting tidings; and he took a boat, and the three mariners were set therein, and the Valar drove them away into the East with a great wind. But they took Vingilot, and hallowed it, and bore it away through Valinor to the uttermost rim of the world; and there it passed through the Door of Night and was lifted up even into the oceans of heaven.

Now fair and marvellous was that vessel made, and it was filled with a wavering flame, pure and bright; and Eärendil the Mariner sat at the helm, glistening with dust of elven-gems, and the Silmaril was bound upon his brow. Far he journeyed in that ship, even into the starless voids; but most often was he seen at morning or at evening, glimmering in sunrise or sunset, as he came back to Valinor from voyages beyond the confines of the world.

On those journeys Elwing did not go, for she might not endure the cold and the pathless voids, and she loved rather the earth and the sweet winds that blow on sea and hill. Therefore there was built for her a white tower northward upon the borders of the Sundering Seas; and thither at times all the sea-birds of the earth repaired. And it is said that Elwing learned the tongues of birds, who herself had once worn their shape; and they taught her the craft of flight, and her wings were of white and silver-grey. And at times, when Eärendil returning drew near again to Arda, she would fly to meet him, even as she had flown long ago, when she was rescued from the sea. Then the far-sighted among the Elves that dwelt in the Lonely Isle would see her like a white bird, shining, rose-stained in the sunset, as she soared in joy to greet the coming of Vingilot to haven.

Now when first Vingilot was set to sail in the seas of heaven, it rose unlooked for, glittering and bright; and the people of Middle-earth beheld it from afar and wondered, and they took it for a sign, and called it Gil-Estel, the Star of High Hope. And when this new star was seen at evening, Maedhros spoke to Maglor his brother, and he said: 'Surely that is a Silmaril that shines now in the West?'

And Maglor answered: 'If it be truly the Silmaril which we saw cast into the sea that rises again by the power of the Valar, then let us be glad; for its glory is seen now by many, and is yet secure from all evil.' Then the Elves looked up, and despaired no longer; but Morgoth was filled with doubt.

Yet it is said that Morgoth looked not for the assault that came upon him from the West; for so great was his pride become that he deemed that none would ever again come with open war against him. Moreover he thought that he had for ever estranged the Noldor from the Lords of the West, and that content in their blissful realm the Valar would heed no more his kingdom in the world without; for to him that is pitiless the deeds of pity are ever strange and beyond reckoning. But the host of the Valar prepared for battle; and beneath their white banners marched the Vanyar, the people of Ingwë, and those also of the Noldor who never departed from Valinor, whose leader was Finarfin the son of Finwë. Few of the Teleri were willing to go forth to war, for they remembered the slaying at the Swanhaven, and the rape of their ships; but they hearkened to Elwing, who was the daughter of Dior Eluchíl and come of their own kindred, and they sent mariners enough to sail the ships that bore the host of Valinor east over the sea. Yet they stayed aboard their vessels, and none of them set foot upon the Hither Lands.

Of the march of the host of the Valar to the north of Middle-earth little is said in any tale; for among them went none of those Elves who had dwelt and suffered in the Hither Lands, and who made the histories of those days that still are known; and tidings of these things they only learned long afterwards from their kinsfolk in Aman. But at the last the might of Valinor came up out of the West, and the challenge of the trumpets of Eönwë filled the sky; and Beleriand was ablaze with the glory of their arms, for the host of the Valar were arrayed in forms young and fair and terrible, and the mountains rang beneath their feet.

The meeting of the hosts of the West and of the North is named the Great Battle, and the War of Wrath. There was marshalled the whole power of the Throne of Morgoth, and it had become great beyond count, so that Anfauglith could not contain it; and all the North was aflame with war.

But it availed him not. The Balrogs were destroyed, save some few that fled and hid themselves in caverns inaccessible at the roots of the earth; and the uncounted legions of the Orcs perished like straw in a great fire, or were swept like shrivelled leaves before a burning wind. Few remained to trouble the world for long years after. And such few as were left of the three houses of the Elf-friends, Fathers of Men, fought upon the part of the Valar; and they were avenged in those days for Baragund and Barahir, Galdor and Gundor, Huor and Húrin, and many others of their lords. But a great part of the sons of Men, whether of the people of Uldor or others new-come out of the east, marched with the Enemy; and the Elves do not forget it.

Then, seeing that his hosts were overthrown and his power dispersed, Morgoth quailed, and he dared not to come forth himself. But he loosed upon his foes the last desperate assault that he had prepared, and out of the pits of Angband there issued the winged dragons, that had not before been seen; and so sudden and ruinous was the onset of that dreadful fleet that the host of the Valar was driven back, for the coming of the dragons was with great thunder, and lightning, and a tempest of fire.

But Eärendil came, shining with white flame, and about Vingilot were gathered all the great birds of heaven and Thorondor was their captain, and there was battle in the air all the day and through a dark night of doubt. Before the rising of the sun Eärendil slew Ancalagon the Black, the mightiest of the dragon-host, and cast him from the sky; and he fell upon the towers of Thangorodrim, and they were broken in his ruin. Then the sun rose, and the host of the Valar prevailed, and well-nigh all the dragons were destroyed; and all the pits of Morgoth were broken and unroofed, and the might of the Valar descended into the deeps of the earth. There Morgoth stood at last at bay, and yet unvaliant. He fled into the deepest of his mines, and sued for peace and pardon; but his feet were hewn from under him, and he was hurled upon his face. Then he was bound with the chain Angainor which he had worn aforetime, and his iron crown they beat into a collar for his neck, and his head was bowed upon his knees. And the two

Silmarils which remained to Morgoth were taken from his crown, and they shone unsullied beneath the sky; and Eönwë took them, and guarded them.

Thus an end was made of the power of Angband in the North, and the evil realm was brought to naught; and out of the deep prisons a multitude of slaves came forth beyond all hope into the light of day, and they looked upon a world that was changed. For so great was the fury of those adversaries that the northern regions of the western world were rent asunder, and the sea roared in through many chasms, and there was confusion and great noise; and rivers perished or found new paths, and the valleys were upheaved and the hills trod down; and Sirion was no more.

Then Eönwë as herald of the Elder King summoned the Elves of Beleriand to depart from Middle-earth. But Maedhros and Maglor would not hearken, and they prepared, though now with weariness and loathing, to attempt in despair the fulfilment of their oath; for they would have given battle for the Silmarils, were they withheld, even against the victorious host of Valinor, even though they stood alone against all the world. And they sent a message therefore to Eönwë, bidding him yield up now those jewels which of old Fëanor their father made and Morgoth stole from him.

But Eönwë answered that the right to the work of their father, which the sons of Fëanor formerly possessed, had now perished, because of their many and merciless deeds, being blinded by their oath, and most of all because of their slaying of Dior and the assault upon the Havens. The light of the Silmarils should go now into the West, whence it came in the beginning; and to Valinor must Maedhros and Maglor return, and there abide the judgement of the Valar, by whose decree alone would Eönwë yield the jewels from his charge. Then Maglor desired indeed to submit, for his heart was sorrowful, and he said: 'The oath says not that we may not bide our time, and it may be that in Valinor all shall be forgiven and forgot, and we shall come into our own in peace.'

But Maedhros answered that if they returned to Aman but the favour of the Valar were withheld from them, then their oath would still remain, but its fulfilment be beyond all hope; and he said: 'Who can tell to what dreadful doom we shall come, if we disobey the Powers in their own land, or purpose ever to bring war again into their holy realm?'

Yet Maglor still held back, saying: 'If Manwë and Varda themselves deny the fulfilment of an oath to which we named them in witness, is it not made void?'

And Maedhros answered: 'But how shall our voices reach to Ilúvatar beyond the Circles of the World? And by Ilúvatar we swore in our madness, and called the Everlasting Darkness upon us, if we kept not our word. Who shall release us?'

'If none can release us,' said Maglor, 'then indeed the Everlasting Darkness shall be our lot, whether we keep our oath or break it; but less evil shall we do in the breaking.'

Yet he yielded at last to the will of Maedhros, and they took counsel together how they should lay hands on the Silmarils. And they disguised themselves, and came in the night to the camp of Eönwë, and crept into the place where the Silmarils were guarded; and they slew the guards, and laid hands on the jewels. Then all the camp was raised against them, and they prepared to die, defending themselves until the last. But Eönwë would not permit the slaying of the sons of Fëanor; and departing unfought they fled far away. Each of them took to himself a Silmaril, for they said: 'Since one is lost to us, and but two remain, and we two alone of our brothers, so is it plain that fate would have us share the heirlooms of our father.'

But the jewel burned the hand of Maedhros in pain unbearable; and he perceived that it was as Eönwë had said, and that his right thereto had become void, and that the oath was vain. And being in anguish and despair he cast himself into a gaping chasm filled with fire, and so ended; and the Silmaril that he bore was taken into the bosom of the Earth.

And it is told of Maglor that he could not endure the pain with which the Silmaril tormented him; and he cast it at last into the Sea, and thereafter he wandered ever upon the shores, singing in pain and regret beside the waves. For Maglor was mighty among the singers of old, named only after Daeron of Doriath; but he came never back among the people of the Elves. And thus it came to pass that the Silmarils found their long homes: one in the airs of heaven, and one in the fires of the heart of the world, and one in the deep waters.

In those days there was a great building of ships upon the shores of the Western Sea; and thence in many a fleet the Eldar set sail into the West, and came never back to the lands of weeping and of war. And the Vanyar returned beneath their white banners, and were borne in triumph to Valinor; but their joy in victory was diminished, for they returned without the Silmarils from Morgoth's crown, and they knew that those jewels could not be found or brought together again unless the world be broken and remade.

And when they came into the West the Elves of Beleriand dwelt upon Tol Eressëa, the Lonely Isle, that looks both west and east; whence they might come even to Valinor. They were admitted again to the love of Manwë and the pardon of the Valar; and the Teleri forgave their ancient grief, and the curse was laid to rest.

Yet not all the Eldalië were willing to forsake the Hither Lands where they had long suffered and long dwelt; and some lingered many an age in Middle-earth. Among those were Círdan the Shipwright, and Celeborn of Doriath, with Galadriel his wife, who alone remained of those who led the Noldor to exile in Beleriand. In Middle-earth dwelt also Gil-galad the High King, and with him was Elrond Half-elven, who chose, as was granted to him, to be numbered among the Eldar; but Elros his brother chose to abide with Men. And from these brethren alone has come among Men the blood of the Firstborn and a strain of the spirits divine that were before Arda; for they were the sons of Elwing, Dior's daughter, Lúthien's son, child of Thingol and Melian; and Eärendil their father was the son of Idril Celebrindal, Turgon's daughter of Gondolin.

But Morgoth himself the Valar thrust through the Door of Night beyond the Walls of the World, into the Timeless Void; and a guard is set for ever on those walls, and Eärendil keeps watch upon the ramparts of the sky. Yet the lies that Melkor, the mighty and accursed, Morgoth Bauglir, the Power of Terror and of Hate, sowed in the hearts of Elves and Men are a seed that does not die and cannot be destroyed; and ever and anon it sprouts anew, and will bear dark fruit even unto the latest days.

Here ends the SILMARILLION. If it has passed from the high and the beautiful to darkness and ruin, that was of old the fate of Arda Marred; and if any change shall come and the Marring be amended, Manwë and Varda may know; but they have not revealed it, and it is not declared in the dooms of Mandos.

AKALLABÊTH

AKALLABÊTH

The Downfall of Númenor

It is said by the Eldar that Men came into the world in the time of the Shadow of Morgoth, and they fell swiftly under his dominion; for he sent his emissaries among them, and they listened to his evil and cunning words, and they worshipped the Darkness and yet feared it. But there were some that turned from evil and left the lands of their kindred, and wandered ever westward; for they had heard a rumour that in the West there was a light which the Shadow could not dim. The servants of Morgoth pursued them with hatred, and their ways were long and hard; yet they came at last to the lands that look upon the Sea, and they entered Beleriand in the days of the War of the Jewels. The Edain these were named in the Sindarin tongue; and they became friends and allies of the Eldar, and did deeds of great valour in the war against Morgoth.

Of them was sprung, upon the side of his fathers, Bright Eärendil; and in the *Lay of Eärendil* it is told how at the last, when the victory of Morgoth was almost complete, he built his ship Vingilot, that Men called Rothinzil, and voyaged upon the unsailed seas, seeking ever for Valinor; for he desired to speak before the Powers on behalf of the Two Kindreds, that the Valar might have pity on them and send them help in their uttermost need. Therefore by Elves and Men he is called Eärendil the Blessed, for he achieved his quest after long labours and many perils, and from Valinor there came the host of the Lords of the West. But Eärendil came never back to the lands that he had loved.

In the Great Battle when at last Morgoth was overthrown and Thangorodrim was broken, the Edain alone of the kindreds of Men fought for the Valar, whereas many others fought for Morgoth. And after the victory of the Lords of the West those of the evil Men who were not destroyed fled back into the east, where many of their race were still wandering in the unharvested lands, wild and lawless, refusing alike the summons of the Valar and of Morgoth. And the evil Men came among them, and cast over them a shadow of fear, and they took them for kings. Then the Valar forsook for a time the Men of Middle-earth who had refused their summons and had taken the friends of Morgoth to be their masters; and Men dwelt in darkness and were troubled by many evil things that Morgoth had devised in the days of his dominion: demons, and dragons, and misshapen beasts, and the unclean Orcs that are mockeries of the Children of Ilúvatar. And the lot of Men was unhappy.

But Manwë put forth Morgoth and shut him beyond the World in the Void that is without; and he cannot himself return again into the World, present and visible, while the Lords of the West are still enthroned. Yet the seeds that he had planted still grew and sprouted, bearing evil fruit, if any would tend them. For his will remained and guided his servants, moving them ever to thwart the will of the Valar and to destroy those that obeyed them. This the Lords of the West knew full well. When therefore Morgoth had been thrust forth, they held council concerning the ages that should come after. The Eldar they summoned to return into the West, and those that hearkened to the summons dwelt in the Isle of Eressëa; and there is in that land a haven that is named Avallónë, for it is of all cities the nearest to Valinor, and the tower of Avallónë is the first sight that the mariner beholds when at last he draws nigh to the Undying Lands over the leagues of the Sea. To the Fathers of Men of the three faithful houses rich reward also was given. Eönwë came among them and taught them; and they were given wisdom and power and life more enduring than any others of mortal race have possessed. A land was made for the Edain to dwell in, neither part of Middle-earth nor of Valinor, for it was sundered from either by a wide sea; yet it was nearer to Valinor. It was raised by Ossë out of the depths of the Great Water, and it was established by Aulë and enriched by Yavanna; and the Eldar brought thither flowers and fountains out of Tol Eressëa. That land the Valar called Andor, the Land of Gift; and the Star of Eärendil shone bright in the West as a token that all was made ready, and as a guide over the sea; and Men marvelled to see that silver flame in the paths of the Sun.

Then the Edain set sail upon the deep waters, following the Star; and the Valar laid a peace upon the sea for many days, and sent sunlight and a sailing wind, so that the waters glittered before the eyes of the Edain like rippling glass, and the foam flew like snow before the stems of their ships. But so bright was Rothinzil that even at morning Men could see it glimmering in the West, and in the cloudless night it shone alone, for no other star could stand beside it. And setting their course towards it the Edain came at last over leagues of sea and saw afar the land that was prepared for them, Andor, the Land of Gift, shimmering in a golden haze. Then they went up out of the sea and found a country fair and fruitful, and they were glad. And they called that land Elenna, which is Starwards; but also Anadûnê, which is Westernesse, Númenórë in the High Eldarin tongue.

This was the beginning of that people that in the Grey-elven speech are called the Dúnedain: the Númenóreans, Kings among Men. But they did not thus escape from the doom of death that Ilúvatar had set upon all Mankind, and they were mortal still, though their years were long, and they knew no sickness, ere the shadow fell upon them. Therefore they grew wise and glorious, and in all things more like to the Firstborn than any other of the kindreds of Men; and they were tall, taller than the tallest of the sons of Middle-earth; and the light of their eyes was like the bright stars. But their numbers increased only slowly in the land, for though daughters and sons were born to them, fairer than their fathers, yet their children were few.

Of old the chief city and haven of Númenor was in the midst of its western coasts, and it was called Andúnië because it faced the sunset. But in the midst of the land was a mountain tall and steep, and it was named the Meneltarma, the Pillar of Heaven, and upon it was a high place that was hallowed to Eru Ilúvatar, and it was open and unroofed, and no other temple or fane was there in the land of the Númenóreans. At the feet of the mountain were built the tombs of the Kings, and hard by upon a hill was Armenelos, fairest of cities, and there stood the tower and the citadel that was raised by Elros son of Eärendil, whom the Valar appointed to be the first King of the Dúnedain.

Now Elros and Elrond his brother were descended from the Three Houses of the Edain, but in part also both from the Eldar and the Maiar; for Idril of Gondolin and Lúthien daughter of Melian were their foremothers. The Valar indeed may not withdraw the gift of death, which comes to Men from Ilúvatar, but in the matter of the Half-elven Ilúvatar gave to them the judgement; and they judged that to the sons of Eärendil should be given choice of their own destiny. And Elrond chose to remain with the Firstborn, and to him the life of the Firstborn was granted. But to Elros, who chose to be a king of Men, still a great span of years was allotted, many times that of the Men of Middle-earth; and all his line, the kings and lords of the royal house, had long life even according to the measure of the Númenóreans. But Elros lived five hundred years, and ruled the Númenóreans four hundred years and ten.

Thus the years passed, and while Middle-earth went backward and light and wisdom faded, the Dúnedain dwelt under the protection of the Valar and in the friendship of the Eldar, and they increased in stature both of mind and body. For though this people used still their own speech, their kings and lords knew and spoke also the Elven tongue, which they had learned in the days of their alliance, and thus they held converse still with the Eldar, whether of Eressëa or of the westlands of Middle-earth. And the loremasters among them learned also the High Eldarin tongue of the Blessed Realm, in which much story and song was preserved from the beginning of the world; and they made letters and scrolls and books, and wrote in them many things of wisdom and wonder in the high tide of their realm, of which all is now forgot. So it came to pass that, beside their own names, all the lords of the Númenóreans had also Eldarin names; and the like with the cities and fair places that they founded in Númenor and on the shores of the Hither Lands.

For the Dúnedain became mighty in crafts, so that if they had had the mind they could easily have surpassed the evil kings of Middle-earth in the making of war and the forging of weapons; but they were become men of peace. Above all arts they nourished ship-building and sea-craft, and they became mariners whose like shall never be again since the world was diminished; and voyaging upon the wide seas was the chief feat and adventure of their hardy men in the gallant days of their youth.

But the Lords of Valinor forbade them to sail so far westward that the coasts of Númenor could no longer be seen; and for long the Dúnedain were content, though they did not fully understand the purpose of this ban. But the design of Manwë was that the Númenóreans should not be tempted to seek for the Blessed Realm, nor desire to overpass the limits set to their bliss, becoming enamoured of the immortality of the Valar and the Eldar and the lands where all things endure.

For in those days Valinor still remained in the world visible, and there Ilúvatar permitted the Valar to maintain upon Earth an abiding place, a memorial of that which might have been if Morgoth had not cast his shadow on the world. This the Númenóreans knew full well; and at times, when all the air was clear and the sun was in the east, they would look out and descry far off in the west a city white-shining on a distant shore, and a great harbour and a tower. For in those days the Númenóreans were far-sighted; yet even so it was only the keenest eyes among them that could see this vision, from the Meneltarma, maybe, or from some tall ship that lay off their western coast as far as it was lawful for them to go. For they did not dare to break the Ban of the Lords of the West. But the wise among them knew that this distant land was not indeed the Blessed Realm of Valinor, but was Avallónë, the haven of the Eldar upon Eressëa, easternmost of the Undying Lands. And thence at times the Firstborn still would come sailing to Númenor in oarless boats, as white birds flying from the sunset. And they brought to Númenor many gifts: birds of song, and fragrant flowers, and herbs of great virtue. And a seedling they brought of Celeborn, the White Tree that grew in the midst of Eressëa; and that was in its turn a seedling of Galathilion the Tree of Túna, the image of Telperion that Yavanna gave to the Eldar in the Blessed Realm. And the tree grew and blossomed in the courts of the King in Armenelos; Nimloth it was named, and flowered in the evening, and the shadows of night it filled with its fragrance.

Thus it was that because of the Ban of the Valar the voyages of the Dúnedain in those days went ever eastward and not westward, from the darkness of the North to the heats of the South, and beyond the South to the Nether Darkness; and they came even into the inner seas, and sailed about Middle-earth and glimpsed from their high prows the Gates of Morning in the East. And the Dúnedain came at times to the shores of the Great Lands, and they took pity on the forsaken world of Middle-earth; and the Lords of Númenor set foot again upon the western shores in the Dark Years of Men, and none yet dared to withstand them. For most of the Men of that age that sat under the Shadow were now grown weak and fearful. And coming among them the Númenóreans taught them many things. Corn and wine they brought, and they instructed Men in the sowing of seed and the grinding of grain, in the hewing of wood and the shaping of stone, and in the ordering of their life, such as it might be in the lands of swift death and little bliss.

Then the Men of Middle-earth were comforted, and here and there upon the western shores the houseless woods drew back, and Men shook off the yoke of the offspring of Morgoth, and unlearned their terror of the dark. And they revered the memory of the tall Sea-kings, and when they had departed they called them gods, hoping for their return; for at that time the Númenóreans dwelt never long in Middle-earth, nor made there as yet any habitation of their own. Eastward they must sail, but ever west their hearts returned.

Now this yearning grew ever greater with the years; and the Númenóreans began to hunger for the undying city that they saw from afar, and the desire of everlasting life, to escape from death and the ending of delight, grew strong upon them; and ever as their power and glory grew greater their unquiet increased. For though the Valar had rewarded the Dúnedain with long life, they could not take from them the weariness of the world that comes at last, and they died, even their kings of the seed of Eärendil; and the span of their lives was brief in the eyes of the Eldar. Thus it was that a shadow fell upon them: in which maybe the will of Morgoth was at work that still moved in the world. And the Númenóreans began to murmur, at first in their hearts, and then in open words, against the doom of Men, and most of all against the Ban which forbade them to sail into the West.

And they said among themselves: 'Why do the Lords of the West sit there in peace unending, while we must die and go we know not whither, leaving our home and all that we have made? And the Eldar die not, even those that rebelled against the Lords. And since we have mastered all seas, and no water is so wild or so wide that our ships cannot overcome it, why should we not go to Avallónë and greet there our friends?'

And some there were who said: 'Why should we not go even to Aman, and taste there, were it but for a day, the bliss of the Powers? Have we not become mighty among the people of Arda?'

The Eldar reported these words to the Valar, and Manwë was grieved, seeing a cloud gather on the noon-tide of Númenor. And he sent messengers to the Dúnedain, who spoke earnestly to the King, and to all who would listen, concerning the fate and fashion of the world.

'The Doom of the World,' they said, 'One alone can change who made it. And were you so to voyage that escaping all deceits and snares you came indeed to Aman, the Blessed Realm, little would it profit you. For it is not the land of Manwë that makes its people deathless, but the Deathless that dwell therein have hallowed the land; and there you would but wither and grow weary the sooner, as moths in a light too strong and steadfast.'

But the King said: 'And does not Eärendil, my forefather, live? Or is he not in the land of Aman?'

To which they answered: 'You know that he has a fate apart, and was adjudged to the Firstborn who die not; yet this also is his doom that he can never return again to mortal lands. Whereas you and your people are not of the Firstborn, but are mortal Men as Ilúvatar made you. Yet it seems that you desire now to have the good of both kindreds, to sail to Valinor when you will, and to return when you please to your homes. That cannot be. Nor can the Valar take away the gifts of Ilúvatar. The Eldar, you say, are unpunished, and even those who rebelled do not die. Yet that is to them neither reward nor punishment, but the fulfilment of their being. They cannot escape, and are bound to this world, never to leave it so long as it lasts, for its life is theirs. And you are punished for the rebellion of Men, you say, in which you had small part, and so it is that you die. But that was not at first appointed for a punishment. Thus you escape, and leave the world, and are not bound to it, in hope or in weariness. Which of us therefore should envy the others?'

And the Númenóreans answered: 'Why should we not envy the Valar, or even the least of the Deathless? For of us is required a blind trust, and a hope without assurance, knowing not what lies before us in a little while. And yet we also love the Earth and would not lose it.'

Then the Messengers said: 'Indeed the mind of Ilúvatar concerning you is not known to the Valar, and he has not revealed all things that are to come. But this we hold to be true, that your home is not here, neither in the Land of Aman nor anywhere within the Circles of the World. And the Doom of Men, that they should depart, was at first a gift of Ilúvatar. It became a grief to them only because coming under the shadow of Morgoth it seemed to them that they were surrounded by a great darkness, of which they were afraid; and some grew wilful and proud and would not yield, until life was reft from them. We who bear the ever-mounting burden of the years do not clearly understand this; but if that grief has returned to trouble you, as you say, then we fear that the Shadow arises once more and grows again in your hearts. Therefore, though you be the Dúnedain, fairest of Men, who escaped from the Shadow of old and fought valiantly against it, we say to you: Beware! The will of Eru may not be gainsaid; and the Valar bid you earnestly not to withhold the trust to which you are called, lest soon it become again a bond by which you are constrained. Hope rather that in the end even the least of your desires shall have fruit. The love of Arda was set in your hearts by Ilúvatar, and he does not plant to no purpose. Nonetheless, many ages of Men unborn may pass ere that purpose is made known; and to you it will be revealed and not to the Valar.'

These things took place in the days of Tar-Ciryatan the Shipbuilder, and of Tar-Atanamir his son; and they were proud men, eager for Wealth, and they laid the men of Middle-earth under tribute, taking now rather than giving. It was to Tar-Atanamir that the Messengers came; and he was the thirteenth King, and in his day the Realm of Númenor had endured for more than two thousand years, and was come to the zenith of its bliss, if not yet of its power. But Atanamir was ill pleased with the counsel of the Messengers and gave little heed to it, and the greater part of his people followed him; for they wished still to escape death in their own day, not waiting upon hope. And Atanamir lived to a great age, clinging to his life beyond the end of all joy; and he was the first of the Númenóreans to do this, refusing to depart until he was witless and unmanned, and denying to his son the kingship at the height of his days. For the Lords of Númenor had been wont to wed late in their long lives and to depart and leave the mastery to their sons when these were come to full stature of body and mind.

Then Tar-Ancalimon, son of Atanamir, became King, and he was of like mind; and in his day the people of Númenor became divided. On the one hand was the greater party, and they were called the King's Men, and they grew proud and were estranged from the Eldar and the Valar. And on the other hand was the lesser party, and they were called the Elendili, the Elf-friends; for though they remained loyal indeed to the King and the House of Elros, they wished to keep the friendship of the Eldar, and they hearkened to the counsel of the Lords of the West. Nonetheless even they, who named themselves the Faithful, did not wholly escape from the affliction of their people, and they were troubled by the thought of death.

Thus the bliss of Westernesse became diminished; but still its might and splendour increased. For the kings and their people had not yet abandoned wisdom, and if they loved the Valar no longer at least they still feared them. They did not dare openly to break the Ban or to sail beyond the limits that had been appointed. Eastwards still they steered their tall ships. But the fear of death grew ever darker upon them, and they delayed it by all means that they could; and they began to build great houses for their dead, while their wise men laboured unceasingly to discover if they might the secret of recalling life, or at the least of the prolonging of Men's days. Yet they achieved only the art of preserving incorrupt the dead flesh of Men, and they filled all the land with silent tombs in which the thought of death was enshrined in the darkness. But those that lived turned the more eagerly to pleasure and revelry, desiring ever more goods and more riches; and after the days of Tar-Ancalimon the offering of the first fruits to Eru was neglected, and men went seldom any more to the Hallow upon the heights of Meneltarma in the midst of the land.

Thus it came to pass in that time that the Númenóreans first made great settlements upon the west shores of the ancient lands; for their own land seemed to them shrunken, and they had no rest or content therein, and they desired now wealth and dominion in Middle-earth, since the West was denied. Great harbours and strong towers they made, and there many of them took up their abode; but they appeared now rather as lords and masters and gatherers of tribute than as helpers and teachers. And the great ships of the Númenóreans were borne east on the winds and returned ever laden, and the power and majesty of their kings were increased; and they drank and they feasted and they clad themselves in silver and gold.

In all this the Elf-friends had small part. They alone came now ever to the north and the land of Gil-galad, keeping their friendship with the Elves and lending them aid against Sauron; and their haven was Pelargir above the mouths of Anduin the Great. But the King's Men sailed far away to the south; and the lordships and strongholds that they made have left many rumours in the legends of Men.

In this Age, as is elsewhere told, Sauron arose again in Middle-earth, and grew, and turned back to the evil in which he was nurtured by Morgoth, becoming mighty in his service. Already in the days of Tar-Minastir, the eleventh King of Númenor, he had fortified the land of Mordor and had built there the Tower of Barad-dûr, and thereafter he strove ever for the dominion of Middle-earth, to become a king over all kings and as a god unto Men. And Sauron hated the Númenóreans, because of the deeds of their fathers and their ancient alliance with the Elves and allegiance to the Valar; nor did he forget the aid that Tar-Minastir had rendered to Gil-galad of old, in that time when the One Ring was forged and there was war between Sauron and the Elves in Eriador. Now he learned that the kings of Númenor had increased in power and splendour, and he hated them the more; and he feared them, lest they should invade his lands and wrest from him the dominion of the East. But for a long time he did not dare to challenge the Lords of the Sea, and he withdrew from the coasts.

Yet Sauron was ever guileful, and it is said that among those whom he ensnared with the Nine Rings three were great lords of Númenórean race. And when the Úlairi arose that were the Ring-wraiths, his servants, and the strength of his terror and mastery over Men had grown exceedingly great, he began to assail the strong places of the Númenóreans upon the shores of the sea.

In those days the Shadow grew deeper upon Númenor; and the lives of the Kings of the House of Elros waned because of their rebellion, but they hardened their hearts the more against the Valar. And the nineteenth king took the sceptre of his fathers, and he ascended the throne in the name of Adûnakhor, Lord of the West, forsaking the Elven-tongues and forbidding their use in his hearing. Yet in the Scroll of Kings the name Herunúmen was inscribed in the High-elven speech, because of ancient custom, which the kings feared to break utterly, lest evil befall. Now this title seemed to the Faithful over-proud, being the title of the Valar; and their hearts were sorely tried between their loyalty to the House of Elros and their reverence of the appointed Powers. But worse was yet to come. For Ar-Gimilzôr the twenty-second king was the greatest enemy of the Faithful. In his day the White Tree was untended and began to decline; and he forbade utterly the use of the Elven-tongues, and punished those that welcomed the ships of Eressëa, that still came secretly to the west-shores of the land.

Now the Elendili dwelt mostly in the western regions of Númenor; but Ar-Gimilzôr commanded all that he could discover to be of this party to remove from the west and dwell in the east of the land; and there they were watched. And the chief dwelling of the Faithful in the later days was thus nigh to the harbour of Rómenna; thence many set sail to Middle-earth, seeking the northern coasts where they might speak still with the Eldar in the kingdom of Gil-galad. This was known to the kings, but they hindered it not, so long as the Elendili departed from their land and did not return; for they desired to end all friendship between their people and the Eldar of Eressëa, whom they named the Spies of the Valar, hoping to keep their deeds and their counsels hidden from the Lords of the West. But all that they did was known to Manwë, and the Valar were wroth with the Kings of Númenor, and gave them counsel and protection no more; and the ships of Eressëa came never again out of the sunset, and the havens of Andúnië were forlorn.

Highest in honour after the house of the kings were the Lords of Andúnië; for they were of the line of Elros, being descended from Silmarien, daughter of Tar-Elendil the fourth king of Númenor. And these lords were loyal to the kings, and revered them; and the Lord of Andúnië was ever among the chief councillors of the Sceptre. Yet also from the beginning they bore especial love to the Eldar and reverence for the Valar; and as the Shadow grew they aided the Faithful as they could. But for long they did not declare themselves openly, and sought rather to amend the hearts of the lords of the Sceptre with wiser counsels.

There was a lady Inzilbêth, renowned for her beauty, and her mother was Lindórië, sister of Eärendur, the Lord of Andúnië in the days of Ar-Sakalthôr father of Ar-Gimilzôr. Gimilzôr took her to wife, though this was little to her liking, for she was in heart one of the Faithful, being taught by her mother; but the kings and their sons were grown proud and not to be gainsaid in their wishes. No love was there between Ar-Gimilzôr and his queen, or between their sons. Inziladûn, the elder, was like his mother in mind as in body; but Gimilkhâd, the younger, went with his father, unless he were yet prouder and more wilful. To him Ar-Gimilzôr would have yielded the sceptre rather than to the elder son, if the laws had allowed.

But when Inziladûn acceded to the sceptre, he took again a title in the Elven-tongue as of old, calling himself Tar-Palantir, for he was far-sighted both in eye and in mind, and even those that hated him feared his words as those of a true-seer. He gave peace for a while to the Faithful; and he went once more at due seasons to the Hallow of Eru upon the Meneltarma, which Ar-Gimilzôr had forsaken. The White Tree he tended again with honour; and he prophesied, saying that when the Tree perished, then also would the line of the Kings come to its end. But his repentance was too late to appease the anger of the Valar with the insolence of his fathers, of which the greater part of his people did not repent. And Gimilkhâd was strong and ungentle, and he took the leadership of those that had been called the King's Men and opposed the will of his brother as openly as he dared, and yet more in secret. Thus the days of Tar-Palantir became darkened with grief; and he would spend much of his time in the west, and there ascended often the ancient tower of King Minastir upon the hill of Oromet nigh to Andúnië, whence he gazed westward in yearning, hoping to see, maybe, some sail upon the sea. But no ship came ever again from the West to Númenor, and Avallónë was veiled in cloud.

Now Gimilkhâd died two years before his two hundredth year (which was accounted an early death for one of Elros' line even in its waning), but this brought no peace to the King. For Pharazôn son of Gimilkhâd had become a man yet more restless and eager for wealth and power than his father. He had fared often abroad, as a leader in the wars that the Númenóreans made then in the coastlands of Middle-earth, seeking to extend their dominion over Men; and thus he had won great renown as a captain both by land and by sea. Therefore when he came back to Númenor, hearing of his father's death, the hearts of the people were turned to him; for he brought with him great wealth, and was for the time free in his giving.

And it came to pass that Tar-Palantir grew weary of grief and died. He had no son, but a daughter only, whom he named Míriel in the Elven-tongue; and to her now by right and the laws of the Númenóreans came the sceptre. But Pharazôn took her to wife against her will, doing evil in this and evil also in that the laws of Númenor did not permit the marriage, even in the royal house, of those more nearly akin than cousins in the second degree. And when they were wedded, he seized the sceptre into his own hand, taking the title of Ar-Pharazôn (Tar-Calion in the Elven-tongue); and the name of his queen he changed to Ar-Zimraphel.

The mightiest and proudest was Ar-Pharazôn the Golden of all those that had wielded the Sceptre of the Sea-Kings since the foundation of Númenor; and three and twenty Kings and Queens had ruled the Númenóreans before, and slept now in their deep tombs under the mount of Meneltarma, lying upon beds of gold.

And sitting upon his carven throne in the city of Armenelos in the glory of his power, he brooded darkly, thinking of war. For he had learned in Middle-earth of the strength of the realm of Sauron, and of his hatred of Westernesse. And now there came to him the masters of ships and captains returning out of the East, and they reported that Sauron was putting forth his might, since Ar-Pharazôn had gone back from Middle-earth, and he was pressing down upon the cities by the coasts; and he had taken now the title of King of Men, and declared his purpose to drive the Númenóreans into the sea, and destroy even Númenor, if that might be.

Great was the anger of Ar-Pharazôn at these tidings, and as he pondered long in secret, his heart was filled with the desire of power unbounded and the sole dominion of his will. And he determined without counsel of the Valar, or the aid of any wisdom but his own, that the title of King of Men he would himself claim, and would compel Sauron to become his vassal and his servant; for in his pride he deemed that no king should ever arise so mighty as to vie with the Heir of Eärendil. Therefore he began in that time to smithy great hoard of weapons, and many ships of war he built and stored them with his arms; and when all was made ready he himself set sail with his host into the East.

And men saw his sails coming up out of the sunset, dyed as with scarlet and gleaming with red and gold, and fear fell upon the dwellers by the coasts, and they fled far away. But the fleet came at last to that place that was called Umbar, where was the mighty haven of the Númenóreans that no hand had wrought. Empty and silent were all the lands about when the King of the Sea marched upon Middle-earth. For seven days he journeyed with banner and trumpet, and he came to a hill, and he went up, and he set there his pavilion and his throne; and he sat him down in the midst of the land, and the tents of his host were ranged all about him, blue, golden, and white, as a field of tall flowers. Then he sent forth heralds, and he commanded Sauron to come before him and swear to him fealty.

And Sauron came. Even from his mighty tower of Barad-dûr he came, and made no offer of battle. For he perceived that the power and majesty of the Kings of the Sea surpassed all rumour of them, so that he could not trust even the greatest of his servants to withstand them; and he saw not his time yet to work his will with the Dúnedain. And he was crafty, well skilled to gain what he would by subtlety when force might not avail. Therefore he humbled himself before Ar-Pharazôn and smoothed his tongue; and men wondered, for all that he said seemed fair and wise.

But Ar-Pharazôn was not yet deceived, and it came into his mind that, for the better keeping of Sauron and of his oaths of fealty, he should be brought to Númenor, there to dwell as a hostage for himself and all his servants in Middle-earth. To this Sauron assented as one constrained, yet in his secret thought he received it gladly, for it chimed indeed with his desire. And Sauron passed over the sea and looked upon the land of Númenor, and on the city of Armenelos in the days of its glory, and he was astounded; but his heart within was filled the more with envy and hate.

Yet such was the cunning of his mind and mouth, and the strength of his hidden will, that ere three years had passed he had become closest to the secret counsels of the King; for flattery sweet as honey was ever on his tongue, and knowledge he had of many things yet unrevealed to Men. And seeing the favour that he had of their lord all the councillors began to fawn upon him, save one alone, Amandil lord of Andúnië. Then slowly a change came over the land, and the hearts of the Elf-friends were sorely troubled, and many fell away out of fear; and although those that remained still called themselves the Faithful, their enemies named them rebels. For now, having the ears of men, Sauron with many arguments gainsaid all that the Valar had taught; and he bade men think that in the world, in the east and even in the west, there lay yet many seas and many lands for their winning, wherein was wealth uncounted. And still, if they should at the last come to the end of those lands and seas, beyond all lay the Ancient Darkness. 'And out of it the world was made. For Darkness alone is worshipful, and the Lord thereof may yet make other worlds to be gifts to those that serve him, so that the increase of their power shall find no end.'

And Ar-Pharazôn said: 'Who is the Lord of the Darkness?'

Then behind locked doors Sauron spoke to the King, and he lied, saying: 'It is he whose name is not now spoken; for the Valar have deceived you concerning him, putting forward the name of Eru, a phantom devised in the folly of their hearts, seeking to enchain Men in servitude to themselves. For they are the oracle of this Eru, which speaks only what they will. But he that is their master shall yet prevail, and he will deliver you from this phantom; and his name is Melkor, Lord of All, Giver of Freedom, and he shall make you stronger than they.'

Then Ar-Pharazôn the King turned back to the worship of the Dark, and of Melkor the Lord thereof, at first in secret, but ere long openly and in the face of his people; and they for the most part followed him. Yet there dwelt still a remnant of the Faithful, as has been told, at Rómenna and in the country near, and other few there were here and there in the land. The chief among them, to whom they looked for leading and courage in evil days, was Amandil, councillor of the King, and his son Elendil, whose sons were Isildur and Anárion, then young men by the reckoning of Númenor. Amandil and Elendil were great ship-captains; and they were of the line of Elros Tar-Minyatur, though not of the ruling house to whom belonged the crown and the throne in the city of Armenelos. In the days of their youth together Amandil had been dear to Pharazôn, and though he was of the Elf-friends he remained in his council until the coming of Sauron. Now he was dismissed, for Sauron hated him above all others in Númenor. But he was so noble, and had been so mighty a captain of the sea, that he was still held in honour by many of the people, and neither the King nor Sauron dared to lay hands on him as yet.

Therefore Amandil withdrew to Rómenna, and all that he trusted still to be faithful he summoned to come thither in secret; for he feared that evil would now grow apace, and all the Elf-friends were in peril. And so it soon came to pass. For the Meneltarma was utterly deserted in those days; and though not even Sauron dared to defile the high place, yet the King would let no man, upon pain of death, ascend to it, not even those of the Faithful who kept Ilúvatar in their hearts. And Sauron urged the King to cut down the White Tree, Nimloth the Fair, that grew in his courts, for it was a memorial of the Eldar and of the light of Valinor.

At the first the King would not assent to this, since he believed that the fortunes of his house were bound up with the Tree, as was forespoken by Tar-Palantir. Thus in his folly he who now hated the Eldar and the Valar vainly clung to the shadow of the old allegiance of Númenor. But when Amandil heard rumour of the evil purpose of Sauron he was grieved to the heart, knowing that in the end Sauron would surely have his will. Then he spoke to Elendil and the sons of Elendil, recalling the tale of the Trees of Valinor; and Isildur said no word, but went out by night and did a deed for which he was afterwards renowned. For he passed alone in disguise to Armenelos and to the courts of the King, which were now forbidden to the Faithful; and he came to the place of the Tree, which was forbidden to all by the orders of Sauron, and the Tree was watched day and night by guards in his service. At that time Nimloth was dark and bore no bloom, for it was late in the autumn, and its winter was nigh; and Isildur passed through the guards and took from the Tree a fruit that hung upon it, and turned to go. But the guard was aroused, and he was assailed, and fought his way out, receiving many wounds; and he escaped, and because he was disguised it was not discovered who had laid hands on the Tree. But Isildur came at last hardly back to Rómenna and delivered the fruit to the hands of Amandil, ere his strength failed him. Then the fruit was planted in secret, and it was blessed by Amandil; and a shoot arose from it and sprouted in the spring. But when its first leaf opened then Isildur, who had lain long and come near to death, arose and was troubled no more by his wounds.

None too soon was this done; for after the assault the King yielded to Sauron and felled the White Tree, and turned then wholly away from the allegiance of his fathers. But Sauron caused to be built upon the hill in the midst of the city of the Númenóreans, Armenelos the

Golden, a mighty temple; and it was in the form of a circle at the base, and there the walls were fifty feet in thickness, and the width of the base was five hundred feet across the centre, and the walls rose from the ground five hundred feet, and they were crowned with a mighty dome. And that dome was roofed all with silver, and rose glittering in the sun, so that the light of it could be seen afar off; but soon the light was darkened, and the silver became black. For there was an altar of fire in the midst of the temple, and in the topmost of the dome there was a louver, whence there issued a great smoke. And the first fire upon the altar Sauron kindled with the hewn wood of Nimloth, and it crackled and was consumed; but men marvelled at the reek that went up from it, so that the land lay under a cloud for seven days, until slowly it passed into the west.

Thereafter the fire and smoke went up without ceasing; for the power of Sauron daily increased, and in that temple, with spilling of blood and torment and great wickedness, men made sacrifice to Melkor that he should release them from Death. And most often from among the Faithful they chose their victims; yet never openly on the charge that they would not worship Melkor, the Giver of Freedom, rather was cause sought against them that they hated the King and were his rebels, or that they plotted against their kin, devising lies and poisons. These charges were for the most part false; yet those were bitter days, and hate brings forth hate.

But for all this Death did not depart from the land, rather it came sooner and more often, and in many dreadful guises. For whereas aforetime men had grown slowly old, and had laid them down in the end to sleep, when they were weary at last of the world, now madness and sickness assailed them; and yet they were afraid to die and go out into the dark, the realm of the lord that they had taken; and they cursed themselves in their agony. And men took weapons in those days and slew one another for little cause; for they were become quick to anger, and Sauron, or those whom he had bound to himself, went about the land setting man against man, so that the people murmured against the King and the lords, or against any that had aught that they had not; and the men of power took cruel revenge.

Nonetheless for long it seemed to the Númenóreans that they prospered, and if they were not increased in happiness, yet they grew more strong, and their rich men ever richer. For with the aid and counsel of Sauron they multiplied their possessions, and they devised engines, and they built ever greater ships. And they sailed now with power and armoury to Middle-earth, and they came no longer as bringers of gifts, nor even as rulers, but as fierce men of war. And they hunted the men of Middle-earth and took their goods and enslaved them, and many they slew cruelly upon their altars. For they built in their fortresses temples and great tombs in those days; and men feared them, and the memory of the kindly kings of the ancient days faded from the world and was darkened by many a tale of dread.

Thus Ar-Pharazôn, King of the Land of the Star, grew to the mightiest tyrant that had yet been in the world since the reign of Morgoth, though in truth Sauron ruled all from behind the throne. But the years passed, and the King felt the shadow of death approach, as his days lengthened; and he was filled with fear and wrath. Now came the hour that Sauron had prepared and long had awaited. And Sauron spoke to the King, saying that his strength was now so great that he might think to have his will in all things, and be subject to no command or ban.

And he said: 'The Valar have possessed themselves of the land where there is no death; and they lie to you concerning it, hiding it as best they may, because of their avarice, and their fear lest the Kings of Men should wrest from them the deathless realm and rule the world in their stead. And though, doubtless, the gift of life unending is not for all, but only for such as are worthy, being men of might and pride and great lineage, yet against all justice is it done that this gift, which is his due, should be withheld from the King of Kings, Ar-Pharazôn, mightiest of the sons of Earth, to whom Manwë alone can be compared, if even he. But great kings do not brook denials, and take what is their due.'

Then Ar-Pharazôn, being besotted, and walking under the shadow of death, for his span was drawing towards its end, hearkened to Sauron; and he began to ponder in his heart how he might make war upon the Valar. He was long preparing this design, and he spoke not openly of it, yet it could not be hidden from all. And Amandil, becoming aware of the purposes of the King, was dismayed and filled with a great dread, for he knew that Men could not vanquish the Valar in war, and that ruin must come upon the world, if this war were not stayed. Therefore he called his son, Elendil, and he said to him:

'The days are dark, and there is no hope for Men, for the Faithful are few. Therefore I am minded to try that counsel which our forefather Eärendil took of old, to sail into the West, be there ban or no, and to speak to the Valar, even to Manwë himself, if may be, and beseech his aid ere all is lost.'

'Would you then betray the King?' said Elendil. 'For you know well the charge that they make against us, that we are traitors and spies, and that until this day it has been false.'

'If I thought that Manwë needed such a messenger,' said Amandil, 'I would betray the King. For there is but one loyalty from which no man can be absolved in heart for any cause. But it is for mercy upon Men and their deliverance from Sauron the Deceiver that I would plead, since some at least have remained faithful. And as for the Ban, I will suffer in myself the penalty, lest all my people should become guilty.'

'But what think you, my father, is like to befall those of your house whom you leave behind, when your deed becomes known?'

'It must not become known,' said Amandil. 'I will prepare my going in secret, and I will set sail into the east, whither daily the ships depart from our havens; and thereafter, as wind and chance may allow, I will go about, through south or north, back into the west, and seek what I may find. But for you and your folk, my son, I counsel that you should prepare yourselves other ships, and put aboard all such things as your hearts cannot bear to part with; and when the ships are ready, you should lie in the haven of Rómenna, and give out among men that you purpose, when you see your time, to follow me into the east. Amandil is no longer so dear to our kinsman upon the throne that he will grieve over much, if we seek to depart, for a season or for good. But let it not be seen that you intend to take many men, or he will be troubled, because of the war that he now plots, for which he will need all the force that he may gather. Seek out the Faithful that are known still to be true, and let them join you in secret, if they are willing to go with you, and share in your design.'

'And what shall that design be?' said Elendil.

'To meddle not in the war, and to watch,' answered Amandil. 'Until I return I can say no more. But it is most like that you shall fly from the Land of the Star with no star to guide you; for that land is defiled. Then you shall lose all that you have loved, foretasting death in life, seeking a land of exile elsewhere. But east or west the Valar alone can say.'

Then Amandil said farewell to all his household, as one that is about to die. 'For,' said he, 'it may well prove that you will see me never again; and that I shall show you no such sign as Eärendil showed long ago. But hold you ever in readiness, for the end of the world that we have known is now at hand.'

It is said that Amandil set sail in a small ship at night, and steered first eastward, and then went about and passed into the west. And he took with him three servants, dear to his heart, and never again were they heard of by word or sign in this world, nor is there any tale or guess of their fate. Men could not a second time be saved by any such embassy, and for the treason of Númenor there was no easy absolving.

But Elendil did all that his father had bidden, and his ships lay off the east coast of the land; and the Faithful put aboard their wives and their children, and their heirlooms, and great store of goods. Many things there were of beauty and power, such as the Númenóreans had contrived in the days of their wisdom, vessels and jewels, and scrolls of lore written in scarlet and black. And Seven Stones they had, the gift of the Eldar; but in the ship of Isildur was guarded the young tree, the scion of Nimloth the Fair. Thus Elendil held himself in readiness, and did not meddle in the evil deeds of those days; and ever he looked for a sign that did not come. Then he journeyed in secret to the western shores and gazed out over the sea, for sorrow and yearning were upon him, and he greatly loved his father. But naught could he descry save the fleets of Ar-Pharazôn gathering in the havens of the west.

Now aforetime in the isle of Númenor the weather was ever apt to the needs and liking of Men: rain in due season and ever in measure; and sunshine, now warmer, now cooler, and winds from the sea. And when the wind was in the west, it seemed to many that it was filled with a fragrance, fleeting but sweet, heart-stirring, as of flowers that bloom for ever in undying meads and have no names on mortal shores. But all this was now changed; for the sky itself was darkened, and there were storms of rain and hail in those days, and violent winds; and ever and anon a great ship of the Númenóreans would founder and return not to haven, though such a grief had not till then befallen them since the rising of the Star. And out of the west there would come at times a great cloud in the evening, shaped as it were an eagle, with pinions spread to the north and the south; and slowly it would loom up, blotting out the sunset, and then uttermost night would fall upon Númenor. And some of the eagles bore lightning beneath their wings, and thunder echoed between sea and cloud.

Then men grew afraid. 'Behold the Eagles of the Lords of the West!' they cried. 'The Eagles of Manwë are come upon Númenor!' And they fell upon their faces.

Then some few would repent for a season, but others hardened their hearts, and they shook their fists at heaven, saying: 'The Lords of the West have plotted against us. They strike first. The next blow shall be ours!' These words the King himself spoke, but they were devised by Sauron.

Now the lightnings increased and slew men upon the hills, and in the fields, and in the streets of the city; and a fiery bolt smote the dome of the Temple and shore it asunder, and it was wreathed in flame. But the Temple itself was unshaken, and Sauron stood there upon the pinnacle and defied the lightning and was unharmed; and in that hour men called him a god and did all that he would. When therefore the last portent came they heeded it little. For the land shook under them, and a groaning as of thunder underground was mingled with the roaring of the sea, and smoke issued from the peak of the Meneltarma. But all the more did Ar-Pharazôn press on with his armament.

In that time the fleets of the Númenóreans darkened the sea upon the west of the land, and they were like an archipelago of a thousand isles; their masts were as a forest upon the mountains, and their sails like a brooding cloud; and their banners were golden and black. And all things waited upon the word of Ar-Pharazôn; and Sauron withdrew into the inmost circle of the Temple, and men brought him victims to be burned.

Then the Eagles of the Lords of the West came up out of the dayfall, and they were arrayed as for battle, advancing in a line the end of which diminished beyond sight; and as they came their wings spread ever wider, grasping the sky. But the West burned red behind them, and they glowed beneath, as though they were lit with a flame of great anger, so that all Númenor was illumined as with a smouldering fire; and men looked upon the faces of their fellows, and it seemed to them that they were red with wrath.

Then Ar-Pharazôn hardened his heart, and he went aboard his mighty ship, Alcarondas, Castle of the Sea. Many-oared it was and many-masted, golden and sable; and upon it the throne of Ar-Pharazôn was set. Then he did on his panoply and his crown, and let raise his standard, and he gave the signal for the raising of the anchors; and in that hour the trumpets of Númenor outrang the thunder.

Thus the fleets of the Númenóreans moved against the menace of the West; and there was little wind, but they had many oars and many strong slaves to row beneath the lash. The sun went down, and there came a great silence. Darkness fell upon the land, and the sea was still, while the world waited for what should betide. Slowly the fleets passed out of the sight of the watchers in the havens, and their lights faded, and night took them; and in the morning they were gone.

For a wind arose in the east and it wafted them away; and they broke the Ban of the Valar, and sailed into forbidden seas, going up with war against the Deathless, to wrest from them everlasting life within the Circles of the World.

But the fleets of Ar-Pharazôn came up out of the deeps of the sea and encompassed Avallónë and all the isle of Eressëa, and the Eldar mourned, for the light of the setting sun was cut off by the cloud of the Númenóreans. And at last Ar-Pharazôn came even to Aman, the Blessed Realm, and the coasts of Valinor; and still all was silent, and doom hung by a thread. For Ar-Pharazôn wavered at the end, and almost he turned back. His heart misgave him when he looked upon the soundless shores and saw Taniquetil shining, whiter than snow, colder than death, silent, immutable, terrible as the shadow of the light of Ilúvatar. But pride was now his master, and at last he left his ship and strode upon the shore, claiming the land for his own, if none should do battle for it. And a host of the Númenóreans encamped in might about Túna, whence all the Eldar had fled.

Then Manwë upon the Mountain called upon Ilúvatar, and for that time the Valar laid down their government of Arda. But Ilúvatar showed forth his power, and he changed the fashion of the world; and a great chasm opened in the sea between Númenor and the Deathless Lands, and the waters flowed down into it, and the noise and smoke of the cataracts went up to heaven, and the world was shaken. And all the fleets of the Númenóreans were drawn down into the abyss, and they were drowned and swallowed up for ever. But Ar-Pharazôn the King and the mortal warriors that had set foot upon the land of Aman were buried under falling hills: there it is said that they lie imprisoned in the Caves of the Forgotten, until the Last Battle and the Day of Doom.

But the land of Aman and Eressëa of the Eldar were taken away and removed beyond the reach of Men for ever. And Andor, the Land of Gift, Númenor of the Kings, Elenna of the Star of Eärendil, was utterly destroyed. For it was nigh to the east of the great rift, and its foundations were overturned, and it fell and went down into darkness, and is no more. And there is not now upon Earth any place abiding where the memory of a time without evil is preserved. For Ilúvatar cast back the Great Seas west of Middle-earth, and the Empty Lands east of it, and new lands and new seas were made; and the world was diminished, for Valinor and Eressëa were taken from it into the realm of hidden things.

In an hour unlooked for by Men this doom befell, on the nine and thirtieth day since the passing of the fleets. Then suddenly fire burst from the Meneltarma, and there came a mighty wind and a tumult of the earth, and the sky reeled, and the hills slid, and Númenor went down into the sea, with all its children and its wives and its maidens and its ladies proud; and all its gardens and its halls and its towers, its tombs and its riches, and its jewels and its webs and its things painted and carven, and its laughter and its mirth and its music, its wisdom and its lore: they vanished for ever. And last of all the mounting wave, green and cold and plumed with foam, climbing over the land, took to its bosom Tar-Míriel the Queen, fairer than silver or ivory or pearls. Too late she strove to ascend the steep ways of the Meneltarma to the holy place; for the waters overtook her, and her cry was lost in the roaring of the wind.

But whether or no it were that Amandil came indeed to Valinor and Manwë hearkened to his prayer, by grace of the Valar Elendil and his sons and their people were spared from the ruin of that day. For Elendil had remained in Rómenna, refusing the summons of the King when he set forth to war; and avoiding the soldiers of Sauron that came to seize him and drag him to the fires of the Temple, he went aboard his ship and stood off from the shore, waiting on the time. There he was protected by the land from the great draught of the sea that drew all towards the abyss, and afterwards he was sheltered from the first fury of the storm. But when the devouring wave rolled over the land and Númenor toppled to its fall, then he would have been overwhelmed and would have deemed it the lesser grief to perish, for no wrench of death could be more bitter than the loss and agony of that day; but the great wind took him, wilder than any wind that Men had known, roaring from the west, and it swept his ships far away; and it rent their sails and snapped their masts, hunting the unhappy men like straws upon the water.

Nine ships there were: four for Elendil, and for Isildur three, and for Anárion two; and they fled before the black gale out of the twilight of doom into the darkness of the world. And the deeps rose beneath them in towering anger, and waves like unto mountains moving with great caps of writhen snow bore them up amid the wreckage of the clouds, and after many days cast them away upon the shores of Middle-earth. And all the coasts and seaward regions of the western world suffered great change and ruin in that time; for the seas invaded the lands, and shores foundered, and ancient isles were drowned, and new isles were uplifted; and hills crumbled and rivers were turned into strange courses.

Elendil and his sons after founded kingdoms in Middle-earth; and though their lore and craft was but an echo of that which had been ere Sauron came to Númenor, yet very great it seemed to the wild men of the world. And much is said in other lore of the deeds of the heirs of Elendil in the age that came after, and of their strife with Sauron that not yet was ended.

For Sauron himself was filled with great fear at the wrath of the Valar, and the doom that Eru laid upon sea and land. It was greater far than aught he had looked for, hoping only for the death of the Númenóreans and the defeat of their proud king. And Sauron, sitting in his black seat in the midst of the Temple, had laughed when he heard the trumpets of Ar-Pharazôn sounding for battle; and again he had laughed when he heard the thunder of the storm; and a third time, even as he laughed at his own thought, thinking what he would do now in the world, being rid of the Edain for ever, he was taken in the midst of his mirth, and his seat and his temple fell into the abyss. But Sauron was not of mortal flesh, and though he was robbed now of that shape in which he had wrought so great an evil, so that he could never again appear fair to the eyes of Men, yet his spirit arose out of the deep and passed as a shadow and a black wind over the sea, and came back to Middle-earth and to Mordor that was his home. There he took up again his great Ring in Barad-dûr, and dwelt there, dark and silent, until he wrought himself a new guise, an image of malice and hatred made visible; and the Eye of Sauron the Terrible few could endure.

But these things come not into the tale of the Drowning of Númenor, of which now all is told. And even the name of that land perished, and Men spoke thereafter not of Elenna, nor of Andor the Gift that was taken away, nor of Númenórë on the confines of the world; but the exiles on the shores of the sea, if they turned towards the West in the desire of their hearts, spoke of Mar-nu-Falmar that was whelmed in the waves, Akallabêth the Downfallen, Atalantë in the Eldarin tongue.

Among the Exiles many believed that the summit of the Meneltarma, the Pillar of Heaven, was not drowned for ever, but rose again above the waves, a lonely island lost in the great waters; for it had been a hallowed place, and even in the days of Sauron none had defiled it. And some there were of the seed of Eärendil that afterwards sought for it, because it was said among loremasters that the farsighted men of old could see from the Meneltarma a glimmer of the Deathless Land. For even after the ruin the hearts of the Dúnedain were still set westwards; and though they knew indeed that the world was changed, they said: 'Avallónë is vanished from the Earth and the Land of Aman is taken away, and in the world of this present darkness they cannot be found. Yet once they were, and therefore they still are, in true being and in the whole shape of the world as at first it was devised.'

For the Dúnedain held that even mortal Men, if so blessed, might look upon other times than those of their bodies' life; and they longed ever to escape from the shadows of their exile and to see in some fashion the light that dies not; for the sorrow of the thought of death had pursued them over the deeps of the sea. Thus it was that great mariners among them would still search the empty seas, hoping to come upon the Isle of Meneltarma, and there to see a vision of things that were. But they found it not. And those that sailed far came only to the new lands, and found them like to the old lands, and subject to death. And those that sailed furthest set but a girdle about the Earth and returned weary at last to the place of their beginning; and they said: 'All roads are now bent.'

Thus in after days, what by the voyages of ships, what by lore and star-craft, the kings of Men knew that the world was indeed made round, and yet the Eldar were permitted still to depart and to come to the Ancient West and to Avallónë, if they would. Therefore the loremasters of Men said that a Straight Road must still be, for those that were permitted to find it. And they taught that, while the new world fell away, the old road and the path of the memory of the West still went on, as it were a mighty bridge invisible that passed through the air of breath and of flight (which were bent now as the world was bent), and traversed Ilmen which flesh unaided cannot endure, until it came to Tol Eressëa, the Lonely Isle, and maybe even beyond, to Valinor, where the Valar still dwell and watch the unfolding of the story of the world. And tales and rumours arose along the shores of the sea concerning mariners and men forlorn upon the water who, by some fate or grace or favour of the Valar, had entered in upon the Straight Way and seen the face of the world sink below them, and so had come to the lamplit quays of Avallónë, or verily to the last beaches on the margin of Aman, and there had looked upon the White Mountain, dreadful and beautiful, before they died.

OF THE RINGS OF POWER AND THE THIRD AGE

OF THE RINGS OF POWER AND THE THIRD AGE

in which these tales come to their end

Of old there was Sauron the Maia, whom the Sindar in Beleriand named Gorthaur. In the beginning of Arda Melkor seduced him to his allegiance, and he became the greatest and most trusted of the servants of the Enemy, and the most perilous, for he could assume many forms, and for long if he willed he could still appear noble and beautiful, so as to deceive all but the most wary.

When Thangorodrim was broken and Morgoth overthrown, Sauron put on his fair hue again and did obeisance to Eönwë, the herald of Manwë, and abjured all his evil deeds. And some hold that this was not at first falsely done, but that Sauron in truth repented, if only out of fear, being dismayed by the fall of Morgoth and the great wrath of the Lords of the West. But it was not within the power of Eönwë to pardon those of his own order, and he commanded Sauron to return to Aman and there receive the judgement of Manwë. Then Sauron was ashamed, and he was unwilling to return in humiliation and to receive from the Valar a sentence, it might be, of long servitude in proof of his good faith; for under Morgoth his power had been great. Therefore when Eönwë departed he hid himself in Middle-earth; and he fell back into evil, for the bonds that Morgoth had laid upon him were very strong.

In the Great Battle and the tumults of the fall of Thangorodrim there were mighty convulsions in the earth, and Beleriand was broken and laid waste; and northward and westward many lands sank beneath the waters of the Great Sea. In the east, in Ossiriand, the walls of Ered Luin were broken, and a great gap was made in them towards the south, and a gulf of the sea flowed in. Into that gulf the River Lhûn fell by a new course, and it was called therefore the Gulf of Lhûn. That country had of old been named Lindon by the Noldor, and this name it bore thereafter; and many of the Eldar still dwelt there, lingering, unwilling yet to forsake Beleriand where they had fought and laboured long. Gil-galad son of Fingon was their king, and with him was Elrond Half-elven, son of Eärendil the Mariner and brother of Elros first king of Númenor.

Upon the shores of the Gulf of Lhûn the Elves built their havens, and named them Mithlond; and there they held many ships, for the harbourage was good. From the grey Havens the Eldar ever and anon set sail, fleeing from the darkness of the days of Earth; for by the mercy of the Valar the Firstborn could still follow the Straight Road and return, if they would, to their kindred in Eressëa and Valinor beyond the encircling seas.

Others of the Eldar there were who crossed the mountains of Ered Luin in that age and passed into the inner lands. Many of these were Teleri, survivors of Doriath and Ossiriand; and they established realms among the Silvan Elves in woods and mountains far from the sea, for which nonetheless they ever yearned in their hearts. Only in Eregion, which Men called Hollin, did Elves of Noldorin race establish a lasting realm beyond the Ered Luin. Eregion was nigh to the great mansions of the Dwarves that were named Khazad-dûm, but by the Elves Hadhodrond, and afterwards Moria. From Ost-in-Edhil, the city of the Elves, the highroad ran to the west gate of Khazad-dûm, for a friendship arose between Dwarves and Elves, such as has never elsewhere been, to the enrichment of both those peoples. In Eregion the craftsmen of the Gwaith-i-Mírdain, the People of the Jewel-smiths, surpassed in cunning all that have ever wrought, save only Fëanor himself; and indeed greatest in skill among them was Celebrimbor, son of Curufin, who was estranged from his father and remained in Nargothrond when Celegorm and Curufin were driven forth, as is told in the *Quenta Silmarillion*.

Elsewhere in Middle-earth there was peace for many years; yet the lands were for the most part savage and desolate, save only where the people of Beleriand came. Many Elves dwelt there indeed, as they had dwelt through the countless years, wandering free in the wide lands far from the Sea; but they were Avari, to whom the deeds of Beleriand were but a rumour and Valinor only a distant name. And in the south and in the further east Men multiplied; and most of them turned to evil, for Sauron was at work.

Seeing the desolation of the world, Sauron said in his heart that the Valar, having overthrown Morgoth, had again forgotten Middle-earth; and his pride grew apace. He looked with hatred on the Eldar, and he feared the Men of Númenor who came back at whiles in their ships to the shores of Middle-earth; but for long he dissembled his mind and concealed the dark designs that he shaped in his heart.

Men he found the easiest to sway of all the peoples of the Earth; but long he sought to persuade the Elves to his service, for he knew that the Firstborn had the greater power; and he went far and wide among them, and his hue was still that of one both fair and wise. Only to Lindon he did not come, for Gil-galad and Elrond doubted him and his fair-seeming, and though they knew not who in truth he was they would not admit him to that land. But elsewhere the Elves received him gladly, and few among them hearkened to the messengers from Lindon bidding them beware; for Sauron took to himself the name of Annatar, the Lord of Gifts, and they had at first much profit from his friendship. And he said to them: 'Alas, for the weakness of the great! For a mighty king is Gil-galad, and wise in all lore is Master Elrond, and yet they will not aid me in my labours. Can it be that they do not desire to see other lands become as blissful as their own? But wherefore should Middle-earth remain for ever desolate and dark, whereas the Elves could make it as fair as Eressëa, nay even as Valinor? And since you have not returned thither, as you might, I perceive that you love this Middle-earth, as do I. Is it not then our task to labour together for its enrichment, and for the raising of all the Elven-kindreds that wander here untaught to the height of that power and knowledge which those have who are beyond the Sea?'

It was in Eregion that the counsels of Sauron were most gladly received, for in that land the Noldor desired ever to increase the skill and subtlety of their works. Moreover they were not at peace in their hearts, since they had refused to return into the West, and they desired both to stay in Middle-earth, which indeed they loved, and yet to enjoy the bliss of those that had departed. Therefore they hearkened to Sauron, and they learned of him many things, for his knowledge was great. In those days the smiths of Ost-in-Edhil surpassed all that they had contrived before; and they took thought, and they made Rings of Power. But Sauron guided their labours, and he was aware of all that they did; for his desire was to set a bond upon the Elves and to bring them under his vigilance.

Now the Elves made many rings; but secretly Sauron made One Ring to rule all the others, and their power was bound up with it, to be subject wholly to it and to last only so long as it too should last. And much of the strength and will of Sauron passed into that One Ring; for the power of the Elven-rings was very great, and that which should govern them must be a thing of surpassing potency; and Sauron forged it in the Mountain of Fire in the Land of Shadow. And while he wore the One Ring he could perceive all the things that were done by means of the lesser rings, and he could see and govern the very thoughts of those that wore them.

But the Elves were not so lightly to be caught. As soon as Sauron set the One Ring upon his finger they were aware of him; and they knew him, and perceived that he would be master of them, and of all that they wrought. Then in anger and fear they took off their rings. But he, finding that he was betrayed and that the Elves were not deceived, was filled with wrath; and he came against them with open war, demanding that all the rings should be delivered to him, since the Elven-smiths could not have attained to their making without his lore and counsel. But the Elves fled from him; and three of their rings they saved, and bore them away, and hid them.

Now these were the Three that had last been made, and they possessed the greatest powers. Narya, Nenya, and Vilya, they were named, the Rings of Fire, and of Water, and of Air, set with ruby and adamant and sapphire; and of all the Elven-rings Sauron most desired to possess them, for those who had them in their keeping could ward off the decays of time and postpone the weariness of the world. But Sauron could not discover them, for they were given into the hands of the Wise, who concealed them and never again used them openly while Sauron kept the Ruling Ring. Therefore the Three remained unsullied, for they were forged by Celebrimbor alone, and the hand of Sauron had never touched them; yet they also were subject to the One.

From that time war never ceased between Sauron and the Elves; and Eregion was laid waste, and Celebrimbor slain, and the doors of Moria were shut. In that time the stronghold and refuge of Imladris, that Men called Rivendell, was founded by Elrond Half-elven; and long it endured. But Sauron gathered into his hands all the remaining Rings of Power; and he dealt them out to the other peoples of Middle-earth, hoping thus to bring under his sway all those that desired secret power beyond the measure of their kind. Seven rings he gave to the Dwarves; but to Men he gave nine, for Men proved in this matter as in others the readiest to his will. And all those rings that he governed he perverted, the more easily since he had a part in their making, and they were accursed, and they betrayed in the end all those that used them. The Dwarves indeed proved tough and hard to tame; they ill endure the domination of others, and the thoughts of their hearts are hard to fathom, nor can they be turned to shadows. They used their rings only for the getting of wealth; but wrath and an overmastering greed of gold were kindled in their hearts, of which evil enough after came to the profit of Sauron. It is said that the foundation of each of the Seven Hoards of the Dwarf-kings of old was a golden ring; but all those hoards long ago were plundered and the Dragons devoured them, and of the Seven Rings some were consumed in fire and some Sauron recovered.

Men proved easier to ensnare. Those who used the Nine Rings became mighty in their day, kings, sorcerers, and warriors of old. They obtained glory and great wealth, yet it turned to their undoing. They had, as it seemed, unending life, yet life became unendurable to them. They could walk, if they would, unseen by all eyes in this world beneath the sun, and they could see things in worlds invisible to mortal men; but too often they beheld only the phantoms and delusions of Sauron. And one by one, sooner or later, according to their native strength and to the good or evil of their wills in the beginning, they fell under the thraldom of the ring that they bore and under the domination of the One, which was Sauron's. And they became for ever invisible save to him that wore the Ruling Ring, and they entered into the realm of shadows. The Nazgûl were they, the Ringwraiths, the Enemy's most terrible servants; darkness went with them, and they cried with the voices of death.

Now Sauron's lust and pride increased, until he knew no bounds, and he determined to make himself master of all things in Middle-earth, and to destroy the Elves, and to compass, if he might, the downfall of Númenor. He brooked no freedom nor any rivalry, and he named himself Lord of the Earth. A mask he still could wear so that if he wished he might deceive the eyes of Men, seeming to them wise and fair. But he ruled rather by force and fear, if they might avail; and those who perceived his shadow spreading over the world called him the Dark Lord and named him the Enemy; and he gathered again under his government all the evil things of the days of Morgoth that remained on earth or beneath it, and the Orcs were at his command

and multiplied like flies. Thus the Black Years began, which the Elves call the Days of Flight. In that time many of the Elves of Middle-earth fled to Lindon and thence over the seas never to return; and many were destroyed by Sauron and his servants. But in Lindon Gil-galad still maintained his power, and Sauron dared not as yet to pass the Mountains of Ered Luin nor to assail the Havens; and Gil-galad was aided by the Númenóreans. Elsewhere Sauron reigned, and those who would be free took refuge in the fastnesses of wood and mountain, and ever fear pursued them. In the east and south well nigh all Men were under his dominion, and they grew strong in those days and built many towns and walls of stone, and they were numerous and fierce in war and armed with iron. To them Sauron was both king and god; and they feared him exceedingly, for he surrounded his abode with fire.

Yet there came at length a stay in the onslaught of Sauron upon the westlands. For, as is told in the *Akallabêth*, he was challenged by the might of Númenor. So great was the power and splendour of the Númenóreans in the noontide of their realm that the servants of Sauron would not withstand them, and hoping to accomplish by cunning what he could not achieve by force, he left Middle-earth for a while and went to Númenor as a hostage of Tar-Calion the King. And there he abode, until at the last by his craft he had corrupted the hearts of most of that people, and set them at war with the Valar, and so compassed their ruin, as he had long desired. But that ruin was more terrible than Sauron had foreseen, for he had forgotten the might of the Lords of the West in their anger. The world was broken, and the land was swallowed up, and the seas rose over it, and Sauron himself went down into the abyss. But his spirit arose and fled back on a dark wind to Middle-earth, seeking a home. There he found that the power of Gil-galad had grown great in the years of his absence, and it was spread now over wide regions of the north and west, and had passed beyond the Misty Mountains and the Great River even to the borders of Greenwood the Great, and was drawing nigh to the strong places where once he had dwelt secure. Then Sauron withdrew to his fortress in the Black Land and meditated war.

In that time those of the Númenóreans who were saved from destruction fled eastward, as is told in the *Akallabêth*. The chief of these were Elendil the Tall and his sons, Isildur and Anárion. Kinsmen of the King they were, descendants of Elros, but they had been unwilling to listen to Sauron, and had refused to make war on the Lords of the West. Manning their ships with all who remained faithful they forsook the land of Númenor ere ruin came upon it. They were mighty men and their ships were strong and tall, but the tempests overtook them, and they were borne aloft on hills of water even to the clouds, and they descended upon Middle-earth like birds of the storm.

Elendil was cast up by the waves in the land of Lindon, and he was befriended by Gil-galad. Thence he passed up the River Lhûn, and beyond Ered Luin he established his realm, and his people dwelt in many places in Eriador about the courses of the Lhûn and the Baranduin; but his chief city was at Annúminas beside the water of Lake Nenuial. At Fornost upon the North Downs also the Númenóreans dwelt, and in Cardolan, and in the hills of Rhudaur; and towers they raised upon Emyn Beraid and upon Amon Sûl; and there remain many barrows and ruined works in those places, but the towers of Emyn Beraid still look towards the sea.

Isildur and Anárion were borne away southwards, and at the last they brought their ships up the Great River Anduin, that flows out of Rhovanion into the western sea in the Bay of Belfalas; and they established a realm in those lands that were after called Gondor, whereas the Northern Kingdom was named Arnor. Long before in the days of their power the mariners of Númenor had established a haven and strong places about the mouths of Anduin, in despite of Sauron in the Black Land that lay nigh upon the east. In the later days to this haven came only the Faithful of Númenor, and many therefore of the folk of the coastlands in that region were in whole or in part akin to the Elf-friends and the people of Elendil, and they welcomed his sons. The chief city of this southern realm was Osgiliath, through the midst of which the Great River flowed; and the Númenóreans built there a great bridge, upon which there were towers and houses of stone wonderful to behold, and tall ships came up out of the sea to the quays of the city. Other strong places they built also upon either hand: Minas Ithil, the Tower of the Rising Moon, eastward upon a shoulder of the Mountains of Shadow as a threat to Mordor; and to the westward Minas Anor, the Tower of the Setting Sun, at the feet of Mount Mindolluin, as a shield against the wild men of the dales. In Minas Ithil was the house of Isildur, and in Minas Anor the house of Anárion, but they shared the realm between them and their thrones were set side by side in the Great Hall of Osgiliath. These were the chief dwellings of the Númenóreans in Gondor, but other works marvellous and strong they built in the land in the days of their power, at the Argonath, and at Aglarond, and at Erech; and in the circle of Angrenost, which Men called Isengard, they made the Pinnacle of Orthanc of unbreakable stone.

Many treasures and great heirlooms of virtue and wonder the Exiles had brought from Númenor; and of these the most renowned were the Seven Stones and the White Tree. The White Tree was grown from the fruit of Nimloth the Fair that stood in the courts of the King at Armenelos in Númenor, ere Sauron burned it; and Nimloth was in its turn descended from the Tree of Tirion, that was an image of the Eldest of Trees, White Telperion which Yavanna caused to grow in the land of the Valar. The Tree, memorial of the Eldar and of the light of Valinor, was planted in Minas Ithil before the house of Isildur, since he it was that had saved the fruit from destruction; but the Stones were divided.

Three Elendil took, and his sons each two. Those of Elendil were set in towers upon Emyn Beraid, and upon Amon Sûl, and in the city of Annúminas. But those of his sons were at Minas Ithil and Minas Anor, and at Orthanc and in Osgiliath. Now these Stones had this virtue that those who looked therein might perceive in them things far off, whether in place or in time. For the most part they revealed only things near to another kindred Stone, for the Stones each called to each; but those who possessed great strength of will and of mind might learn to direct their gaze whither they would. Thus the Númenóreans were aware of many things that their enemies wished to conceal, and little escaped their vigilance in the days of their might.

It is said that the towers of Emyn Beraid were not built indeed by the Exiles of Númenor, but were raised by Gil-galad for Elendil, his friend; and the Seeing Stone of Emyn Beraid was set in Elostirion, the tallest of the towers. Thither Elendil would repair, and thence he would gaze out over the sundering seas, when the yearning of exile was upon him; and it is believed that thus he would at whiles see far away even the Tower of Avallónë upon Eressëa, where the Master-stone abode, and yet abides. These stones were gifts of the Eldar to Amandil, father of Elendil, for the comfort of the Faithful of Númenor in their dark days, when the Elves might come no longer to that land under the shadow of Sauron. They were called the Palantíri, those that watch from afar; but all those that were brought to Middle-earth long ago were lost.

Thus the Exiles of Númenor established their realms in Arnor and in Gondor; but ere many years had passed it became manifest that their enemy, Sauron, had also returned. He came in secret, as has been told, to his ancient kingdom of Mordor beyond the Ephel Dúath, the Mountains of Shadow, and that country marched with Gondor upon the east. There above the valley of Gorgoroth was built his fortress vast and strong, Barad-dûr, the Dark Tower; and there was a fiery mountain in that land that the Elves named Orodruin. Indeed for that reason Sauron had set there his dwelling long before, for he used the fire that welled there from the heart of the earth in his sorceries and in his forging; and in the midst of the Land of Mordor he had fashioned the Ruling Ring. There now he brooded in the dark, until he had wrought for himself a new shape; and it was terrible, for his fair semblance had departed for ever when he was cast into the abyss at the drowning of Númenor. He took up again the great Ring and clothed himself in power; and the malice of the Eye of Sauron few even of the great among Elves and Men could endure.

Now Sauron prepared war against the Eldar and the Men of Westernesse, and the fires of the Mountain were wakened again. Wherefore seeing the smoke of Orodruin from afar, and perceiving that Sauron had returned, the Númenóreans named that mountain anew Amon Amarth, which is Mount Doom. And Sauron gathered to him great strength of his servants out of the east and the south; and among them were not a few of the high race of Númenor. For in the days of the sojourn of Sauron in that land the hearts of well nigh all its people had been turned towards darkness. Therefore many of those who sailed east in that time and made fortresses and dwellings upon the coasts were already bent to his will, and they served him still gladly in Middle-earth. But because of the power of Gil-galad these renegades, lords both mighty and evil, for the most part took up their abodes in the southlands far away; yet two there were, Herumor and Fuinur, who rose to power among the Haradrim, a great and cruel people that dwelt in the wide lands south of Mordor beyond the mouths of Anduin.

When therefore Sauron saw his time he came with great force against the new realm of Gondor, and he took Minas Ithil, and he destroyed the White Tree of Isildur that grew there. But Isildur escaped, and taking with him a seedling of the Tree he went with his wife and his sons by ship down the River, and they sailed from the mouths of Anduin seeking Elendil. Meanwhile Anárion held Osgiliath against the Enemy, and for that time drove him back to the mountains; but Sauron gathered his strength again, and Anárion knew that unless help should come his kingdom would not long stand.

Now Elendil and Gil-galad took counsel together, for they perceived that Sauron would grow too strong and would overcome all his enemies one by one, if they did not unite against him. Therefore they made that League which is called the Last Alliance, and they marched east into Middle-earth gathering a great host of Elves and Men; and they halted for a while at Imladris. It is said that the host that was there assembled was fairer and more splendid in arms than any that has since been seen in Middle-earth, and none greater has been mustered since the host of the Valar went against Thangorodrim.

From Imladris they crossed the Misty Mountains by many passes and marched down the River Anduin, and so came at last upon the host of Sauron on Dagorlad, the Battle Plain, which lies before the gate of the Black Land. All living things were divided in that day, and some of every kind, even of beasts and birds, were found in either host, save the Elves only. They alone were undivided and followed Gil-galad. Of the Dwarves few fought upon either side; but the kindred of Durin of Moria fought against Sauron.

The host of Gil-galad and Elendil had the victory, for the might of the Elves was still great in those days, and the Númenóreans were strong and tall, and terrible in their wrath. Against Aeglos the spear of Gil-galad none could stand; and the sword of Elendil filled Orcs and Men with fear, for it shone with the light of the sun and of the moon, and it was named Narsil.

Then Gil-galad and Elendil passed into Mordor and encompassed the stronghold of Sauron; and they laid siege to it for seven years, and suffered grievous loss by fire and by the darts and bolts of the Enemy, and Sauron sent many sorties against them. There in the valley of Gorgoroth Anárion son of Elendil was slain, and many others. But at the last the siege was so strait that Sauron himself came forth; and he wrestled with Gil-galad and Elendil, and they both were slain, and the sword of Elendil broke under him as he fell. But Sauron also was thrown down, and with the hilt-shard of Narsil Isildur cut the Ruling Ring from the hand of Sauron and took it for his own. Then Sauron was for that time vanquished, and he forsook his body, and his spirit fled far away and hid in waste places; and he took no visible shape again for many long years.

Thus began the Third Age of the World, after the Eldest Days and the Black Years; and there was still hope in that time and the memory of mirth, and for long the White Tree of the Eldar flowered in the courts of the Kings of Men, for the seedling which he had saved Isildur planted in the citadel of Anor in memory of his brother, ere he departed from Gondor. The servants of Sauron were routed and dispersed, yet they were not wholly destroyed; and though many Men turned now from evil and became subject to the heirs of Elendil, yet many more remembered Sauron in their hearts and hated the kingdoms of the West. The Dark Tower was levelled to the ground, yet its foundations remained, and it was not forgotten. The Númenóreans indeed set a guard upon the land of Mordor, but none dared dwell there because of the terror of the memory of Sauron, and because of the Mountain of Fire that stood nigh to Barad-dûr; and the valley of Gorgoroth was filled with ash. Many of the Elves and many of the Númenóreans and of Men who were their allies had perished in the Battle and the Siege; and Elendil the Tall and Gil-galad the High King were no more. Never again was such a host assembled, nor was there any such league of Elves and Men; for after Elendil's day the two kindreds became estranged.

The Ruling Ring passed out of the knowledge even of the Wise in that age; yet it was not unmade. For Isildur would not surrender it to Elrond and Círdan who stood by. They counselled him to cast it into the fire of Orodruin nigh at hand, in which it had been forged, so that it should perish, and the power of Sauron be for ever diminished, and he should remain only as a shadow of malice in the wilderness. But Isildur refused this counsel, saying: 'This I will have as weregild for my father's death, and my brother's. Was it not I that dealt the Enemy his death-blow?' And the Ring that he held seemed to him exceedingly fair to look on; and he would not suffer it to be destroyed. Taking it therefore he returned at first to Minas Anor, and there planted the White Tree in memory of his brother Anárion. But soon he departed, and after he had given counsel to Meneldil, his brother's son, and had committed to him the realm of the south, he bore away the Ring, to be an heirloom of his house, and marched north from Gondor by the way that Elendil had come; and he forsook the South Kingdom, for he purposed to take up his father's realm in Eriador, far from the shadow of the Black Land.

But Isildur was overwhelmed by a host of Orcs that lay in wait in the Misty Mountains; and they descended upon him at unawares in his camp between the Greenwood and the Great River, nigh to Loeg Ningloron, the Gladden Fields, for he was heedless and set no guard, deeming that all his foes were overthrown. There well nigh all his people were slain, and among them were his three elder sons, Elendur, Aratan, and Ciryon; but his wife and his youngest son, Valandil, he had left in Imladris when he went to the war. Isildur himself escaped by means of the Ring, for when he wore it he was invisible to all eyes; but the Orcs hunted him by scent and slot, until he came to the River and plunged in. There the Ring betrayed him and avenged its maker, for it slipped from his finger as he swam, and it was lost in the water. Then the Orcs saw him as he laboured in the stream, and they shot him with many arrows, and that was his end. Only three of his people came ever back over the mountains after long wandering; and of these one was Ohtar his esquire, to whose keeping he had given the shards of the sword of Elendil.

Thus Narsil came in due time to the hand of Valandil, Isildur's heir, in Imladris; but the blade was broken and its light was extinguished, and it was not forged anew. And Master Elrond foretold that this would not be done until the Ruling Ring should be found again and Sauron should return; but the hope of Elves and Men was that these things might never come to pass.

Valandil took up his abode in Annúminas, but his folk were diminished, and of the Númenóreans and of the Men of Eriador there remained now too few to people the land or to maintain all the places that Elendil had built; in Dagorlad, and in Mordor, and upon the Gladden Fields many had fallen. And it came to pass after the days of Eärendur, the seventh king that followed Valandil, that the Men of Westernesse, the Dúnedain of the North, became divided into petty realms and lordships, and their foes devoured them one by one. Ever they dwindled with the years, until their glory passed, leaving only green mounds in the grass. At length naught was left of them but a strange people wandering secretly in the wild, and other men knew not their homes nor the purpose of their journeys, and save in Imladris, in the house of Elrond, their ancestry was forgotten. Yet the shards of the sword were cherished during many lives of Men by the heirs of Isildur; and their line, from father to son, remained unbroken.

In the south the realm of Gondor endured, and for a time its splendour grew, until it recalled the wealth and majesty of Númenor ere it fell. High towers the people of Gondor built, and strong places, and havens of many ships; and the Winged Crown of the Kings of Men was held in awe by people of many lands and tongues. For many a year the White Tree grew before the King's house in Minas Anor, the seed of that tree which Isildur brought out of the deeps of the sea from Númenor; and the seed before that came from Avallónë, and before that from Valinor in the Day before days when the world was young.

Yet at the last, in the wearing of the swift years of Middle-earth,

Gondor waned, and the line of Meneldil son of Anárion failed. For the blood of the Númenóreans became much mingled with that of other men, and their power and wisdom was diminished, and their life-span was shortened, and the watch upon Mordor slumbered. And in the days of Telemnar, the third and twentieth of the line of Meneldil, a plague came upon dark winds out of the east, and it smote the King and his children, and many of the people of Gondor perished. Then the forts on the borders of Mordor were deserted, and Minas Ithil was emptied of its people; and evil entered again into the Black Land secretly, and the ashes of Gorgoroth were stirred as by a cold wind, for dark shapes gathered there. It is said that these were indeed the Úlairi, whom Sauron called the Nazgûl, the Nine Ringwraiths that had long remained hidden, but returned now to prepare the ways of their Master, for he had begun to grow again.

And in the days of Eärnil they made their first stroke, and they came by night out of Mordor over the passes of the Mountains of Shadow, and took Minas Ithil for their abode; and they made it a place of such dread that none dared to look upon it. Thereafter it was called Minas Morgul, the Tower of Sorcery; and Minas Morgul was ever at war with Minas Anor in the west. Then Osgiliath, which in the waning of the people had long been deserted, became a place of ruins and a city of ghosts. But Minas Anor endured, and it was named anew Minas Tirith, the Tower of Guard; for there the kings caused to be built in the citadel a white tower, very tall and fair, and its eye was upon many lands. Proud still and strong was that city, and in it the White Tree still flowered for a while before the house of the Kings; and there the remnant of the Númenóreans still defended the passage of the River against the terrors of Minas Morgul and against all the enemies of the West, Orcs and monsters and evil Men; and thus the lands behind them, west of Anduin, were protected from war and destruction.

Still Minas Tirith endured after the days of Eärnur, son of Eärnil, and the last King of Gondor. He it was that rode alone to the gates of Minas Morgul to meet the challenge of the Morgul-lord; and he met him in single combat, but he was betrayed by the Nazgûl and taken alive into the city of torment, and no living man saw him ever again. Now Eärnur left no heir, but when the line of the Kings failed the Stewards of the house of Mardil the Faithful ruled the city and its ever-shrinking realm; and the Rohirrim, the Horsemen of the North, came and dwelt in the green land of Rohan, which before was named Calenardhon and was a part of the kingdom of Gondor; and the

Rohirrim aided the Lords of the City in their wars. And northward, beyond the Falls of Rauros and the Gates of Argonath, there were as yet other defences, powers more ancient of which Men knew little, against whom the things of evil did not dare to move, until in the ripening of time their dark lord, Sauron, should come forth again. And until that time was come, never again after the days of Eärnil did the Nazgûl dare to cross the River or to come forth from their city in shape visible to Men.

In all the days of the Third Age, after the fall of Gil-galad, Master Elrond abode in Imladris, and he gathered there many Elves, and other folk of wisdom and power from among all the kindreds of Middle-earth, and he preserved through many lives of Men the memory of all that had been fair; and the house of Elrond was a refuge for the weary and the oppressed, and a treasury of good counsel and wise lore. In that house were harboured the Heirs of Isildur, in childhood and old age, because of the kinship of their blood with Elrond himself, and because he knew in his wisdom that one should come of their line to whom a great part was appointed in the last deeds of that Age. And until that time came the shards of Elendil's sword were given into the keeping of Elrond, when the days of the Dúnedain darkened and they became a wandering people.

In Eriador Imladris was the chief dwelling of the High Elves; but at the Grey Havens of Lindon there abode also a remnant of the people of Gil-galad the Elvenking. At times they would wander into the lands of Eriador, but for the most part they dwelt near the shores of the sea, building and tending the elven-ships wherein those of the Firstborn who grew weary of the world set sail into the uttermost West. Círdan the Shipwright was lord of the Havens and mighty among the Wise.

Of the Three Rings that the Elves had preserved unsullied no open word was ever spoken among the Wise, and few even of the Eldar knew where they were bestowed. Yet after the fall of Sauron their power was ever at work, and where they abode there mirth also dwelt and all things were unstained by the griefs of time. Therefore ere the Third Age was ended the Elves perceived that the Ring of Sapphire was with Elrond, in the fair valley of Rivendell, upon whose house the stars of heaven most brightly shone; whereas the Ring of Adamant was in the Land of Lórien where dwelt the Lady Galadriel. A queen she was of the woodland Elves, the wife of Celeborn of Doriath, yet she herself was of the Noldor and remembered the Day before days in Valinor, and she was the mightiest and fairest of all the Elves that remained in Middle-earth. But the Red Ring remained hidden until the end, and none save Elrond and Galadriel and Círdan knew to whom it had been committed.

Thus it was that in two domains the bliss and beauty of the Elves remained still undiminished while that Age endured: in Imladris; and in Lothlórien, the hidden land between Celebrant and Anduin, where the trees bore flowers of gold and no Orc or evil thing dared ever come. Yet many voices were heard among the Elves foreboding that, if Sauron should come again, then either he would find the Ruling Ring that was lost, or at the best his enemies would discover it and destroy it; but in either chance the powers of the Three must then fail and all things maintained by them must fade, and so the Elves should pass into the twilight and the Dominion of Men begin.

And so indeed it has since befallen: the One and the Seven and the Nine are destroyed; and the Three have passed away, and with them the Third Age is ended, and the Tales of the Eldar in Middle-earth draw to their close. Those were the Fading Years, and in them the last flowering of the Elves east of the Sea came to its winter. In that time the Noldor walked still in the Hither Lands, mightiest and fairest of the children of the world, and their tongues were still heard by mortal ears. Many things of beauty and wonder remained on earth in that time, and many things also of evil and dread: Orcs there were and trolls and dragons and fell beasts, and strange creatures old and wise in the woods whose names are forgotten; Dwarves still laboured in the hills and wrought with patient craft works of metal and stone that none now can rival. But the Dominion of Men was preparing and all things were changing, until at last the Dark Lord arose in Mirkwood again.

Now of old the name of that forest was Greenwood the Great, and its wide halls and aisles were the haunt of many beasts and of birds of bright song; and there was the realm of King Thranduil under the oak and the beech. But after many years, when well nigh a third of that age of the world had passed, a darkness crept slowly through the wood from the southward, and fear walked there in shadowy glades; fell beasts came hunting, and cruel and evil creatures laid there their snares.

Then the name of the forest was changed and Mirkwood it was called, for the nightshade lay deep there, and few dared to pass through, save only in the north where Thranduil's people still held the evil at bay. Whence it came few could tell, and it was long ere even the Wise could discover it. It was the shadow of Sauron and the sign of his return. For coming out of the wastes of the East he took up his abode in the south of the forest, and slowly he grew and took shape there again; in a dark hill he made his dwelling and wrought there his sorcery, and all folk feared the Sorcerer of Dol Guldur, and yet they knew not at first how great was their peril.

Even as the first shadows were felt in Mirkwood there appeared in the west of Middle-earth the Istari, whom Men called the Wizards. None knew at that time whence they were, save Círdan of the Havens, and only to Elrond and to Galadriel did he reveal that they came over the Sea. But afterwards it was said among the Elves that they were messengers sent by the Lords of the West to contest the power of Sauron, if he should arise again, and to move Elves and Men and all living things of good will to valiant deeds. In the likeness of Men they appeared, old but vigorous, and they changed little with the years, and aged but slowly, though great cares lay on them; great wisdom they had, and many powers of mind and hand. Long they journeyed far and wide among Elves and Men, and held converse also with beasts and with birds; and the peoples of Middle-earth gave to them many names, for their true names they did not reveal. Chief among them were those whom the Elves called Mithrandir and Curunír, but Men in the North named Gandalf and Saruman. Of these Curunír was the eldest and came first, and after him came Mithrandir and Radagast, and others of the Istari who went into the east of Middle-earth, and do not come into these tales. Radagast was the friend of all beasts and birds; but Curunír went most among Men, and he was subtle in speech and skilled in all the devices of smithcraft. Mithrandir was closest in counsel with Elrond and the Elves. He wandered far in the North and West and made never in any land any lasting abode; but Curunír journeyed into the East, and when he returned he dwelt at Orthanc in the Ring of Isengard, which the Númenóreans made in the days of their power.

Ever most vigilant was Mithrandir, and he it was that most doubted the darkness in Mirkwood, for though many deemed that it was wrought by the Ringwraiths, he feared that it was indeed the first shadow of Sauron returning; and he went to Dol Guldur, and the Sorcerer fled from him, and there was a watchful peace for a long while. But at length the Shadow returned and its power increased; and in that time was first made the Council of the Wise that is called the White Council, and therein were Elrond and Galadriel and Círdan, and other lords of the Eldar, and with them were Mithrandir and Curunír. And Curunír (that was Saruman the White) was chosen to be their chief, for he had most studied the devices of Sauron of old. Galadriel indeed had wished that Mithrandir should be the head of the Council, and Saruman begrudged them that, for his pride and desire of mastery was grown great; but Mithrandir refused the office, since he would have no ties and no allegiance, save to those who sent him, and he would abide in no place nor be subject to any summons. But Saruman now began to study the lore of the Rings of Power, their making and their history.

Now the Shadow grew ever greater, and the hearts of Elrond and Mithrandir darkened. Therefore on a time Mithrandir at great peril went again to Dol Guldur and the pits of the Sorcerer, and he discovered the truth of his fears, and escaped. And returning to Elrond he said:

'True, alas, is our guess. This is not one of the Úlairi, as many have long supposed. It is Sauron himself who has taken shape again and now grows apace; and he is gathering again all the Rings to his hand; and he seeks ever for news of the One, and of the Heirs of Isildur, if they live still on earth.'

And Elrond answered: 'In the hour that Isildur took the Ring and would not surrender it, this doom was wrought, that Sauron should return.'

'Yet the One was lost,' said Mithrandir, 'and while it still lies hid, we can master the Enemy, if we gather our strength and tarry not too long.'

Then the White Council was summoned; and Mithrandir urged them to swift deeds, but Curunír spoke against him, and counselled them to wait yet and to watch.

'For I believe not,' said he, 'that the One will ever be found again in Middle-earth. Into Anduin it fell, and long ago, I deem, it was rolled to the Sea. There it shall lie until the end, when all this world is broken and the deeps are removed.'

Therefore naught was done at that time, though Elrond's heart misgave him, and he said to Mithrandir: 'Nonetheless I forebode that the One will yet be found, and then war will arise again, and in that war this Age will be ended. Indeed in a second darkness it will end, unless some strange chance deliver us that my eyes cannot see.'

'Many are the strange chances of the world,' said Mithrandir, 'and help oft shall come from the hands of the weak when the Wise falter.'

Thus the Wise were troubled, but none as yet perceived that Curunír had turned to dark thoughts and was already a traitor in heart: for he desired that he and no other should find the Great Ring, so that he might wield it himself and order all the world to his will. Too long he had studied the ways of Sauron in hope to defeat him, and now he envied him as a rival rather than hated his works. And he deemed that the Ring, which was Sauron's, would seek for its master as he became manifest once more; but if he were driven out again, then it would lie hid. Therefore he was willing to play with peril and let Sauron be for a time, hoping by his craft to forestall both his friends and the Enemy, when the Ring should appear.

He set a watch upon the Gladden Fields; but soon he discovered that the servants of Dol Guldur were searching all the ways of the River in that region. Then he perceived that Sauron also had learned of the manner of Isildur's end, and he grew afraid and withdrew to Isengard and fortified it; and ever he probed deeper into the lore of the Rings of Power and the art of their forging. But he spoke of none of this to the Council, hoping still that he might be the first to hear news of the Ring. He gathered a great host of spies, and many of these were birds; for Radagast lent him his aid, divining naught of his treachery, and deeming that this was but part of the watch upon the Enemy.

But ever the shadow in Mirkwood grew deeper, and to Dol Guldur evil things repaired out of all the dark places of the world; and they were united again under one will, and their malice was directed against the Elves and the survivors of Númenor. Therefore at last the Council was again summoned and the lore of the Rings was much debated; but Mithrandir spoke to the Council, saying:

'It is not needed that the Ring should be found, for while it abides on earth and is not unmade, still the power that it holds will live, and Sauron will grow and have hope. The might of the Elves and the Elf-friends is less now than of old. Soon he will be too strong for you, even without the Great Ring; for he rules the Nine, and of the Seven he has recovered three. We must strike.'

To this Curunír now assented, desiring that Sauron should be thrust from Dol Guldur, which was nigh to the River, and should have leisure to search there no longer. Therefore, for the last time, he aided the Council, and they put forth their strength; and they assailed Dol Guldur, and drove Sauron from his hold, and Mirkwood for a brief while was made wholesome again.

But their stroke was too late. For the Dark Lord had foreseen it, and he had long prepared all his movements; and the Úlairi, his Nine Servants, had gone before him to make ready for his coming. Therefore his flight was but a feint, and he soon returned, and ere the Wise could prevent him he re-entered his kingdom in Mordor and reared once again the dark towers of Barad-dûr. And in that year the White Council met for the last time, and Curunír withdrew to Isengard, and took counsel with none save himself.

Orcs were mustering, and far to the east and the south the wild peoples were arming. Then in the midst of gathering fear and the rumour of war the foreboding of Elrond was proved true, and the One Ring was indeed found again, by a chance more strange than even Mithrandir had foreseen; and it was hidden from Curunír and from Sauron. For it had been taken from Anduin long ere they sought for it, being found by one of the small fisher-folk that dwelt by the River, ere the Kings failed in Gondor; and by its finder it was brought beyond search into dark hiding under the roots of the mountains. There it dwelt, until even in the year of the assault upon Dol Guldur it was found again, by a wayfarer, fleeing into the depths of the earth from the pursuit of the Orcs, and passed into a far distant country, even to the land of the Periannath, the Little People, the Halflings, who dwelt in the west of Eriador. And ere that day they had been held of small account by Elves and by Men, and neither Sauron nor any of the Wise save Mithrandir had in all their counsels given thought to them.

Now by fortune and his vigilance Mithrandir first learned of the Ring, ere Sauron had news of it; yet he was dismayed and in doubt. For too great was the evil power of this thing for any of the Wise to wield, unless like Curunír he wished himself to become a tyrant and a dark lord in his turn; but neither could it be concealed from Sauron for ever, nor could it be unmade by the craft of the Elves. Therefore with the help of the Dúnedain of the North Mithrandir set a watch upon the land of the Periannath and bided his time. But Sauron had many ears, and soon he heard rumour of the One Ring, which above all things he desired, and he sent forth the Nazgûl to take it. Then war was kindled, and in battle with Sauron the Third Age ended even as it had begun.

But those who saw the things that were done in that time, deeds of valour and wonder, have elsewhere told the tale of the War of the Ring, and how it ended both in victory unlooked for and in sorrow long foreseen. Here let it be said that in those days the Heir of Isildur arose in the North, and he took the shards of the sword of Elendil, and in Imladris they were reforged; and he went then to war, a great captain of Men. He was Aragorn son of Arathorn, the nine and thirtieth heir in the right line from Isildur, and yet more like to Elendil than any before him. Battle there was in Rohan, and Curunír the traitor was thrown down and Isengard broken; and before the City of Gondor a great field was fought, and the Lord of Morgul, Captain of Sauron, there passed into darkness; and the Heir of Isildur led the host of the West to the Black Gates of Mordor.

In that last battle were Mithrandir, and the sons of Elrond, and the King of Rohan, and lords of Gondor, and the Heir of Isildur with the Dúnedain of the North. There at the last they looked upon death and defeat, and all their valour was in vain; for Sauron was too strong. Yet in that hour was put to the proof that which Mithrandir had spoken, and help came from the hands of the weak when the Wise faltered. For, as many songs have since sung, it was the Periannath, the Little People, dwellers in hillsides and meadows, that brought them deliverance.

For Frodo the Halfling, it is said, at the bidding of Mithrandir took on himself the burden, and alone with his servant he passed through peril and darkness and came at last in Sauron's despite even to Mount Doom; and there into the Fire where it was wrought he cast the Great Ring of Power, and so at last it was unmade and its evil consumed.

Then Sauron failed, and he was utterly vanquished and passed away like a shadow of malice; and the towers of Barad-dûr crumbled in ruin, and at the rumour of their fall many lands trembled. Thus peace came again, and a new Spring opened on earth; and the Heir of Isildur was crowned King of Gondor and Arnor, and the might of the Dúnedain was lifted up and their glory renewed. In the courts of Minas Anor the White Tree flowered again, for a seedling was found by Mithrandir in the snows of Mindolluin that rose tall and white above the City of Gondor; and while it still grew there the Elder Days were not wholly forgotten in the hearts of the Kings.

Now all these things were achieved for the most part by the counsel and vigilance of Mithrandir, and in the last few days he was revealed as a lord of great reverence, and clad in white he rode into battle; but not until the time came for him to depart was it known that he had long guarded the Red Ring of Fire. At the first that Ring had been entrusted to Círdan, Lord of the Havens; but he had surrendered it to Mithrandir, for he knew whence he came and whither at last he would return.

'Take now this Ring,' he said; 'for thy labours and thy cares will be heavy, but in all it will support thee and defend thee from weariness. For this is the Ring of Fire, and herewith, maybe, thou shalt rekindle hearts to the valour of old in a world that grows chill. But as for me, my heart is with the Sea, and I will dwell by the grey shores, guarding the Havens until the last ship sails. Then I shall await thee.'

White was that ship and long was it a-building, and long it awaited the end of which Círdan had spoken. But when all these things were done, and the Heir of Isildur had taken up the lordship of Men, and the dominion of the West had passed to him, then it was made plain that the power of the Three Rings also was ended, and to the Firstborn the world grew old and grey. In that time the last of the Noldor set sail from the Havens and left Middle-earth for ever. And latest of all the Keepers of the Three Rings rode to the Sea, and Master Elrond took there the ship that Círdan had made ready. In the twilight of autumn it sailed out of Mithlond, until the seas of the Bent World fell away beneath it, and the winds of the round sky troubled it no more, and borne upon the high airs above the mists of the world it passed into the Ancient West, and an end was come for the Eldar of story and of song.

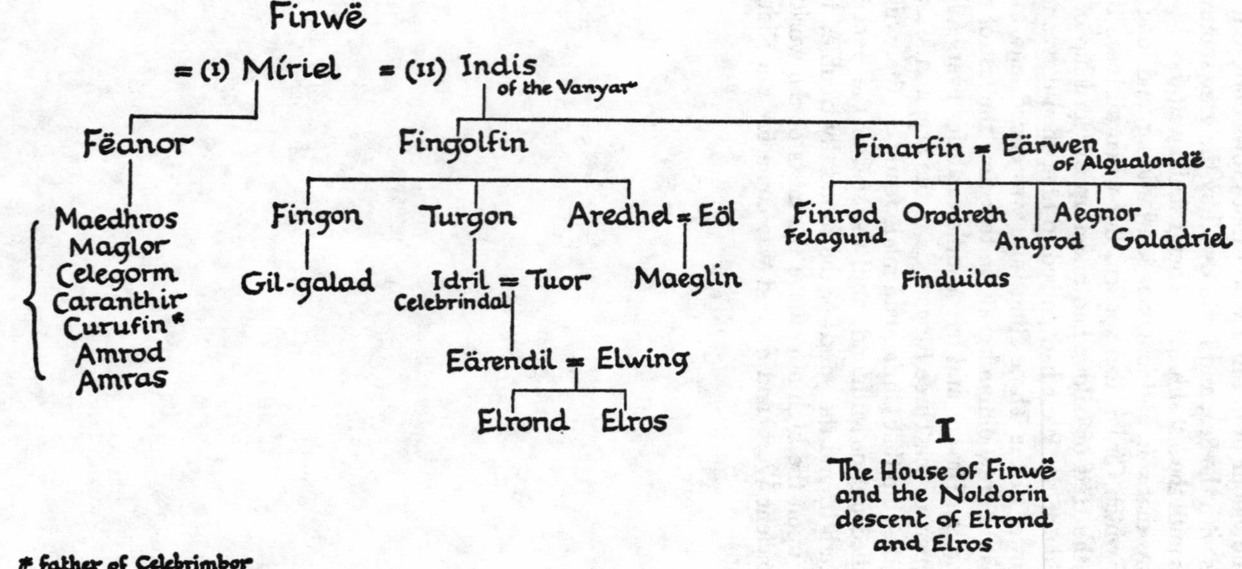

I

The House of Finwë and the Noldorin descent of Elrond and Elros

* father of Celebrimbor

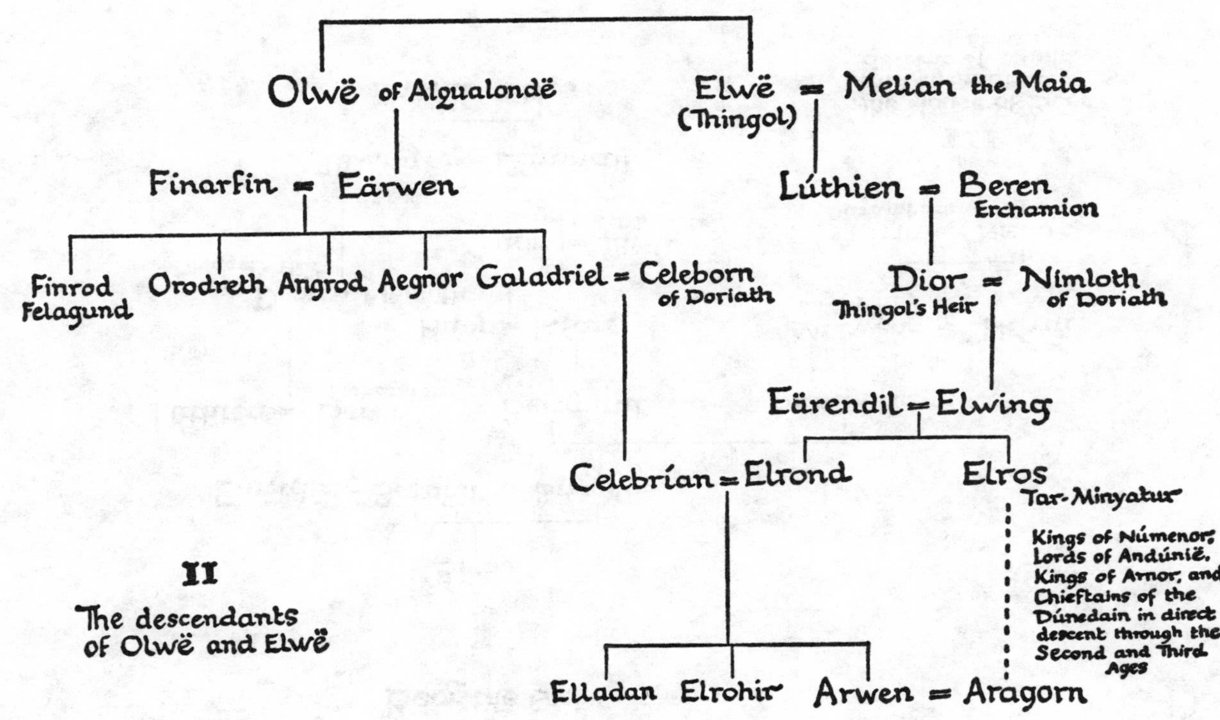

II

The descendants of Olwë and Elwë

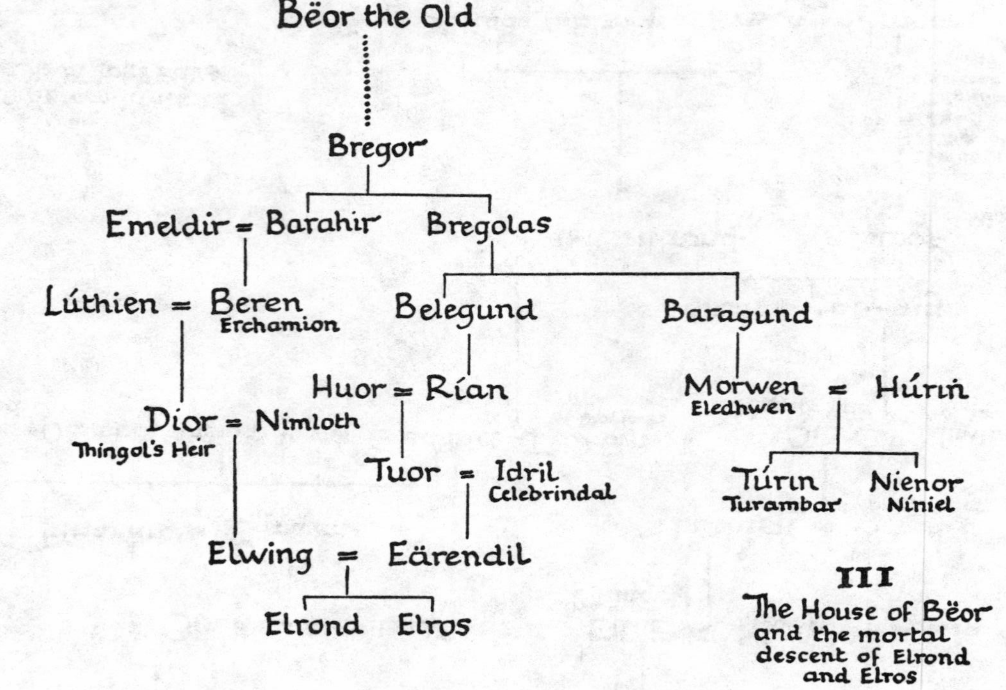

III
The House of Bëor and the mortal descent of Elrond and Elros

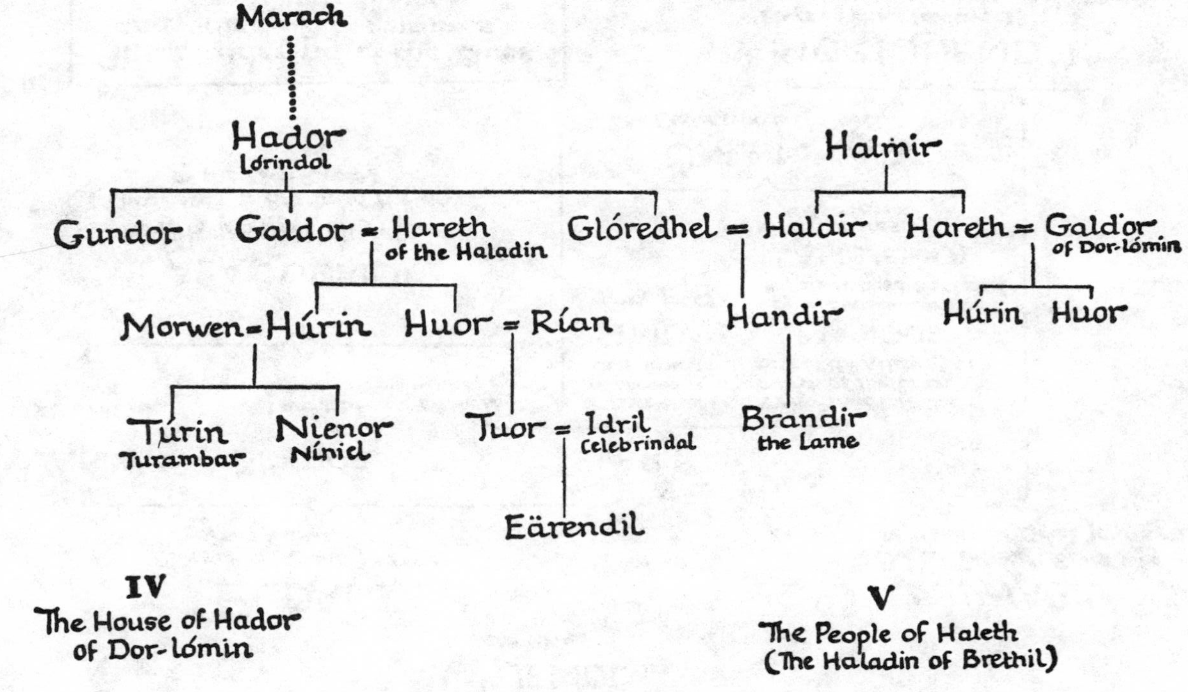

IV

The House of Hador of Dor-lómin

V

The People of Haleth (The Haladin of Brethil)

QUENDI
The Elves

ELDAR
Elves of the Great Journey from Cuiviénen

AVARI
'The Unwilling': Elves who refused the Great Journey

VANYAR
All went to Aman

NOLDOR
All went to Aman

TELERI

Those that went to Aman

Those that remained in Beleriand:
SINDAR
Grey-elves

Those that left the march of the Teleri east of the Misty Mts.:
NANDOR
of whom some after-wards entered Beleriand:
LAIQUENDI
Green-elves of Ossiriand

CALAQUENDI
'Elves of the Light' (High Elves)
(They came to Aman in the days of the Two Trees)

ÚMANYAR
The Eldar who were 'not of Aman'

MORIQUENDI
'Elves of the Darkness'
(They never saw the Light of the Trees)

The Sundering of the Elves and some of the names given to their divisions

NOTE ON PRONUNCIATION

The following note is intended simply to clarify a few main features in the pronunciation of names in the Elvish languages, and is by no means exhaustive. For full information on the subject see *The Lord of the Rings* Appendix E.

CONSONANTS

C always has the value of *k,* never of *s;* thus *Celeborn* is *'Keleborn',* not *'Seleborn'.* In a few cases, as *Tulkas, Kementári* a *k* has been used in the spelling in this book.

CH always has the value of *ch* in Scotch *loch* or German *buch,* never that of *ch* in English *church.* Examples are *Carcharoth, Erchamion.*

DH is always used to represent the sound of a voiced ('soft') *th* in English, that is the *th* in *then,* not the *th* in *thin.* Examples are *Maedhros, Aredhel, Haudh-en-Arwen.*

G always has the sound of English g in *get;* thus *Region, Eregion* are not pronounced like English *region,* and the *first* syllable of *Ginglith* is as in English *begin,* not as in *gin.*

Consonants written twice are pronounced long; thus *Yavanna* has the long *n* heard in English *unnamed, penknife,* not the short *n* in *unaimed, penny.*

VOWELS

AI has the sound of English *eye;* thus the second syllable of *Edain* is like English *dine,* not *Dane.*

AU	has the value of English *ow* in *town;* thus the first syllable of *Aulë* is like English *owl,* and the first syllable of *Sauron* is like English *sour,* not *sore.*
EI	as in *Teiglin* has the sound of English *grey.*
IE	should not be pronounced as in English *piece,* but with both the vowels *i* and *e* sounded, and run together; thus *Ni-enna,* not *'Neena'.*
UI	as in *Uinen* has the sound of English *ruin.*
AE	as in *Aegnor, Nirnaeth,* and OE as in *Noegyth, Loeg,* are combinations of the individual vowels, *a-e, o-e,* but *ae* may be pronounced in the same way as *ai,* and *oe* as in English *toy.*
EA and EO	are not run together, but constitute two syllables; these combinations are written *ëa* and *ëo* (or, when they begin names, *Eä* and *Eö: Eärendil, Eönwë*).
Ú	in names like *Húrin, Túrin, Túna* should be pronounced *oo;* thus *'Toorin',* not *'Tyoorin'.*
ER, IR, UR	before a consonant (as in *Nerdanel, Círdan, Gurthang*) or at the end of a word (as in *Ainur*) should not be pronounced as in English *fern, fir, fur,* but as in English *air, eer, oor.*
E	at the end of words is always pronounced as a distinct vowel, and in this position is written *ë.* It is likewise always pronounced in the middle of words like *Celeborn, Menegroth.*

A circumflex accent in stressed monosyllables in Sindarin denotes the particularly long vowel heard in such words (thus *Hîn Húrin*); but in Adúnaic (Númenórean) and Khuzdul (Dwarvish) names the circumflex is simply used to denote long vowels.

INDEX OF NAMES

Since the number of names in the book is very large, this index provides, in addition to page-references, a short statement concerning each person and place. These statements are not epitomes of all that is said in the text, and for most of the central figures in the narrative are kept extremely brief; but such an index is inevitably bulky, and I have reduced its size in various ways.

The chief of these concerns the fact that very often the English translation of an Elvish name is also used as the name independently; thus for example the dwelling of King Thingol is called both *Menegroth* and 'The Thousand Caves' (and also both together). In most such cases I have combined the Elvish name and its translated meaning under one entry, with the result that the page-references are not restricted to the name that appears as the heading (e.g., those under *Echoriath* include those to 'Encircling Mountains'). The English renderings are given separate headings, but only with a simple direction to the main entry, and only if they occur independently. Words in inverted commas are translations; many of these occur in the text (as *Tol Eressëa* 'the Lonely Isle'), but I have added a great many others. Information about some names that are not translated is contained in the Appendix.

With the many titles and formal expressions in English whose Elvish originals are not given, such as 'the Elder King' and 'the Two Kindreds', I have been selective, but the great majority are registered. The references are in intention complete (and sometimes include pages where the subject of the entry occurs but is not actually mentioned by name) except in a very few cases where the name occurs very frequently indeed, as *Beleriand, Valar.* Here the word *passim* is used, but selected references are given to important passages; and in the entries for some of the Noldorin princes the many occurrences of the name that relate only to their sons or their houses have been eliminated.

References to *The Lord of the Rings* are by title of the volume, book, and chapter.

APPENDIX

ELEMENTS IN QUENYA AND SINDARIN NAMES

These notes have been compiled for those who take an interest in the Eldarin languages, and *The Lord of the Rings* is extensively drawn upon for illustration. They are necessarily very compressed, giving an air of certainty and finality that is not altogether justified; and they are very selective, this depending both on considerations of length and the limitations of the editor's knowledge. The headings are not arranged systematically by roots or in Quenya or Sindarin forms, but somewhat arbitrarily, the aim being to make the component elements of names as readily identifiable as possible.

adan (plural *Edain*) in *Adanedhel, Aradan, Dúnedain.* For its meaning and history see *Atani* in the Index.

aelin 'lake, pool' in *Aelin-uial;* cf. *lin* (1).

aglar 'glory, brilliance' in *Dagor Aglareb, Aglarond.* The form in Quenya, *alkar,* has transposition of the consonants: to Sindarin *aglareb* corresponds *Alkarinquë.* The root is *kal-* 'shine', q.v.

aina 'holy' in *Ainur, Ainulindalë.*

alda 'tree' (Quenya) in *Aldaron, Aldudenië, Malinalda,* corresponding to Sindarin *galadh* (seen in *Caras Galadon* and the *Galadrim* of Lothlórien).

alqua 'swan' (Sindarin *alph*) in *Alqualondë;* from a root *alak-* 'rushing' occurring also in *Ancalagon.*

amarth 'doom' in *Amon Amarth, Cabed Naeramarth, Ūmarth,* and in the Sindarin form of Túrin's name 'Master of Doom', *Turamarth.* The Quenya form of the word appears in *Turambar.*

amon 'hill', a Sindarin word occurring as the first element of many names; plural *emyn* in *Emyn Beraid.*

anca 'jaws' in *Ancalagon* (for the second element in this name see *alqua*).

an(d) 'long' in *Andram, Anduin;* also in *Anfalas* ('Langstrand') in Gondor, *Cair Andros* ('ship of long-foam') an island in Anduin, and *Angerthas* 'long rune-rows'.

andúnë 'sunset, west' in *Andúnië,* to which corresponds in Sindarin *annûn,* cf. *Annúminas,* and *Henneth Annûn* 'window of the sunset' in Ithilien. The ancient root of these words, *ndu,* meaning 'down, from on high', appears also in Quenya *númen* 'the way of the sunset, west' and in Sindarin *dûn* 'west', cf. *Dúnedain.* Adûnaic *adûn* in *Adûnakhor, Anadûnê* was a loan from Eldarin speech.

anga 'iron', Sindarin *ang,* in *Angainor, Angband, Anghabar, Anglachel, Angrist, Angrod, Anguirel, Gurthang; angren* 'of iron' in *Angrenost,* plural *engrin* in *Ered Engrin.*

anna 'gift' in *Annatar, Melian, Yavanna;* the same stem in *Andor* 'Land of Gift'.

annon 'great door or gate', plural *ennyn,* in *Annon-in-Gelydh;* cf. *Morannon* the 'Black Gate' of Mordor and *Sirannon* the 'Gate-stream' of Moria.

ar- 'beside, outside' (whence Quenya *ar* 'and', Sindarin *a*), probably in *Araman* 'outside Aman'; cf. also (*Nirnaeth*) *Arnoediad* '(Tears) without reckoning'.

ar(a)- 'high, noble, royal' appears in a great many names, as *Aradan, Aredhel, Argonath, Arnor,* etc.; extended stem *arat-* appearing in *Aratar,* and in *aráto* 'champion, eminent man', e.g. *Angrod* from *Angaráto* and *Finrod* from *Findaráto;* also *aran* 'king' in *Aranrúth. Ereinion* 'scion of kings' (name of Gil-galad) has the plural of *aran;* cf. *Fornost Erain* 'Norbury of the Kings' in Arnor. The prefix *Ar-* of the Adûnaic names of the Kings of Númenor was derived from this.

arien (the Maia of the Sun) is derived from a root *as-* seen also in Quenya *árë* 'sunlight'.

atar 'father' in *Atanatári* (see *Atani* in Index), *Ilúvatar.*

band 'prison, duress' in *Angband;* from original *mbando,* of which the Quenya form appears in *Mandos* (Sindarin *Angband* = Quenya *Angamando*).

bar 'dwelling' in *Bar-en-Danwedh.* The ancient word *mbár* (Quenya *már,* Sindarin *bar*) meant the 'home' both of persons and of peoples, and thus appears in many place-names, as *Brithombar, Dimbar* (the first element of which means 'sad, gloomy'), *Eldamar, Val(i)mar, Vinyamar, Mar-nu-Falmar. Mardil,* name of the first of the Ruling Stewards of Gondor, means 'devoted to the house' (i.e. of the Kings).

barad 'tower' in *Barad-dûr, Barad Eithel, Barad Nimras;* the plural in *Emyn Beraid.*

beleg 'mighty' in *Beleg, Belegaer, Belegost, Laer Cú Beleg.*

bragol 'sudden' in *Dagor Bragollach.*

brethil probably means 'silver birch'; cf. *Nimbrethil* the birchwoods in Arvernien, and *Fimbrethil,* one of the Entwives.

brith 'gravel' in *Brithiach, Brithombar, Brithon.*

(*For many names beginning with C see entries under K*)

calen (galen) the usual Sindarin word for 'green', in *Ard-galen, Tol Galen, Calenardhon;* also in *Parth Galen* ('Green Sward') beside Anduin and *Pinnath Gelin* ('Green Ridges') in Gondor. See *kal-.*

cam (from *kambā*) 'hand', but specifically of the hand held cupped in the attitude of receiving or holding, in *Camlost, Erchamion.*

carak- This root is seen in Quenya *carca* 'fang', of which the Sindarin form *carch* occurs in *Carcharoth,* and also in *Carchost* ('Fang Fort', one of the Towers of the Teeth at the entrance to Mordor). Cf. *Caragdûr, Carach Angren* ('Iron Jaws', the rampart and dike guarding the entrance to Udûn in Mordor), and *Helcaraxë.*

caran 'red', Quenya *carnë,* in *Caranthir, Carnil, Orocarni;* also in *Caradhras,* from *caran-rass,* the 'Red-horn' in the Misty Mountains, and *Carnimírië* 'red-jewelled', the rowan-tree in Treebeard's song. The translation of *Carcharoth* in the text as 'Red Maw' must depend on association with this word; see *carak-.*

celeb 'silver' (Quenya *telep, telpë,* as in *Telperion*) in *Celeborn, Celebrant, Celebros. Celebrimbor* means 'silver-fist', from the adjective *celebrin* 'silver' (meaning not 'made of silver' but 'like silver, in hue or worth') and *paur* (Quenya *quárë*) 'fist', often used to mean 'hand'; the Quenya form of the name was *Telperinquar. Celebrindal* has *celebrin* and *tal, dal* 'foot'.

coron 'mound' in *Corollairë* (also called *Coron Oiolairë,* which latter word appears to mean 'Ever-summer', cf. *Oiolossë*); cf. *Cerin Amroth,* the great mound in Lothlórien.

cú 'bow' in *Cúthalion, Dor Cúarthol, Laer Cú Beleg.*

cuivië 'awakening' in *Cuiviénen* (Sindarin *Nen Echui*). Other derivatives of the same root are *Dor Firn-i-Guinar; coirë,* the first beginning of Spring, Sindarin *echuir, The Lord of the Rings* Appendix D; and *coimas* 'life-bread', Quenya name of *lembas.*

cul- 'golden-red' in *Culúrien.*

curu 'skill' in *Curufin(wë), Curunír.*

dae 'shadow' in *Dor Daedeloth,* and perhaps in *Daeron.*

dagor 'battle'; the root is *ndak-*, cf. *Haudh-en-Ndengin.* Another derivative is *Dagnir* (*Dagnir Glaurunga* 'Glaurung's Bane').

del 'horror' in *Deldúwath; deloth* 'abhorrence' in *Dor Daedeloth.*

dîn 'silent' in *Dor Dínen;* cf. *Rath Dínen,* the Silent Street in Minas Tirith, and *Amon Dîn,* one of the beacon-hills of Gondor.

dol 'head' in *Lórindol;* often applied to hills and mountains, as in *Dol Guldur, Dolmed, Mindolluin* (also *Nardol,* one of the beacon-hills of Gondor, and *Fanuidhol,* one of the Mountains of Moria).

dôr 'land' (i.e. dry land as opposed to sea) was derived from *ndor;* it occurs in many Sindarin names, as *Doriath, Dorthonion, Eriador, Gondor, Mordor,* etc. In Quenya the stem was blended and confused with a quite distinct word *nórë* meaning 'people'; in origin *Valinórë* was strictly 'the people of the Valar', but *Valandor* 'the land of the Valar', and similarly *Númen(n)órë* 'people of the West', but *Númendor* 'land of the West'. Quenya *Endor* 'Middle-earth' was from *ened* 'middle' and *ndor;* this in Sindarin became *Ennor* (cf. *ennorath* 'middle lands' in the chant *A Elbereth Gilthoniel*).

draug 'wolf' in *Draugluin.*

dú 'night, dimness' in *Deldúwath, Ephel Dúath.* Derived from earlier *dōmē,* whence Quenya *lómë;* thus Sindarin *dúlin* 'nightingale' corresponds to *lómelindë.*

duin '(long) river' in *Anduin, Baranduin, Esgalduin, Malduin, Taur-im-Duinath.*

dûr 'dark' in *Barad-dûr, Caragdûr, Dol Guldur;* also in *Durthang* (a castle in Mordor).

ëar 'sea' (Quenya) in *Eärendil, Eärrámë,* and many other names. The Sindarin word *gaer* (in *Belegaer*) is apparently derived from the same original stem.

echor in *Echoriath* 'Encircling Mountains' and *Orfalch Echor;* cf. *Rammas Echor* 'the great wall of the outer circle' about the Pelennor Fields at Minas Tirith.

edhel 'elf' (Sindarin) in *Adanedhel, Aredhel, Glóredhel, Ost-in-Edhil;* also in *Peredhil* 'Half-elven'.

eithel 'well' in *Eithel Ivrin, Eithel Sirion, Barad Eithel;* also in *Mitheithel,* the river Hoarwell in Eriador (named from its source). See *kel-.*

êl, elen 'star'. According to Elvish legend, *ele* was a primitive exclamation 'behold!' made by the Elves when they first saw the stars. From this origin derived the ancient words *êl* and *elen,* meaning 'star', and the adjectives *elda* and *elena,* meaning 'of the stars'. These elements appear in a great many names. For the later use of the name *Eldar* see the Index. The Sindarin equivalent of *Elda* was *Edhel* (plural *Edhil*), q.v.; but the strictly corresponding form was *Eledh,* which occurs in *Eledhwen.*

er 'one, alone', in *Amon Ereb* (cf. *Erebor,* the Lonely Mountain), *Erchamion, Eressëa, Eru.*
ereg 'thorn, holly' in *Eregion, Region.*
esgal 'screen, hiding' in *Esgalduin.*

falas 'shore, line of surf' (Quenya *falassë*) in *Falas, Belfalas;* also *Anfalas* in Gondor. Cf. *Falathar, Falathrim.* Another derivative from the root was Quenya *falma* '(crested) wave', whence *Falmari, Mar-nu-Falmar.*
faroth is derived from a root meaning 'hunt, pursue'; in the Lay of Leithian the *Taur-en-Faroth* above Nargothrond are called 'the Hills of the Hunters'.
faug- 'gape' in *Anfauglir, Anfauglith, Dor-nu-Fauglith.*
fëa 'spirit' in *Fëanor, Fëanturi.*
fin- 'hair' in *Finduilas, Fingon, Finrod, Glorfindel.*
formen 'north' (Quenya) in *Formenos;* Sindarin *forn* (also *for, forod*) in *Fornost.*
fuin 'gloom, darkness' (Quenya *huinë*) in *Fuinur, Taur-nu-Fuin.*

gaer 'sea' in *Belegaer* (and in *Gaerys,* Sindarin name of Ossë). Said to derive from the stem *gaya* 'awe, dread', and to have been the name made for the vast and terrifying Great Sea when the Eldar first came to its shores.
gaur 'werewolf' (from a root *ngwaw-* 'howl') in *Tol-in-Gaurhoth.*
gil 'star' in *Dagor-nuin-Giliath, Osgiliath* (*giliath* 'host of stars'); *Gil-Estel, Gil-galad.*
girith 'shuddering' in *Nen Girith;* cf. also *Girithron,* name of the last month of the year in Sindarin (*The Lord of the Rings* Appendix D).
glîn 'gleam' (particularly applied to the eyes) in *Maeglin.*
golodh is the Sindarin form of Quenya *Noldo;* see *gûl.* Plural *Golodhrim,* and *Gelydh* (in *Annon-in-Gelydh*).
gond 'stone' in *Gondolin, Gondor, Gonnhirrim, Argonath, seregon.* The name of the hidden city of King Turgon was devised by him in Quenya as *Ondolindë* (Quenya *ondo* = Sindarin *gond,* and *lindë* 'singing, song'); but it was known always in legend in the Sindarin form *Gondolin,* which was probably interpreted as *gond-dolen* 'Hidden Rock'.
gor 'horror, dread' in *Gorthaur, Gorthol; goroth* of the same meaning, with reduplicated *gor,* in *Gorgoroth, Ered Gorgoroth.*
groth (*grod*) 'delving, underground dwelling' in *Menegroth, Nogrod* (probably also in *Nimrodel,* 'lady of the white cave'). *Nogrod* was originally *Novrod* 'hollow delving' (hence the translation *Hollowbold*), but was altered under the influence of *naug* 'dwarf'.
gûl 'sorcery' in *Dol Guldur, Minas Morgul.* This word was derived from

the same ancient stem *ngol-* that appears in *Noldor;* cf. Quenya *nólë* 'long study, lore, knowledge'. But the Sindarin word was darkened in sense by its frequent use in the compound *morgul* 'black arts'.

gurth 'death' in *Gurthang* (see also *Melkor* in the Index).

gwaith 'people' in *Gwaith-i-Mírdain;* cf. *Enedwaith* 'Middle-folk', name of the land between the Greyflood and the Isen.

gwath, wath 'shadow' in *Deldúwath, Ephel Dúath;* also in *Gwathló,* the river Greyflood in Eriador. Related forms in *Ered Wethrin, Thuringwethil.* (This Sindarin word referred to dim light, not to the shadows of objects cast by light: these were called *morchaint* 'dark shapes'.)

hadhod in *Hadhodrond* (translation of *Khazad-dûm*) was a rendering of *Khazâd* into Sindarin sounds.

haudh 'mound' in *Haudh-en-Arwen, Haudh-en-Elleth,* etc.

heru 'lord' in *Herumor, Herunúmen;* Sindarin *hîr* in *Gonnhirrim, Rohirrim, Barahir; híril* 'lady' in *Hírilorn.*

him 'cool' in *Himlad* (and *Himring?*).

híni 'children' in *Eruhíni* 'Children of Eru'; *Narn i Hîn Húrin.*

hîth 'mist' in *Hithaeglir, Hithlum* (also in *Nen Hithoel,* a lake in Anduin). *Hithlum* is Sindarin in form, adapted from the Quenya name *Hísilómë* given by the Noldorin exiles (Quenya *hísië* 'mist', cf. *Hísimë,* the name of the eleventh month of the year, *The Lord of the Rings* Appendix D).

hoth 'host, horde' (nearly always in a bad sense) in *Tol-in-Gaurhoth;* also in *Loss(h)oth,* the Snowmen of Forochel (*The Lord of the Rings* Appendix A (I, iii)) and *Glamhoth* 'din-horde', a name for Orcs.

hyarmen 'south' (Quenya) in *Hyarmentir;* Sindarin *har-, harn, harad.*

iâ 'void, abyss' in *Moria.*

iant 'bridge' in *Iant Iaur.*

iâth 'fence' in *Doriath.*

iaur 'old' in *Iant Iaur;* cf. the Elvish name of Bombadil, *Iarwain.*

ilm- This stem appears in *Ilmen, Ilmarë,* and also in *Ilmarin* ('mansion of the high airs', the dwelling of Manwë and Varda upon Oiolossë).

ilúvë 'the whole, the all' in *Ilúvatar.*

kal- (*gal-*) This root, meaning 'shine', appears in *Calacirya, Calaquendi, Tar-calion; galvorn, Gil-galad, Galadriel.* The last two names have no connexion with Sindarin *galadh* 'tree', although in the case of Galadriel such a connexion was often made, and the name altered to *Galadhriel.* In the High-elven speech her name was *Al(a)táriel,* derived from *alata* 'radiance' (Sindarin *galad*) and *riel* 'garlanded maiden' (from a root *rig-* 'twine, wreathe'): the whole meaning 'maiden crowned with a radiant garland', referring to her hair. *calen* (*galen*) 'green' is etymologically 'bright', and derives from this root; see also *aglar*.

káno 'commander': this Quenya word is the origin of the second element in *Fingon* and *Turgon*.

kel- 'go away', of water 'flow away, flow down', in *Celon;* from *et-kelē* 'issue of water, spring' was derived, with transposition of the consonants, Quenya *ehtelë*, Sindarin *eithel*.

kemen 'earth' in *Kementári;* a Quenya word referring to the earth as a flat floor beneath *menel*, the heavens.

khelek- 'ice' in *Helcar, Helcaraxë* (Quenya *helka* 'icy, ice-cold'). But in *Helevorn* the first element is Sindarin *heledh* 'glass', taken from Khuzdul *kheled* (cf. *Kheled-zâram* 'Mirrormere'); *Helevorn* means 'black glass' (cf. *galvorn*).

khil- 'follow' in *Hildor, Hildórien, Eluchil.*

kir- 'cut, cleave' in *Calacirya, Cirth, Angerthas, Cirith* (*Ninniach, Thoronath*). From the sense 'pass swiftly through' was derived Quenya *círya* 'sharp-prowed ship' (cf. English *cutter*), and this meaning appears also in *Círdan, Tar-Ciryatan,* and no doubt in the name of Isildur's son *Círyon.*

lad 'plain, valley' in *Dagorlad, Himlad; imlad* a narrow valley with steep sides, in *Imladris* (cf. also *Imlad Morgul* in the Ephel Dúath).

laurë 'gold' (but of light and colour, not of the metal) in *Laurelin;* the Sindarin forms in *Glóredhel, Glorfindel, Loeg Ningloron, Lórindol, Rathlóriel.*

lhach 'leaping flame' in *Dagor Bragollach,* and probably in *Anglachel* (the sword made by Eöl of meteoric iron).

lin (1) 'pool, mere' in *Linaewen* (which contains *aew* (Quenya *aiwë*) 'small bird'), *Teiglin;* cf. *aelin.*

lin- (2) This root, meaning 'sing, make a musical sound', occurs in *Ainulindalë, Laurelin, Lindar, Lindon, Ered Lindon, lómelindi.*

lith 'ash' in *Anfauglith, Dor-nu-Fauglith;* also in *Ered Lithui,* the Ashen Mountains, forming the northern border of Mordor, and *Lithlad* 'Plain of Ashes' at the feet of Ered Lithui.

lok- 'bend, loop' in *Urulóki* (Quenya (*h*)*lókë* 'snake, serpent', Sindarin *lhûg*).

lóm 'echo' in *Dor-lómin, Ered Lómin;* related are *Lammoth, Lanthir Lamath.*

lómë 'dusk' in *Lómion, lómelindi;* see *dú.*

londë 'land-locked haven' in *Alqualondë;* the Sindarin form *lond* (*lonn*) in *Mithlond.*

los 'snow' in *Oiolossë* (Quenya *oio* 'ever' and *lossë* 'snow, snow-white'); Sindarin *loss* in *Amon Uilos* and *Aeglos.*

loth 'flower' in *Lothlórien, Nimloth;* Quenya *lótë* in *Ninquelótë, Vingilótë.*
luin 'blue' in *Ered Luin, Helluin, Luinil, Mindolluin.*

maeg 'sharp, piercing' (Quenya *maika*) in *Maeglin.*
mal- 'gold' in *Malduin, Malinalda;* also in *mallorn,* and in the Field of *Cormallen,* which means 'golden circle' and was named from the *culumalda* trees that grew there (see *cul-*).
mān- 'good, blessed, unmarred' in *Aman, Manwë;* derivatives of *Aman* in *Amandil, Araman, Úmanyar.*
mel- 'love' in *Melian* (from *Melyanna* 'dear gift'); this stem is seen also in the Sindarin word *mellon* 'friend' in the inscription on the West-gate of Moria.
men 'way' in *Númen, Hyarmen, Rómen, Formen.*
menel 'the heavens' in *Meneldil, Menelmacar, Meneltarma.*
mereth 'feast' in *Mereth Aderthad;* also in *Merethrond,* the Hall of Feasts in Minas Tirith.
minas 'tower' in *Annúminas, Minas Anor, Minas Tirith,* etc. The same stem occurs in other words referring to isolated, prominent, things, e.g. *Mindolluin, Mindon;* probably related is Quenya *minya* 'first' (cf. *Tar-Minyatur,* the name of Elros as first King of Númenor).
mîr 'jewel' (Quenya *mírë*) in *Elemmírë, Gwaith-i-Mírdain, Míriel, Nauglamír, Tar-Atanamir.*
mith 'grey' in *Mithlond, Mithrandir, Mithrim;* also in *Mitheithel,* the river Hoarwell in Eriador.
mor 'dark' in *Mordor, Morgoth, Moria, Moriquendi, Mormegil, Morwen,* etc.
moth 'dusk' in *Nan Elmoth.*

nan(d) 'valley' in *Nan Dungortheb, Nan Elmoth, Nan Tathren.*
nár 'fire' in *Narsil, Narya;* present also in the original forms of *Aegnor* (*Aikanáro* 'Sharp Flame' or 'Fell Fire') and *Fëanor* (*Fëanáro* 'Spirit of Fire'). The Sindarin form was *naur,* as in *Sammath Naur,* the Chambers of Fire in Orodruin. Derived from the same ancient root (*a*)*nar* was the name of the Sun, Quenya *Anar* (also in *Anárion*), Sindarin *Anor* (cf. *Minas Anor, Anórien*).
naug 'dwarf' in *Naugrim;* see also *Nogrod* in entry *groth.* Related is another Sindarin word for 'dwarf', *nogoth,* plural *noegyth* (*Noegyth Nibin* 'Petty-dwarves') and *nogothrim.*
-(*n*)*dil* is a very frequent ending of personal names, *Amandil, Eärendil* (shortened *Eärnil*), *Elendil, Mardil,* etc.; it implies 'devotion', 'disinterested love' (see *Mardil* in entry *bar*).
-(*n*)*dur* in names such as *Eärendur* (shortened *Eärnur*) is similar in meaning to -(*n*)*dil.*

neldor 'beech' in *Neldoreth;* but it seems that this was properly the name of Hírilorn, the great beech-tree with three trunks (*neldë* 'three' and *orn*).

nen 'water', used of lakes, pools, and lesser rivers, in *Nen Girith, Nenning, Nenuial, Nenya; Cuiviénen, Uinen;* also in many names in *The Lord of the Rings,* as *Nen Hithoel, Bruinen, Emyn Arnen, Núrnen. Nîn* 'wet' in *Loeg Ningloron;* also in *Nindalf.*

nim 'white' (from earlier *nimf, nimp*) in *Nimbrethil, Nimloth, Nimphelos, niphredil* (*niphred* 'pallor'), *Barad Nimras, Ered Nimrais.* The Quenya form was *ninquë;* thus *Ninquelótë* = *Nimloth.* Cf. also *Taniquetil.*

orn 'tree' in *Celeborn, Hírilorn;* cf. *Fangorn* 'Treebeard', and *mallorn,* plural *mellyrn,* the trees of Lothlórien.

orod 'mountain' in *Orodruin, Thangorodrim; Orocarni, Oromet.* Plural *ered* in *Ered Engrin, Ered Lindon,* etc.

os(*t*) 'fortress' in *Angrenost, Belegost, Formenos, Fornost, Mandos, Nargothrond* (from *Narog-ost-rond*), *Os*(*t*)*giliath, Ost-in-Edhil.*

palan (Quenya) 'far and wide' in *palantíri, Tar-Palantir.*

pel- 'go round, encircle' in *Pelargir, Pelóri,* and in the *Pelennor,* the 'fenced land' of Minas Tirith; also in *Ephel Brandir, Ephel Dúath* (*ephel* from *et-pel* 'outer fence').

quen- (*quet-*) 'say, speak' in *Quendi* (*Calaquendi, Laiquendi, Moriquendi*), *Quenya, Valaquenta, Quenta Silmarillion.* The Sindarin forms have *p* (or *b*) for *qu;* e.g. *pedo* 'speak' in the inscription on the West-gate of Moria, corresponding to the Quenya stem *quet-,* and Gandalf's words before the gate, *lasto beth lammen* 'listen to the words of my tongue', where *beth* 'word' corresponds to Quenya *quetta.*

ram 'wall' (Quenya *ramba*) in *Andram, Ramdal;* also in *Rammas Echor,* the wall about the Pelennor Fields at Minas Tirith.

ran- 'wander, stray' in *Rána,* the Moon, and in *Mithrandir, Aerandir;* also in the river *Gilraen* in Gondor.

rant 'course' in the river-names *Adurant* (with *adu* 'double') and *Celebrant* ('Silverlode').

ras 'horn' in *Barad Nimras,* also in *Caradhras* ('Redhorn') and *Methedras* ('Last Peak') in the Misty Mountains; plural *rais* in *Ered Nimrais.*

rauko 'demon' in *Valaraukar;* Sindarin *raug, rog* in *Balrog.*

ril 'brilliance' in *Idril, Silmaril;* also in *Andúril* (the sword of Aragorn) and in *mithril* (Moria-silver). Idril's name in Quenya form was *Itarillë* (or *Itarildë*), from a stem *ita-* 'sparkle'.

rim 'great number, host' (Quenya *rimbë*) was commonly used to form collective plurals, as *Golodhrim, Mithrim* (see the Index), *Naugrim, Thangorodrim,* etc.

ring 'cold, chill' in *Ringil, Ringwil, Himring;* also in the river *Ringló* in Gondor, and in *Ringarë,* Quenya name of the last month of the year (*The Lord of the Rings* Appendix D).

ris 'cleave' appears to have blended with the stem *kris-* of similar meaning (a derivative of the root *kir-* 'cleave, cut', q.v.); hence *Angrist* (also *Orcrist* 'Orc-cleaver', the sword of Thorin Oakenshield), *Crissaegrim, Imladris.*

roch 'horse' (Quenya *rokko*) in *Rochallor, Rohan* (from *Rochand* 'land of horses'), *Rohirrim;* also in *Roheryn* 'horse of the lady' (cf. *heru*), Aragorn's horse, which was so called because given to him by Arwen (*The Return of the King* V 2).

rom- A stem used of the sound of trumpets and horns which appears in *Oromë* and *Valaróma;* cf. *Béma,* the name of this Vala in the language of Rohan as translated into Anglo-Saxon in *The Lord of the Rings* Appendix A (II): Anglo-Saxon *bēme* 'trumpet'.

rómen 'uprising, sunrise, east' (Quenya) in *Rómenna.* The Sindarin words for 'east', *rhûn* (in *Talath Rhúnen*) and *amrûn,* were of the same origin.

rond meant a vaulted or arched roof, or a large hall or chamber so roofed; so *Nargothrond* (see *ost*), *Hadhodrond, Aglarond.* It could be applied to the heavens, hence the name *Elrond* 'star-dome'.

ros 'foam, spindrift, spray' in *Celebros, Elros, Rauros;* also in *Cair Andros,* an island in the river Anduin.

ruin 'red flame' (Quenya *rúnya*) in *Orodruin.*

rûth 'anger' in *Aranrúth.*

sarn '(small) stone' in *Sarn Athrad* (*Sarn Ford* on the Brandywine is a half-translation of this); also in *Sarn Gebir* ('stone-spikes': *ceber,* plural *cebir* 'stakes'), rapids in the river Anduin. A derivative is *Serni,* a river in Gondor.

sereg 'blood' (Quenya *serkë*) in *seregon.*

sil- (and variant *thil-*) 'shine (with white or silver light)' in *Belthil, Galathilion, Silpion,* and in Quenya *Isil,* Sindarin *Ithil,* the Moon (whence *Isildur, Narsil; Minas Ithil, Ithilien*). The Quenya word *Silmarilli* is said to derive from the name *silima* that Fëanor gave to the substance from which they were made.

sîr 'river', from root *sir-* 'flow', in *Ossiriand* (the first element is from the stem of the numeral 'seven', Quenya *otso,* Sindarin *odo*), *Sirion;* also in *Sirannon* (the 'Gate-stream' of Moria) and *Sirith* ('a flowing', as *tirith* 'watching' from *tir*), a river in Gondor. With change of *s* to *h* in the middle of words it is present in *Minhiriath* 'between the rivers', the region between the Brandywine and the Greyflood; in *Nanduhirion* 'vale of dim streams', the Dimrill Dale (see *nan(d)* and *dú*); and in *Ethir Anduin*, the outflow or delta of Anduin (from *et-sîr*).

sûl 'wind' in *Amon Sûl, Súlimo;* cf. *súlimë*, Quenya name of the third month of the year (*The Lord of the Rings* Appendix D).

tal (*dal*) 'foot' in *Celebrindal*, and with the meaning 'end' in *Ramdal.*

talath 'flat lands, plain' in *Talath Dirnen, Talath Rhúnen.*

tar- 'high' (Quenya *tára* 'lofty'), prefix of the Quenya names of the Númenórean Kings; also in *Annatar*. Feminine *tári* 'she that is high, Queen' in *Elentári, Kementári.* Cf. *tarma* 'pillar' in *Meneltarma.*

tathar 'willow'; adjective *tathren* in *Nan-tathren;* Quenya *tasarë* in *Tasarinan, Nan-tasarion* (see *Nan-tathren* in the Index).

taur 'wood, forest' (Quenya *taurë*) in *Tauron, Taur-im-Duinath, Taur-nu-Fuin.*

tel- 'finish, end, be last' in *Teleri.*

thalion 'strong, dauntless' in *Cúthalion, Thalion.*

thang 'oppression' in *Thangorodrim*, also in *Durthang* (a castle in Mordor). Quenya *sanga* meant 'press, throng', whence *Sangahyando* 'Throng-cleaver', name of a man in Gondor (*The Lord of the Rings* Appendix A (I, iv)).

thar- 'athwart, across' in *Sarn Athrad, Thargelion;* also in *Tharbad* (from *thara-pata* 'crossway') where the ancient road from Arnor and Gondor crossed the Greyflood.

thaur 'abominable, abhorrent' in *Sauron* (from *Thauron*), *Gorthaur.*

thin(*d*) 'grey' in *Thingol;* Quenya *sinda* in *Sindar, Singollo* (*Sindacollo: collo* 'cloak').

thôl 'helm' in *Dor Cúarthol, Gorthol.*

thôn 'pine-tree' in *Dorthonion.*

thoron 'eagle' in *Thorondor* (Quenya *Sorontar*), *Cirith Thoronath.* The Quenya form is perhaps present in the constellation-name *Soronúmë.*

til 'point, horn' in *Taniquetil, Tilion* ('the Horned'); also in *Celebdil* 'Silvertine', one of the Mountains of Moria.

tin- 'sparkle' (Quenya *tinta* 'cause to sparkle', *tinwë* 'spark') in *Tintallë;* also in *tindómë* 'starry twilight' (*The Lord of the Rings* Appendix D), whence *tindómerel* 'daughter of the twilight', a poetic name for the nightingale (Sindarin *Tinúviel*). It appears also in Sindarin *ithildin* 'starmoon', the substance of which the devices on the West-gate of Moria were made.

tir 'watch, watch over' in *Minas Tirith, palantíri, Tar-Palantir, Tirion.*

tol 'isle' (rising with sheer sides from the sea or from a river) in *Tol Eressëa, Tol Galen,* etc.

tum 'valley' in *Tumhalad, Tumladen;* Quenya *tumbo* (cf. Treebeard's *tumbalemorna* 'black deep valley', *The Two Towers* III 4). Cf. *Utumno,* Sindarin *Udûn* (Gandalf in Moria named the Balrog 'Flame of Udûn'), a name afterwards used of the deep dale in Moria between the Morannon and the Isenmouthe.

tur 'power, mastery' in *Turambar, Turgon, Túrin, Fëanturi, Tar-Minyatur.*

uial 'twilight' in *Aelin-uial, Nenuial.*

ur- 'heat, be hot' in *Urulóki;* cf. *Urimë* and *Urui,* Quenya and Sindarin names of the eighth month of the year (*The Lord of the Rings* Appendix D). Related is the Quenya word *aurë* 'sunlight, day' (cf. Fingon's cry before the Nirnaeth Arnoediad), Sindarin *aur,* which in the form *Or-* is prefixed to the names of the days of the week.

val- 'power' in *Valar, Valacirca, Valaquenta, Valaraukar, Val(i)mar, Valinor.* The original stem was *bal-,* preserved in Sindarin *Balan,* plural *Belain,* the Valar, and in *Balrog.*

wen 'maiden' is a frequent ending, as in *Eärwen, Morwen.*

wing 'foam, spray' in *Elwing, Vingelot* (and only in these two names).

yávë 'fruit' (Quenya) in *Yavanna;* cf. *Yavannië,* Quenya name of the ninth month of the year, and *yávië* 'autumn' (*The Lord of the Rings* Appendix D).